THE BEST OF
WITNESS
1987–2004

EDITED BY PETER STINE
AND DOUG HAGLEY

Michigan State University Press
East Lansing

⊚ The paper used in this publication meets the minimum requirements of ANSI/NISO Z39.48-1992 (R 1997) (Permanence of Paper).

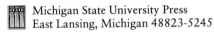 Michigan State University Press
East Lansing, Michigan 48823-5245

Printed and bound in the United States of America.

14 13 12 11 10 09 08   1 2 3 4 5 6 7 8 9 10

ISBN: 978-0-87013-829-4

Library of Congress Cataloging-in-Pubication Data
The best of witness, 1987–2004 / edited by Peter Stine and Doug Hagley.
       p. cm.
   Includes bibliographical references.
   ISBN 978-0-87103-829-4 (pbk. : alk. paper)
   1.   American literature—20th century. 2.   American literature—21st century.   I. Stine, Peter. II. Hagley, Doug, 1952- III. Witness (Farmington Hills, Mich.)
   PS536.2.B475 2008
   810.8'0054—dc22   2007051504

Acknowledgments:
"Oxygen," from *A Kind of Flying: Selected Stories* by Ron Carlson. Copyright © 2003, 1997, 1992, 1987 by Ron Carlson. Used by permission of W. W. Norton & Company, Inc. "Newborn Is Thrown in Trash and Dies," from *All Stories Are True* by John Edgar Wideman. Copyright © 1992 by John Edgar Wideman. Used by permission of Pantheon Books, a division of Random House, Inc. "On Wanting to Grow Horns," from *Nerve Storm* by Amy Gerstler. Copyright © 1993 by Amy Gerstler. Used by permission of Penguin, a division of Penguin Group (USA) Inc. "She Wipes Out Time," from *Dear Ghosts* by Tess Gallagher. Copyright © 2006 Tess Gallagher. Used by permission of Graywolf Press, St. Paul, Minnesota. "The Psychic Detective: Fantasy," from *Dread* by Ai. Copyright © 2003 by Ai. Used by permission of W.W. Norton & Company, Inc. "The Clan of One-breasted Women," from *Refuge: An Unnatural History of Family and Place* by Terry Tempest Williams. Copyright © 1991 by Terry Tempest Williams. Used by permission of Pantheon Books, a division of Random House, Inc.

Book and cover design: Doug Hagley

g green press INITIATIVE   Michigan State University Press is a member of the Green Press Initiative and is committed to developing and encouraging ecologically responsible publishing practices. For more information about the Green Press Initiative and the use of recycled paper in book publishing, please visit www.greenpressinitiative.org.

Visit Michigan State University Press on the World Wide Web at:
www.msupress.msu.edu

Contents

Poetry

Nonfiction

■ ■ ■ ■ ■ ■ ■ ■ ■ ■ ■

Editor's Comment

Peter Stine

I n 1987 I was approached by a philanthropic businessman in Detroit, Dr. Sidney Lutz, who asked if I might be interested in starting an "intellectual journal." At the time I was collecting unemployment while writing ghost testimonials for a pyramid weight-loss company, whose two CEOs were rebounding from a failed scheme running guns between India and Pakistan. I embraced Dr. Lutz's unlikely offer, eager to return to the world of respectability. Within four years his company too would fail, but the new journal was successfully launched and in 1991 found a rescuing angel in Oakland Community College, located north of Detroit. This teaching institution has provided a haven and financial support, enabling *Witness* to earn a place as one of America's most respected literary journals.

People have often asked me what is meant by "writer-as-witness" in the case of *Witness*. I have struggled to come up with an answer that seems entirely adequate. The root word is "wit"—*to know*—and acts of witness can be found in religious experience, the law, and even meditation. Like the religious witness, a writer reveals through performance—the act of writing—the values by which he or she lives. Like the legal witness, a writer is both observer and reporter, ready and equipped to speak out boldly, often on issues of grave moral concern. Yet this "testimony" is never objective, for a writer is engaged in the event, whether real or imaginary, and achieves credibility only through a successful aesthetic rendering. Finally, as in meditation, a writer, with enough luck and patience and passive receptivity to the world, is witness to what is beyond the self and gains access to a universality of perception that we associate with genuine creativity.

Ultimately, such analogies suggest that what literary art does at its best is cast the *reader* as witness to events otherwise not experienced. Bertrand Russell remarked that we know things either by "acquaintance" or "description," and it is through the latter that writing can expand our knowing. As editor of *Witness*, I have tried to present our readers with writings that might illuminate those issues of conscience that have defined our historical moment. Whether turning to the Holocaust, Vietnam, civil rights, private victimization, political oppression, the natural world, sports, cities, rural America, work, religion, crime, American families, love, aging, or ethnic America, *Witness* has featured, free of ideology, the essence of bearing literary witness.

This retrospective issue of *Witness* presents a selection of the "best" fiction, poetry, and nonfiction to appear in the journal over eighteen years. It was gratifying to return to these pieces and find them as alive as when I first read them as submissions pulled from manila envelopes. The process of selection was difficult, if only because I could have assembled another, equally strong issue of the "best" of *Witness* from an entirely different group of contributors. Perhaps because of its focus on social themes, perhaps because of its maverick identity, *Witness* has been lucky from the start in attracting so many established writers, so much new talent. Three earlier special issues of *Witness* have been reissued as books from university presses, and our contributors have regularly appeared in annual honorary anthologies such as *The O. Henry Awards*, *The Best American Poetry*, *The Pushcart Prize*, and *The Best American Essays*.

I would like to take this opportunity to thank to several institutions and people. Without the generous support of Oakland Community College, *Witness* would have died in 1990. Since 1988, the National Endowment for the Arts has awarded *Witness* more grants than any other literary journal in the country, thus ensuring its survival. With virtually no funds for promotion, *Witness* has been forced to rely on word of mouth, and many of our contributors — Joyce Carol Oates, John Balaban, Stuart Dybek, Terry Tempest Williams, and others — have spoken up publicly on the journal's behalf. Doug Hagley, the art director of *Witness* from the beginning, and the only real staff member the journal has ever had, has made the success of this publication possible. Finally, I am very grateful to Michigan State University Press for reprinting *Our Best: 1987-2004*, thereby making the anthology available to a new and wider circle of readers.

FICTION

■■■■■■■■■■■

Oxygen

Ron Carlson

I n 1967, the year before the year that finally cracked the twentieth century once and for all, I had as my summer job delivering medical oxygen in Phoenix, Arizona. I was a sophomore at the University of Montana in Missoula, but my parents lived in Phoenix, and my father, as a welding engineer, used his contacts to get me a job at Dye Oxygen Company. I started there doing what I called dumbbell maintenance, the kind of make-work assigned to college kids. I cleared debris from the back lot, mainly crushed packing crates that had been discarded. That took a week and on the last day, as I was raking, I put a nail through the bottom of my foot and had to go for a tetanus shot. Next, I whitewashed the front of the supply store and did such a good job that I began a month of painting my way around the ten-acre plant.

These were good days for me. I was nineteen years old and this was the hardest work I had ever done. The days were stunning, starting hot and growing insistently hotter. My first week two of the days had been a hundred and sixteen. The heat was a pure physical thing, magnified by the steel and pavement of the plant, and in that first week, I learned what not to touch, where not to stand, and I found the powerhouse heat simply bracing. I lost some of the winter dormitory fat and could feel myself browning and getting into shape.

Of course, during this time I was living at home, that is arriving home from work sometime after six and then leaving for work sometime before seven the next morning. My parents and I had little use for each other. They were in their mid-forties then, an age that I've since found out can be oddly taxing, and besides they were in the middle of a huge career decision which would make their fortune and allow them to live the way they live now. I was nineteen, as I said, which in this country is not a real age at all.

I was having a hard ride through the one relationship I had begun during the school year. Her name was Linda Enright, a classmate, and we had made the mistake of sleeping together that spring, just once, but it wrecked absolutely everything. We were dreamy beforehand, the kind of couple who walked real close, bumping foreheads. We read each other's papers. I'm not making this up: we read poetry on the library lawn under a tree. I had met her in a huge section of Western Civilization taught by a young firebrand named Whisner, whose credo was "Western civilization is what you personally are doing." Linda and I had taken it seriously, the way we took all things, I guess, and we joined the Democratic Student Alliance and worked on a grape boycott, though it didn't seem that there were that many grapes to begin with in Montana that chilly spring.

And then one night in her dorm room we went ahead with it, squirming out of our clothes on her hard bed and we did something for about a minute that changed everything. After that we weren't even the same people. She wasn't she and I wasn't I; we were two young citizens in the wrong country. I see now that a great deal of it was double- and triple-think, that is I thought she thought it was my fault and I thought that she might be right with that thought and I should be sorry and that I was sure she didn't know how sorry I was already, regret like a big burning house on the hill of my conscience, or something like that, and besides all I could think through all my sorrow and compunction was that I wanted it to happen again, soon. It was confusing. All I could remember from the incident itself was Linda stopping once and undoing my belt and saying, "Here, I'll get it."

The coolness of that practical phrase repeated in my mind after I'd said good-bye to Linda and she'd gone off to Boulder where her summer job was working in her parents' cookie shop. I called her every Sunday from a pay phone at an Exxon station on Indian School Road, and we'd fight and if you asked me what we fought about I couldn't tell you. We both felt misunderstood. I'd slump outside the door as far as the steel cord allowed, my skin running to chills in the heat, and we'd argue until the operator came on and then I'd dump eight dollars of quarters into the blistering mechanism and go home.

The radio that summer played the number one song, "Little Red Riding Hood," by Sam the Sham and the Pharaohs over and over along with songs by the Animals, even "Sky Pilot." This was not great music and I knew it at the time, but it all set me on edge. After work I'd shower and throw myself on the couch in my parents' dark and cool living room and read and sleep and watch the late movies.

About the third week of June, I burned myself. I'd graduated to the paint sprayer and was coating the caustic towers in the oxygen plant. I was forty feet up an extension ladder reaching right and left to spray the tops of the tanks. Beneath me was the pump station that ran the operation, a nasty tangle of motors, belts and valving. The mistake I made was to spray where the ladder arms met the curved surface of the tank and as I reached out then to hit the last and furthest spot, I felt the ladder slide in the new paint. Involuntarily I threw my arms straight out in a terrific hug against the superheated steel. Oddly I didn't feel the burn at first nor did I drop the spray gun. It certainly would have killed me to fall. After a moment, long enough to stabilize my heartbeat and sear my cheekbone and the inside of both elbows, I slid one foot down one rung and began to descend.

All the burns were the shapes of little footballs, the one on my face a three-inch oval below my left eye, but after an hour with the doctor that afternoon, I didn't miss a day of work. They've all healed extraordinarily well, though they darken first if I'm not careful with the sun. That summer I was proud of them, the way I was proud not to have dropped the spray gun, and proud of my growing strength, of the way I'd broken in my work shoes, and proud in a strange way of my loneliness.

Where does loneliness live in the body? How many kinds of loneliness are there? Mine was the loneliness of the college student in a summer job at once very far from and very close to the thing he will become. I thought my parents were hopelessly bourgeoisie, my girlfriend a separate race, my body a thing of wonder and terror, and as I went through the days, my loneliness built. Where? In my heart? It didn't feel like my heart. The loneliness in me was a dryness in the back of my mouth that could not be slaked.

And what about lust, that thing that seemed to have defeated me that spring, undermined my sense of the good boy I'd been, and rinsed the sweetness from my relationship with Linda? Lust felt related to the loneliness, part of the dry, bittersweet taste in the lava-hot air. It went with me like an aura as I strode with my burns across the paved yard of Dye Oxygen Company, and I felt it as a certain tension in the tendons in my legs, behind the knees, a tight, wired feeling that I knew to be sexual.

The loading dock at Dye Oxygen was a huge rotting concrete slab under an old corrugated metal roof. After I burned my face, I was transferred there. Mr. Mac Bonner ran the dock with two Hispanic guys that I got to know pretty well, Victor and Jesse, and they kept the place clean and well organized in a kind of military way. Industrial and medical trucks were always delivering full or empty cylinders or taking them away and the tanks had to be lodged in neat squadrons which would not be in the way. Victor, who was the older man, taught me how to roll two cylinders at once while I walked, turning my hands on the caps and kick-turning the bottom of the rear one. As soon as I could do that, briskly moving two at a time, I was accepted there and fell into a week of work with them, loading and unloading trucks. They were quiet men who knew the code and didn't have to speak or call instructions when a truck backed in. I followed their lead.

There were dozens of little alcoves amid the gas cylinders standing on the platform and that is where I ate my lunches now. Victor and Jesse had milk crates and they found one for me and we'd sit out of sight up there from 11:30 to noon and eat. There was a certain uneasiness at first, as if they weren't sure if I should be joining them, but then Victor saw it was essentially a necessity. I wasn't going to get my lunch out of the old fridge on the dock and walk across the yard to eat with the supply people. On the dock was where I learned the meaning of *whitebread*, the way it's used now. I'd open my little bag: two tuna sandwiches and a baggie of chips, and then I'd watch the two men open their huge sacks of burritos and tacos and other items I didn't know the names of and which I've never seen since. During these lunches Victor would talk a little, telling me where to keep my gloves so that the drivers didn't pick them up, and where not to sit even on break. One day Jesse handed me a burrito rolled in white paper, I was on the inside now; they'd taken me in.

That afternoon there was a big Linde Oxygen semi backed against the dock and we were rolling the hot cylinders off when I heard a crash. Jesse yelled from back in the dock and I saw his arms flash and Victor, who was in front of me, lay the two tanks he was rolling on the deck of the truck and jumped off the side and ran into the open yard. I saw the first rows of tanks start to tumble wildly, a chain reaction, a murderous thundering domino chase. As the cylinders fell off the dock, they cartwheeled into the air crazily, heavily tearing clods from the cement dock ledge and thudding into the tarry asphalt. A dozen plummeted onto somebody's Dodge rental car parked too close to the action. It was crushed. The noise was ponderous, painful, and the session continued through a minute until there was only one lone bank of brown nitrogen cylinders standing like a little jury on the back corner of the loading dock. The space looked strange that empty.

The yard was full of people standing back in a crescent. Then I saw Victor step forward and walk toward where I stood on the back of the semi. I still had my hands on the tanks.

He looked what? Scared, disgusted, and a little amused. "Mi amigo," he said, climbing back on the truck. "When they go like that, run away." He pointed back to where all of the employees of Dye Oxygen Company were watching us. "Away, get it?"

"Yes, sir," I told him. "I do."

"Now you can park those," he said, tapping the cylinders in my hand. "And we'll go pick up all these others."

It took the rest of the day and still stands as the afternoon during which I lifted more weight than any other in this life. It felt a little funny setting the hundreds of cylinders back on the old pitted concrete. "They should repour this," I said to Victor as we were finishing.

"They should," he said. "But if accidents are going to follow you, a new floor won't help." I wondered if he meant that I'd been responsible for the catastrophe.

"I'm through with accidents," I told him. "Don't worry. This is my third. I'm finished."

The next day I was drafted to drive one of the two medical oxygen trucks. One of the drivers had quit and our foreman Mac Bonner came out onto the dock in the morning and told me to see Nadine, who ran Medical, in her little office building out front. She was a large woman who had one speed: gruff. I was instructed in a three-minute speech to go get my commercial driver's license that afternoon and then stop by the uniform shop on Bethany Home and get two sets of brown trousers and short-sleeve yellow shirts worn by the delivery people. On my way out I went by and got my lunch and saw Victor. "They want me to drive the truck. Dennis quit, I guess."

"Dennis wouldn't last," Victor said. "We'll have the Ford loaded for you by nine."

The yellow shirt had a name oval over the heart pocket: David. And the brown pants had a crease that will outlast us all. It felt funny going to work in those clothes and when I came up to the loading dock after picking up the truck keys and my delivery list, Jesse and Victor came out of the forest of cylinders grinning. Jesse saluted. I was embarrassed and uneasy. "One of you guys take the truck," I said.

"No way, David." Victor stepped up and pulled my collar straight. "You look too good. Besides, this job needs a white guy." I looked helplessly at Jesse.

"Better you than me," he said. They had the truck loaded: two groups of ten medical blue cylinders chain-hitched into the front of the bed. These tanks were going to be in people's bedrooms. Inside each was the same oxygen as in the dinged-up green cylinders that the welding shops used.

I climbed in the truck and started it up. Victor had already told me about allowing a little more stopping time because of the load. "Here he comes, ladies," Jesse called. I could see his hand raised in the rearview mirror as I pulled onto McDowell and headed for Sun City.

At that time, Sun City was set alone in the desert, a weird theme park for retired white people, and from the beginning it gave me an eerie feeling. The streets were like toy streets, narrow and clean, running in huge circles. No cars, no garage doors open, and, of course, in the heat, no pedestrians. As I made my rounds, wheeling the hot blue tanks up the driveways and through the carpeted houses to the bedroom, uncoupling the old tank, connecting the new one, I felt peculiar. In the houses I was met by the wife or the husband and was escorted along the way. Whoever was sick was in the other room. It was all very proper. These people had come here from the Midwest and the East. They had been doctors and professors and lawyers and wanted to live among their own kind. No one under twenty could reside in Sun City. When I'd made my six calls, I fled that town, heading east on old Bell Road, which in those days was miles and miles of desert and orchards, not two traffic lights all the way to Scottsdale Road.

Mr. Rensdale was the first of my customers I ever saw in bed. He lived in one of the many blocks of townhouses they were building in Scottsdale. These were compact units with two stories and a pool in the small private yard. All of Scottsdale shuddered under bulldozers that year; it was dust and construction delays, as the little town began to see the future. I rang the bell and was met by a young woman in a long silk shirt who saw me and said, "Oh, yeah. Come on in. Where's Dennis?"

I had the hot blue cylinder on the single dolly and pulled it up the step and into the dark, cool space. I had my pocket rag and wiped the wheels as soon as she shut the door. I could see her knees and they seemed to glow in the near dark. "I'm taking his route for a while," I said, standing up. I couldn't see her face, but she had a hand on one hip.

"Right," she said. "He got fired."

"I don't know about that," I said. I pointed down the hall. "Is it this way?"

"No, upstairs, first door on your right. He's awake, David." She said my name just the way you read names off shirts. Then she put her hand on my sleeve and said, "Who hit you?" My burn was still raw across my cheekbone.

"I got burned."

"Cute," she said. "They're going to love that back at . . . where?"

"University of Montana."

"University of what?" she said. "There's a university there?" She cocked her head at me. I couldn't tell what she was wearing under that shirt. She smiled. "I'm kidding. I'm a snob, but I'm kidding. What year are you?"

"I'll be a junior," I said.

"I'm a senior at Penn," she said. I nodded, my mind whipping around for something clever. I didn't even know where Penn was.

"Great," I said. I started up the stairs.

"Yeah," she said, turning. "Great."

I drew the dolly up the carpeted stair carefully, my first second-story, and entered the bedroom. It was dim in there, but I could see the other cylinder beside the bed and a man in the bed, awake. He was wearing pajamas, and immediately upon seeing me, said, "Good. Open the blinds will you?"

"Sure thing," I said, and I went around the bed and turned the mini-blind wand. The Arizona day fell into the room. The young woman I'd spoken to walked out to the pool beneath me. She took her shirt off and hung it on one of the chairs. Her breasts were white in the sunlight. She set out her magazine and drink by one of the lounges and lay face down in a shiny green bikini bottom.

While I was disconnecting the regulator from the old tank and setting up the new one, Mr. Rensdale introduced himself. He was a thin, handsome man with dark hair and mustache and he looked like about three or four of the actors I was seeing those nights in late movies after my parents went to bed. He wore an aspirator with the two small nostril tubes, which he removed while I changed tanks. I liked him immediately.

"Yeah," he went on, "it's good you're going back to college. Though there's a future, believe me, in this stuff." He knocked the oxygen tank with his knuckle.

"What field are you in?" I asked him. He seemed so absolutely worldly there, his wry eyes and his East-coast accent, and he seemed old the way people did then, but I realize now he wasn't fifty.

"I, lad, am the owner of Rensdale Foundations, which my father founded," his whisper was rich with humor, "and which supplies me with more money than my fine daughters will ever be able to spend." He turned his head toward me. "We make ladies' undergarments, lots of them."

The dolly was loaded and I was ready to go. "Do you enjoy it? Has it been a good thing to do?"

"Oh, for chrissakes," he wheezed, a kind of laugh, "give me a week on that, will you? I didn't know this was going to be an interview. Come after four and it's worth a martini to you, kid, and we'll do some career counseling."

"You all set?" I said as I moved to the door.

"Set," he whispered now, rearranging his aspirator. "Oh absolutely. Go get them, champ." He gave me a thin smile and I left. Letting myself out of the dark downstairs, I did an odd thing. I stood still in the house. I had talked to her right here. I saw her breasts again in the bright light. No one knew where I was.

From the truck I called Nadine telling her I was finished with Scottsdale and was heading — on schedule — to Mesa. The heat in the early afternoon as I dropped through the river bottom was gigantic, an enormous, unrelenting thing and I took a kind of perverse pleasure from it. I could feel a heartbeat in my healing burns. My truck was not air-conditioned, a thing that wouldn't fly now, but then I drove with my arm out the window through the traffic of these desert towns.

Half the streets in Mesa were dirt, freshly bladed into the huge grid which now is paved wall to wall. I made several deliveries and ended up at the torn edge of the known world, the road just a track, a year maybe two at most from the first ripples of the growth which would swallow hundreds of miles of the desert. The house was an old block home gone to seed, the lawn dirt, the shrubs dead, the windows brown with dust and cobwebs. From the front yard I had a clear view of the Santan Mountains to the south. I was fairly sure I had a wrong address and that the property was abandoned. I knocked on the greasy door and after five minutes a stooped, red-haired old man answered. This was Gil, and I have no idea how old he was that summer, but it was as old as you get. Plus he was sick with emphysema and liver disease. His skin, stretched tight and translucent on his gaunt body, was splattered with brown spots. On his hand several had been picked raw.

I pulled my dolly into the house, dark inside against the crushing daylight and was hit by the roiling smell of dog hair and urine. I didn't kneel to wipe the wheels. "Right in here," the old man said, leading me back into the house toward a yellow light in the small kitchen where I could hear a radio chattering. He had his oxygen set up in the corner of the kitchen; it looked like he lived in the one room. There was a fur of fine red dust on everything, the range, the sink, except half the kitchen table where he had his things arranged, some brown vials of prescription medicine, two decks of cards, a pencil or two on a small pad, a warped issue of *Field and Stream*, a little red Bible, and a box of cough drops. In the middle of the table was a fancy painted plate, maybe a seascape, with a line of Oreos on it. I got busy changing out the tanks.

Meanwhile the old man sat down at the kitchen table and started talking. "I'm Gil Benson," his speech began, "and I'm glad to see you, David. My lungs got burned in France in 1944 and it took them twenty years to buckle." He spoke, like so many of my customers, in a hoarse whisper. "I've lived all over the world including the three A's: Africa, Cairo, Australia, Burberry, and Alaska, Point Barrow. My favorite place was Montreal, Canada because I was in love there and married the woman, had children. She's dead. My least favorite place is right here because of this. One of my closest friends was Jack Kramer, the tennis player. That was many years ago. I've flown every plane made between the years 1938 and 1958. I don't fly anymore with all this." He indicated the oxygen equipment. "Sit down. Have a cookie."

I had my dolly ready. "I shouldn't, sir," I said. "I've got a schedule and better keep it."

"Grab that pitcher out of the fridge before you sit down. I made us some Koolaid. It's good."

I opened his refrigerator. Except for the Tupperware pitcher, it was empty. Nothing. I put the pitcher on the table. "I really have to go," I said. "I'll be late."

Gil lifted the container of Koolaid and raised it into a jittery hover above the two plastic glasses. There was going to be an accident. His hands were covered with purple scabs. I took the pitcher from him and filled the glasses.

"Sit down," he said. "I'm glad you're here, young fella." When I didn't move he said, "Really. Nadine said you were a good-looking kid. This is your last stop today. Have a snack."

So began my visits with the old Gil Benson. He was my last delivery every fourth day that summer, and as far as I could tell, I was the only one to visit his wretched house. On one occasion I placed one of the Oreos he gave me on the comer of my chair as I left and it was there next time when I returned. Our visits became little three-part dramas: my arrival and the bustle of intrusion; the snack and his monologue; his hysteria and weeping.

The first time he reached for my wrist across the table as I was standing up to go, it scared me. Things had been going fine. He'd told me stories in an urgent voice, one story spilling into the other without a seam, because he didn't want me to interrupt. I had *I've got to go* all over my face, but he wouldn't read it. He spoke as if placing each word in the record, as if I were going to write it all down when I got home. It always started with a story of long ago, an airplane, a homemade repair, an emergency landing, a special cargo, an odd coincidence, each part told with pride, but his voice would gradually change, slide into a kind of whine as he began an escalating series of complaints about his doctors, the insurance, his children, naming each of the four and relating their indifference, petty greed or cruelty. I nodded through all of this: *I've got to go.* He leaned forward and picked at the back of his hands. When he tired after forty minutes, I'd slide my chair back and he'd grab my wrist.

By then I could understand his children pushing him away and moving out of state. I wanted out. But I'd stand — while he still held me — and say, "That's interesting. Save some of these cookies for next time." And then I'd move to the door, hurrying the dolly, but never fast enough to escape. Crying softly and carrying his little walker bottle of oxygen, he'd see me to the door and then out into the numbing heat to the big white pickup. He'd continue his monologue while I chained the old tank in the back and while I climbed in the cab and started the engine and then while I'd start to pull away. I cannot describe how despicable I felt doing that, gradually moving away from old Gil on that dirt lane, and when I hit the corner and turned west for the shop, I tromped it: forty-five, fifty, fifty-five, raising a thick red dust train along what would some day be Chandler Boulevard.

Backing up to the loading dock late on those days with a truck of empties, I was full of animal happiness. The sun was at its worst, blasting the sides of everything and I moved with the measured deliberation the full day had given me. My shirt was crusted with salt, but I wasn't sweating anymore. When I bent to the metal fountain beside the dock, gulping the water, I could feel it bloom on my back and chest and come out along my hairline. Jesse or Victor would help me sort the cylinders and reload for tomorrow. I spent eight dollars every Sunday calling Linda Enright. I became tight and fit, my burns finally scabbed up so that by mid-July I looked like a young boxer, and I tried not to think about anything.

A terrible thing happened in my phone correspondence with Linda. We stopped fighting. We'd talk about her family; the cookie business was taking off, but her father wouldn't let her take the car. He was stingy. I told her about my deliveries, the heat. She was looking forward to getting the fall bulletin. Was I going to major in geology as I'd planned? As I listened to us talk, I stood and wondered: who are these people? The other me wanted to interrupt, to ask: hey, didn't we have sex? I mean, was that sexual intercourse? Isn't the world a little different for you now? But I chatted with her. When the operator came on, I was crazy with Linda's indifference, but unable to say anything but, "Take care, I'll call."

Meanwhile the summer assumed a regularity that was nothing but comfort. I drove my routes: hospitals Mondays, rest homes Tuesdays, residences the rest of the week. Sun City, Scottsdale, Mesa. Nights I'd stay up and watch the old movies, keeping a list of titles and great lines. It was as much of a life of the mind as I wanted. Then it would be six a.m. and I'd have Sun City, Scottsdale, Mesa. I was hard and brown and lost in the routine.

I was used to sitting with Gil Benson and hearing his stories, pocketing the Oreos secretly to throw them from the truck later; I was used to the new carpet smell of all the little homes in Sun City, everything clean, quiet and polite; I was used to Elizabeth Rensdale showing me her white breasts, posturing by the pool whenever she knew I was upstairs with her father. By the end of July I had three or four of her little moves memorized, the way she rolled on her back, the way she kneaded them with oil sitting with her long legs on each side of the lounge chair. Driving the valley those long summer days, each window of the truck a furnace, listening to "Paperback Writer" and "Last Train to Clarksville," I delivered oxygen to the paralyzed and dying, and I felt so alive and on edge at every moment that I could have burst. I liked the truck, hopping up unloading the hot cylinders at each address and then driving to the next stop. I knew what I was doing and wanted no more.

Rain broke the summer. The second week in August I woke to the first clouds in ninety days. They massed and thickened and by the time I left Sun City, it had begun, a crashing downpour. I didn't want to be late at the Rensdales'. I was wiping down the tank in the covered entry when Elizabeth opened the door and disappeared back into the dark house. I was wet from the warm rain and coming into the air-conditioned house ran a chill along my sides. The blue light of the television pulsed against the darkness. When my eyes adjusted and I started backing up the stairway with the new cylinder, I saw Elizabeth sitting on the couch in the den, her knees together up under her chin, watching me. She was looking right at me.

"This is the worst summer of my entire life," she said.

"Sorry," I said, coming down a step. "What'd you say?"

"David! Is that you?" Mr. Rensdale called from his room. His voice was a ghost. I liked him very much and it had become clear over the summer that he was not going back to Pennsylvania.

Elizabeth Rensdale whispered across the room to me, "I don't want to be here." She closed her eyes and rocked her head. I stood the cylinder on the dolly and went over to her. I didn't like leaving it there on the carpet. It wasn't what I wanted to do. She was sitting in her underpants on the couch. "He's dying," she said to me.

"Oh," I said, trying to make it simply a place holder, let her know that I'd heard her. She put her face in her hands and lay over on the couch. I dropped to a knee and, putting my hand on her shoulder, I said, "What can I do?"

This was the secret side that I suspected from this summer. Elizabeth Rensdale put her hand on mine and turned her face to mine so slowly that I felt my heart drop a gear, grinding now heavily uphill in my chest. The rain was like a pressure on the roof.

Mr. Rensdale called my name again. Elizabeth's face on mine so close and open made it possible for me to move my hand around her back and pull her to me. It was like I knew what I was doing. I didn't take my eyes from hers when she rolled onto her back and guided me onto her. It was different in every way from what I had imagined. The dark room closed around us. Her mouth came to mine and stayed there. This wasn't education; this was need. And later, when I felt her hand on my bare ass, her heels rolling in the back of my knees, I knew it was the mirror of my cradling her in both my arms. We rocked along the edge of the couch, moving it finally halfway across the den as I pushed into her. I wish I could get this right here, but there is no chance. We stayed together for a moment afterward and my eyes opened and focused. She was still looking at me, holding me, and her look was simply serious.

Her father called, "David?" from upstairs again, and I realized he must have been calling steadily. Still, we were slow to move. I stood without embarrassment and dressed, tucking my shirt in. That we were intent, that we were still rapt made me confident in a way I'd never been. I grabbed the dolly and ascended the stairs.

Mr. Rensdale lay white and twisted in the bed. He looked the way the dying look, his face parched and sunken, the mouth a dry orifice, his eyes little spots of water. I saw him acknowledge me with a withering look, more power than you'd think could rise from such a body. I felt it a cruel scolding, and I moved in the room deliberate with shame, avoiding his eyes. The rain drummed against the window in waves. After I had changed out the tanks, I turned to him and said, "There you go."

He rolled his hand in a little flip toward the bed table and his glass of water. His chalky mouth was in the shape of an O, and I could hear him breathing, a thin rasp. Who knows what happened in me then, because I stood in the little bedroom with Mr. Rensdale and then I just rolled the dolly and the expired tank out and down the stairs. I didn't go to him; I didn't hand him the glass of water. I burned: who would ever know what I had done?

When I opened the door downstairs on the world of rain, Elizabeth came out of the dark again, naked, to stand a foot or two away. I took her not speaking as just part of the intensity I felt and the way she stood with her arms easy at her sides was the way I felt when I'd been naked before her. We looked at each other for a moment; the rain was already at my head and the dolly and tank were between us in the narrow entry, and then something happened that sealed the way I feel about myself even today. She came up and we met beside the tank and there was no question the way we went for each other about what was going on. I pushed by the oxygen equipment and followed her onto the entry tile, then a moment later turning in adjustment so that she could climb me, get her bare back off the floor.

So the last month of that summer I began seeing Elizabeth Rensdale every day. My weekly visits to the townhouse continued, but then I started driving out to Scottsdale nights. I told my parents I was at the library, because I wanted it to sound like a lie and have them know it was a lie. I came in after midnight; the library closed at nine.

Elizabeth and I were hardy and focused lovers. I relished the way every night she'd meet my knock at the door and pull me into the room and then, having touched, we didn't stop. Knowing we had two hours, we used every minute of it and we became experts at each other. For me these nights were the first nights in my new life, I mean, I could tell then that there was no going back, that I had changed my life forever and I could not stop it. We never went out for a Coke, we never took a break for a glass of water, we rarely spoke. There was admiration and curiosity in my touch and affection and gratitude in hers or so I assumed, and I was pleased, even proud at the time that there was so little need to speak.

On the way home with my arm out in the hot night, I drove like the young king of the desert. Looking into my car at a traffic light, other drivers could read it all on my face and the way I held my head cocked back. I was young those nights, but I was getting over it.

Meanwhile Gil Benson had begun clinging to me worse than ever and those prolonged visits were full of agony and desperation. As the Arizona monsoon season continued toward Labor Day, the rains played hell with his old red road, and many times I pulled up in the same tracks I'd left the week before. He now considered me so familiar that cookies weren't necessary. A kind of terror had inhabited him, and it was fed by the weather. Now most days I had to go west to cross the flooded Salt River at the old Mill Avenue Bridge to get to Mesa late and by the time I arrived, Gil would be on the porch, frantic. Not because of oxygen deprivation; he only needed to use the stuff nights. But I was his oxygen now, his only visitor, his only companion. I'd never had such a thing happen before and until it did I thought of myself as a compassionate person. I watched myself arrive at his terrible house and wheel the tank toward the door and I searched myself for compassion, the smallest shred of fellow feeling, kindness, affection, pity, but all I found was repulsion, impatience. I thought, surely I would be kind, but that was a joke, and I saw that compassion was a joke too, along with fidelity and chastity and all the other notions I'd run over this summer. Words, I thought, big words. Give me the truck keys and a job to do, and the words can look out for themselves. I had no compassion for Gil Benson. His scabby hands, the dried spittle in the ruined corners of his mouth, his crummy weeping in his stinking house. He always grabbed my wrist with both hands, and I shuffled back toward the truck. His voice was so nakedly plaintive it embarrassed me. I wanted to push him down in the mud and weeds of his yard and drive away, but I never did that. What I finally did was worse.

The summer already felt nothing but old as Labor Day approached, the shadows in the afternoon gathering reach although the temperature was always a hundred and five. I could see it when I backed into the dock late every day, the banks of cylinders stark in the slanted sunlight, Victor and Jesse emerging from a world which was only black and white, sun and long shadow. The change gave me a feeling that I can only describe as anxiety. Birds flew overhead, three and four at a time, headed somewhere. There were huge banks of clouds in the sky every afternoon and after such a long season of blanched white heat, the shadows beside things seemed ominous. The cars and buildings and the massive tin roof of the loading dock were just things, but their shadows seemed like meanings. Summer, whatever it had meant, was ending.

I sensed this all through a growing curtain of fatigue. The long hot days and the sharp extended nights with Elizabeth began to shave my energy. At first it took all the extra that I had being nineteen, and then I started to cut into the principal. I couldn't feel it mornings which passed in a flurry, but afternoons, my back solid sweat against the seat of my truck, I felt it as a weight, my body going leaden as I drove the streets of Phoenix.

"Oy, amigo," Jesse said one day late in August when I rested against the shipping desk in back of the dock. "Que pasa?"

"Nothing but good things," I said. "How're you doing?"

He came closer and looked at my face, concerned. "You sick?"

"No, I'm great. Long day."

Victor appeared with the cargo sheet and handed me the clipboard to sign. He and Jesse exchanged glances. I looked up at them. Victor put his hand on my chin and let it drop. "Too much tail." He was speaking to Jesse. "He got the truck and forgot what I told him. Remember?" He turned to me. "Remember? Watch what you're doing." Victor took the clipboard back and tapped it against his leg. "When the tanks start to fall, run the *other* way."

But it was a hot heedless summer and I showered every night like some animal born of it, heedless and hot, and I pulled a cotton T-shirt over my ribs, combed my wet hair back, and without a word to my parents, who were wary of me now it seemed, drove to Scottsdale and buried myself in Elizabeth Rensdale.

The Sunday before Labor Day, I didn't call Linda Enright. I rousted around the house, finally raking the yard, sweeping the garage, and washing all three of the cars, before rolling onto the couch in the den and watching some of the sad, throwaway television of a summer Sunday. In each minute of the day, Linda Enright was in my mind. I saw her there in her green sweater by her father's rolltop. We always talked about what we were wearing and she always said the green sweater, saying innocently as if wearing the sweater that I'd helped pull over her head that night in her dorm room was of little note, a coincidence, and not the most important thing that she'd say in the whole eight-dollar call, and I'd say just Levi's and a T-shirt, hoping she'd imagine the belt, the buckle, the trouble it could all be in the dark. I saw her sitting still in the afternoon shadow, maybe writing some notes in her calendar or reading, and right over there, the telephone. I could get up and hit the phone booth in less than ten minutes and make that phone ring, have her reach for it, but I didn't. It was the most vivid Linda had appeared to me the entire summer.

Green sweater in the study through the endless day. I let her sit there until the last sunlight rocked through the den, broke and disappeared.

Elizabeth Rensdale and I kept at it. Over the Labor Day weekend, I stayed with her overnight and we worked and reworked ourselves long past satiation. She was ravenous and my appetite for her was relentless. That was how I felt it all: relentless. Moments after coming hard into her, I would begin to palm her bare hip as if dreaming and then still dreaming begin to mouth her ear and her hand would play over my genitals lightly and then move in dreamily sorting me around in the dark and we would shift to begin again. I woke from a brief nap sometime after four in the morning with Elizabeth across me, a leg between mine, her face in my neck, and I felt a heaviness in my arm as I slid it down her tight back that reminded me of what Victor had said. I was tired in a way I'd never known. My blood stilled and I could feel a pressure running in my head like sand, and still my hand descended in the dark. There was no stopping. Soon I felt her hand, as I had every night for a month, and we labored toward dawn.

In the morning, Sunday, I didn't go home, but drove way down by Dye Oxygen Company to the Roadrunner, the truckstop there on McDowell adjacent to the freeway. It was the first day I'd ever been sore and I walked carefully to the coffee shop. I sat alone at the counter, eating eggs and bacon and toast and coffee, feeling the night tick away in every sinew the way a car cools after a long drive. It was an effort to breathe and at times I had to stop and gulp some air, adjusting myself on the counter stool. Around me it was only truck drivers who had driven all night from Los Angeles, Sacramento, Albuquerque, Salt Lake City. There was only one woman in the place, a large woman in a white waitress dress who moved up and down the counter pouring coffee. When she poured mine, I looked up at her and our eyes locked, I mean her head tipped and her face registered something I'd never seen before. If I used such words I'd call it horror, but I don't. My old heart bucked. I thought of my professor Whisner and Western Civ; if it was what I was personally doing, then it was in tough shape. The gravity of the moment between the waitress and myself was such that I was certain to my toenails I'd been seen: she knew all about me.

That week I gave Nadine my notice, reminding her that I would be leaving in ten days, mid-September, to go back to school. "Well Sonnyboy, I hope we didn't work your wheels off."

"No, ma'am. It's been a good summer."

"We think so, too," she said. "Come by and I'll have your last check cut early, so we don't have to mail it."

"Thanks, Nadine." I moved to the door; I had a full day of deliveries.

"Old Gil Benson is going to miss you, I think."

"I've met a lot of nice people," I said. I wanted to deflect this and get going.

"No," she said. "You've been good to him; it's important. Some of these old guys don't have much to look forward to. He's called several times. I might as well tell you. Mr. Dye heard about it and is writing you a little bonus."

I stepped back toward her. "What?"

"Congratulations." She smiled. "Drive carefully."

Some of my customers knew I was leaving and made kind remarks or shook my hand or had their wife hand me an envelope with a twenty in it. I smiled and nodded gratefully and then turned businesslike to the dolly and left. These were strange good-byes, because there was no question that we would ever see each other again. It had been a summer and I had been their oxygen guy. But there was more: I was young and they were ill. I stood in the bedroom doors in Sun City and said, "Take care," and I moved to the truck and felt something, but I couldn't even today tell you what it was. The people who didn't know, who said, "See you next week, David," I didn't correct them. I said, "See you," and I left their homes too. It all had me on edge.

The last day of my job in the summer of 1967, I drove to work under a cloud cover as thick as twilight in winter and still massing. It began to rain early and I made the quick decision to beat the Salt River flooding by hitting Mesa first and Scottsdale in the afternoon. I had known for a week that I did not want Gil Benson to be my last call for the summer, and this rain, steady but light, gave me the excuse I wanted. The traffic was colossal, and I crept in a huge column of cars east across the river noting it was twice as bad coming back, everyone trying to get to Phoenix for the day. What I am saying is that I had time to think about it all, this summer, myself, and it was a powerful stew. I imagined it raining in the hills of Boulder, Linda Enright selling cookies in her apron in a shop with curtains, a Victorian tearoom, ten years ahead of itself as it turned out, her sturdy face with no expression telling she wasn't a virgin anymore, and that now she had been for thirty days betrayed. I thought, and this is the truth, I thought for the first time of what I was going to say *last* to Elizabeth Rensdale. I tried to imagine it, and my imagination failed. When I climbed from her bed the nights I'd gone to her, it was just that, climbing out, dressing and crossing to the door. She didn't get up. This wasn't "Casablanca" or "High Noon," or "Captain Blood," which I had seen this summer, this was getting fucked in a hot summer desert town by your father's oxygen delivery man. There was no way to make it anything else.

Even driving slowly, I fishtailed through the red clay along Gil's road. The rain moved in for the day, persistent and even, and the temperature stalled and hovered at about a hundred. I thought Gil would be pleased to see me so soon in the day, because he was always glad to see me, welcomed me, but I surprised him this last Friday knocking at the door for five full minutes before he unlocked the door looking scared. Though I had told him I would eventually be going back to college, I hadn't told him this was my last day.

Shaken up like he was, things went differently. There was no chatter right off the bat, no sitting down at the table. He just moved things out of the way as I wheeled the oxygen in and changed tanks. He stood to one side, leaning against the counter. When I finished, he made no move to keep me there, so I just kept going. I wondered for a moment if he knew who I was or if he was just waking up. At the front door, I said, "There you go, good luck, Gil." His name quickened him and he came after me with short steps in his slippers.

"Well, yes," he started as always. "I wouldn't need this stuff at all if I'd stayed out of the war." And he was off and cranking. But when I went outside, he followed me into the rain. "Of course, I was strong as a horse and came back and got right with it. I mean, there wasn't any sue-the-government then. It was late in 1945. We were happy to be home. I was happy." He went on, the rain pelting us both. His slippers were all muddy.

"You gotta go," I told him. "It's wet out here." His wet skin in the flat light looked raw, the spots on his forehead brown and liquid; under his eyes the skin was purple. I'd let him get too close to the truck and he'd grabbed the door handle.

"I wasn't sick a day in my life," he said. "Not as a kid, not in the Navy. Ask my wife. When this came on," he patted his chest, "it came on bang! Just like that and here I am. Somewhere." I put my hand on his on the door handle and I knew that I wasn't going to be able to pry it off without breaking it.

Then there was a hitch in the rain, a gust of wet wind, and hail began to rattle through the yard, bouncing up from the mud, bouncing off the truck and our heads. "Let me take you back inside," I said. "Quick, Gil, let's get out of this weather." Gil Benson pulled the truck door open, and with surprising dexterity he stepped up into the vehicle, sitting on all my paperwork. He wasn't going to budge and I hated pleading with him. I wouldn't do it. Now the hail had tripled, quadrupled in a crashfest off the hood. I looked at Gil, shrunken and purple in the darkness of the cab; he looked like the victim of a fire.

"Well, at least we're dry in here, right?" I said. "We'll give it a minute." And that's what it took, about sixty seconds for the hail to abate, and after a couple of heavy curtains of the rain ripped across the hood as if they'd been thrown from somewhere, the world went silent and we could hear only the patter of the last faint drops. "Gil," I said. "I'm late. Let's go in." I looked at him but he did not look at me. "I've got to go." He sat still, his eyes timid, frightened, smug. It was an expression you use when you want someone to hit you.

I started the truck, hoping that would scare him, but he did not move. His eyes were still floating and it looked like he was grinning, but it wasn't a grin. I crammed the truck into gear and began to fishtail along the road. At the corner we slid in the wet clay across the street and stopped.

I kicked my door open and jumped down into the red mud and went around the front of the truck. When I opened his door, he did not turn or look at me, which was fine with me. I lifted Gil like a bride and he clutched me, his wet face against my face. I carried him to the weedy corner lot. He was light and bony like an old bird and I was strong and I felt strong, but I could tell this was an insult the old man didn't need. When I stood him there he would not let go, his hands clasped around my neck and I peeled his hands apart carefully, easily, and I folded them back toward him so he wouldn't snag me again. "Good-bye, Gil," I said. He was an old wet man alone in the desert. He did not acknowledge me.

I ran to the truck and eased ahead for traction and when I had traction, I floored it, throwing mud behind me like a rocket.

By the time I lined up for the Tempe Bridge, the sky was torn with blue vents. The Salt River was nothing but muscle, a brown torrent four feet over the river bottom roadway. The traffic was thick. A ten-mile rainbow had emerged over the McDowell Mountains.

I radioed Nadine that the rain had slowed me up and I wouldn't make it back before five.

"No problem, Sonnyboy," she said. "I'll leave your checks on my desk. Have you been to Scottsdale yet? Over."

"Just now," I said. "I'll hit the Rensdales' and on in. Over."

"Sonnyboy," she said. "Just pick up there. Mr. Rensdale died yesterday. Remember the portable unit, OK? And good luck at school. Stop in if you're down for Christmas break. Over."

I waited a minute to over-and-out to Nadine while the news subsided in me. It was on Scottsdale Road at Camelback where I turned right. That corner will always be that radio call. "Copy. Over," I said.

I just drove. Now the sky was ripped apart the way I've learned only a western sky can be, the glacial cloud cover broken and the shreds gathering against the Superstition Mountains, the blue air a color you don't see twice a summer in the desert, icy and clear, no dust or smoke. All the construction crews in Scottsdale had given it up and the bright lumber on the sites sat dripping in the afternoon sun.

In front of the Rensdales' townhouse I felt odd going to the door with the empty dolly. I rang the bell and after a moment, Elizabeth appeared. She was barefoot in jeans and a T-shirt, and she just looked at me. "I'm sorry about your father," I said. "This is tough." She stared at me and I held the gaze. "I mean it. I'm sorry."

She drifted back into the house. It felt for the first time strange and cumbersome to be in the dark little townhouse. She had the air conditioning cranked way up so that I could feel the edge of a chill on my arms and neck as I pulled the dolly up the stairs to Mr. Rensdale's room. It had been taken apart a little bit, the bed stripped, our gear all standing in the corner. With Mr. Rensdale gone you could see what the room was, just a little box in the desert. Looking out the window over the pool and the two dozen tiled roofs before the edge of the Indian Reservation and the sage and creosote bushes, it seemed clearly someplace to come and die. The mountains now all rinsed by rain were red and purple, a pretty lie.

"I'm going back Friday." Elizabeth had come into the room. "I guess I'll go back to school."

"Good," I said. "Good idea." I didn't know what I was saying. The space in my heart about returning to school was nothing but dread.

"They're going to bury him tomorrow." She sat on the bed. "Out here somewhere."

I started to say something about that, but she pointed at me. "Don't come. Just do what you do, but don't come to the funeral. You don't have to."

"I want to," I said. Her tone had hurt, made me mad.

"My mother and sister will be here tonight," she said.

"I want to," I said. I walked to the bed and put my hands on her shoulders.

"Don't."

I bent and looked into her face.

"Don't."

I went to pull her toward me to kiss and she leaned away sharply. "Don't, David." But I followed her over onto the bed, and though she squirmed, tight as a knot, I held her beside me, adjusting her, drawing her back against me. We'd struggled in every manner, but not this. Her arms were tight cords and it took more strength that I'd ever used to pin them both against her chest while I opened my mouth on her neck and ran my other hand flat inside the front of her pants. I reached deep and she drew a sharp breath and stretched her legs out along mine, bumping at my ankles with her heels. Then she gave way and I knew I could let go of her arms. We lay still that way, nothing moving but my finger. She rocked her head back.

About a minute later she said, "What are you doing?"

"It's OK," I said.

Then she put her hand on my wrist, stopping it. "Don't," she said. "What are you doing?"

"Elizabeth," I said, kissing at her nape. "This is what we do. Don't you like it?"

She rose to an elbow and looked at me, her face rock hard, unfamiliar. "This is what we do?" Our eyes were locked. "Is this what you came for?" She lay back and thumbed off her pants until she was naked from the waist down. "Is it?"

"Yes," I said. It was the truth and there was pleasure in saying it.

"Then go ahead. Here." She moved to the edge of the bed, a clear display. The moment had fused and I held her look and I felt seen. I felt known. I stood and undid my belt and went at her, the whole time neither of us changing expression, eyes open, though I studied her as I moved looking for a signal of the old ways, the pleasure, a lowered eyelid, the opening mouth, but none came. Her mouth was open but as a challenge to me, and her fists gripped the mattress but simply so she didn't give ground. She didn't move when I pulled away, just lay there looking at me. I remember it as the moment in this life when I was farthest from any of my feelings. I gathered the empty cylinder and the portable gear with the strangest thought: *It's going to take me twenty years to figure out who I am now.*

I could feel Elizabeth Rensdale's hatred, as I would feel it dozens of times a season for many years. It's a kind of dread for me that has become a rudder and kept me out of other troubles. That next year at school, I used it to treat Linda Enright correctly, as a gentleman, and keep my distance, though I came to know I was in love with her and had been all along. I had the chance to win her back and I did not take it. We worked together several times with the Democratic Student Alliance, and it is public record that our organization brought Robert Kennedy to the Houck Center on campus that March. Professor Whisner introduced him that night, and at the reception I shook Robert Kennedy's hand. It felt, for one beat, like Western Civilization.

That bad day at the Rensdales' I descended the stair, carefully, not looking back and I let myself out of the townhouse for the last time. The mud on the truck had dried in brown fans along the sides and rear. The late afternoon in Scottsdale had been scrubbed and hung out to dry, and the elongated shadows of the short new imported palms along the street printed themselves eerily in the wet lawns. Today those trees are as tall as those weird shadows. I just wanted to close this whole show down.

But as I drove through Scottsdale, block by block, west toward Camelback Mountain, I was torn by a nagging thought of Gil Benson. I shouldn't have left him out there. At a dead-end by the Indian School canal I stopped and turned off the truck. The grapefruit grove there was being bladed under. Summer was over; I was supposed to be happy.

Back at Dye Oxygen, I told Gene, the swingman, to forget it and I unloaded the truck myself. It was the one good hour of that day, one hour of straight work, lifting and rolling my empties into the ranks at the far end of the old structure. Victor and Jesse would find them tomorrow. They would be the last gas cylinders I would ever handle. I locked the truck and walked to the office in my worn-out work shoes. I found two envelopes on Nadine's desk: my check and the bonus check. It was two hundred and fifty dollars. I put them in my pocket and left my keys, pulling the door locked behind me.

I left for my junior year of college at Missoula three days later. The evening before my flight, my parents took me to dinner at a steakhouse on a mesa, a western place where they cut your tie off if you wear one. The barn-plank walls were covered with the clipped ends of ties. It was a good dinner, hearty, the baked potatoes big as melons and the charred edges of the steaks dropping off the plates. My parents were giddy, ebullient because their business plans which had so consumed them were looking good. They were proud of me, they said, working hard like this all summer away from my friends. I was changing, they said, and they could tell it was for the better.

After dinner we went back to the house and had a drink on the back terrace, which was a new thing in our lives. I didn't drink very much and

I had never had a drink with my parents. My father made a toast to my success at school and then my mother made a toast to my success at school, and then she stood and threw her glass out back and we heard it shatter against the stucco wall. A moment later she hugged me and she and my father went in to bed.

I cupped my car keys and went outside. I drove the dark streets. The radio played a steady rotation of exactly the same songs heard today on every 50,000-watt station in this country; every fifth song was the Supremes. I knew where I was going. Beyond the bright rough edge of the lights of Mesa I drove until the pavement ended, and then I dropped onto the red clay roads and found Gil Benson's house. It was as dark as some final place, and there was no disturbance in the dust on the front walk or in the network of spider webs inside the broken storm door. I knocked and called for minutes. Out back, I kicked through the debris and weeds until I found one of the back bedroom windows unlocked and I slid it open and climbed inside. In the stale heat, I knew immediately that the house was abandoned. I called Gil's name and picked my way carefully to the hall. The lights did not work, and in the kitchen when I opened the fridge, the light was out and the humid stench hit me and I closed the door. I wasn't scared, but I was something else. Standing in that dark room where I had palmed old Oreos all summer long, I now had proof, hard proof that I had lost Gil Benson. He hadn't made it back and I couldn't wish him back.

Outside, the bright dish of Phoenix glittered to the west. I drove toward it carefully. Nothing had cooled down. In every direction the desert was being torn up, and I let the raw night rip through the open car window, the undiminished heat like a pulse at my neck. At home my suitcases were packed. I eased along the empty roadways trying simply to gather what was left, to think, but it was like trying to fold a big blanket alone. I kept having to start over.

■■■■■■■■■■

English as a Second Language

Lucy Honig

Inside Room 824, Maria parked the vacuum cleaner, fastened all the locks and the safety chain and kicked off her shoes. Carefully she lay a stack of fluffy towels on the bathroom vanity. She turned the air conditioning up high and the lights down low. Then she hoisted up the skirt of her uniform and settled all the way back on the king-sized bed with her legs straight out in front of her. Her feet and ankles were swollen. She wriggled her toes. She threw her arms out in each direction and still her hands did not come near the edges of the bed. From here she could see, out the picture window, the puffs of green treetops in Central Park, the tiny people circling along the paths below. She tore open a small foil bag of cocktail peanuts and ate them very slowly, turning each one over separately with her tongue until the salt dissolved. She snapped on the TV with the remote control and flipped channels.

The big-mouth game show host was kissing and hugging a woman playing on the left-hand team. Her husband and children were right there with her, and *still* he encircled her with his arms. Then he sidled up to the daughter, a girl younger than her own Giuliette, and *hugged* her and kept *holding* her, asking questions. None of his business, if this girl had a boyfriend back in Saginaw!

"Mama, you just don't understand." That's what Jorge always said when she watched TV at home. He and his teenaged friends would sit around in their torn blue jeans dropping potato chips between the cushions of her couch and laughing, writhing with laughter while she sat like a stone.

Now the team on the right were hugging each other, squealing, jumping up and down. They'd just won a whole new kitchen — refrigerator, dishwasher, clothes washer, microwave, *everything!* Maria could win a

33

whole new kitchen too, someday. You just spun a wheel, picked some words. She could do that.

She saw herself on TV with Carmen and Giuliette and Jorge. Her handsome children were so quick to press the buzzers the other team never had a chance to answer first. And they got every single answer right. Her children shrieked and clapped and jumped up and down each time the board lit up. They kissed and hugged that man whenever they won a prize. That man put his hands on her beautiful young daughters. That man pinched and kissed *her,* an old woman, in front of the whole world! Imagine seeing *this* back home! Maria frowned, chewing on the foil wrapper. There was nobody left at home in Guatemala, nobody to care if a strange man squeezed her wrinkled flesh on the TV.

"Forget it, Mama. They don't let poor people on these programs," Jorge said one day.

"But poor people need the money, they can win it here!"

Jorge sighed impatiently. "They don't give it away because you *need* it!"

It was true, she had never seen a woman with her kids say on a show: My husband's dead. Jorge knew. They made sure before they invited you that you were the right kind of people and you said the right things. Where would she put a new kitchen in her cramped apartment anyway? No hookups for a washer, no space for a two-door refrigerator...

She slid sideways off the bed, carefully smoothed out the quilted spread, and squeezed her feet into her shoes. Back out in the hall she counted the bath towels in her cart to see if there were enough for the next wing. Then she wheeled the cart down the long corridor, silent on the deep blue rug.

Maria pulled the new pink dress on over her head, eased her arms into the sleeves, then let the skin slide into place. In the mirror she saw a small dark protrusion from a large pink flower. She struggled to zip up in back, then she fixed the neck, attaching the white collar she had crocheted. She pinned the rhinestone brooch on next. Shaking the pantyhose out of the package, she remembered the phrase: the cow before the horse, wasn't that it? She should have put these on first. Well, so what. She rolled down the left leg of the nylons, stuck her big toe in, and drew the sheer fabric around her foot, unrolling it up past her knee. Then she did the right foot, careful not to catch the hose on the small flap of scar.

The right foot bled badly when she ran over the broken glass, over what had been the only window of the house. It had shattered from gunshots across the dirt yard. The chickens dashed around frantically, squawking, trying to fly, spraying brown feathers into the air. When she had seen Pedro's head turn to blood and the two oldest boys dragged away, she swallowed every word, every cry, and ran with the two girls. The fragments of glass stayed in her foot for all the days of hiding. They ran and ran and ran and somehow Jorge caught up and they were found by their own side and smuggled out. And still she was silent, until the nurse at the border went after the glass and drained the mess inside her foot. Then she had sobbed and screamed, "Aaiiiee!"

M ama, stop thinking and get ready," said Carmen.
"It is too short, your skirt," Maria said in Spanish. "What will they say?"

Carmen laughed. "It's what they all wear, except for you old ladies."
"Not to work! Not to school!"
"Yes, to work, to school! And Mama, you are going for an award for your English, for all you've learned, so please speak English!"

Maria squeezed into the pink high heels and held each foot out, one by one, so she could admire the beautiful slim arch of her own instep, like the feet of the American ladies on Fifth Avenue. Carmen laughed when she saw her mother take the first faltering steps, and Maria laughed too. How much she had already practiced in secret, and still it was so hard! She teetered on them back and forth from the kitchen to the bedroom, trying to feel steady, until Carmen finally sighed and said, "Mama, quick now or you'll be late!"

S he didn't know if it was a good omen or a bad one, the two Indian women on the subway. They could have been sitting on the dusty ground at the market in San ____, selling corn or clay pots, with the bright-colored striped shawls and full skirts, the black hair pulled into two braids down each back, the deeply furrowed square faces set in those impassive expressions, seeing everything, seeing nothing. They were exactly as they must have been back home, but she was seeing them *here*, on the downtown IRT from the Bronx, surrounded by businessmen in suits, kids with big radio boxes, girls in skin-tight jeans and dark purple lipstick. Above them, advertisements for family planning and TWA. They were like stone-age men sitting on the train in loincloths made from animal skins, so out of place, out of time. Yet timeless, Maria thought, they are timeless guardian spirits, here to accompany me to my honors. Did anyone else see them? As strange as they were, nobody looked. Maria's heart pounded faster. The boys with the radios were standing right over them and never saw them. They were invisible to everyone but her: Maria was utterly convinced of it. The spirit world had come back to life, here on the number 4 train! It was a miracle!

"Mama, look, you see the grandmothers?" said Carmen.

"Of course I see them," Maria replied, trying to hide the disappointment in her voice. So Carmen saw them too. They were not invisible. Carmen rolled her eyes and smirked derisively as she nodded in their direction, but before she could put her derision into words, Maria became stern. "Have respect," she said. "They are the same as your father's people." Carmen's face sobered at once.

She panicked when they got to the big school by the river. "Like the United Nations," she said, seeing so much glass and brick, an endless esplanade of concrete.

"It's only a college, Mama. People learn English here, too. And more, like nursing, electronics. This is where Anna's brother came for computers."

"Las Naciones Unidas," Maria repeated, and when the guard stopped them to ask where they were going, she answered in Spanish: to the literacy award ceremony.

"*English*, Mama!" whispered Carmen.

But the guard also spoke in Spanish: take the escalator to the third floor.

"See, he knows," Maria retorted.

"That's not the point," murmured Carmen, taking her mother by the hand.

Every inch of the enormous room was packed with people. She clung to Carmen and stood by the door paralyzed until Cheryl, her teacher, pushed her way to them and greeted Maria with a kiss. Then she led Maria back through the press of people to the small group of award winners from other programs. Maria smiled shakily and nodded hello.

"They're all here now!" Cheryl called out. A photographer rushed over and began to move the students closer together for a picture.

"Hey Bernie, wait for the Mayor!" someone shouted to him. He spun around, called out some words Maria did not understand, and without even turning back to them, he disappeared. But they stayed there, huddled close, not knowing if they could move. The Chinese man kept smiling, the tall black man stayed slightly crouched, the Vietnamese woman squinted, confused, her glasses still hidden in her fist. Maria saw all the cameras along the sides of the crowd, and the lights, and the people from television with video machines, and more lights. Her stomach began to jump up and down. Would she be on television, in the newspapers? Still smiling, holding his pose, the Chinese man next to her asked, "Are you nervous?"

"Oh yes," she said. She tried to remember the expression Cheryl had taught them. "I have worms in my stomach," she said.

He was a much bigger man than she had imagined from seeing him on TV. His face was bright red as they ushered him into the room and quickly through the crowd, just as it was his turn to take the podium. He said hello to the other speakers and called them by their first names. The crowd drew closer to the little stage, the people standing farthest in the back pushed in. Maria tried hard to listen to the Mayor's words. "Great occasion . . . pride of our city . . . ever since I created the program . . . people who have worked so hard . . . overcoming hardship . . . come so far." Was that them? Was he talking about them already? Why were the people out there all starting to laugh? She strained to understand, but still caught only fragments of his words. "My mother used to say . . . and I said. Look, Mama . . . " He was talking about *his* mother now; he called her Mama, just like Maria's kids called *her*. But everyone laughed so hard. At his mother? She forced herself to smile; up front, near the podium, everyone could see her. She should seem to pay attention and understand. Looking out into the crowd she felt dizzy. She tried to find Carmen among all the pretty young women with big eyes and dark hair. There she was! Carmen's eyes met Maria's; Carmen waved. Maria beamed out at her. For a moment she felt like she belonged there, in this crowd. Everyone was smiling, everyone was so happy while the Mayor of New York stood at the podium telling jokes. How happy Maria felt too!

Maria Perez grew up in the countryside of Guatemala, the oldest daughter in a family of nineteen children," read the Mayor as Maria stood quaking by his side. She noticed he made a slight wheezing noise when he breathed between words. She saw the hairs in his nostrils, black and white and wiry. He paused. "Nineteen children!" he exclaimed, looking at the audience. A small gasp was passed along through the crowd. Then the Mayor looked back at the sheet of paper before him. "Maria never had a chance to learn to read and write, and she was already the mother of five children of her own when she fled Guatemala in 1980 and made her way to New York for a new start."

It was her own story, but Maria had a hard time following. She had to stand next to him while he read it, and her feet had started to hurt, crammed into the new shoes. She shifted her weight from one foot to the other.

"At the age of forty-five, while working as a chambermaid and sending her children through school, Maria herself started school for the first time. In night courses she learned to read and write in her native Spanish. Later, as she was pursuing her G.E.D. in Spanish, she began studying English as a Second Language. This meant Maria was going to school five nights a week! Still she worked as many as 60 hours cleaning rooms at the Plaza Hotel.

"Maria's ESL teacher, Cheryl Sands, says — and I quote — 'Maria works harder than any student I have ever had. She is an inspiration to her classmates. Not only has she learned to read and write in her new language, but she initiated an oral history project in which she taped and transcribed interviews with other students, who have told their stories from around the world.' Maria was also one of the first in New York to apply for amnesty under the 1986 Immigration Act. Meanwhile, she has passed her enthusiasm for education to her children: her son is now a junior in high school, her youngest daughter attends the State University, and her oldest daughter, who we are proud to have with us today, is in her second year of law school on a scholarship."

Two older sons were dragged through the dirt, chickens squawking in mad confusion, feathers flying. She heard more gunshots in the distance, screams, chickens squawking. She heard, she ran. Maria looked down at her bleeding feet. Wedged tightly into the pink high heels, they throbbed.

The Mayor turned toward her. "Maria, I think it's wonderful that you have taken the trouble to preserve the folklore of students from so many countries." He paused. Was she supposed to say something? Her heart stopped beating. What was folklore? What was preserved? She smiled up at him, hoping that was all she needed to do.

"Maria, tell us now, if you can, what was one of the stories you collected in your project?"

This was definitely a question, meant to be answered. Maria tried to smile again. She strained on tiptoes to reach the microphone, pinching her toes even more tightly in her shoes. "Okay," she said, setting off a high-pitched ringing from the microphone.

The Mayor said, "Stand back," and tugged at his collar. She quickly stepped away from the microphone.

"Okay," she said again, and this time there was no shrill sound. "One of my stories, from Guatemala. You want to hear?"

The Mayor put his arm around her shoulder and squeezed hard. Her first impulse was to wriggle away, but he held tight. "Isn't she wonderful?" he asked the audience. There was a slow ripple of applause. "Yes, we want to hear!"

She turned and looked up at his face. Perspiration was shining on his forehead and she could see by the bright red bulge of his neck that his collar was too tight. "In my village in Guatemala," she began, "the mayor did not go along — get along — with the government so good."

"Hey, Maria," said the Mayor, "I know exactly how he felt!" The people in the audience laughed. Maria waited until they were quiet again.

"One day our mayor met with the people in the village. Like you meet people here. A big crowd in the square."

"The people liked him, your mayor?"

"Oh, yes," said Maria. "Very much. He was very good. He tried for more roads, more doctors, new farms. He cared very much about his people."

The Mayor shook his head up and down. "Of course," he said, and again the audience laughed.

Maria said, "The next day after the meeting, the meeting in the square with all the people, soldiers come and shoot him dead."

For a second there was total silence. Maria realized she had not used the past tense and felt a deep, horrible stab of shame for herself, shame for her teacher. She was a disgrace! But she did not have more than a second of this horror before the whole audience began to laugh. What was happening? They couldn't be laughing at her bad verbs? They couldn't be laughing at her dead mayor! They laughed louder and louder and suddenly flashbulbs were going off around her, the TV cameras swung in close, too close, and the Mayor was grabbing her by the shoulders again, holding her tight, posing for one camera after another as the audience burst into wild applause. But she hadn't even finished! Why were they laughing?

"What timing, huh?" said the Mayor over the uproar. "What d'ya think, the Republicans put her here, or maybe the Board of Estimate?" Everyone laughed even louder and he still clung to her and cameras still moved in close, lights kept going off in her face and she could see nothing but the sharp white poof! of light over and over again. She looked for Carmen and Cheryl, but the white poof! poof! poof! blinded her. She closed her eyes and listened to the uproar, now beginning to subside, and in her mind's eye saw chickens trying to fly, chickens fluttering around the yard littered with broken glass.

He squeezed her shoulders again and leaned into the microphone. "There are ways to get rid of mayors, and ways to get rid of mayors, huh Maria?"

The surge of laughter rose once more, reached a crescendo, and then began to subside again. "But wait," said the Mayor. The cameramen stepped back a bit, poising themselves for something new.

"I want to know just one more thing, Maria," said the Mayor, turning to face her directly again. The crowd quieted. He waited a few seconds more, then asked his question. "It says here nineteen children. What was it like growing up in a house with nineteen children? How many *bathrooms* did you have?"

Her stomach dropped and twisted as the mayor put his hand firmly on the back of her neck and pushed her toward the microphone again. It was absolutely quiet now in the huge room. Everyone was waiting for her to speak. She cleared her throat and made the microphone do the shrill hum. Startled, she jumped back. Then there was silence. She took a big, trembling breath.

"We had no bathrooms there, Mister Mayor," she said. "Only the outdoors."

The clapping started immediately, then the flashbulbs burning up in her face. The Mayor turned to her, put a hand on each of her shoulders, bent lower and kissed her! Kissed her on the cheek!

"Isn't she terrific?" he asked the audience, his hand on the back of her neck again, drawing her closer to him. The audience clapped louder, faster. "Isn't she just the greatest?"

She tried to smile and open her eyes, but the lights were still going off—poof! poof!—and the noise was deafening.

M ama, look, your eyes were closed *there*, too," chided Jorge, sitting on the floor in front of the television set.

Maria had watched the camera move from the announcer at the studio desk to her own stout form in bright pink, standing by the Mayor.

"In my village in Guatemala," she heard herself say, and the camera showed her wrinkled face close up, eyes open now but looking nowhere. Then the mayor's face filled the screen, his forehead glistening, and then suddenly all the people in the audience, looking ahead, enrapt, took his place. Then there was her wrinkled face again, talking without a smile. ". . . soldiers come and shoot him dead." Maria winced, hearing the wrong tense of her verbs. The camera shifted from her face to the Mayor. In the brief moment of shamed silence after she'd uttered those words, the Mayor drew his finger like a knife across his throat. And the audience began to laugh.

"Turn it off!" she yelled to Jorge. "Off! This minute!"

L ate that night she sat alone in the unlighted room, soaking her feet in Epsom salts. The glow of the television threw shadows across the wall, but the sound was off. The man called Johnny was on the screen, talking. The people in the audience and the men in the band and the movie stars sitting on the couch all had their mouths wide open in what she knew were screams of laughter while Johnny wagged his tongue. Maria heard nothing except brakes squealing below on the street and the lonely clanging of garbage cans in the alley.

She thought about her English class and remembered the pretty woman, Ling, who often fell asleep in the middle of a lesson. The other Chinese students all teased her. Everyone knew that she sewed coats in a sweatshop all day. After the night class she took the subway to the Staten Island Ferry, and after the ferry crossing she had to take a bus home. Her parents were old and sick and she did all their cooking and cleaning late at night. She struggled to keep awake in class; it seemed to take all her energy simply to smile and listen. She said very little and the teacher never forced her, but she fell further and further behind. They called her the Quiet One.

One day just before the course came to an end the Quiet One asked to speak. There was no reason, no provocation—they'd been talking informally about their summer plans—but Ling spoke with a sudden urgency. Her English was very slow. Seeing what a terrible effort it was for her, the classmates all tried to help when she searched for words.

"In my China village there was a teacher," Ling began. "Man teacher." She paused. "All children love him. He teach mathematic. He very—" She stopped and looked up toward the ceiling. Then she gestured with her fingers around her face.

"Handsome!" said Charlene, the oldest of the three Haitian sisters in the class.

Ling smiled broadly. "Handsome! Yes, he very handsome. Family very rich before. He have sister go to Hong Kong who have many, many money."

"*Much* money," said Maria.

"Much, much money," repeated Ling thoughtfully. "Teacher live in big house."

"In China? Near you?"

"Yes. Big house with much old picture." She stopped and furrowed her forehead, as if to gather words inside of it.

"Art? Paint? Pictures like that?" asked Xavier.

Ling nodded eagerly. "Yes. In big house. Most big house in village."

"But big house, money, rich like that, bad in China," said Fu Wu. "Those year. Government bad to you. How they let him do?"

"In *my* country," said Carlos, "government bad to you if you got *small* house, *no* money."

"Me too," said Maria.

"Me too," said Charlene.

The Chinese students laughed.

Ling shrugged and shook her head. "Don't know. He have big house. Money gone, but keep big house. Then I am little girl." She held her hand low to the floor.

"I *was* a little girl," Charlene said gently.

"I *was*," said Ling. "Was, was." She giggled for a moment, then seemed to spend some time in thought. "We love him. All children love — all children did loved him. He giving tea in house. He was — was — so handsome!" She giggled. All the women in the class giggled. "He very nice. He learn music, he go . . . he went to school far away."

"America?"

Ling shook her head. "Oh no, no. You know, another . . . west."

"Europa!" exclaimed Maria proudly. "Espain!"

"No, no, another."

"France!" said Patricia, Charlene's sister. "He went to school in France?"

"Yes, France," said Ling. Then she stopped again, this time for a whole minute. The others waited patiently. No one said a word. Finally she continued. "But big boys in more old school not like him. He too handsome."

"Oooh!" sang out a chorus of women. "Too handsome!"

"The boys were jealous," said Carlos.

Ling seized the word. "Jealous! Jealous! They very jealous. He handsome, he study France, he very nice to children, he give cake in big house, he show picture on wall." Her torrent of words came to an end and she began to think again, visibly, her brow furrowing. "Big school boys, they . . . " She stopped.

"Jealous!" sang out the others.

"Yes," she said, shaking her head "no." "But more. More bad. Hate. They hate him."

"That's bad," said Patricia.

"Yes, very bad." Ling paused, looking at the floor. "And they heat."

"Hate."

"No, they heat."

All the class looked puzzled. Heat? Heat? They turned to Cheryl.

The teacher spoke for the first time. "Hit? Ling, do you mean hit? They hit him?" Cheryl slapped the air with her hand.

Ling nodded, her face somehow serious and smiling at the same time. "Hit many time. And also so." She scooted her feet back and forth along the floor.

"Oooh," exclaimed Charlene, frowning. "They kicked him with the feet."

"Yes," said Ling. "They kicked him with the feet and hit him with the hands, many many time they hit, they kick."

"Where this happened?" asked Xavier.

"In school. In classroom like . . . " She gestured to mean their room.

"In the school?" asked Xavier. "But other people were they there? They say stop, no?"

"No. Little children in room. They cry, they . . . " She covered her eyes with her hand, then uncovered them. "Big boys kick and hit. No one stop. No one help."

Everyone in class fell silent. Maria remembered: they could not look at one another then. They could not look at their teacher.

Ling continued. "They break him, very hurt much place." She stopped. They all fixed their stares on Ling, they could bear looking only at her. "Many place," she said. Her face had not changed, it was still half smiling. But now there were drops coming from her eyes, a single tear down each side of her nose. Maria would never forget it. Ling's face did not move or wrinkle or frown. Her body was absolutely still. Her shoulders did not quake. Nothing in the shape or motion of her eyes or mouth changed. None of the things that Maria had always known happen when you cry happened when Ling shed tears. Just two drops rolled slowly down her two pale cheeks as she smiled.

"He very hurt. He *was* very hurt. He blood many place. Boys go away. Children cry. Teacher break and hurt. Later he in hospital. I go there visit him." She stopped, looking thoughtful. "I went there." One continuous line of wetness glistened down each cheek. "My mother, my father say don't go, but I see him. I say, 'You be better?' But he hurt. Doctors no did helped. He alone. No doctor. No nurse. No medicine. No family."

She stopped. They all stared in silence for several moments.

Finally Carlos said, "Did he went home?"

Ling shook her head. "He go home but no walk." She stopped. Maria could not help watching those single lines of tears moving down the pale round face. "A year, more, no walk. Then go."

"Go where?"

"End."

Again there was a deep silence. Ling looked down, away from them, her head bent low.

"Oh, no," murmured Charlene. "He died."

Maria felt the catch in her throat, the sudden wetness of tears on her own two cheeks, and when she looked up she saw that all the other students, men and women both, were crying too.

Maria wiped her eyes. Suddenly all her limbs ached, her bones felt stiff and old. She took her feet from the basin and dried them with a towel. Then she turned off the television and went to bed.

■■■■■■■■■■■

Newborn Is Thrown in Trash and Dies

John Edgar Wideman

They say you see your whole life pass in review the instant before you die. How would *they* know? If you die after the instant replay, you aren't around to tell anybody anything. So much for they and what they say. So much for the wish to be a movie star for once in your life because I think that's what people are hoping, what people are pretending when they say you see your life that way at the end. Death doesn't turn your life into a five-star production. The end is the end. And what you know at the end goes down the tube with you. I can speak to you now only because I haven't reached bottom yet. I'm on my way, faster than I want to be traveling and my journey won't take long, but I'm just beginning the countdown to zero. Zero's where I started also so I know a little about zero. Know what they say isn't necessarily so. In fact the opposite's true. You begin and right in the eye of that instant storm your life plays itself out for you in advance. That's the theater of your fate, there's where you're granted a preview, the coming attractions of everything that must happen to you. Your life rolled into a ball so dense, so super heavy it would drag the universe down to hell if this tiny, tiny lump of whatever didn't dissipate as quickly as it formed. Quicker. The weight of it is what you recall some infinitesimal fraction of when you stumble and crawl through your worst days on earth.

Knowledge of what's coming gone as quickly as it flashes forth. Quicker. Faster. Gone before it gets here, so to speak. Any other way and nobody would stick around to play out the cards they're dealt. No future in it. You begin forgetting before the zero's entirely wiped off the clock face, before the next digit materializes. What they say is assbackwards, a saying by the way, assbackwards itself. Whether or not you're treated to a summary at the end, you get the whole damn thing handed to you, neatly packaged as you begin. Then you forget it. Or try to forget. Live your life as if it hasn't happened before, as if the tape has not been pre-punched full of holes, the die cast.

I remember because I won't receive much of a life. A measure of justice in the world, after all. I receive a compensatory bonus. Since the time between my wake-up call and curfew is so cruelly brief, the speeded-up preview of what will come to pass, my life, my portion, my destiny, my, my, my career, slowed down just enough to let me peek. Not slow enough for me to steal much, but I know some of what it contains, its finality, the groaning, fatal weight of it around my neck.

Call it a trade-off. A stand-off. Intensity for duration. I won't get much and this devastating flash isn't much either, but I get it. Zingo.

But the future remains mysterious. Room in the flash for my life and everybody else's, too much for everyone alive now or who has ever been alive to understand, even if we all put our heads together and became one gigantic brain, a brain lots smarter than the sum of each of our smarts, an intelligence as great as the one that guides ants, whales or birds, because they're smarter, they figure things out not one by one, each individual locked in the cell of its head, its mortality, but collectively, doing what the group needs to do to survive, relate to the planet. If we were smarter even than birds and bees, we'd still have only a clue about what's inside the first flash of being. I know it happened and that I receive help from it. Scattered help. Sometimes I catch on. Sometimes I don't. But stuff from it's being pumped out always. I know things I have no business knowing. Things I haven't been around long enough to learn myself. For instance, many languages. A vast palette of feelings. The names of unseen things. Nostalgia for a darkness I've never experienced, a darkness another sense I can't account for assures me I will enter again. Larger matters. Small ones. Naked as I am I'm dressed so to speak for my trip. Down these ten swift flights to oblivion.

Floor Ten. Nothing under the sun, they say, is new. This time they're right. They never stop talking so percentages guarantee they'll be correct sometimes. Especially since they speak out of both sides of their mouths at once: *Birds of a feather flock together. Opposites attract.* Like the billion billion monkeys at typewriters who sooner or later will bang out this story I think is uniquely mine. Somebody else, a Russian, I believe, with a long, strange-sounding name, has already written about his life speeding past as he topples slow motion from a window high up in a tall apartment building. But it was in another country. And alas, the Russian's dead.

Floor Nine. In this building they shoot craps. One of the many forms of gambling proliferating here. Very little new wealth enters this cluster of buildings that are like high-rise covered wagons circled against the urban night, so what's here is cycled and recycled by games of chance, by murder and other violent forms of exchange. Kids do it. Adults. Birds and bees. The law here is the same one ruling the jungle, they say. They say this is a jungle of the urban asphalt concrete variety. Since I've never been to Africa or the Amazon I can't agree or disagree. But you know what I think about what they say.

Seven come eleven. Snake-eyes. Boxcars. Fever in the funkhouse searching for a five. Talk to me, baby. Talk. Talk. Please. Please. Please.

They cry and sing and curse and pray all night long over these games. On one knee they chant magic formulas to summon luck. They forget luck is rigged. Some of the men carry a game called Three Card Monte downtown. They cheat tourists who are stupid enough to trust in luck. Showmen with quick hands shuffling cards to a blur, fast feet carrying them away from busy intersections when cops come to break up their scam or hit on them for a cut. Flimflam artists, con men who daily use luck as bait and hook, down on their knees in a circle of other men who also should know better, trying to sweet-talk luck into their beds. Luck is the card you wish for, the card somebody else holds. You learn luck by its absence. Luck is what separates you from what you want. Luck is always turning its back and you lose.

Like other potions and powders they sell and consume here luck creates dependency. In their rooms people sit and wait for a hit. A yearning unto death for more, more, more till the little life they've been allotted dies in a basket on the doorstep where they abandoned it.

The Floor of Facts. Seventeen stories in this building. The address is 2950 West 23rd Street. My mother is nineteen years old. The trash chute down which I was dropped is forty-five feet from the door of the apartment my mother was visiting. I was born and will die Monday, August 12, 1991. The small door in the yellow cinder block wall is maroon. I won't know till the last second why my mother pushes it open. In 1990 nine discarded babies were discovered in New York City's garbage. As of August this year seven have been found. 911 is the number to call if you find a baby in the trash. Ernesto Mendez, 44, a Housing Authority caretaker, will notice my head, shoulders, and curly hair in a black plastic bag he slashes open near the square entrance of the trash compactor on the ground floor of this brown-brick public housing project called the Gerald J. Carey Gardens. Gardens are green places where seeds are planted, tended, nurtured. The headline above my story reads "Newborn Is Thrown in Trash and Dies." The headline will remind some readers of a similar story with a happy ending that appeared in March. A baby rescued and surviving after she was dropped down a trash chute by her twelve-year-old mother. The reporter, a Mr. George James who recorded many of the above facts, introduced my unhappy story in the Metropolitan Section of the *New York Times* on Wednesday, August 14, with this paragraph: "A young Brooklyn woman gave birth on Monday afternoon in a stairwell in a Coney Island housing project and then dropped the infant down a trash chute into a compactor 10 stories below, the police said yesterday." And that's about it. What's fit to print. My tale in a nutshell followed by a relation of facts obtained by interview and reading official documents. Trouble is I could not be reached for comment. No one's fault. Certainly no negligence on the reporter's part. He gave me sufficient notoriety. Many readers must have shaken their heads in dismay or sighed or blurted Jesus Christ, did you see this, handing the Metro section across the breakfast table or passing it to somebody at work. As grateful as I am to have my story made public you should be able to understand why I feel cheated, why the newspaper account is not enough, why I want my voice to be part of the record. The awful silence is not truly broken until we speak for ourselves. One chance to speak was snatched away. Then I didn't cry out as I plunged through the darkness. I didn't know any better. Too busy thinking to myself, *This is how it is, this is how it is, how it is* . . . accustoming myself to what it seemed life brings, what life is. Spinning, tumbling, a breathless rush, terror, exhilaration and wonder, wondering is this it, am I doing it right. I didn't know any better. The floors, the other lives packed into this building were going on their merry way as I flew past them in the darkness of my tunnel. No one waved. No one warned me. Said hello or good-bye. And of course I was too busy flailing, trying to catch my breath, trying to stop shivering in the sudden, icy air, welcoming almost the thick, pungent draft rushing up at me as if another pair of thighs were opening below to replace the ones from which I'd been ripped.

In the quiet dark of my passage I did not cry out. Now I will not be still.

A Floor of Questions. Why.

A Floor of Opinions. I believe the floor of fact should have been the ground floor, the foundation, the solid start, the place where all else is firmly rooted. I believe there should be room on the floor of fact for what

I believe, for this opinion and others I could not venture before arriving here. I believe some facts are unnecessary and that unnecessary borders on untrue. I believe facts sometimes speak for themselves but never speak for us. They are never anyone's voice and voices are what we must learn to listen to if we wish ever to be heard. I believe my mother did not hate me. I believe somewhere I have a father, who if he is reading this and listening carefully will recognize me as his daughter and be ashamed, heartbroken. I must believe these things. What else do I have? Who has made my acquaintance or noticed or cared or forgotten me? How could anyone be aware of what hurtles by faster than light, blackly, in a dark space beyond the walls of the rooms they live in, beyond the doors they lock, shades they draw when they have rooms and the rooms have windows and the windows have shades and the people believe they possess something worth concealing?

In my opinion my death will serve no purpose. The street lamps will pop on. Someone will be run over by an expensive car in a narrow street and the driver will hear a bump but consider it of no consequence. Junkies will leak out the side doors of this gigantic mound, nodding, buzzing, greeting their kind with hippy-dip vocalizations full of despair and irony and stylized to embrace the very best that's being sung, played and said around them. A young woman will open a dresser drawer and wonder whose baby that is sleeping peacefully on a bed of dishtowels, T-shirts, a man's ribbed sweat socks. She will feel something slither through the mud of her belly and splash into the sluggish river that meanders through her. She hasn't eaten for days, so that isn't it. Was it a deadly disease? Or worse, some new life she must account for? She opens and shuts the baby's drawer, pushes and pulls, opens and shuts.

I believe all floors are not equally interesting. Less reason to notice some than others. Equality would become boring, predictable. Though we may slight some and rattle on about others, that does not change the fact that each floor exists and the life on it is real, whether we pause to notice or not. As I gather speed and weight during my plunge, each floor adds its share. When I hit bottom I will bear witness to the truth of each one.

Floor of Wishes. I will miss Christmas. They say no one likes being born on Christmas. You lose your birthday, they say. A celebration already on December 25th and nice things happen to everyone on that day anyway, you give and receive presents, people greet you smiling and wish you peace and good will. The world is decorated. Colored bulbs draped twinkling in windows and trees, doorways hung with wild berries beneath

which you may kiss a handsome stranger. Music everywhere. Even
wars truced for 24 hours and troops served home-cooked meals, almost.
Instead of at least two special days a year, if your birthday falls on
Christmas, you lose one. Since my portion's less than a day, less than
those insects called ephemera receive, born one morning dead the next,
and I can't squeeze a complete life cycle as they do into the time allotted,
I wish today were Christmas. Once would be enough. If it's as special
as they say. And in some matters we yearn to trust them. Need to trust
something, someone, so we listen, wish what they say is true. The holiday
of Christmas seems to be the best time to be on earth, to be a child and
awaken with your eyes full of dreams and expectations and believe for
a while at least that all good things are possible — peace, good will, love,
merriment, the raven-maned rocking horse you want to ride forever.
No conflict of interest for me. I wouldn't lose a birthday to Christmas.
Rather than this smoggy heat I wish I could see snow. The city, this
building snug under a blanket of fresh snow. No footprints of men
running, men on their knees, men bleeding. No women forced out into
halls and streets, away from their children. I wish this city, this tower
were stranded in a gentle snowstorm and Christmas happens day after
day and the bright fires in every hearth never go out, and the carols ring
true chorus after chorus, and the gifts given and received precipitate
endless joys. The world trapped in Christmas for a day dancing on
forever. I wish I could transform the ten flights of my falling into those
12 days in the Christmas song. *On the first day of Christmas my true
love said to me* . . . angels, a partridge in a pear tree, ten maids a-milking,
five gold rings, two turtledoves. I wish those would be the sights greeting
me instead of darkness, the icy winter heart of this August afternoon I
have been pitched without a kiss through a maroon door.

Floor of Power. El Presidente inhabits this floor. Some say he owns
the whole building. He believes he owns it, collects rents, treats the building
and its occupants with contempt. He is a bold-faced man. Cheeks slotted
nose to chin like a puppet's. Cold, slitty eyes. Chicken lips. This floor
is entirely white. A floury, cracked white some say used to gleam. El
Presidente is white also. Except for the pink dome of his forehead. Once,
long ago, his flesh was pink from head to toe. Then he painted himself
white to match the white floor of power. Paint ran out just after the brush
stroke that permanently sealed the closed bulbs of his eyes. Since El
Presidente is cheap and mean he refused to order more paint. Since El
Presidente is vain and arrogant he pretended to look at his unfinished
self in the mirror and proclaimed he liked what he saw, the coat of cakey

white, the raw, pink dome pulsing like a bruise.

El Presidente often performs on TV. We can watch him jog, golf, fish, travel, lie, preen, mutilate the language. But these activities are not his job; his job is keeping things in the building as they are, squatting on the floor of power like a broken generator or broken furnace or broken heart, occupying the space where one that works should be.

Floor of Regrets. One thing bothers me a lot. I regret not knowing what is on the floors above the one where I began my fall. I hope it's better up there. Real gardens perhaps or even a kind of heaven for the occupants lucky enough to live above the floors I've seen. Would one of you please mount the stairs, climb slowly up from floor ten, examine carefully, one soft, warm night, the topmost floors and sing me a lullaby of what I missed?

Floor of Love. I'm supposed to be sleeping. I could be sleeping. Early morning and my eyes don't want to open and legs don't want to push me out of bed yet. Two rooms away I can hear Mom in the kitchen. She's fixing breakfast. Daddy first, then I will slump into the kitchen Mom has made bright and smelling good already this morning. Her perkiness, the sizzling bacon, water boiling, wheat bread popping up like jack-in-the-box from the shiny toaster, the Rice Crispies crackling, fried eggs hissing, the FM's sophisticated patter and mincing string trios would wake the dead. And it does. Me and Daddy slide into our places. Hi, Mom. Good morning, Dearheart. The day begins. Smells wonderful. I awaken now to his hand under the covers with me, rubbing the baby fat of my tummy where he's shoved my nightgown up past my panties. He says I shouldn't wear them. Says it ain't healthy to sleep in your drawers. Says no wonder you get those rashes. He rubs and pinches. Little nips. Then the flat of his big hand under the elastic waistband wedges my underwear down. I raise my hips a little to help. No reason not to. The whole thing be over with sooner. Don't do no good to try and stop him or slow him down. He said my Mama knows. He said go on fool and tell her she'll smack you for talking nasty. He was right. She beat me in the kitchen. Then took me into their room and he stripped me butt-naked and beat me again while she watched. So I kinda hump up, wiggle, and my underwear's down below my knees, his hand's on its way back up to where I don't even understand how to grow hairs yet.

The Floor that Stands for All the Other Floors Missed or Still to Come. My stepbrother Tommy was playing in the school yard and they shot him dead. Bang. Bang. Gang banging and poor Tommy caught a cap in his chest. People been in and out the apartment all day. Sorry. Sorry.

51

Everybody's so sorry. Some brought cakes, pies, macaroni casseroles, lunch meat, liquor. Two Ebony Cobras laid a joint on Tommy's older brother who hadn't risen from the kitchen chair he's straddling, head down, nodding, till his boys bop through the door. They know who hit Tommy. They know tomorrow what they must do. Today one of those everybody-in-the-family and friends-in-dark-clothes funeral days, the mothers, sisters, aunts, grandmothers weepy, the men mother-fucking everybody from god on down. You can't see me among the mourners. My time is different from this time. You can't understand my time. Or name it. Or share it. Tommy is beginning to remember me. To join me where I am falling unseen through your veins and arteries down down to where the heart stops, the square opening through which trash passes to the compactor.

■ ■ ■ ■ ■ ■ ■ ■ ■ ■

My Dog Roscoe

Bonnie Jo Campbell

Ever since my sister was convicted of growing marijuana plants in the basement of her psychic bookstore, she and I have been especially close. From her cell in the Kalamazoo Women's Institute for Corrections, she listened to me complain about my boyfriend, Oscar, and she was completely supportive when, after Oscar gave me a venereal disease, I swore to break up with him once and for all. Things turned out differently, however, once Oscar explained that he had contracted the offending bacteria from an exercise bicycle. To avoid my sister's skepticism, I skipped my weekly visit, sending in my place a note saying I had the flu and laryngitis. Lydia probably would already have known how events unfolded with Oscar and me, except that as a result of her cell mate's complaints that Lydia was consorting with Satan, the authorities had taken away her tarot cards. A few days later, my sister called me. "Sarah!" she said. "I made a new tarot deck from toilet-paper squares, and as soon as I focused on your photo, the devil and the fool came up. You have broken up with Oscar, haven't you?"

"I, um, I'm in the process of breaking up with him." Why, I wanted to ask, did she always assume the fool referred to me.

"What do you mean 'in the process'?"

"It's hard to do all at once. I'm easing us apart."

"Sarah," she said, "this guy gave you chlamydia. And this is the guy who not only fooled around with that cheerleader last summer—he did it in your car."

"His was in the shop."

Sure, Oscar was a real piece of crap, but he was my first love, and that's not something to throw away like so many Big Game lottery tickets. For most of our ten years together, I was convinced that Oscar was the only man for me, that destiny had tossed us together like a couple of fuzzy dice. Ever since we'd served up our virginity to each other at sixteen, the neon pink cord connecting us had repeatedly stretched, but it had always sprung back. On good days I felt certain we'd been reincarnated from Romeo and Juliet or some lesser known but equally romantic couple of centuries past. Bad days made me wonder if I might once have been Romeo's dog.

Because I was a Libra and wanted balance in my life, naturally I'd be attracted to a Scorpio who needed adventure and risk, and for whom Virgo was rising, which lent method to his madness. And besides, whenever Oscar apologized for his transgressions, his puppy eyes melted even my strongest resolve. He had straight white teeth—they'd cost his parents no small fortune—and a well-developed musculature from working out at the health club he managed. Over the last few years, he'd taken to slicking back his dark hair in a Latin thug look which was very flattering. Oh, and he danced like a gigolo, his hands all over me, or all over whoever he happened to be with. Wherever we went, the jealousy from other women seeped across the room like a green goo, and it made me proud that he was with me.

Our fighting had gotten worse, though, until almost every evening Oscar and I spent together climaxed in some sort of argument. Take the afternoon I sprained my ankle falling off a stair-stepper which stopped suddenly when Oscar—never handy with utilities—accidentally turned off the power at the health club. Oscar and I had already planned to go out that evening to Dingo Alley, and so I limped along and parked myself at a table. I was hoping for a little sympathy, but Oscar spent the night dirty-dancing with a skinny blonde. I distracted myself by drinking too many gin-and-tonics and eating four bar bags of sour-cream-and-onion potato chips. As soon as we got back to my apartment, I passed out on the couch.

The next morning I let him have it. "How could you dance that way with that woman, Oscar? While I was sitting there with a broken ankle? The stars in the heavens spell out our names, and you'd rather stare at a cheap little fluorescent bulb."

Oscar was already showered and dressed, combing his neat beard in the hall mirror next to my statuette of Shiva, god of destruction. "Oh, I was just having fun." His eyes met mine in the mirror and shone briefly with sincerity. "Anyway, you were talking to that friend of your sister."

I looked from him to many-armed Shiva, who had been cast in bronze with a rather feminine figure. "That 'friend' was the waitress," I said, "and she was busy, and I only know her because she turned in Lydia for growing pot."

"And you ate those stinky chips. How can I get close to you when you smell like onion powder?"

"Do you think I enjoy smelling that blonde on you? She had the aura of a saucepan of molding pea soup."

"You can't see auras."

I crossed my arms. He had me confused for a second—his usual tactic when we fought. "I didn't say I *saw* her aura—I smelled it." Besides, some people, like Lydia, *could* see auras.

He slid his comb into its plastic sleeve. "You say you don't want to control me."

"Oscar, you just plain don't respect me. It's that simple." My arms fell to my sides.

"I do respect you, Sarah. I especially respect your beautiful breasts." He cupped both hands and held them toward me. "Bring those baby pumpkins over here. Come to papa, girls."

"Oscar, just go home."

"Fine," he said. "If that's what you want."

He slammed the door, then returned a moment later for his leather jacket, checking the pocket for his sunglasses before slamming the door again. He never seemed to mind when I made him leave. He probably felt it gave him license to do whatever he wanted until we made up. We'd fought like this a thousand times, and I wondered whether this time could possibly be any different. Next time I saw him, he'd wear a guilt-ridden expression, and he would apologize sweetly, but for that I would have to wait.

I'm making Oscar out to be a terrible jerk, and he was, but he was also beautiful, especially while he slept, and he was usually charming and gracious, and had a kind, brave heart, particularly when it came to animals. Early one summer, when we were visiting friends at Duck Lake, he'd stripped to his red bikini underwear and swum out to save a little dog that was floating away on a raft some kids had tied together with water lily stems—he did this despite chilly water and the risk of swimmer's itch. Afterwards, whenever I doubted Oscar, I clung to that vision of him rising from the water, flecked with algae, the shivering toy poodle in his arms. The dog's eyes bulged beneath its soggy forelocks, and Oscar's privates had shriveled inside his wet underpants.

A little before noon, as was my habit, I called his apartment and apologized to his machine, but my heart wasn't in it. Then I went around

the corner to do my laundry, where I met a stranger, Pete, who was sitting
in the only plastic chair with his legs crossed on a washing machine. He
was reading the science section of the *Detroit Free Press*, while his load
of white T-shirts, white socks, and white underwear sudsed. When he
stood, tall and broad-shouldered, to offer me his seat, I didn't yet know
that I was meeting a union electrician who conducted his daily affairs
with an honest simplicity as constant as the flow of electrons through
insulated cables. Pete arrived in my life a plainly wrapped gift from a
wholesome, uncomplicated deity. He ate the same cereal every morning,
Cheerios, and if we went out for breakfast instead, he always ordered
a mushroom-and-cheese omelet with sausage on the side. And when
he loved a woman as much as he came to love me, he desired only the
one woman. During the dryer cycle, Pete and I went for coffee at the
gas-station cafe across the street. Each time our knees touched under the
table, a current passed through me, so that by the time we returned to
our hot, dry clothes, my skin was glowing. We would be married seven
months later. I broke the news to Oscar in bed.

"We can't do this anymore, Oscar."

"Why not?"

"Because I'm getting married next week. My fate is now bound to
that of another."

"Is that what you want, Sarah? To get married? You and I should get
married, then."

"How could you even say that? We've been engaged for eight years."

"Then what's your hurry?"

"I've fallen in love with another man, one who treats me like a goddess,
one who will forsake all others for me."

"How can you do this to me, baby? Girls, tell her not to do this."

I tipped his face up. "Oscar, I'm marrying another man."

He looked down again. "Don't listen to her, girls. Fight it. You know
I love you."

I'd been meaning to tell Oscar it was over, but there was something
in the air surrounding him, a magic spell or an aphrodisiacal potpourri
of pheromones, undetectable on a conscious level. Every time I had tried
to broach the subject of our breakup, I grew dizzy, and Oscar had never
been so passionate and considerate as he was in those last few months.

I shook my head in the mock-despair that a woman feels when she is
loved by two men, and when one is in the process of kissing her from
her armpit to her elbow to her wrist. Had there been some way to stay
friends after marriage, I would have tried, but communicating at all with

Oscar would lead to the bedroom, which would be guaranteed to screw up the karma in my new married life.

"I'm sorry, Oscar. I really am. But I'm marrying a nice guy who will be true to me. I want to start a family." I pushed him away, afraid of losing my resolve should he begin licking the inside of my wrist, which was very sensitive, perhaps because in some tragic past life I had been a suicide, maybe even a crucifixion.

"We could start a family, you and me," Oscar said. He got out of bed and leaned naked against the door frame, displaying all I would be denying myself. He held in his stomach and puffed out his chest.

"We've talked about this, Oscar." Rather, I had talked, and he had stared at golf on TV or contorted himself in order to scratch his back against the door frame as he was starting to do now. He affected a sweet and sad expression. "I'd do anything to keep you in my life." He spoke with such sincerity that I almost believed him, but then he began to massage his back against the wood in earnest. "Anything," he said, as he rocked back and forth, sighing with pleasure.

Oscar did love me, but he didn't know how to behave. Take the woman from Benton Harbor who showed up outside his apartment early one morning with four-inch heels and ratted hair. The arrival of her rusty Chevy in the no-parking zone out front had seemed as ominous as the nine of swords — a tarot card depicting a woman with nine heavy, sharp weapons dangling above her bed. From the bathroom window I watched the Benton Harbor woman open the back door of her car and lift a tiny, hairy twin in each arm. She chewed gum in an athletic but careful manner which didn't muss her lipstick. Oscar acted as though he had never seen her before. "Who are you, baby? What do you want with me?" He continued to play innocent for months ("I've never seen her before, Sarah, I swear"), until the DNA test said, sure enough, the kids were his, a one-in-a-billion match. I had never wanted children out of wedlock, but I'd been jealous nonetheless.

"I can't afford any more children," he'd said. "I've got two already."

"It just pisses me off that you hump a big-haired stranger once, and she gets to entwine her life with yours for all eternity, while we've been together all these years and have nothing to show for it. We've never even planted a flower together. Those should be my children, Oscar."

"It's not the children's fault. Why blame it on the children?"

"I'm not. I'm blaming it on you."

"Girls, tell her to lighten up on me. You know I'm doing my best."

Because I had lived like this — suspicious, guilt-ridden, compromised —

for all of my adult life, I hadn't realized there was an alternative. What a joy, then, to learn there was another man in the universe for me, a tall, shining man who respected me, who spoke to my face. The Department of Corrections authorities allowed my sister one hour of freedom to attend my wedding at the county courthouse. Perhaps it was merely that she hadn't seen or touched a man (other than guards) in months, but she gushed over Pete.

"Your aura is bright purple," she said. "That's very rare in a man."

"Is it?"

"You're the perfect king of cups," she said.

"Thank you." Pete blushed.

Even as the guards were putting Lydia in the back seat of the county cruiser, she and Pete continued arguing about the nature of electricity.

Pete and I moved an hour north to Grand Rapids, which made it easier to sever ties with Oscar. Pete worked on a new hospital building and took another class toward his engineering degree, and my old supervisor helped me get a job as an administrative assistant in an office furniture manufacturing company where the boss thought herself fortunate to have me in her employ. I liked work, and I looked forward each evening to returning home to Pete. He never schemed to get away from me, and when he told me something, say, that he had to work late, I could believe him. Compared to Oscar, he was a pitiful dancer, but he was willing to go with me a couple of times a month, and he was gradually loosening up. Pete was the kind of guy who, when you introduce him to your girlfriends, they say, "He's so nice. Cute too." Oscar had been the kind of guy you avoided introducing to your girlfriends altogether.

Pete was a generous, hard-working Gemini, a sign conducive to electricity, which in combination with his job might explain his aura. His only fault was that he was a little dull. Left to his own devices, if he didn't have to study, he fell asleep by 9:30. In romantic matters, he was a well-equipped and passionate man, but he had a tendency to be too gentle, as though accustomed to women who hadn't spent the last decade lifting weights with their acrobatic ex-boyfriends. And he really did wear only white T-shirts and blue jeans, even when we went out.

Before we enjoined our souls in the holy bonds of matrimony, Pete had told me about his ex-girlfriends, one of whom was a sad alcoholic. In exchange, I spoke in general terms about Oscar, but neglected to mention that I still hadn't managed to break up with him. The last time I saw Oscar was two days before the wedding, when he came to my apartment. "One more for the road," he'd said. "It's over for real this time," I told him afterwards, and if I hadn't been so caught up in the excitement of my wedding, I might have mirrored the agony Oscar seemed to be feeling.

It was months into my marriage when I really started to feel the loss of my old sweetheart. Sometimes when the phone rang, I grabbed it and waited breathlessly to hear Oscar's voice. Instead, it was usually a telemarketer pushing phone service or cemetery plots, or else Lydia calling collect from jail.

Spring turned lushly to summer, and when the blossoms fell from the trees in our yard, fruit grew in their places and birds perched on the branches. But even in this garden of bliss, I began to feel unsettled. Some warm evenings, I sat on the porch beside Pete and stroked the insides of my wrists, trying to puzzle through my feelings for Oscar.

Half a year into our marriage, I learned I was two months pregnant, and it was about this time that a stray dog—bigger than a cocker spaniel, smaller than a retriever, black with white pepper spots—showed up at the back door of the house we were renting with an option to buy. The dog's collar had no identification tags, but "Roscoe" was written on the fabric in alcohol marker. At first I tried to shoo him away, but he was persistent, and I quickly became attached to him. Pete didn't know if he wanted a dog, he said, though he could see getting a puppy a year or two after the baby was born. For about a week, I worked to change Pete's mind, all the while feeding the dog on the back porch. When Pete finally agreed that we could keep Roscoe, I bathed his coat with flea shampoo, took him to the veterinarian for shots, and, on Dr. Wellborn's advice, made an appointment for the surgical neutering.

Not even I understood why I was so adamant about the dog, but I somehow knew the fellow was meant to share his life with me. A worldly light showed in Roscoe's eyes, and he gazed at me with a beautiful and sad expression which revealed he had known pain. Perhaps he had even suffered with me in a past life—maybe we'd been on a Roman slave ship, chained side-by-side to our oars. Or if I had been Cleopatra, then he might've been some Nile-side employee whom I'd hardly noticed, but whose love for me was so overwhelming that it had resulted in, say, his killing himself outside my bedroom window. Or perhaps he had died by throwing his body between me and an assassin. In any case, I knew I must care for him now.

Roscoe was somewhat wary around Pete, but when the dog and I were alone he had a habit of rolling onto his back and opening his legs. One day as I scratched his chest, which was surprisingly muscular for a little mongrel, his tongue snaked out to lick the underside of my wrist.

Probably this dog and I had been very close in the previous life, I thought. Maybe those slave ship captains had severely whipped Roscoe when he voiced his opinions about human rights, and maybe I then revived Roscoe with fresh water from my own meager rations.

Roscoe the dog stood up and walked to the doorway, rubbed his back deliberately against the door frame, then continued into the kitchen. I followed him and kneeled to look into his face. Couldn't be. Ridiculous. Plenty of dogs lick women's wrists and rub their backs against door frames. How could I even think such a thing? Roscoe took a nugget of dry food in his mouth and crunched it, then settled into licking his privates.

Later, while I was undressing to get into the shower, I looked down to see Roscoe gazing at my breasts with his tongue hanging out. "Stop it," I scolded. The dog had been smiling, but he then lowered his eyes with a look of guilt I knew all too well. My stomach was just starting to swell by then, and I had felt proud, but Roscoe was making me embarrassed. I wrapped my bathrobe around my body and stepped over him.

Later, while Pete studied at his desk in the bedroom, I reclined on the couch and opened a bag of Be-Mo sour-cream-and-onion potato chips. Although Pete preferred plain salted chips, he took no offense at my eating any kind of snack foods whatsoever—he encouraged me to indulge my cravings and had recently allowed me to spell out the letters of baby names on his stomach in cheese doodles. As I lifted one chip after another from the bag to my mouth, Roscoe's eyes followed my hand. When I finally offered him a chip, Roscoe stretched up to take it in his mouth. I breathed a sigh of relief. Oscar had always hated chips, especially the onion kind. But this dog liked them, and that was that, and the whole resemblance had been my imagination. When Roscoe sauntered into the kitchen, I leaned off the couch and caught sight of him spitting out the chip, then lapping water from his dish, as if to wash the taste away.

"Oscar?" I said.

The dog stopped drinking.

"Is that you?" I asked.

The dog trotted back to me and tilted his head sideways. This was a darling gesture, because one ear lifted while the other sagged, probably due to nerve damage from frostbite according to Dr. Wellborn. Roscoe opened his mouth and let his tongue hang over his small bottom teeth.

I said, "You couldn't live without me, could you?" The dog pushed his nose under my hand, and I smoothed his hair over his head, then patted the couch. "Come up here, big guy." The dog jumped onto the couch and lay with his head resting on my right breast. He watched my face for a while, then focused on the television with a gaze far too intent for a dumb animal. I pushed him away only when his drool soaked through my nightie.

Over the course of the next few days, I noticed that my old boyfriend had changed. Oscar had always been a prime rib and filet mignon man, yet Roscoe preferred his Waggy Meals and Chew Bites in poultry flavors. To my relief, he had also changed his taste in television—Oscar used to roll his eyes whenever I turned on my ten o'clock police-and-lawyer dramas, but Roscoe seemed content to watch, never suggesting that he'd prefer news or wrestling. On the negative side, while Oscar had been fastidious about his personal cleanliness, Roscoe never missed an opportunity to rummage through neighbors' garbage bags or to roll on the carcasses of animals that had been hit and killed along the road. As for bathing, he rarely bothered to lick anything other than his privates.

When I got up the nerve to call Oscar's number in Kalamazoo, two rings were followed by a recording, "This number is not in service." My heart beat faster, and I had to sit down. I didn't understand the transmigration of souls any better than the average Midwestern plumber's daughter, so I didn't know whether Oscar's inhabitation of this dog's body was temporary or permanent. Surely the old Oscar hadn't died, for my sister, who read all the regional papers, would have phoned me, but that slick, muscular body I knew so well was more than likely now inhabited by the soul of a mixed-breed canine. Probably Oscar had been so despondent at losing me that he paid some local sorcerer to swap his identity with Roscoe's, or perhaps he managed to net a magic fish in Duck Lake and got three wishes. Knowing how those wishes can backfire, this might be the fulfillment of a wish to be with me.

That night I lay in bed with Pete at my side and the dog near my feet. "Maybe we shouldn't get him neutered," I said.

"Why not?"

"Is that really fair? What if he wants to have a family? What gives human beings the right to impose their wills on other species?"

"Sarah, you're not dominating him. You're rescuing him. If not for you, he'd probably have gotten hit on the road or gassed at the pound already."

After I kissed Pete off to work the next morning at 6:45, I called the dog to my feet. During the sleepless night I had come to the conclusion that the nagging sinkhole of emptiness I felt wasn't from missing Oscar— after all, here he was. Rather, I needed closure on our relationship. Oscar needed to know exactly how I felt about our years together. "You've been very bad," I said, pointing into his face. Over the course of the next half hour I reminded him of some of his worst behavior, including his frolic with that mean librarian. Oscar had denied any such encounter, but after the evening in question, the woman continually renewed his books so he never had to pay late fines, while she required of me the strictest compliance. "You've been very, very bad," I said.

Roscoe closed his mouth and whined briefly. "Hah!" I said. "You admit your guilt!" Of course he'd admitted guilt before, but this time he couldn't talk back, couldn't disagree about dirty-dancing with blondes, couldn't explain away the lady from Benton Harbor, couldn't charm me into forgetting the cheerleader stains on my upholstery, couldn't make me feel guilty for screaming at him about his not showing up for the six-course birthday dinner I made him. He couldn't reach the door knob, let alone storm out. He gazed at my finger intently and with regret, until suddenly his head whipped around and he gnawed at his back leg, pretending to bite a flea.

"Look at me when I talk to you," I said, grabbing his nose. "You can't avoid me, Oscar, Roscoe, whatever you call yourself." When I let him go, he lay his speckled nose between his paws.

"That's better," I said, satisfied that for the next ten years, I would have control in this relationship. Here at last was the balance I'd sought. Now that I knew what it was to be loved by a good man, I was aware of how badly Oscar had treated me, and he must pay for it . Still, neutering him seemed over the top, unreasonably cruel, not to mention stupid should I ever want Oscar to be human again, say if something happened to Pete while he was working on the twentieth floor of a new office building. Who knew what kind of deal Oscar had made with that magic fish?

When my sister called me at work later that morning, I told her that Oscar had come back to find me.

"So he's sniffing around your door again, is he?"

"Sort of," I said.

"Listen, Sarah, I did the tarot for you this morning."

"You mean the toilet-tissue tarot?" I still wasn't certain this homemade deck of hers was legitimate.

"Listen, I drew the lovers, upside-down. I drew it last night too, with the fool." The lovers card is not necessarily bad, but it suggests temptation, choice, the struggle between sacred and profane love, and upside-down it warns of the wrong choice. "You resist him, Sweetie. Tell him you've moved on to better things. If he doesn't go away, let me know and I'll put some kind of curse on him."

"You don't understand," I protested. "He's come to me in the form of a stray dog, and I've taken him in." I presented her with all the evidence.

My sister was usually an open-minded person, and despite her dislike of Oscar she had always been restrained in her condemnations, but she was surprisingly harsh with me on the phone. "Get a grip!" she demanded. "Your Pete is an angel, a bright knight standing high above the rabble. You are the luckiest person in the world to have found true love with a good man, so shut up about Oscar and shut up about that damned dog."

I listened, stunned, wondering if maybe they'd slipped lard into the crust of her vegetarian pot pies again.

"And your potato chip test is stupid," she said. "If I could bust out of here, I'd come over and kick your ass right now."

I held the phone slightly away from my ear and looked around the office to see if anyone was staring at me. I'd been planning to transfer money into her account and to send her a book I'd found about improving the Feng Shui of very small spaces. Instead I told her thanks for being so supportive, next time I'd call the Psychic Friends Network, and hung up. On Wednesday afternoon I left a message at the clinic canceling the Friday neutering.

Thursday morning, Roscoe whined to go outside earlier than usual, while Pete was showering. I dragged myself out of bed and fiddled to straighten the leash. A wave of nausea flushed through me as I opened the door, so I had to grab my stomach and bend forward, and in my moment of inattention, Roscoe took off. He pumped his legs faster and faster across our yard, around a basswood tree and past our neighbor's house, toward the main road. I ran after him but was slowed by my slippers and robe. Roscoe took the road at a shallow angle. If he'd been paying any attention, he'd have noticed the approaching menace of the blue car which braked and swerved but couldn't avoid slamming — whomp — into Roscoe, throwing his body into the air, then onto the dirt shoulder. In pursuit, I didn't hesitate to run after Roscoe, out in front of the car, which halted within a foot of me. My heart stopped momentarily, and the world took on a greenish tinge as I realized I had just risked extinguishing not only my own light but also the three-month-old spark of life inside me.

At the sight of Roscoe's lifeless body, however, I once again forgot about the future. I kneeled beside him. Before us, in a kennel opening out of a garage attached to a ranch-style house, perched the object of Roscoe's desire — a black female chow dog with lush fur and a ridiculously curly tail, rubbing herself against the side of her pen. Three other neighborhood dogs scratched and whimpered at the chain link, and as I watched, a loopy-eared Irish setter crossed the road safely and joined the other males.

The woman who'd hit Roscoe got out of the car and stood beside me in the kind of ugly, padded shoes librarians wear. "He just ran out in front of me," she said. "I'm so sorry. I have two dogs of my own. I love dogs."

I put my face into the lifeless fur and began to weep. A rough tongue unrolled itself onto my face. "He's alive!" I shouted.

Roscoe pulled away from me and maneuvered himself slowly to a sitting position, then pulled his body up with great difficulty and stood shaking on three legs. When I touched the fourth leg, he winced. "Go get my husband," I yelled to the librarian. "Down that road, the yellow house, third on the left."

Roscoe sank to the ground again, heaving a sigh.

"You never could be true, could you?" I said. "Now do you see what comes from philandering?" Momentarily, Roscoe's ears both sagged, but then he sniffed the air in the direction of the cage and the one ear lifted. I was thinking that it ought to be illegal to let females out when they smelled that way—they were little more than death traps—but in my heart I knew it wasn't the bitch's fault. It was a wonder something hadn't happened before now, something to do with a jealous prizefighter husband or a father with a shotgun. I didn't need to punish Oscar any more, because his karma had caught up with him at last. "You just couldn't be good," I said, shaking my head.

Roscoe continued to watch the cage even after somebody called the female dog inside. As the other males dispersed to sniff stupidly around the yard, Roscoe turned and looked at me through the most regretful, guileless eyes in the world, and I knew that at last he understood how bad he had been.

"Sarah, honey, we'd better get him into the truck," said Pete from behind me. "I called Dr. Wellborn, and she's coming in early for us. He's really bleeding."

I hadn't heard Pete's truck pull up, and I somehow hadn't even noticed the pool of blood on the dirt shoulder. It was hard to tell how much blood Roscoe had lost, but I imagined the worst. Now that he knew the error of his ways, I was losing him. If something happened to Pete, if he was shocked with two thousand volts in a freak electrical accident, Oscar could not transform and take me back. Pete lifted Roscoe into the truck as the lady who had hit him watched sadly and patiently, as though she could stand there all day in those comfortable shoes. Though Pete argued it was unsafe, not to mention illegal, I insisted on riding in the truck bed with the dog. Pete drove slowly and carefully, and I stroked Roscoe's head.

As we coasted to a stop outside the clinic, I opened the tailgate and lugged myself out, feeling the heaviness of pregnancy for the very first time. I pulled Roscoe toward me and was grateful when Pete helped me carry him. The veterinarian's assistant held the door for us.

"He's bruised and traumatized," said Dr. Wellborn after the examination. She was a serious dark-eyed woman with her hair pulled back, a Queen of Pentacles, rich with practical talents and probably a Capricorn, too. "But nothing seems to be broken. He's almost stopped bleeding, but I'd like to stitch that gash."

"Oh, Doctor," I said. "Thank you."

"He's going to do it again, though, unless he's neutered." She studied a yellow chart. "It says here you canceled your Friday appointment."

"Why did you cancel the appointment?" Pete turned to me.

"I just couldn't bring him in at that time, that's all."

Pete stared at me, genuinely puzzled. While I may have misled him slightly about Oscar before the wedding, I'd never told Pete an outright lie before. I swore to myself that I'd never lie to Pete again, at least not about anything important.

"Your aura or horoscope or something?" Pete suggested. He wanted to believe me.

"We've still got a surgical opening for tomorrow morning," said Wellborn. "You can leave him here overnight. That way we'll keep an eye on him."

Until death do us part, I'd told Pete. I thought I'd already committed to him, and yet I'd been keeping alive the possibility of getting into my Toyota and driving to Oscar, where I'd tear off my clothes and jump into his bed, leaving my new life behind as though it had been a pleasant dream. But castration was so very final—even if one could transmigrate back into one's old body, there would be residual effects on the soul, and Oscar would always know I'd done this to him.

"Miss?" asked the assistant, her pen ready.

On the other hand, as a dog, he provided companionship and reliable affection in a way he never had as a human. The last few weeks with Roscoe had been happier than any such period I'd spent with Oscar in the last ten years. And even if something did happen to Pete, I knew I could never return to the daily frustration and insecurity of being Oscar's girl. He was a far better dog than he'd ever been a boyfriend.

"Ma'am? Do you want that appointment?"

Pete was screwing up his eyes looking at me, as if waiting for me to explain — to confess myself to be an adulterer or to grow a purple horn out of the middle of my forehead.

Roscoe was looking pained, but I didn't meet his eyes. He'd been given plenty of chances to make things right, and after ten years, it was just too late. And however he got to be a dog, his well-being was now in my hands. I placed one of my hands on my belly, where I sensed a prick of energy like a tiny sigh of relief.

"Of course, we'll take the appointment," I said and smiled at Pete.

■ ■ ■ ■ ■ ■ ■ ■ ■ ■ ■

Jerry's Kid

Robert Schirmer

I would like to speak on behalf of my son," the father said.
"That's not necessary," I told him.
"No," he said. "It is. Every word is necessary."

It was 3:30 a.m. and I had been asked to sit with the family. The hospital was short-handed, this was Labor Day weekend, and when cutting to the bone of the matter, what did I have in my life that was more pressing?

A doctor actually asked me this, a pale, old man whose lesioned skin cast an odor like soft fruit. The sad truth was, I couldn't answer him.

The family were parents to the boy who held up a Quik-Mart on the L-section of highway that connected the yellow fields of throat-high corn to the town lumberyards and smokestacks. Seventeen, face shining with doped-up glory, the boy had waited until the store was free of truck drivers and marginals and quarreling lovers who couldn't find their way on the map, then he thrust a gun at the cash clerk's temple and said, "I've got a bullet here just waiting to set up house."

Only the clerk packed a gun, too, in a side drawer he kept always open. He was Fully Prepared, he told me later, when I first arrived on the scene with Len, my partner, and we clamored into the store with our oxygen and tubes and stretcher... he was Fully Prepared for the moment any fucked-up someone busted into *his* store and tried to make off with *his* life.

"Yes," I said. I was the first to kneel beside the boy sprawled across the tiles, in both hands clutching his heart, which had slipped outside the hole in his chest. I ran my fingers through the boy's sweating hair. This situation had me stumped. I was a paramedic, not Christ. The blood was everywhere — pooled over the tiles, settled beneath the beef jerky and magazine racks, stained across potato chip bags and cigarette cartons. Drops of it had already bloomed across the front of my uniform. If I were Christ — and I couldn't help thinking this — the spilled blood would be wine now, and instead of his own choking tongue, the boy's mouth would be filled with bread, rich whole bread I had conjured out of nothing more than my own desire to change things. Inside my head I would hear music and parables, not static. I couldn't let go of these thoughts.

"Jesus," Len said, shaking a blanket over the boy's body, covering his face and the silver gun lying beside him. "This one's a scene."

I folded the blanket back down around the boy's neck. "He's not dead," I said. Len stared in bafflement and located the pulse in his own throat. He had only one more year before retirement.

"My father owned a home furnishings store," the clerk said. He was rearranging items on a rack — packets of gum, spotted jelly beans, licorice sticks, red and black. I nodded and, with Len's help, hoisted the boy onto the stretcher. He was heavy to lift, but once in our arms, so very light I envied him such weightlessness. The boy mumbled to the angels I was certain had already descended upon the room. I could see them, or nearly, aglow around us, shouldering me out. "He knew the names of his customers," the clerk continued. "He sold rugs and velvet armchairs, he sold them sofa cushions and weed killer for their gardens."

The clerk was not a bad man. He had his business, his memories. As Len and I carried the broken boy out the door, the clerk cried after us, desperately, "What's your hurry?"

Now I stood on assignment in the echoing hospital hall with the boy's father, waiting to hear his son's fate. The clerk, I was certain, was telling his father's story to the police by now. Len had gone home, and the boy's mother had wandered off somewhere. I drank lukewarm coffee from a styrofoam cup and watched as the father stared out the window, breathing barely onto the glass where his fingertips lightly rested. Outside there was nothing much to see but lampposts, lighted windows, vacant buildings. For a moment I saw the giant shadow of something moving, and imagined a helicopter rising out of the darkness, or a prehistoric bird someone had forgotten to tell me about, but in the end it was just a billboard of the Marlboro Man, shivering in the wind to the joys of nicotine.

"He would never have pulled the trigger." The father turned to face me with this watershed.

"All right."

"No. I know you've heard this before. A man of your profession, the things you must have heard. All the excuses. But my boy . . . "

The father groped for the precise words. I couldn't look him in the face because it was unlike any I'd stared into before. Grief, regret, rage, denial, too many emotions to name were jumbled together, competing for expression, so that his face looked constantly in flux. I was looking right at him and I could not have told you the shape of his head, for example, or the color of his hair or his eyes. How could eyes be expected to hold such fevered emotion and color too?

"I don't care what you think of me," he said. "But you must not judge him as a son. He was a good boy. He didn't mistreat us."

"I wasn't thinking about him in any way as a son," I said.

"A boy picks up a gun, you think he means to use it? You think that's what he means?"

"I'm not a father."

"Guns, knives, what ends up in a boy's hand, that's not the point. It's not what's *real*. The real him." The father's eyes seemed to be burning down to some base element — liquid mercury, quicksilver. "Even a good boy, a first-rate son, will do these things, he will hold these objects, destructive things in his hands, a test of some kind, a challenge maybe, but it's not what he *means* to be doing — "

The father stopped for nothing more than a rattling breath, which I supposed fanned the flame inside him. "So don't tell me he meant to steal, he needed that money, hell, I have money, my wife and I would have given him the money, anything he wanted with all of our hands — "

"I believe you," I said.

The father struck me once in the jaw, hard enough to land me at his feet. I lay in surrender for a moment across the cool tiles, surveying the angles of the world from this position. I felt shot up with Novocaine, everything drugged and out of reach, not such an unpleasant feeling. The father leaned over, I thought he would drop across me like a sawed tree.

"Now you're sorry!" Veins popped out in his neck, those stinging eyes. "Now aren't you sorry?"

I stood up and walked away from him. I might as well have shot the boy myself, the way I was feeling. I had seen men on fire before, racing away from an exploding railcar as if they believed they still had a chance. Children sawed out of twisted car wrecks were placed in my arms, in their delirium mistaking me for a parent carrying them off to sleep. "Night," they breathed out of their swollen mouths and tried to turn over. And there were the old women with broken hips and collarbones and femurs, who mumbled gratitude as I lifted them off their floors or bathtubs or even the blue ice in the back yards of their lonely, unheated homes.

I'd seen good things, too, of course, and occasionally a wonderful thing. Once I saw a man and woman so frenzied with passion they danced atop a moving streetcar in a rainstorm while stripping away their office wear. Tie, blazer, shirt, nylons, all were cast down over the rails where the car had just been. The woman kicked off a shoe and it spiraled into my hands. I don't remember many things better than this.

My secret: during a rainstorm, I often open my window and hold the shoe out until it's filled. I drink from the woman's heel. You can't find water that good beneath your feet or at the crest of a mountain.

In this state, I wandered into the TV lounge. I didn't realize until I was seated that a woman occupied the far end of the sofa. She was maybe forty and sat erect, unflinching, something beautifully numb about her, yet she clutched the sofa arm like she was spinning in a cup on an amusement park ride, and her mascara was streaked. I saw so much of the dying boy in her drawn face that I didn't feel the need for introductions. She stared at the Labor Day Telethon on TV. No one distinct was doing their act at four in the morning, because who would be awake enough to notice them? A fat woman who looked obliquely like she had once been a casual celebrity sang the high notes of some Broadway show tune. Applause was followed by a plea for donations. The telethon, we were reminded, fought a disease that rendered children motionless, digesting bone and muscle down to putty. I studied the phone volunteers in the background—smiling and drowsy-eyed, young and old—searching for someone I may have serviced once who was now doing well.

"Amazing, isn't it, how many people are up at four in the morning, willing to lend a hand?" I said. I could not feel my teeth or bottom lip. We were alone in the room except for an old woman in a far corner chair, squeezing medicated drops into her eyes.

"I don't know any of them," the mother said. She looked over at me. "Your lip's swollen."

"Your husband hit me."

"Yes, he would. Uniforms don't mean much to him. They've become the enemy." She looked as if she were fully ready to say more or fully ready to stand and go to him, but she ended up doing neither. She turned back to the TV. A boy in a wheelchair was brandished onto the stage, head a paperweight his wilting neck could not hold. While the boy struggled to articulate his name, the host brushed hair off the boy's forehead and managed a teary smile. The fat woman clasped her hands to her chest and nodded, yes, yes. "Well," the mother said. "Do you

70

suppose those two rented the emotions along with the suits?"

"They mean well," I said. "Their hearts are in the right place," I added after a silence. Then this seemed like exactly the wrong thing to have said, so I let the silence alone after that.

"I don't know," she said vaguely. Her hands sought her own throat, stroked her veins, her collarbone, and for a moment I thought she meant to claw herself, until I understood she was moving more from exhaustion than panic. "I've known three children who have died over the past two years," she continued. "Can you imagine? Three. One was a friend of Tom's. Naturally I've read about dozens more in the papers. Not one has died from this disease, not one. Do you think I've missed something?"

Tom. This was the first I'd heard the boy's name spoken. At the bottom of the TV a list of donor names ran like ticker tape. Tom Gibbons passed over the screen, E. Gaylord, $40. I imagined this Tom with his wife and two children. He was up so late or so early because his own son had the flu or maybe a cold and Tom Gibbons had to feed his boy children's aspirin and talk him back to sleep. He called in his donation on a whim, because he'd turned on the TV for a few moments, saw the boy in the wheelchair, and thought, *Children's aspirin can't make the crippled children walk.* $40 was the price for banishing forever from his mind the image of the boy deteriorating in a chair, freeing Tom Gibbons to concentrate once again on the small comforts of his own son's minor, passing virus.

"I will tell you this," the mother continued. "One of Tom's friends had a heart attack. When he was twelve—*they* were twelve—he swam across a pool, and when he stepped out into the breeze, he dropped on the ground in a seizure. This was not the friend who died. The doctors said it was heredity, this heart attack, but his parents' hearts were strong as racehorses."

By now I had run out of things to even pretend to say.

"The point is, of course, that when Tom came to me later, and asked how he could tell if he was getting a heart attack, how would he know the signs, do you know what I answered him?"

"No," I said.

"Neither do I. For the life of me, I can't . . . I was probably busy doing something else. In the back garden, maybe. There was sun. Wasps. He probably waited for a minute and then walked away."

Down the hall, Tom's father began screaming. It was a sound of grief so terrible it bordered on rapture, a sound that could turn lives around and begin them again in a new place. I thought, I should not hear this, and yet I listened, even with relief. We knew what it meant without anyone's explanation. I turned to the mother as the reality of this moment struck her and lodged deep; she bowed slowly inward, wrapping her arms around herself as if she were her own child. All the while she did not tear her eyes from the TV. A drum rolled. The dollar signs flipped over into the next million. Bright lights flashed, the fat woman jumped up and down and wept. The host embraced her, the two swaying mightily above the displaced boy, who stared out from the screen upon us all. "Shame," the mother said.

■■■■■■■■■■

The Immaculate Conception

John Addiego

When Giuseppe Verbicaro was eighty-nine years old he married Maria Guadalupe Diego, a seventeen-year-old prostitute from the Latino barrio of the Mission District. He stepped out of Molinari's on Columbus, a little tipsy, and stood on the steps of the church overlooking Washington Square. This is when he first got the notion that God wanted him to remarry, as he stood on the steps and watched the pigeons circle the spires and fluted alcoves overhead. And even though Giuseppe was currently married, God told him it was time to do it again.

Maria was working North Beach when she spotted Giuseppe shuffling across the park in a forty-year-old, three-piece, pin-striped suit. Two months pregnant by God only knew which salesman from Tulsa or sailor from San Diego, she heard the child speak to her and express its desire to live. This was three days before Manuel and one of his girls were supposed to take her for the abortion. She lay on the grass in Washington Square watching a cloud the shape of a woman's face while two men played a flute and a clarinet, and the child said *I want this* from her stomach. Hijo, she thought, I need a husband. Some rich old geezer who will leave me alone.

When she approached Giuseppe on the church steps three pigeons hovered inches above his hat and shoulders. Maria began to ask for directions, but laughed unavoidably when the birds landed on the old-timer's hat and shoulders. He shook his head and arms, then found himself laughing, too. A few minutes later they were speaking a mixture of Spanish, Italian and pidgin English, punctuated by Giuseppe's extreme chivalry.

"My wife has passed away," he lied in Italian because this was what God probably wanted him to say. As he brushed a tear from his eye, his gold-plated wristwatch flashed.

"I am so very sorry for you," she lied in Spanish. She wore a white dress and leather sandals. A blue rebozo draped her head and shoulders. The consoling touch of her small hand on his was no more than a feather.

Giuseppe's wife of sixty years, Rosari, was informed of the bigamy by their daughter, Francesca, a week after the marriage.

"They even got his birth date in Calabria," Francesca said. She leaned over the *Chronicle*, which was spread across her broad lap. "Look at that, Ma. It can't be him. You think it's him? Or else somebody found his I.D. in some saloon?"

Rosari pulled on the hem of her black dress. The two women sat facing the street, on the porch of the family house in the East Bay. They were silent for some time. Then Rosari said, "Well, that cuts it. Enough is enough."

Giuseppe's children and grandchildren were astounded by his September romance across the bay. It wasn't just embarrassing, even disgusting when you actually thought about it, but wasn't it also illegal, they asked each other. You think they check the records on people? You think in San Francisco they care if an old goat marries a child? In San Francisco?

"Who is this little goldbrick? Who is this home-wrecker?" Francesca shrieked.

"I thought Pop was the home-wrecker," her simple-minded older brother, Narciso, answered. This was because Giuseppe had truly taken up as a wrecker after the Great Earthquake set its example and threw his family into the streets in 1906. Up until that moment he'd spent most of his years in America shining shoes in the Majestic Theater on Ninth and Market, but the seismic convulsion changed his life forever. With a mixture of terror and awe he witnessed the enormous brick edifice, with its roof seventy-five feet above the floor, burst open like a pig on a spit as he stood holding his box of rags and wax. America was burning and falling around him. God was telling rich and poor alike: He was not pleased.

Rubble needed to be cleared. Charred and half-toppled houses needed to be demolished to open lots for new buildings. Giuseppe was not a big man, but he was sinewy and tall for an Italian peasant, and he could swing a sledgehammer like an ape. For decades afterward his children and grandchildren would tell stories of houses he toppled like trees, buildings he chopped down and removed from the face of the earth by his own hand. They would speak in hushed tones of banks and offices, wrought of brick and wood, returned to dust by their father.

Precisely where Maria came from is unclear, but it was said she had family who tended sheep and rainy farmland for a land baron in the red and green mountains in the Oaxaca department of Mexico. Her older brother had snuck into California with her and died from a foot infection soon after. The curandera who attended the ailing boy with herbs and incantations realized a week before his death that there was nothing to be done to keep him alive, and she told Maria this on a fog-shrouded summer morning on Valencia Street, stirring instant coffee at the card table. The girl, then only fourteen, decided that afternoon that she would have to become a prostitute in order to survive.

She was dark and exquisite, even at that age, with deep eyes that flowed into a fierce anger and then, instantly, ebbed into the sorrow of a confused child. Hustling for a dope peddler named Manuel near hotels, bars, and night clubs in North Beach cost her the little affection and sympathy she'd had from neighboring women. She endured their vehemence, avoided their church and markets, and slept frequently in unlocked cars. Her hatred of men, of their rankness and animal minds, almost matched her self-hatred, the disgust she felt toward the small, elegant body she was trapped inside of.

A woman who also worked Broadway and North Beach found their marriage the funniest thing she'd seen in years, but Maria saw little humor in the undertaking. She listened to the child's need inside of her. To Giuseppe she was a virgin and remained so, in spite of the pregnancy, throughout their years together.

It may have been senility. It may have been the overwhelming purity of her beauty in his eyes. Some of the family attributed it to vermouth and closed the book there. Regardless, Giuseppe had not felt such harmony with the world around him, the eucalyptus trees and the junipers, the carved stones, the gleam of oil on the bay at dusk, for as long as memory. And God had often dealt Giuseppe a mysterious hand, giving him bread for destruction instead of craft, making him appear the rake in the bars and social clubs of Little Italy with a wife conveniently stirring pots across the bay when, as He and he only knew, he'd been struck impotent some twenty years earlier after an injury and a disgusting encounter in the Tenderloin. And now God had told Giuseppe Verbicaro, brittle-boned old sinner with a limp sex, drinker and dreamer with a big fedora and wandering brogans, to provide for this angel.

Maria's cappuccino-colored skin, her sudden laughter and eyes black as midnight, made him smile like a baby. The smell of her hair was from another world. So when she informed him that she was with child, about two months after the courthouse wedding, he asked simply how and by whom. She answered with a steady voice: *Dios sabe* and *Nadie*. God knows. Nobody.

He accepted the miracle. Maybe he remembered the story, told by another Italian shoeshine before the earthquake, about a woman in the old Sutro Baths at the Cliff House. Sperm, thrashing madly upstream in public pools, could make things unsafe for women anywhere outside of their own bathrooms. Maybe he took it the way he received the columns of sunlight finding him through morning fog on a long walk to the liquor store on Grant, as something too beautiful to ask questions about.

One night he decided that God had slipped between Maria's thighs while she slept and planted His seed with a penis as thin as a thread of gold. God's penis was incredibly thin, but it was also unbelievably long. It stretched through the open window of their flat on Green Street, past the top of the Coit Tower; it reached down from the sky where a full moon hung beside it like a testicle filled with celestial semen. Giuseppe chuckled as he found his way to the toilet in the dark. God has only one ball, he said to himself.

The marriage turned out better than Maria had expected, due in large part to Giuseppe's impotence, but also to his generosity. He gave her money for nice clothes and food, for movies and tickets to the Funhouse and Playland at the beach. He watched her make dolls out of cornhusks and yarn. That first summer, learning that she craved fresh cherries, he walked a few miles with her to the Japanese Tea Garden and picked his fedora full amidst bonsai maples and miniature pagodas.

In many respects she was still a child, coerced at an early age into selling her body and her childhood. A pimp named Manuel had seen her potential and made her a lucrative product. He injected her with drugs, raped and sodomized her, beat her with his fists until she thought of the dark water and the peace of falling from the Golden Gate. It was the unborn infant who saved her, who gave her a reason to find a way to live.

News of the pregnancy put the frosting on Giuseppe's disgrace. What could there be under the sun to shock and disgust you more than this, his children wanted to know. But the birth inspired a sea change. Without plan or announcement his daughters and grandchildren came to Green Street with gifts, with ravioli and a whole salmon and fig cookies for the mother, with a flannel bunting and bibs for the baby. They held the child and marveled at his beautiful skin, same as his mother's, at his perfect oval face and black eyes. They took Maria shopping at Macy's and made her eat so her hips and breasts could get bigger. Francesca's daughter Susan struggled to understand Maria's Spanish, even the name of her son. "Hey-

Zeus, you call him?"

"*Si, Jesus,*" she replied.

"He's a little miracle, that's for sure."

They baby-sat while Maria went to the Funhouse and flew down the wooden slide on a potato sack or lost herself among the mirrors. They scolded Giuseppe for being a skinflint, and they threw out his liquor bottles. They shook their heads and sighed, imagining the old man's faux virility. They walked around the kitchen holding the little miracle to their breasts, singing old show tunes.

One morning between three and four Giuseppe had trekked out of bed to the toilet when he heard a rattling. Somebody was trying the door. He stood behind it a moment, then cleared his throat. The rattling stopped.

"Hey," Giuseppe whispered. He thought it might be old Desiderio, locked out for the night by his angry wife. "Che cosa?"

A man's voice on the other side spoke in English and Spanish. He said he was Maria's family. Giuseppe opened the door.

The fellow was young with slicked-back hair, and he kept sniffing like he had a cold. Giuseppe made espresso. The two men tiptoed around the kitchen, to Maria's bedroom door where they could see mother and babe sleeping. The man sniffed and chuckled. His hands and eyes moved constantly. They returned to the kitchen.

Giuseppe pulled the salmon, two feet long and stiff as a plank, from the ice box and placed it in a pan to thaw. He moved slowly, as if most of his joints were as frozen as the fish, crushing garlic and basil leaves into a bowl. The young man asked why in the hell Maria had chosen him to fleece. Giuseppe didn't understand his English. There was a pistol, shiny as tinsel, in the young man's hand. This he understood. What the fuck did this *anciano* think he was doing? Ancient old man in pajamas holding a fish.

In the old stories, in the Good Book which Giuseppe couldn't read, the Lord made a man and a woman and kicked them out of paradise for being nosey. Later, in Giuseppe's recollection, He sent a child to save us all. It was a strange plan when you thought about it. He gets with child a Virgin, then appoints some old man to look after them.

The young man said he needed Maria because she brought it in fast and because nobody ducks out on him. He laughed. "You can buy it on the street next week, if I don't kill you."

The gun barrel was less than a yard from Giuseppe's face. The flat

77

was silent, save the ticking of a clock and the occasional bleating of ships on the bay. Giuseppe wondered what God might have up His sleeve. Was it time for him to die? Was it time for Maria and her little miracle to die? And at that moment the little miracle screamed.

It was a scream like an ice pick in the head, like a siren to wake the dead out of Hell. The young man covered his ears, and Giuseppe made like DiMaggio at Seal's Stadium. He made like he was bringing down the house with one swing, with a fish as his hammer. The man's shiny head cracked like a walnut against the door frame. Blood seeped from its ears and mouth. Maria knelt and picked up the pistol. "Gracias," she whispered to Giuseppe.

He fit into a large burlap sack, but it took both of them to carry him to the pier. Already the produce trucks were arriving with their many gifts from the fields and valleys of California, with dates and avocados, with oranges bright as the sun from the south. And the child on his mother's hip pointed the way, singing in his own tongue as Maria and Giuseppe slouched under the weight of our world and trudged through the darkness to the water.

■■■■■■■■■■■

Berna's Place

Jane McCafferty

My husband and I worked together so that the house would be presentable for our only son and his new girlfriend. "It's serious, this time," our son had told me. "I think I've found my life." Life, he said, not wife. But really, he'd found the whole package.

Jude, my husband, was a newly retired art professor, and an artist — working in oil and acrylic and over the years our entire house had turned into a studio. We had paint thinner on the back of our toilet, smocks on the railing, art magazines piled into the corners of the dining room. I told myself this was inevitable: how could a man like Jude be contained in one room? Even the front porch had been conquered by his old cans, the dried brushes piled in a heap below the swing, the scrappy canvases he never seemed to move out to the curb for the trash collectors leaning against the wall by the door. (I'd given up.) In his art he was somewhat successful; the best galleries in Philadelphia had shown his work, and Jude was gratified by a number of fellow artists who seemed to think he was some kind of genius. Articles in the 1970s about his early neo-Expressionism said as much. Though he'd never admit it, and often made the joke that he was a has-been that never was, I knew Jude needed to think he was a genius. In his heart he still wrestled with that tiresome affliction that most men trade in for a kind of reluctant humility by the time they turn fifty. Jude, at sixty-four, was still going strong, sometimes painting all night long in the attic, Billie Holiday or Bach for company, a view of the skyline out the window.

He was also very kind. He knew when I was tired from a day at work, where I sat behind a counter in a crowded hospital trying to help exasperated, sometimes furious people figure out their health care insurance. When I was mopping the floor to prepare the house for our son and his girlfriend, Jude climbed out of the cave of his work and told me to go take a nap. He'd clean, he said, his eyes still glazed with his art. And I knew he'd apply the same fierce, concentrated energy to housework as he did to his painting. The place would shine.

My son rang the doorbell that evening at dusk; I was struck by that since usually he burst through the door with no warning. I was used to him raiding the refrigerator as if he were still in high school. This night was different, though. This was the night we were to meet his girlfriend.

I was the one to answer. There they stood in the dusk, my handsome son in his maroon sweater and ponytail, a twenty-five-year-old young man who liked his dog, reading, Buddhist meditation, and hiking, and beside him, holding his hand, stood his girlfriend, as he'd been calling her, despite the fact that she was, at least compared to him, old. Sixty, I'd soon learn. Sixty. Nine years my senior. She wore a beige raincoat, and moccasins. She was very tall, with high cheekbones and lank, dark hair parted on the side, and my first thought was that she looked like my pediatrician from childhood, a woman who'd visited my home when I'd had German measles. The resemblance was so uncanny that for a moment I thought it was her. Doctor Vera Martin! I was almost ready to embrace her, for she had impressed me deeply as a child, with a sense of authority that seemed rooted both in her eloquent silences and the sudden warmth that transformed her serious face when she finally smiled. My son's friend smiled and the resemblance only deepened.

"Hi!" I said, and stared at this woman who I knew could not be my childhood doctor, who was, in fact, long dead. So who was she? Not his girlfriend. Not really.

"Invite us in, Ma," said my son, and I could see he was enjoying my shock. "This is Berna, Ma. Berna, this is Marian, my ma."

Berna reached out to shake my hand. Her eyes were dark and warm. As she opened her coat I saw her sweatshirt was covered with decals of cats.

"I wasn't able to dress appropriately," she said. "I'm coming from work. You'll pardon me, I hope?"

"Work?"

"She's a vet," my son jumped in, beaming at her. He was more animated than I'd seen him in years. "She makes house-calls. A traveling vet. I went with her today. She's excellent. Harry (that was his dog) loved her. That's how we met. She's the only traveling vet in town." He took a deep breath, he seemed filled with a kind of desperate, nervous excitement—

so different from his usual taut calm.

"A traveling vet," I said. "Well well. That's something. Please come in, sit down."

The two of them followed me into the living room. I felt I was dreaming. Berna sat down. She made no noise as she sat. No little groan of pleasure. No sigh. She sat with her long back as straight as the poised tails of the cats on her sweatshirt, her eyes and the eyes of the cats too alert so that I felt like a small crowd was quietly assessing me. Griffin sat beside her, and held her hand, and suddenly I asked him if I could speak to him in the kitchen. I felt toyed with, and wanted him to know.

"Why didn't you mention she was old enough to be your grandmother?" I hadn't meant to hiss at him. In the kitchen light his brown eyes widened.

"What's your problem?" he said. "Did you turn into Dad or something?"

"Griffin, this is ridiculous! Don't act like you're not enjoying the shock value of this! She looks like my childhood pediatrician, who was old then, and dead now!"

He scrunched up his face in a sort of disgusted confusion. All the composure I'd seen for the past two years, composure that had struck me as false, had left him. I knew his palms were sweating. I felt for him, but it struck me as comical, his expecting me to take this in stride.

"I want to marry this woman," he said. "I want to marry her. This has nothing to do with your childhood doctor, or shock value." I saw he was deadly serious. So, I thought, this is how his strangeness has found itself a home. Let's hope it's temporary, a pit stop.

Berna appeared in the doorway, a tall, long-limbed sixty in a cheap, baggy cat sweatshirt that somehow was dignified enough on her.

"Look," she said. "Let's be up front here, shall we? Let's get it all out on the table. Go ahead and tell me what's pressing in on you: I'm old enough to be his mother."

"Grandmother," I said.

"Grandmother then," Berna said, with a kind of pride that lifted her chin. "Though I'd have to have given birth at an awfully young age to make that a true statement." Her voice was soft and steady with confidence.

"I've finally brought Berna here because she's the first woman I've really loved. That needs to be known and digested."

"That's what you're telling her?" I said to him, remembering a string of girls named Cindy, and the three Jens, two of whom I'd become quite friendly with.

"I told her because it's true, Ma. OK? Now it's all out in the open. You want a beer, Bern?"

"Sure," said Bern.

And I heard my husband coming down the steps. Here we go, I thought.

M y husband and son never got along. I used to blame Jude — he'd been so absent during Griffin's childhood, so self-absorbed, and my son had been born, it seemed, awestruck by his father. Terrible combination. In those early years we lived out in the country and Jude painted in a large shed; Griffin was like a dog, waiting too patiently for the master to finally notice him and play. The more absorbed his father was, the keener Griffin's need became; Jude claimed there was something manipulative in this, but my heart broke for my child, and I think I rightly feared his very soul was being shaped by the intensity of his longing. Maybe that can be said of all children.

I'd beg Jude to give the boy a little attention, and he did, but it was the wrong kind. He'd take Griffin to the art museum. He'd try to make him memorize paintings, learn perspective, listen to facts about the artists. Griffin tried his best, and told Jude he wanted to walk into Pierre Bonnard's paintings and live there, but you shouldn't do this with a seven-year-old unless the kid is oddly brilliant, a prodigy, which Griffin never was, and I know this disappointed his father, and I know, also, that his father blamed my genes. I come from a long line of Midwestern farmers. If I said any big words in my mother's presence, she cocked her eyebrow, which meant for me to get down off my damn high horse. Intelligence was a force to be tamed into utility.

After years of rejection, Griffin finally gave up. He was twelve, then. He got a dog for his birthday that year. It seemed to me that all his love for his father got transferred onto the dog, a mutt from the shelter Griff named Roberto, for the great ballplayer Roberto Clemente. Roberto was a bit mangy and looked heartsick, but loved Griffin the way dogs love boys. A simple solution, I thought. Roberto went everywhere with Griffin — they even let that dog into the grocery store. Things were easier for Griffin after that. He became a teenager who said very little to either of us. In high school he found an enormous friend named Jack J. Pree, who wore thick glasses, and who managed to attract certain girls despite his obesity. Jack lived with his aunt and uncle, drove a monstrous, ancient gold Buick, called himself *the fatso existentialist* and called Griff *Brother Soul*. It was the sort of mythology Griff needed. Brother Soul and The Fatso Existentialist spent days just driving around with aging Roberto hanging out the window, the three of them listening to old blues and new punk. Nights they read philosophy books aloud, or had water balloon fights in Jack J. Pree's tiny hedged back yard, which was five doors down from us. Through a hole in the bushes, I spied on them. I loved my son, and I'd become a spy in his life.

Jude walked into the kitchen that evening, and I saw, for a moment, how handsome he was, which still happened when I was aware that someone else would be looking at him for the first time. Griffin, Berna and I had taken seats at the oak table by the glass wall that looked out onto a little patio. Berna had first stood at the window and admired that space. "Lovely," she'd said.

"Hey Griffin," Jude said, and looked at Berna. "Where's your girlfriend?"

Berna got up from the table.

"Hello," she said. "I'm Berna Kateson." She walked over and shook his hand. She was nearly as tall as Jude.

Griffin watched them with utmost seriousness, waiting for his father to do something wrong.

"Griffin and I have been together for quite a while now, so we thought it was time to meet you," Berna said, again with her distinct, almost imperceptible chin-raising pride.

"Uh huh," said my husband. "I see." He shot a look at Griffin, then his eyes settled on my own, and I looked down, away from him, so that he was stranded in his shock. Berna sat back down.

"I realize this isn't a typical scenario," she said. "I realize one might feel a little baffled when faced with the possibility of their son marrying an older woman, even a very successful one."

Jude opened the refrigerator and pulled out a bottle of wine, poured himself a glass, and sat down with us at the table.

"So," he said to Berna, and looked at her with coldly urgent eyes. "Why don't you tell us about yourself. About your success."

"That seems a kind of power-play question," Berna said. "So maybe I should ask it to you. Why don't you tell me about yourself? Your success?"

She smiled back at him, without malice.

I could feel Griffin loving this. Her simple composure must have seemed like real bravery to him.

"Well," said my husband, "I'm sure Griffin here has told you all about me. I'm sure it's been a stellar father-son relationship report. It was all little league and fishing trips with Griff and me."

Berna laughed, generously, I thought. Jude squinted his eyes at her, then looked at me as if to say, are we dreaming?

"We're both wiped out, actually," said Griffin. "We had a day that was hard on the heart, didn't we, Bern? I mean, we should tell the story of our day and put things in perspective, right? Rather than spend more time on this petty American bullshit?"

Whenever Griffin didn't like something he called it American. This had been his habit for years.

"We had to put two cats down, and tell a dog owner that his dog had one week of life left," Berna said. "Nobody took this well. We became on-the-spot grief counselors, which isn't unusual." She massaged her temples. She stuck her limp dark hair behind her ears.

"We?" said my husband. "Did my son go to veterinary school since I last saw him? Or is he simply Granny's sidekick now?"

"He's studying to be an assistant," Berna said. "I'm sorry you're obsessed with age, but I'd have been foolish not to expect it."

Berna sipped her beer. Then a great burst of laughter escaped from her mouth. Very, very odd. A shocking contrast to her whole bearing, which was elegant reserve.

"Excuse me," she said, as if she'd burped. Her eyes flashed, widening; her lips suppressed a smile.

"Can we go into the other room where it's more comfortable?" I said, as if we would all turn into different people if our chairs were softer.

So anyhow," Berna said, almost as soon as we sat down, "Griffin is gifted, utterly gifted with animals. By that I mean he's not only got the brains to be a vet, he's got the heart. He's already on his way to being a certified assistant, but I think that's just the beginning."

Jude sat with his arms crossed in a high-backed green chair, his eyes peering over his glasses. I sat on the couch on one side of Berna, and Griffin sat very close to her on the other side. I was really hoping they didn't do anything like kiss. Griffin had been known to kiss his other girlfriends quite blatantly, with a kind of hostile showmanship in our presence.

"It's easy to find a brain," Berna continued. "And it's easy to find a heart. I've had a whole string of assistants that were all heart. Near disasters, I have to say. The last gal, Peggy, who I thought might be good since she looked exactly like a horse — so often the ones who most resemble animals are good — I know, that's odd — but anyhow, every time we had to go to someone's house and put their pet down, she'd gallop out of the room and sob. The person losing the animal they'd loved for twenty years would be quietly welling up with tears, and then they'd stop, too concerned with Peggy's sobbing to even feel their own sorrow."

"So what happened to Peggy?" I said. I imagined her grazing in a field, chewing on hay. "Did she find another profession?"

"Peggy's all right," Berna said. "Peggy has a job in a bank now. She needs numbers. Numbers don't die."

Jude sighed. It was the sigh that said he wasn't getting enough attention.

"Before Peggy it was Michael Bent. Michael Bent turned out to be a bit of a Nazi. I suppose that's irresponsible of me, using that term when he really did nothing at all. But his eyes had me constantly on the alert. I'd never seen such icy eyes. The eyes of an imprisoned soul. The only time I saw pleasure in those eyes was when he was giving shots. Before Michael Bent it was Barren Sedgewick, a very short, witty man in his fifties who quit a big corporate job to be my assistant, and then after three weeks died of a heart attack one evening in my car. I'm sorry to go on like this. May I go get myself another beer?"

Griffin ran to get her one; now he was back.

"Tell them about Emily Donnerbaum," said Griffin, enraptured, a child hearing stories he already knows.

"Yes, do tell us about Emily Donnerbaum," said Jude, "and then, why don't we start planning your wedding?"

A silence fell.

"How many children will you be having, Griff?" Jude said, smiling, his arms still crossed.

Griffin moved even closer to Berna. He rolled his eyes and gave his father a look of exasperation.

"You think I'd even consider bringing children into *this* world? You think I'd want them sucking down the energy of global terrorism? And as I mentioned to you a few years back, the fact that we have enough children on the globe *already* makes a *difference* to me. I'm not so big on propagating my own genes to gratify my own ego, which I know you think is too big, and you may be right, in fact I *know* you're right, but at least I'm trying to *subdue* it. Not to mention stray animals without homes. Why does everyone I meet have this 1950s American thing about having kids?"

Griffin spoke with such passion that Jude looked at him for a moment with love. We hadn't seen any passion from Griffin for a few years. We'd seen composure. We'd heard descriptions of what he called his "practice." His practice was sitting on a pillow and counting each one of his breaths for one hour a day, before going to work as a telemarketer for Greenpeace. (He'd quit his very lucrative computer job.) His practice purified his thoughts, he said. It helped him deal with "afflictive emotion." It allowed, I suppose, for un-American transcendence.

"And we'll have a house full of animals, that's for certain," Berna said, in a voice that was soothing no matter what she was saying. "I have four cats now, and two dogs, and I've managed this restraint only because it's difficult for one person to have more than this. More than six and you start cheating them out of a superb life. But with a man around the house, especially a good man like Griff, there's no telling how many we'll be able to take in."

"Our grandchildren," I mumbled, and barked out a laugh in spite of myself.

"Actually," Berna suddenly said, looking at Griffin, "it's not in my nature tò lie this way. Nor is it in yours. What were we thinking. Griff? We'd let them down easy?"

Lying?

She looked at us. "Look," she said, holding up her hand to show us the ring. "We're already married. I'm your daughter-in-law now, all right? There will be no big wedding." She smiled over at Griffin.

"OK," said Griffin, "now you know. Bern, tell them about Emily Donnerbaum now! You gotta hear this!"

That night, after they left, I lay in bed in our dark room and started to laugh. Jude sighed, exasperated with me; this wasn't funny. In fact, each time he closed his eyes he said he pictured them in bed, naked together, and it made his skin crawl. At this I laughed harder, then settled down to scold him.

"Jude! That's rather unkind," I said. "She may be getting on in years, but she's not disgusting. Her face is beautiful. Those cheekbones I'd like to have."

"Naked," Jude said. "I keep seeing her naked, and it is disgusting. It's like a fairy-tale image I can't shake. I guess this marks me as pathetic and shallow. I always said you'd eventually discover this."

"No, not pathetic, Jude, but a little harsh. And in ten years I'll be her age. Will I be a fairy-tale image?"

"You'll be you."

"I think old bodies are beautiful," I said, and smiled to myself, my eyes on the twisted black branches of the tree that scraped our window. I had never really thought this before. In fact, I'd always found old bodies disturbing, male or female, but especially female. As a young woman I'd been one to sit on the beach and cringe at the old ladies walking by, I'd been one to promise myself that I'd always stay covered up when I got up in years. But in the darkness that night, remembering Berna's vivid vet stories and my son next to her, holding her hand and waiting to be alone with her, a clenched fist inside of me opened up. I lay there remembering my son's waiting — the feel of his waiting — everything was boring to him near the end of our night because he wanted her, he wanted her alone, and in bed. How long had it been since Jude had experienced that sort of waiting? Waiting to have me? Ten years? Twenty?

"Jude?" I said.

"Mmmm?"

"I think we need to put aside our bias and learn to love Berna. She's highly intelligent, and graceful, and actually quite funny. And she brings out the *life* in Griff. Whether we like it or not, she's going to be part of us."

"You're losing your mind," he grumbled. "A young man doesn't marry a woman thirty-five years older than himself. Thirty-five fucking years! If he does, the parents should step in and interpret it as mental illness, and begin looking for appropriate institutions."

"Jude! He's always been different, but he's never been mentally ill."

"I'd rather he had brought home a little bald Buddhist girl," Jude said. "If I were him right now, some part of me would be hoping my parents would step in."

"Jude, he's an adult, and he's married. We have no power anymore."

"He's a good-looking kid missing out on beautiful young women! He's missing out on the best life has to offer! He's trading all that in — the best years of his life — for an eccentric brain whose dogs probably sit in chairs at the dinner table."

Jude sat up and flicked on the light.

He looked around the room as if he'd never seen it before.

"Why would he do this?" he said, to the wall. "I bet she buys the dogs plaid raincoats like that woman we knew in Sea Isle."

"No, Jude. Berna is not the dog-raincoat type. You know that." I was exhilarated. I was, moment by moment, growing more proud of my son, and less interested in my husband, whom I knew I could taunt right now — I knew I could talk to him about all the men he knew who'd left their wives and married women half their age. (We had two very good friends in fact, who'd done this, and we'd gone to their pretty, hushed, little weddings, and despite my initial cynicism I'd felt moved and happy for everyone.) And I knew I could bring up Anita Defranz, a talented twenty-year-old painter he'd had an affair with eight years ago, a girl he brought to dinner after confessing the affair to me, wanting it all to be in the open, wanting me to like the girl, and I did, I did like her quite a bit even as I wanted her to vanish, even as my face grew hot at the thought of her. But I never told Jude that something ended for me during that dinner, nothing dramatic — but some part of my story with Jude ended as Anita Defranz told me how delicious the casserole was. "May I please have the recipe, please?" she'd said.

Jude had so trusted me to understand him, to understand his longing for Anita Defranz, who indeed was beautiful, with perfect skin and long, shiny dark hair, that I felt oddly touched by that trust, almost as if Jude were a child whose neediness made him a little dense. And now, in bed, feeling Jude's protest fill the room, feeling his confusion thicken the air in the room, I again saw him as a child, a child who could not see beyond its own sense of things. I felt sorry for him, really, and hated that pity, because it was pity that catapulted him from the realm of anyone I could unequivocally desire. Maybe I'd pitied him ever since Anita Defranz in her red silk shirt had sat so primly at our table.

"I'm going out for a walk," Jude said, pulling on his jeans. "I need some fresh air to help me figure this out."

I remember how after he left, and I was alone in the room without his protest, suddenly I was protesting myself. My one boy! This would be his life? This? How sad! Fundamentally sad, and it all must mean something sadder. And what kind of woman would do this? Such presumption! She was crazy, no doubt. My sentimental visions of going to stay with his young wife after the birth of their first child, a girl, of course, the girl I'd never had myself, pressed in on me.

I wept stupid tears knowing I'd stop all this just as soon as Jude came back with the energy of his rant.

I'm a reactor, Griffin once told me, not an actor.

Jude had vaguely obsessive tendencies; it showed up in his painting (one year he painted nothing but unremarkable gray rooms with brown floors), it showed up the year he drove two miles every morning at five a.m. to get a cream donut and black coffee from Winnie's Diner, in the way he had worn only black canvas shoes by day, and construction boots in the evening. He was a man who went on kicks — and I could look back over our life and organize my memories around them. *The tofu jogging year. The gambling year. The year he understood Republicans. The year of Ancient Greece books.*

And now he could not stop visiting my son and his new wife.

"Come on," he'd say. "Let's go on out and see what they're doing tonight."

"We should call ahead of time."

"No," he'd say. "I want to see what they do when they're not prepared."

"That's not polite," I argued, but somehow we'd be on our way by then, in Jude's little Chevy, his head almost touching the ceiling, the radio tuned into a sports show—the one kick he never abandoned, and me looking out the window at the starless city night.

We'd drive nine miles into the country dark, into the wild array of brilliant stars, then up along their bumpy dirt driveway, and we'd see the one lit window in their house—a kitchen window—and invariably we would find the two of them on the Murphy bed—you know, those beds that fold down out of the wall—they had one in their kitchen—someone who'd owned the house long ago had nursed an invalid. So we'd look in through the window and knock and they'd call, "Come in," having no idea who we were. They were fearless; I suppose their love had rendered the whole world benign. Or maybe Berna had always been that way.

We'd step into the dimly lit kitchen. They had a Franklin stove filled with fire for heat. The air felt good. Charged, somehow, with good, unspeakable things. With spirits and spices. Both loved cooking. Griffin, I'd always thought, should have gone to chef school. He'd always seemed most happy at the stove.

"Hi," we'd say, "just thought we'd drop in and say hello." I'd look at Jude regarding them. His face looked so troubled, all mixed up with criticism and deep interest and profound bafflement.

The two of them would be on the Murphy bed in old flannel pajamas and surrounded by three or four cats. They were always so bright-eyed, and tucked under quilts made by Berna's mother, a woman who we'd learn had joined the Peace Corps when she was seventy-four, after teaching mentally retarded adults for thirty-eight years. (My heart lurched forward, hearing this.) They'd quickly slip out of bed, smile at us and tell us to sit down at the table. In the soft light of that kitchen, with the old, creaking wooden floor and the white lace curtains and the enormous spice rack and the big cheap painting of the wild ocean, Berna looked beautiful, I noticed. Not just beautiful for an older person, but beautiful. Griff, who always looked perfect to me, was more so. Under the table, a black dog usually slept, snoring quietly. In the room just beyond the kitchen, a chameleon lived in a plant that touched the ceiling. To feed the chameleon Berna kept crickets in egg cartons on the solar porch in the back; she fed them powdered milk and fruits. You could always hear their song. When you closed your eyes it was as though the memory of a peaceful August night from the heart of childhood had been brought to life.

"Can I get you some tea?" Berna asked us, moving toward the cabinets.

"Tea would be good," I said. She had long, bare feet, and her nails were painted, which surprised me, since she wore no makeup.

"You haven't had tea until you've had Berna's," my son said.

She served us ginger tea in small blue flowered teacups, with lemon and bamboo honey. It was true, the tea was better than any we'd had. She put the teapot on the table, and sat down. Again, I noticed how she never sighed, or groaned as she moved about, as she sat or got up from chairs. (I'd begun groaning in my late thirties.)

"So," Jude wanted to know one fall night, "where are you from, originally?"

"Nova Scotia," she said, her teacup in her hand. She had wrapped herself in an orange and yellow afghan.

"Nova Scotia!" he said. "Such a beautiful place."

"Indeed. I miss it every day, even as I'm utterly rooted here."

"I was there once, in my twenties," Jude said. "We hiked, and slept near the coast, and swam in the lakes. It was stunningly gentle land. That's my memory of it. Damn, I'd like to go back. And that wild water. Nova Scotia! I'll be damned."

"You never told me about that," I said. "I thought I knew everything."

Jude smiled at me, from a Nova Scotian distance.

Was it my imagination, or did discovering that she was from Nova Scotia change everything for Jude? He was mysterious that way — unpredictable just when you started to feel his predictability too keenly.

I remember the red leaves flying beyond the window that night, my son trying not to glare at his father, while Jude leaned in toward Berna, to hear more about her homeland, his eyes warm. She told us of her father, an old fisherman who wrote poetry and was living now in a hut by a lake. A man who coaxed the sweetest carrots out of bad soil. Berna tried to talk to all of us, but really she was speaking to Jude, responding to his own sudden interest. When Jude's interested, it's like he gets a lasso out and ropes the person in.

"We usually hit the hay about now," Griffin finally said that night, because his father and Berna were still talking about Nova Scotia, and some great, irrational fear in him was taking over all his better impulses. He was imagining the object of his desire running off with his father, of course. He was imagining they looked good together. I remembered being in that kind of love, where everyone's a threat. I was far enough away from such pain to envy its intensity.

"Griffin," I whispered in his ear as we were leaving, "relax, she loves you. Nobody is going to take her away. Most certainly not *him*."

His body stiffened at this intrusive intimacy. He had to pretend he was fearless with me. And yet, as we were pulling out of the driveway, he came out onto the stoop and waved, and I felt the wave as an offering of his thanks.

In those early months we had many evenings like this, with Berna, in her silken, dusky, calming voice, telling us stories of her family, or stories involving her work, and my son listening, marveling at this articulate, strange wonder of a wife, and watching us closely, usually. After a while he'd relax, forget to be vigilant, and we'd see his own charm as he told his own story. We saw his youth, his thoughtful eyes, his wild energy for life, his mind, unhinged from worrying about the opinions of others (except maybe ours) and we understood how Berna had fallen for him.

How do I say this? Six months after I met Berna, I became involved with a thirty-year-old groundskeeper named Abraham. Perhaps it's predictable that a mother whose son is married to someone so old would feel she's been granted a kind of license. Many would say it's Freudian, but that's too easy. I only know that after we began to accept the marriage as real, after we had seen them countless times in their Murphy bed in their eccentric pajamas, bizarre but beautiful really, with their animals and radiant regard for each other, after we had spent several Sunday afternoons walking in the woods behind Berna's house, and nights under stars she, like Jude, could name, after all that I felt a kind of penetrating amusement, a profound sort of humor infecting the whole world, and a newfound belief in surprises. I was waiting to be surprised. I was open. I wasn't walking around looking for a younger man — that sort of literal answer wouldn't have appealed to me at all. And yet, the day I visited my friend Noreen in her old home near the graveyard, I knew that when she pointed out the window at a certain groundskeeper named Abraham and said, "Isn't he adorable?" that this certain Abraham was meaningful to me, somehow. He wasn't, for me, adorable, but rather a man, and I liked his name and how he looked in the gray light, with his black eyes and his faded red hooded sweatshirt, and while it's true that I wouldn't have moved beyond a whimsical admiration of the young man had I not known Berna, I stood at the window beside Noreen and felt absolutely fired with lust for a moment. I may have blushed when she told me I shouldn't stare at children that way.

"Speaking of that," Noreen said, "how's Griffin doing with the old lady? Bernadette?"

"Berna," I said. "She's really not that old. She's younger than we are, Noreen, in a way. I mean, her spirit is roughly Griffin's age. And she's got hardly a line in her face. (This part wasn't true and I was embarrassed to find myself lying.) And she moves so gracefully. I understand now, I think."

"God!" Noreen said. "I hate how everyone ends up understanding everything! It's weird, completely weird, and now you think it's normal."

I could have said, "Noreen, look at you, in this lovely old house that you keep so nice, you who fears the water and chooses to get seasick every other weekend so your husband can have his boat and eat it too, you who spends a fortune getting your hair bleached twice a month because you're terrified of looking old, look at all that and then we can talk about normal."

But I said nothing. I was not an aggressive person. I hated to hurt anyone, so avoided challenging conversation. And I was, perhaps, already planning how to talk to Abraham. I'd known Noreen for twenty-six years. We'd pushed children in strollers together. Nothing I could say would make her able to understand what I was feeling about life. She was a dear friend, but all the limits I had to respect with her made me lonely.

Abraham sat in his truck listening to music and eating a piece of bread. I walked up to the truck and said, "How long had you been a landscaper?" I was nervous, and said *had*, rather than *have*, and felt the tips of my ears grow hot.

"A landscaper?" Abraham said. "Is that what I am?"

He looked bored, at first.

"If not that, then what? What do you call yourself?"

"Abraham Horell. And you? What do you call yourself?" The boredom in his face had given way to a kind of bemused smile. It was a windy spring day, with gray light and silence surrounding us. I was aware that I'd relive this moment in memory.

"I haven't come up with a word for myself yet. Don't know what to call myself."

"Oh," he said, flatly, and I worried I'd been too odd.

"My name is Patricia," I said. "Some call me Trisha."

"Trisha," he said. "Nice name."

He got out of his truck. He was tall, in loose khakis. He left the music on. Miles Davis. He asked me why I was standing there at the edge of Noreen's yard. Did I know her?

"She's an old friend."

"Do you know the old man?"

"Not as well as I know Noreen."

"The old man takes her for granted. That's my opinion. And I've only been around him three times. My father would've called him a horse's ass."

That was all I needed. It was fuel. If he could see that much, he could see a lot of things.

I looked toward the massive garden he had planted, the rich soil dark as his hair.

"You do good work," I said. And I stepped closer to him. I looked at his face. My heart was pounding because I knew that even this subtle gesture might look as wildly transparent as it felt.

"Thank you," he said, and I saw he wore a tiny star of an earring on one ear. "If you come back later, you can see the whole garden, the whole thing, finished."

"I think I will," I said. And I tried to imagine that the final look we exchanged demolished any innocence between us.

It didn't. I did come back later, and he walked me around the garden, like a proud boy with a curious parent. My heart sank as I told him how lovely it all was. I came back twice that week, and it wasn't until I brought him coffee the following week that he understood. I could tell by the way he took the coffee, brushed hair out of my eyes, lowered his chin to his chest, and held my gaze.

Later that same day Abraham and I went to a place called The Deluxe Luncheonette. And I got to hear all about the sweet young man who had dropped out of med school five years ago, who was divorced, who had a child named Zoe Clare, whose ex-wife was "remarried to a rich dude" but still demanding child support, whose father, whom he'd adored, had recently died.

Abraham spoke with ease, fueled by the bad, strong coffee of the luncheonette. His legs moved back and forth under the table, knocking against each other. I didn't particularly like his style of conversation — it had that windblown quality, where you feel the person could be talking to anyone, but I didn't admit this to myself at the time.

As it turned out, we were there because Abraham lived upstairs, in a room.

After coffee, and rice pudding, and saltines, and water, up we went. My head felt full of blood. My eyes watered. I bit down on the lipstick I'd applied hours before, then wiped it off on a tissue.

You could stand at the window of his book-lined room and look down on the little main street, the unspeakably mundane work-a-day world, and the view gave me more reason to be there. He came up behind me, placed a kiss on my neck, which felt too cold, too wet, but I was relieved not to have to talk anymore, and relieved that the room was dusky, so that both my body and the pictures of his child framed on the dresser, a girl in a red hat jumping rope, were slightly muted.

"Are you on the pill?" he whispered, and I told him I was, but he should use a condom anyway—diseases, I whispered. I hadn't been on the pill for years, and the truth was, it had been two years since I needed to worry about any of it. The change, as they called it, was something I'd walked through as if it were a simple doorway. What change? I'd wanted to ask someone.

I did not like his kissing—too pointed, almost mock-aggressive. I kept turning my face. But soon after, when he entered me, speaking to me gently, saying "it's OK, it's OK," and I whispered back, "I know it's OK," I did not expect to be weeping with the odd shock of joy that was simply intense sexual pleasure. I clung to him with misplaced emotion, as if he were someone I'd fallen in love with. And since no real love was anywhere in that room, save for in the face of that jump-roping little girl on the dresser, the pleasure ended in embarrassment for me.

For Abraham, I'm not sure. He may have been used to these things. He ran down to the luncheonette and brought me up a coke and a plate of fries. We ate them together in silence, and I kept my eyes wide on the window, and listened to the sound of my own chewing as if it could protect me from thinking things like *here I am, a middle-aged slut!*

As I sat there dipping fries into ketchup, Jude's face, Jude's voice, broke through like a light. I was gratified to feel I missed him. Missed my husband, whoever he was.

I had four more late afternoons just like this one, and put an end to them because I understood how quickly they would put an end to themselves. Abraham's last words to me were so ironic they provoke my laughter even now. "You're wild," he'd said. How unknown I felt, but not as foolish as you might imagine.

I saw Abraham only one other time—two months later, driving through a blue day in his truck, with a dog, and a young woman, whose yellow hair streamed out the window. I honked my horn and waved, in spite of myself, and then he was gone.

Jude," I said one night in the dark. It was raining, and we'd just watched a bad movie on television, both of us enduring insomnia. "I had an affair, you know."

"No, I didn't know."

"He was very young. He worked on Noreen's yard. It ended up meaning very little to me, but I thought I'd tell you. You've always been open with me."

"Have I?"

"As I recall, a girl you loved ate dinner with us. She loved my cooking."

"True. True enough."

"Jude, where are you? I can't feel your reaction."

"I can't either."

"Excuse me?"

"Maybe I'm relieved."

"Relieved?"

"That you're outside the shell of this marriage when I've been outside it for years."

He sat up and put his head in his hands. I felt that he wanted to weep, but had no tears.

"Jude?" My face was red; why had I told him?

"Just don't say you're sorry."

"I won't."

"Because I've been terribly unfaithful. More than once, you know. More than twice. You probably know this. Do you know this?" I didn't say a word, but felt alone now, when I had imagined I'd already been alone. Does loneliness have floors like an endless skyscraper, and you keep descending?

"Four times. Four affairs. The last one ended last year. I've been dying to tell you."

"Really? Why don't we go downstairs and have us a drink, Jude. And you can tell me the story of our lives. You know, the one you forgot to tell me for the past twenty years or so. I'm such a good listener but you'll need to give me some details." I was on this new cold floor in the same old skyscraper and it seemed I had a new voice to go with it, a lower, more detached sort of voice, which was the very opposite of what I felt in the dead center of my heart. It was terror I felt. Because he'd stolen my sense of our past, and I had nothing to replace it with yet.

I got all their names. Besides Anita there was Lisa, the same Lisa again a year later. Savannah, and Lily. I sat and wrote the names down on a yellow tablet. I wrote them in a list, while Jude sat and rubbed his eyes. "Oh," he said, "Patty, I forgot Patty. She was manic-depressive."

"No, Jude, not yet, I don't want the stories yet. Just the names."

"If you count one-nighters there was also Rhonda Jean."

"Rhonda Jean," I murmured, writing it down. "Rhonda Jean! Was she a country-and-western singer, Jude? Was that the year you were always listening to Tanya Tucker?" I held the list up so he could see. "Does that look like all of them?"

He nodded. "You're stooping pretty low with this."

"Just meeting you on your own ground, Jude."

"Certainly. But it's ground well beneath you. You'll probably leave me, too, and that's understandable."

"Is that your hope? That I'll leave you?"

"No, no, of course not." He yawned, and I thought tears filled his eyes. He looked down at his own hands.

I was not ready to baby him. I took it girl by girl. I made columns for the following categories: duration of affair, age, hair color, height, weight, breast size, intelligence, family background, hobbies. This was beneath me, embarrassing even at the time. I was driven by an old fury finally coming to life.

The affairs had happened *before* Anita Defranz, most of them when Jude was in his thirties. Only Lily had been recent.

"So we can start there," I said. "We can start with Lily. You tell me the story, and I'll listen up."

I spoke with calm authority. I spoke in unconscious imitation of Berna.

"Lily is nobody you'd ever want to meet," he said.

"But I need the story, Jude."

"It will mortify me to tell you."

"So be it."

"She was in her twenties, she called herself a poet, I met her at Reed Carone's house, he was her professor at the time, she wore a beaded top, she was nice enough, in the summer she worked with deaf children, she was a *girl*, can we stop now?"

"Jude, it's interesting to me."

"It was physical attraction, that's all. The most elemental kind. I'm sorry. We'd go to her crummy apartment. She was a slob, and I had to endure the presence of her roommate who called me the pig. Finally the roommate said the pig could no longer enter the sty, so it was Howard Johnson's hotel. We went there weekly for seven weeks. Then she fell for a young buck from Cuba, introduced him to me so I'd get the picture of how far up in the world she was moving. I was relieved. And after that I've been faithful, and will be until I die."

"Faithful."

"I certainly love you. Nobody else."

"Nice words, Jude, but who are we? I want to hate you. But then, that would be like hating my life. I don't want to do that. Do I."

My eyes stung with tears. *My life* echoed in my brain, and I saw myself as a little girl running down a road in Indiana, the first time I'd ever felt that sense of *my life!* I'd been stung by a bee. I remembered my father in the doorway of the kitchen, scooping me up. I cried, not from the bee sting but because I knew I had a life, and was alone living it.

"So what did Lily look like?" I said. "Like Anita Defranz?"

"More or less."

"I'd like to hate you, Jude. For all those nights you fell asleep beside me, so exhausted, so spent. You wouldn't even talk to me! I'd like to kick you, and slap you. But I'm a dignified person who is now going out for a walk."

I felt him watch me rise from my chair, and I was gratified that he was speechless.

We lived in silence for nearly a week — avoiding each other when we could, and then 120 roses were delivered to my door, the card simply saying "From Jude Harrison," which made me laugh until tears streamed down my face.

"Jude!" I hollered that day — he was upstairs painting. "Jude Harrison, this lunacy solves absolutely nothing! Where will we put them?"

He came downstairs — I stopped laughing as soon as I saw him, my heart recoiling — and together we quietly found vases and jars for each rose, and the whole house filled up with his apology. For a while, I was touched, and then not so touched. Now we had a friendly silence, sometimes broken with, "Want some scrambled eggs?" or "I need to paint in the kitchen today, if it's all right? I need that light" or "How 'bout we go see Berna and Griff tonight?"

In the car that night Jude and I rode in silence. I felt so eager to get to Griffin's house, as if it were a holiday and I were a child in love with ritual. I knew we'd be served tea, I knew they'd be in pajamas, I knew I'd hear stories, I knew the house would have that inexplicable atmosphere. *Electrified by something*, I thought, *by mystery*, I decided, though even that word did not capture what I felt there.

They had company. It was only the third time we'd come to find them not alone. The first two times it had been old Jack J. Pree, no longer a fatso or an existentialist, but married and the father of twin girls. He was still Jack J. Pree, though, full of loud laughter, and no dull judgments, and when he left he lifted Bern off the ground for a hug. His wife was more like a stunned, wide-eyed owl. You could feel her observations were grist for the mill for the tale she'd tell her friend on the phone the next day.

Tonight the company was a stranger, an old man, very old, who we saw first through the window. I wondered if it was Berna's father.

We stepped inside; the kitchen felt like deep water. Berna's eyes were sad. Griffin was nowhere.

"What happened?"

"This is Charlie Demato," Berna said. "He's staying with Griff and me for a while."

Charlie Demato, the old man, sat at the kitchen table with a bowl of oatmeal in front of him. He had sharp elbows perched on the table's edge, and he smiled up at us. "A pleasure to meet you," he said. "You'll excuse my spirits," he added.

"We had to put down Mr. Demato's dog today. He lost his wife three weeks ago."

Jude and I expressed our sympathy. I felt we should leave. Surely Mr. Demato didn't need strangers like us. I said as much.

The old man looked up at me. "Please," he said. "Please stay. Don't go."

It was as if he were demanding that there be no more departures in life—nobody, ever again, would be leaving.

"Just sit down," he ordered.

Griffin appeared, smiled at us from the doorway.

"Berna," the old man said, "tell these people about Belle. Tell them so they know she wasn't just some dog."

Berna said that he should tell the story. That it would help him.

"Excuse me while I get my album of photographs," said Mr. Demato, and walked into the other room.

"He's staying with us," Griffin said.

"We know."

"It's part of how Bern runs the business. If some old person loses a pet and they live alone and they can't bear it, she invites them out here."

"Doesn't have to be an old person," Berna said. "Loneliness comes in all ages. A girl of twenty lived with me for six months one time. Turned out she had a lot to teach me. She stayed too long, she got herself pregnant, she ate too much, and made it impossible for me to meditate. But she was a teacher for me, I knew that all along."

Mr. Demato was coming back to us, his enormous album in his arms.

"Ain't I a sight for sore eyes?" he mumbled, and laughed. "This goddamn album weighs more than I do."

He sat down in the chair and opened to the first page.

"My wife, six years old!" he said, and clapped. "Deprived child.

Never had a dog. Her mother claimed to be allergic. Her mother was a big liar. She hated me. My wife took after her father. Her father fell off a rooftop and died when he was thirty-two. Broke my wife's heart. Just a little girl. Never the same again."

He flipped through a few pages. His breathing quickened.

"I am unprepared," he said. "I am very unprepared. And I did many things to prepare myself. I rejoined the Catholic church."

We were all looking at him, trying to express something with our faces. Berna was up taking bread out of the oven. I saw that Mr. Demato's hand had started to tremble. "I went into the confession booth. 'Bless me father for I have sinned,' I said. 'But God who made death is the real sinner,' I said. The priest said, 'It is normal to be angry at death, and it's good to express your anger.'"

He looked up at us. He had urgent blue eyes. "You're all too young to understand," he said. "You live with a woman for forty-eight years. Her biggest fault is too much garlic on her food, and maybe she had to get the last word in. Bitchy once a month, even after menopause. We got the dog twenty years ago. A mutt. A pup. She took care of it just like it was a baby. She talked to it that way. We'd had a baby together. A smart girl. The girl grew up and moved to San Diego. The girl got breast cancer when she was forty. Survived. We lived through that together. Luck was on our side. How lucky we were. And look here, she played piano!"

He closed the book of pictures before we could see. He rested one of his hands on top of it, the other hand coming up to cover his eyes. He stood up. "I'm sorry, I am not prepared. I wasn't prepared. For the weight of it. I am sorry to go on. Berna, may I go to my room? I thank you. The dog died a peaceful death in my arms. A lovely way to go. They should do it for human beings. You have a fine son. Good night, now. The dog was named Belle."

As he walked away Jude's hand took my own under the table.

"He's a nice old man," Jude said. "I wish I'd known one good thing to say."

"Yes," I said. "Me too."

Jude squeezed my hand.

Then, we heard the old man singing. Not softly. He was belting it out in there, a song I'd never heard. *All the lilies, all the lilies, lighting up her face!* He had a terrible voice, a comic voice, and who would have thought he could be so loud?

We sat and wondered if we should go to him. If this was a sign of unraveling. But nobody moved.

"The man needs to sing," Berna said. She smiled.

We ate her warm, fresh bread. *The lilies, the lilies, the lilies in the snow!*

We laughed a little. The song did not soften, if anything he got louder and more off key. It went on and on. We almost got used to it.

We learned Griffin had been accepted to veterinary school in Philadelphia. We drank to that — brandy. I kissed him.

When the old man fell silent, we all rose from the table. He's sung himself to death, I thought, as we all seemed to tiptoe toward his room.

But the old man met us halfway there. He was bundled up in a parka. He said he was going out for a walk. He was going to sing in the great outdoors he said. He was not prepared, he said. We saw he was weeping.

I wanted to embrace this man. But he was nobody you could embrace. He was a force for whom you simply had to get out of the way. You had to move aside and let the old man go into the great outdoors, unprepared.

We saw him, later, Jude and I. We were in our car, beginning our ride back home. The old man was headed back to Bern and Griffin's house where he would find fire in the stove, and some companionship, and something else I'd never name. We didn't stop and ask the old man if he needed a ride up the hill.

"If I lost you," Jude said, "I'd be walking like that. I'd be out walking alone for the rest of my life."

His words had the near ring of sincerity, and touched me for a moment, even as I didn't believe them.

"I couldn't stand it," he said. "You're my whole life."

"Well I hope if you sing you sound better than he did," I said, and Jude said nothing, wounded, perhaps, that I wasn't engaging his fears.

For the first time in years, I rested my head on Jude's shoulder as he drove. This was more awkwardness than it was comfort. But it was something. We rode through the dark like that, in a new kind of silence, a silence made of fading echoes, the echo of an old man's song, the echo of pain and resentment and lies that break hearts, the echo of all we'd ever meant to be for one another.

We were hungry. We stopped and had a meal in an all-night diner, Jude and I. The booth was aqua and small. We ate in silence. We could hardly take our eyes off each other. *We are what we are*, we seemed to be saying in that quiet. *We are what we are.*

We were filling up so we could go home to continue our broken, indelicate story.

■ ■ ■ ■ ■ ■ ■ ■ ■ ■ ■

The Tub

Lex Williford

for the James sisters

Every Sunday morning before eleven-o'clock Mass until 1951, when Helen turned sixteen and her mother finally put a stop to it, Helen drew her father a hot bath in their lion-clawed tub, then watched him dance and shave before the bathroom mirror steamed. When she was small and her father took anything—chickens, tomatoes, pies— as full payment for fixing people's cars during the Depression, he tickled her nose with his shaving brush while the deep tub filled to blue, then picked her up, laughing, and rubbed his sandpaper-rough whiskers against her cheeks. When she got too heavy to lift anymore, he taught her the lines he'd memorized the week before from signs scrolling out along East Texas blacktops on his long sales trips to Texarkana and Tyler and Lufkin:

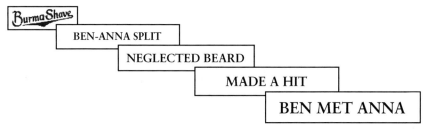

Her father tight-tucked a white terry-cloth bath towel around his waist, and he bobbed and dipped his hips, stropping his straight razor along a thick leather strap, waving it in the air like Glen Miller's baton to the Big Band beat of their walnut Philco blaring "In the Mood" from down the hall. Then he squeezed out a white curl from a blue tube of Burma Shave and whipped up a thick lather, his rosewood shaving brush clop-clopping inside his cracked ceramic cup, to the machine-gun pops of Gene Krupa's syncopated rim shots.

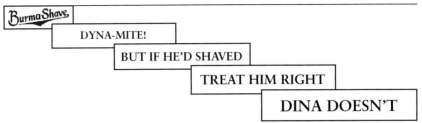

DYNA-MITE!

BUT IF HE'D SHAVED

TREAT HIM RIGHT

DINA DOESN'T

Humming and swinging, her father swirled the brush up under his nose and around his cheeks and chin, a white beard of foam, then scratched his straight razor up his thick black neck-stubble in time with "Boogie-Woogie Bugle Boy from Company B." Helen swung her hips and hummed along, too, but she worried her father might cut his own throat or lose his hip towel, he got so carried away sometimes, turning from the mirror, then turning her, ducking her under his arm, then spinning her laughing out into the hall. She swung with him and danced, ready to cover her eyes at any moment if she had to, but her father's hip towel always stayed. Helen gripped her father's styptic pencil in her damp palm, keeping a close eye out for any welling nick, even the slightest pinprick of blood.

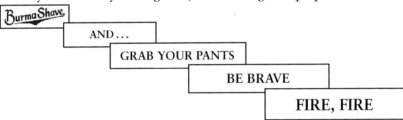

AND...

GRAB YOUR PANTS

BE BRAVE

FIRE, FIRE

"So, Sister, what's the news from our boys on the front?" her father asked her every Sunday morning since 1942, when Helen, seven, heard the news from FDR and ran to the bathroom door, breathless, to tell him the Allies were holding back the Axis advance in North Africa. Her father, thirty-two, had a heart murmur since he was a boy, and the Sunday she told him the news he looked sad and said, "Honey, your old man should be fighting Rommel over there, but he's a 4-F bastard with a hole in his heart."

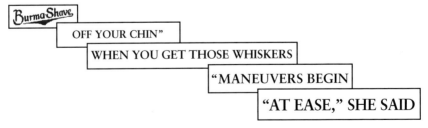

OFF YOUR CHIN"

WHEN YOU GET THOSE WHISKERS

"MANEUVERS BEGIN

"AT EASE," SHE SAID

Her father kept it up throughout the war, even after Truman dropped the bomb and her mother made her father sleep on the living room divan for two months till he promised to shut down his garage next to Lou McVee's bar down on the corner of Beacon and Columbia. Helen missed her father terribly weekdays he was on the road selling engine gaskets for the Monkey Grip Rubber Products Company, but Sundays, as the tub misted the mirror to steam, he was back again, laughing and reciting the lines from the new signs he'd seen just the week before outside Nacogdoches, Texas:

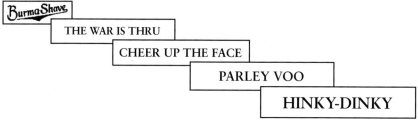

THE WAR IS THRU

CHEER UP THE FACE

PARLEY VOO

HINKY-DINKY

During the long, happy period of peace from '45 till '50, Helen's father still dolloped a dot of shaving cream onto the tip of her nose, still winked at her and asked her the same question — "So what's the news from our boys on the front?"—till she blushed and giggled about the public school boys who passed whistling by the windows of St. James, the all-girls Catholic school in east Dallas. But when her father started helping Kit Keeble, a black-haired boy from down the block, rebuild the engine of his '36 Indian Chief in their carport Saturdays, the word *boys* shifted to the singular and stayed that way for good.

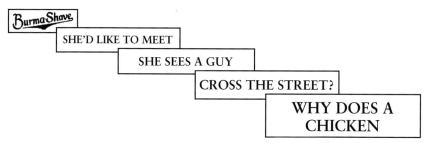

SHE'D LIKE TO MEET

SHE SEES A GUY

CROSS THE STREET?

WHY DOES A
CHICKEN

The day Kit turned sixteen, he showed up at their front door in his jeans and a bomber jacket, a bulge at his shoulder where he'd rolled up a pack of L&Ms in the sleeve of his white T-shirt, and he pleaded with her mother to let him take Helen for a spin around the block on his rebuilt motorcycle, which rumbled and roiled oily smoke from their grass-humped drive.

"This girl's only fourteen," her mother said, almost a shout, "and she'll *never* ride a motorcycle, not so long as *I* live." Then she shut the screened door clapping in Kit's face.

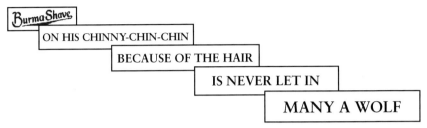

ON HIS CHINNY-CHIN-CHIN

BECAUSE OF THE HAIR

IS NEVER LET IN

MANY A WOLF

For the next two years, Helen held out till her sixteenth birthday, when her mother said she'd *think* about letting Helen go out with Kit, maybe, if Helen was good and she was home by nine p.m. As always, her father lost that argument but never said a word to his wife Hanna when he started paying Kit two bits an hour to come over and help him Saturdays in the small mechanic's shop he'd built behind their carport. Helen spent half the day trying to talk to Kit, who didn't say much, but her father talked to him easily and winked at her, pointing to the screwdrivers and wrenches Kit called out for when he rolled out, grease-smudged, from the creeper under her father's 1940 Chrysler Royal Coupe. Her father believed absolutely in Chrysler and Monkey Grip products, he told Kit, and he pointed out the new Monkey Grip calendar under the shop's single yellow bulb, chimpanzees in suits and ties and green visors, waving cards at each other as they argued over a hand of smoky poker. Her father showed Kit everything he needed to know, how to change the oil and filter every three thousand miles, how to change the points and plugs, how to change a head gasket and set the timing.

"Don't do that, Kit. You'll make another smudge," Helen said when Kit squinched his eyes and scratched his nose with a greasy thumb.

"Well, scratch his nose for him, why don't you?" her father told her. So she did.

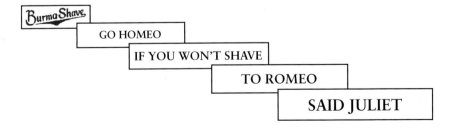

GO HOMEO

IF YOU WON'T SHAVE

TO ROMEO

SAID JULIET

In the bathroom that Sunday, she whispered, "Kit looks just like Monty Clift, don't you think, Pop?" and she listened outside the door for her mother's heavy footsteps on the hall's hardwood floors. She sat on the cool edge of the tub and touched a finger to the scalding bath water, just the way her father liked it, so hot she could barely touch it, and she watched him dry-towel the foam scraped from his pink neck and face, a bloody white tear of toilet paper stuck to his chin. She watched him open his pocketknife to clean out the black crescents of gunk from under his thick, scallopy nails, then stared at all the white flecks under her father's fingernails and her own. White flecks under fingernails were venial sins, her mother had told her once when Helen was ten. She'd done something wrong, she couldn't remember what, and Helen worried about herself and her father, they both had so many.

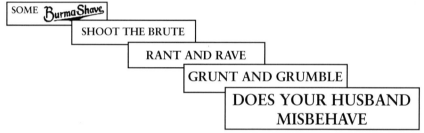

SOME Burma Shave
SHOOT THE BRUTE
RANT AND RAVE
GRUNT AND GRUMBLE
DOES YOUR HUSBAND MISBEHAVE

In her father's dark shop behind the carport, Kit's hands were always too black with grease to see any white flecks under his nails. One Saturday afternoon, without saying a word to her mother, her father chaperoned them both, his treat, to a matinee of *A Place in the Sun*, and the Lakewood Theater was so dark all Helen could see were Kit's knuckle cuts on the armrest next to her, the black crescents under his thick nails, just like her father's. At the end of the movie, when Elizabeth Taylor told Montgomery Clift, "All the same, I'll go on loving you for as long as I live," Kit took Helen's hand into his rough palm, and she sneaked a glance at her father, who smiled a moment, but pretended not to notice, then swallowed in quiet gulps when Montgomery Clift told Elizabeth Taylor, "Love me for the time I have left. Then forget me," then walked down Death Row to his execution.

The Saturday she turned sixteen, Helen's father called out to her from the tub down the hall, asking if she'd mind washing his back. By then her father's beard stubble had gone to gray and he'd lost most of his hair, and the only way he could comb the damp, downy fuzz on top of his head was with a soft, plush towel. Helen sat on the edge of the tub and scrubbed her father's hairy back with a long-handled brush, quiet, glancing up at a mourning dove pecking at their neighbors' roof gravel just outside the bathroom window.

"All right," her father said, "what's the matter? You can tell me." Helen didn't answer and he made his old joke about rotating the crop of hair on his back to the top of his head, then recited the rhymes he'd seen the week before in the high grass shoulders on the way from Longview to the Louisiana line:

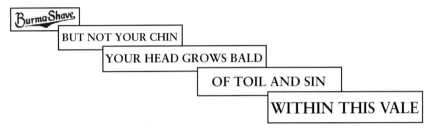

Helen stared off a long time, unable to speak for the tightness in her throat.

"So what's the news from our boys on the front?" her father said, trying to cheer her up. Then she broke down and told him that Truman had drafted Kit for Korea.

"That's it," her father whispered. "Shhh. That's enough. Don't tell me any more. No more news from the front."

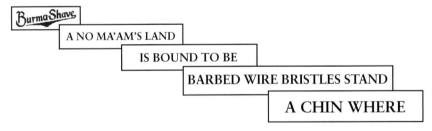

Her mother stood outside the bathroom door, her stomach and bosom heaving in her wire bra and girdle, her heavy arms folded, a white mustache of Nair depilatory on her upper lip. "So, young lady, you want to tell me what's going on in here?"

Helen's throat pinched and throbbed and she couldn't answer. Her mother frowned at her father. "Well? What's she doing in here?"

Helen's father sat up in the tub, sloshing water to the bathroom floor. "She's upset. Can't you see that? They're shipping Kit off to Korea."

"Good for him. Good for us. Get him out of *my* hair for a while.

Keep him from sniffing around here all the time."

"Hanna, for God's sake —" her father started.

"What's your daughter doing in here?" her mother said again, almost a shout. "Girl gone to woman sixteen years today. I'd like to know."

Helen's father flushed in the cooling bath and pulled his knees up to his chest like a child.

"I was just washing his back, Mama," Helen said, blushing, too, staring down at her bare feet in a puddle of her father's bath water.

"You hush. And *you*." Her mother glared at her father, pulling Helen out into the hall by the sleeve of her slip. "Naked. In front of your own grown daughter. What in God's name is wrong with you?" Then she pulled the door shut like a shot.

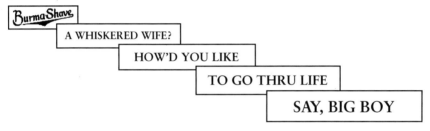

That afternoon, Helen's mother told her no, she couldn't go out with Kit, not tonight or any other night, and so what if he was leaving next week for Fort Hood? Helen would just have to wait a year or two, when Kit came back stateside, and Helen said, "*If*, you mean. *If*." Then she ran out the front door, down the steps and along the cracked walk to her father's old garage down the street like she'd done a thousand times as a girl. She turned the corner of Beacon and Columbia and ran smack into Lou McVee, who leaned against a light post outside her bar smoking a Lucky Strike.

"Hey, honey, why in such a hurry? You all right?"

Helen wiped her eyes and listened for her father's air compressor hissing next door to fill anyone's tires for free, but then she glanced at the QuikStop and remembered her father's garage had been closed down for years, and her father would soon be off hitting golf balls at the Bob-

O-Links to get away from her mother.

"My god, you're Jesse's kid, aren't you? So pretty and all grown up. How's your daddy these days, honey? We miss him around here, you know."

"My pop's off puttering at the putt-putt—" Helen started, but the childish words caught in her throat, and she tried not to stare too long at Lou McVee the first time so close up.

Word had it that Lou McVee had lost her Navy husband early in the war, when a Zero took out an ammunition dump in southern Oahu. December 7, 1941. Naturally blond like Helen, Lou McVee had long, wavy hair, and her eyes were go-light green, her skin smooth as Ivory soap except for the silvery down along the sides of her neck. Lou McVee didn't need any make-up, except a little red lipstick and an eyebrow pencil to darken the mole at the corner of her mouth like Shelly Winters.

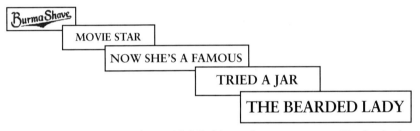

"M . . . ma'am," Helen said, blinking, almost a stutter. She looked through the padded door to the dark her mother had warned her father never to enter and said, "Is it OK I use your phone?"

Lou McVee stepped out her cigarette on the stoop and touched Helen's shoulder, turning her toward the door. "Sure thing, hon."

It was dark inside and cool, and a stubbly-faced man tonging a blue block of ice from his truck laughed and said, "Bringing 'em in here a little young, don't you think, Lou?" and Lou McVee laughed back and said, "Aw, shut up, Donny, and bring us in another one of those blocks of ice. Anything for Jesse's girl." Lou McVee squeezed Helen's shoulders and winked, then led her down a dark hallway. Helen spotted a Monkey Grip calendar and a framed photo on the wall, a man turning and swinging a woman across a dance room floor. The dancing man was laughing, his hat tipped down over his eyes like Fred Astaire.

"That's my dad," Helen said, pointing.

"And guess who *that* is?" Lou McVee pointed to the dancing blonde, her back to the camera.

"Your daddy was kind to me after I lost my Bill at Pearl Harbor. He

and Bill were good friends. And don't let anybody else tell you different."
She pointed Helen to the phone booth next to the women's room and
dropped a bright buffalo nickel into her palm for the call. "Let me tell
you, honey. Your daddy can dance."

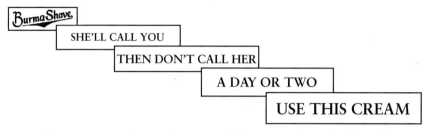

SHE'LL CALL YOU
THEN DON'T CALL HER
A DAY OR TWO
USE THIS CREAM

Helen met Kit at the QuikStop curb, his '36 Indian Chief rumbling
and rattling the storefront windows like summer thunder. When she ran
out of the store to greet him, Lou McVee's lipstick all grown-up strange
on her mouth, Kit ran right past her without noticing and stood turning
a display of balsa gliders and kites.

"Which one you want?" he said, grinning. "It's your birthday. Get
you a sandwich, too, and a Dr. Pepper. Let's have us picnic at White
Rock Lake."

She pointed to a balsa kit with a rubber band and red propeller, then
to a bright green kite, then to another one red, white and blue, and when
she couldn't make up her mind, Kit bought them all, plus a spool of string,
with the money he'd earned just that morning from her father.

They spun out from the curb, tearing through the honeysuckle air past
blurs of greening oaks and honking cars, her eyes watering in the wind
all the way to White Rock Lake. She locked her arms tight around Kit's
skinny waist and shouted, "Slow down!" laughing so hard she almost
peed her pants. Kit laughed, too, and shouted back over his shoulder,
"Don't open your mouth or you'll swallow a bumble bee!"

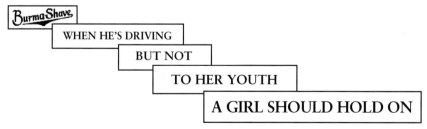

WHEN HE'S DRIVING
BUT NOT
TO HER YOUTH
A GIRL SHOULD HOLD ON

Along the lake's muddy shore, Kit slid the glider wings and rudder
into their balsa slots and held the plane while she wound the propeller's

rubber band tight. Then she let the glider fly out across the road to the fish hatchery, and a wind caught it and swung it back over the cottonwoods and out over White Rock Lake.

"Oh, no!" she shouted, her hands over her eyes.

"Want me to go get it?" Kit said, full of bluster, and laughed when it ditched behind a sailboat, and Helen said, "No, Kit. The water's freezing."

Kit stripped off his bomber jacket, T-shirt and boots anyway, his chest still smooth as a boy's, and he whooped and hollered and cursed as he stumbled in and swam out, snagging the glider and waving it high in the air.

When he got back to shore, the black gumbo mud squelching up between his toes, the wind blew his chest to goose-pimple blue. "What you standing around for?" he said, his teeth chattering. "Warm me up, will you?"

Kit's mouth tasted like Mrs. Baird's bread and chicken salad, L&Ms and tadpoles, she thought, and when she threw his bomber jacket over his shoulders, he zipped it up around her, and she held him so long inside her sweater got all wet. Kit's face was smooth as her father's best chamois, whiskerless as a girl's.

By late afternoon, the two of them had run themselves breathless trying to get their kites up into the air, but the wind that had taken the glider out over the lake had died.

"Here," Kit said, "I got it," and he hopped onto his Indian Chief and kicked it to a grumbling roar, then steered it one-handed up and down the hillside, dragging the red, white and blue kite through the high grass like a folded Stars and Stripes. When he bumped back onto the road, he held the string high up in the air till the kite caught the wind and flew out behind him like a salute.

Kit looked back at the kite far out over his shoulder, then grinned at Helen, kicking his tailpipes like a bronco's flanks, yipping like a cowboy.

When Helen saw the car coming, she shouted back, "Kit!" then covered her eyes with her hands.

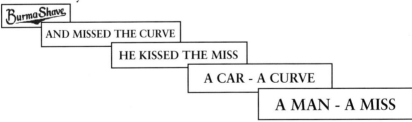

Helen ran across the road and jumped the ditch where Kit's Indian Chief lay on its side in the mud, the back tire still spinning, slinging mud, black exhaust sputtering and burbling from the tail pipe under the ditch's muddy water. She stumbled through the high clover where Kit lay next to a live oak along the shore, his eyes closed, his head turned at a strange angle, his tongue lolling out of his mouth.

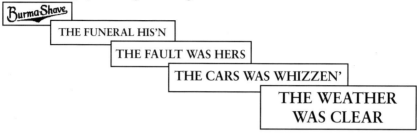

Kit's eyes fluttered a moment when she bent over him and then he began to laugh.

"I'm going to kill you!" she said and slapped him on the arm.

"Ow!" he said. "I've had an accident!"

"I thought you were dead!" she shouted.

Kit grinned at Helen and pulled her down to him in the grass, then pointed up to the sky.

The snagged string had wrapped his wrist, and the kite flew taut out over the lake like a flapping flag.

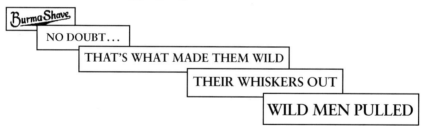

It was just five minutes to nine when Kit dropped Helen off at the QuikStop, another five-minute walk back home. From the front porch, the screened door's rusted spring panged and twinged as her father's grandfather clock tolled nine.

Her father stood up from the divan. "Helen? Thank God."

Her mother sat at the dining room table, staring at the cake's unlit candles, next to it a red-ribboned box in yellow wrapping paper.

Helen's father looked her up and down, his eyes worried, and Helen glanced down to see the grass stains on the knees of her gabardines, her fingers catching in her wind-tangled hair.

"Best now you go to your room," her father said, almost a whisper.

"Let this kettle cool."

Helen turned.

"Wait," her mother said and stood. She walked to Helen by the front door and pressed her fingers and thumb hard between Helen's jaws, turning her face left, then right. She wiped the corner of Helen's mouth with a finger. A red smear of lipstick. "I want you to go across the street to Mr. Yarbrough's yard and strip your father a good willow switch. A good green one, I say, or I'll send you back for another."

"For God's sake, Hanna, there's no way I'm going to — "

"This is *your* fault," her mother told him. "You think I don't know about you bringing that boy around here all the time? Giving him money? You think I can't see? Why do you always have to undermine me?"

"She's sixteen, Hanna. Too old to — "

"Too old, you say, or too young. It's a father's job to discipline."

"You could buy a whole goddamn bundle of switches, for all I care, and I still wouldn't — "

"Don't you talk to me with that filth. Helen, outside. I'll just have to do this myself. Somebody in this house has to."

"No," her father said and gripped Helen by the wrist. "I'll take care of this myself, once and for all." Her father jerked her by the arm down the hall to the bathroom. He unhooked his razor strap from the mirror, and then held it out for his wife to get a good look at it in the hallway. "Here!" he shouted. "Is this good enough for you?" Then he slammed the bathroom door in her face and locked it.

"Who the hell do you think you are, young lady?" he shouted at Helen. "Do you have any idea how much you scared your mother and me? We've called every hospital in Dallas. You *did* go out with that boy, didn't you? And you rode his motorcycle when your mother expressly told you *not* to, am I right? *Answer* me."

"Yes, sir."

"All right, then. This is the first and last time, you understand? I don't want ever to have to do this again. You think I want to do this?"

"No," Helen said.

Her father told her to put her hands on the side of the tub, to keep quiet till he'd finished. Helen stared at him, stunned, trembling by the tub.

Then her father smiled at her and winked.

The slinging strap slapped the side of the tub hard, and her father shouted, "That's for being smart with your mother!" Then he made a pained face.

"Ohh," Helen said, covering her mouth to keep from laughing.

Her father slapped the strap against the tub again, a loud hollow crack. "And *that's* for riding a motorcycle when your mother expressly forbid you to!" Helen's father grimaced, rolled his eyes and grinned.

"Ohhh," Helen said. "Please, Pop, don't hit me again."

"What? I told you to keep quiet, didn't I?" And he strapped the tub twice.

"Oh. Ohhhhh," Helen moaned, covering her mouth, and snorted.

"Jesse?" her mother said just outside the bathroom door. "Jesse! What's going on in there? What are you doing to that girl?"

"This is just what you wanted, right? Here!" And her father slapped the strap against the tub one more time.

"Jesse!" her mother shouted, wiggling the doorknob, then pounding the door. "Open up this door!"

Her mother's heavy footsteps echoed down the hallway's hardwood floors, and Helen could hear her mother pulling down hatboxes from her bedroom closet.

When her mother pushed open the bathroom door moments later, hatpin in door lock, Helen and her father were both sitting on the edge of the tub, red-faced, unable to look at each other without laughing.

Helen's mother stared at them both a long time, her arms folded.

"I want you out of this house," her mother told her father. "Now."

Her father wiped at his eyes. "Oh, come on, Hanna. We're just having us a little fun." But her mother's eyes were hard as marbles.

"It was me, Mama," Helen said, knowing that look, knowing there was no way of changing her mother's mind. "Please, Mama, it was my fault. I'm the one you should — "

"Out," her mother told her father, "out!" and she pointed down the hall to the front door.

For months, Helen's father was on the road seven days a week, staying over weekends at hotels in Little Rock and Marshall and Houston, and Helen's mother refused to talk to him when he called, sometimes two or three times a night. Whenever she heard his voice, she slammed the phone into its cradle. When Helen reached to pick up the receiver herself, thinking it was her father or Kit Keeble calling from Killeen, her mother stood in her way and let the phone ring till it stopped, then refused to talk or even to look at Helen for days.

One evening, Helen found one of Kit's letters from Fort Hood ripped into tiny pieces as she carried out the kitchen trash, and she spent hours taping the pieces back together behind the locked bathroom door.

"What are you doing in there?" her mother said in the hallway. "I said what are you doing?"

Kit had had a good time at White Rock Lake, the letter said. Why hadn't Helen written? He hoped she wasn't mad at him, hoped he hadn't gotten her into too much trouble.

Helen wrote him back right away, saying she was sorry; she'd only gotten the one letter—were there others? Then she told him to call her Saturday nights at eight p.m. before they gave him his marching orders from south Texas to South Korea. She gave him the number of the phone booth she'd called him from that day at White Rock Lake, then told him to address all his correspondence to her care of Lou McVee.

Six months after he'd left Fort Hood, Lou handed Helen Kit's last letter, a blue government issue flimsy as tissue paper from a U.S. base just outside Berlin. They were shipping Kit off to Seoul next week, he wrote, but not to worry. He'd just gotten himself an old '42 Nazi BMW with a sidecar—a bullet-riddled *Volksmotorrad* that had seen action in the Battle of the Bulge—and when Kit shipped the motorcycle back at the end of his tour, he and her father could fix it up like they'd done the Indian Chief, and she could ride with him in the sidecar, where it was safer for a girl.

Kit stopped writing a month or so later, and Helen feared he'd met a Korean girl. It never once occurred to her that he might have gone MIA.

One Sunday morning, after Helen had bathed and dressed for eleven o'clock Mass at St. James, she walked in on her mother sitting at the living room table, covering her mouth with her hands. When her mother looked up and saw her, she wiped at her eyes and stood, touching Helen's shoulder, then pointed down to a short obit in the *Dallas Morning News*. In a blizzard some time after Christmas, an Army cycle had run over a Chinese land mine on a back road just south of Kaesong, and they'd not found the bike or the driver's body till a month later, frozen in a ditch under four feet of snow. Funeral services would be held that morning at Sparkman Hillcrest.

Staring at her mother, Helen remembered Kit lying on his back, playing dead under a live oak along the shore of White Rock Lake, remembered him laughing, wet and shivering, in his bomber jacket, and the same palm that had slapped his arm, then touched his smooth, bare chest in the goosepimple cold, burned with the urge to slap her mother's face.

But her mother had already set their heavy black phone on the living room table, had already begun to dial, asking the operator for a hotel in

Fort Smith, then handed Helen the phone.

When her father answered a moment later, he'd just stepped out of the bathroom steam.

"Pop?" Helen said, the word catching in her throat like whiskers in a drain.

"Helen."

Her father had just cut himself shaving when the telephone rang, and he joked that he just might bleed to death. Then his faint laugh crackled and faded over the line as she told him the last time the latest news from the front.

■■■■■■■■■■

Jackson Stillwell

Richard Currey

She was an old woman, walking with the sheriff in the orchard behind her house.

"We're gonna go on and declare him dead," the sheriff said.

She watched her feet move through fallen leaves.

"What was it, Edna?" the sheriff asked. "Epilepsy?"

She nodded. "Epilepsy," she said. "And not right in the head."

She stopped between two trees and the sheriff stopped beside her.

"That was the most of it," she went on. "Not right in the head. He couldn't have done what he did otherwise."

The sheriff squinted into the distance. "I reckon not."

"You know," Edna said, "this orchard used to be a beautiful place. Jackson would help me out here. He'd drag in apples in burlap sacks." She looked at the sheriff. "That's one thing that boy was good for. He could turn in a day's work."

"Yes ma'am." The sheriff fingered his hat brim.

"After a while," she said, "it just got to be too much for us. No matter how much we worked we couldn't keep up."

The sheriff took a breath. "The land'll do that to you. It can get away from a person."

Edna reached toward a tree, touching it. "Jackson told me he could taste apples when he chewed the skin of these trees." She studied the bark, considering.

The sheriff said he was sure he didn't know, and apologized for needing to leave so soon. He said he had another couple stops farther south.

"Well," she said. "I thank you for coming out."

The sheriff put on his hat, and told her it was no trouble at all. He hesitated a moment before he turned and walked back to his car and left her standing alone in her orchard in a breach of autumn light.

Edna Stillwell delivered her son Jackson into the world in the early summer of 1901. The doctor's solemn announcement confirming the boy's epilepsy and retardation would not come for five years after his birth, and Edna had been fond of telling people the child was born backward, *inside-out and into the hands of the Lord*, the last of her eight children and wrong from the first, haunted by the world like an animal too far from home. Her husband, twenty-one years her senior, had died in his sleep two months after the birth. Her other children grown and gone, Jackson came up alone with his mother, a boy in constant awe staring into empty corners of the old house, standing astonished and bewildered at the windows during rainfall, passing days in his father's fallow barn, a private heaven of musk and bats' dung and the furtive lives of birds, his years falling in time. Alone in the barn he would collapse into seizures, eyes turned and lost in his head, his body locked in trance against a moving darkness. He would hear the voice of a woman and the pealing of bells or smell the approach of animals he had never seen, believing a celestial radiance flooded the barn's loft as he gathered his senses in the aftermath of each episode. He had taken crushing falls. There was a broken arm in an unconscious dive from the hay window, and his face carried the print of a pitchfork's tines, two perfect circles of scar side by side on his left cheek. The doctor rode out to the Stillwell place after the accidents, assessing the damage, comforting Jackson and Edna. On his last visit the doctor accepted a cup of tea, leaving Jackson on the front porch with a triangular bandage over a fractured collarbone.

In the kitchen the doctor stared into his cup. "That bone'll be alright in a few weeks if you can keep him quiet," he said. "You know I can't do anything about the rest."

"Well," Edna said. "It's no fault of yours."

"Still, a doctor wants to do what he can. At least say something of worth. I keep thinking the next time I come out they'll have a cure for epilepsy. A pill. Something Jack could drink once a day." He looked into his cup again, then finished the tea in a swallow.

Edna followed the doctor out and sat on the porch. It was midsummer of 1935 and she watched her son, chipping weeds along a garden row, on his knees with a spade in his left hand.

His right arm swung gently in the sling. He showed no sign of pain.

She sighed, sipped from her teacup. Lately, her ankles had been swelling at the end of a day. Her right eye was clouding over. Her hips ached on cold mornings. She did not ask herself what would become of her son when she was gone. Let the Lord provide.

She was seventy-eight years old.

J ackson Stillwell sat across from his mother in the plain kitchen as they finished a dinner of garden beans and pone. He watched her, studying her chin, her rimless spectacles, considering his question. He was careful with a question: more than once she had put him off, told him he could not hope to understand and he had come to think the answers to his questions would open into some other country to reveal the face of a secret world, that he would discover a road into what everybody else seemed to have. He asked his mother about time and light and rain, where they came from and why. He was fascinated by dreams and Edna struggled with versions of her own truth. *Pictures and voices that come to you while you're sleeping. The visions you receive, that travel through your mind.* Jackson Stillwell was convinced his personal redemption would come in the form of a dream and he asked his mother, "Mama, what was the first dream you ever had?"

He had no memory of dreaming. He believed he had never dreamed, that when he fell asleep he simply vanished.

Edna looked at her son, then at the kitchen's one window. "God, boy," she said. "The first dream I ever had. I don't know as I could truthfully say."

Jackson grinned, waited for her story.

She looked down at her plate. "I know I would dream from the stories my daddy told me," she said. "He'd tell a ghost story and I'd dream about it that night, wake up all shivery, have to go in and sleep with him and Mama. He'd tell a funny story, my brothers'd say I was laughing in my sleep."

She turned again to the window. "Now there's a thing," she went on. "Laughing in your sleep. Course I don't know that's true. Not with my brothers to tell it. But my very first dream? If I ever did know, I surely don't know now."

Jackson gazed at her, weighing what he had heard. Then he said, "Mama, I been thinking about Ramona. Wishing she'd come back."

Edna Stillwell got up from the table and passed through the back door to the pump in the yard. A mongrel was limp in the weathered-out porch shade, watching her, and when she looked at the three-room house she knew her son was inside, alone at the kitchen table, staring at the open doorway she had moved through. She still called him boy, the man with two days' growth of beard who asked about her dreams.

Jackson sailed the south meadow to the east of his mother's house, checking his traps, kicking a yellow down out of the wild alfalfa and sweet clover. He came on a trap full of rabbit, the animal dead at least a day, pulled the lock and drew out the rigid corpse. With the rabbit against a thatch of mustard grass he stretched a front paw clear of the body, cleaving the foot away in one fall of his hatchet and putting the paw in the soft cloth bag his mother had made for him. Standing and walking he felt the sun move in the sky and for a moment he thought he heard someone call his name, a woman's voice. He stopped in the middle of the broad meadow, listening for the bells he heard when he was about to have what his mother always called *a spell*, bells blowing out of the air. He looked up at the glaze of clouds. *Sit down boy* his mother had told him, sit down when you feel a spell coming on and he told her *Sometimes Mama I'm so weak, I can't do nothing, I just want it to come and take me over and be done with it* as if a storm could move up and over the horizon so suddenly he was riveted by the black clouds climbing into the air. Jackson Stillwell stood in his rabbit-trap meadow in a spill of summer as his eyes rolled away from the light, arms pushing out of the seizure and reaching as he fell like a tree coming down, arms and legs rigid in convulsion, his quivering body lifting a feathered mist of pollen.

From where he fell he looked into the sky while his eyes came back to focus and his memory returned in pieces. He watched for pictures and signs in the shapes of the clouds. He sang quietly to himself. He thought of Ramona; the meadow had been a favorite place to play when they were children. For years Ramona's aunt visited Jackson's mother, and Ramona came with her, bringing gifts from town: cut flowers that smelled of jasmine and water, persimmons with their wet bitterness on Jackson's chin, a ball and jacks. On one visit she brought postcards. From France, Ramona told him. Images of the Brittany countryside with peasants bending in wheat, harlequins dancing in front of a fountain, two ladies in a garden with parasols. Ramona told stories to accompany each scene and Jackson took them for true.

They chased across pasture and into forest, hide and seek, Ramona laughing and running ahead under a spackled fall of light in the elder and boxwood and black cherry, pounding ankle-deep across creeks, rolling slopes until the sky swam.

As Ramona grew older her aunt made more visits alone, telling Jackson that Ramona was becoming a young lady, with other things to do, other people to see. Jackson was polite. He wanted to conceal his fear. He never knew how or why he was changing and saw Ramona Snow on his few town trips and felt her distance growing even as she greeted him, smiling, kissing him on the cheek.

At times, and always at night from his bed, Jackson Stillwell heard music. He was convinced he heard music and left his bed to walk from the house into the night in his long underwear and bare feet. Moonlight edged the crowns of maples as he searched for what he had heard, as if he would walk out on the road and turn one way or another and find a musician along the roadside with an instrument on one knee, a dulcimer or a banjo, sitting and playing. The music was a part of the night, inside the night, and Jackson could not be sure but he tried to listen, he bit his lower lip working hard to listen.

There were nights he walked over two miles from the house, walking barefoot until he knew how late it was and how alone he was and that he no longer heard the music. He heard what he knew was there: a slow wind on the move across alfalfa fields and corn rows, crickets, frogs now and again from the direction of water. He tried to remember the music as he walked back to his mother's house, tried to recollect the chain of melody a man could climb if he was listening right. On the night in July when he heard the music again he got out of bed, pulled on his trousers and left the house, turning south at the gate and walking along the dirt lane. He followed the music as far as he could, as far as it took him along the road, along the line of creek that pulled in from the west and off, toward the river. He was taking the music to Ramona. He would remember it and take it to her and sing it to her, standing beside her bed. He would take his gift to Ramona and they would walk together along the road and into the forest and he would have her back again.

The moon was mid-sky, nearly full, bright and cold and clean, and he walked the four miles to the north edge of town, to the Snow house.

As he opened the gate the family dog stood on the porch and barked once, jumped down and came toward him through the grass. Jackson waited, knelt and stroked the animal when it reached him, leaving it contented on its side as he moved in against the back wall of the house, stepping carefully below the windows. The window he remembered as Ramona's was open, a white curtain drifting. He pulled himself up and over the sill until he sat in the windowframe, and dropped quietly inside the room.

The curtain blew across the sill and flattened against his back, lifted away again to billow and fill the window.

When he was a boy he had sat on the floor of this same bedroom with one of Ramona's first powder puffs, batting it over the hardwood. He tried to put it in his mouth and Ramona pulled it away, laughing, *No, silly, you can't eat it.* The room smelled as it had then, of varnished spruce and clean bedding and body powder.

He watched the woman he knew must be Ramona, her hair dark and fanned over the pillow as he let his own breath slip into time with the rise and fall of her body, wondering if she was dreaming. She was on her side and Jackson stared, thinking that if he looked long enough he would see what she was dreaming, he would have a vision of the inside of her night and it would become his own, second sight, the thing he would carry away. He could tell his mother he knew what a dream looked like. That he had one of his own.

She moved in her sleep, groaning softly; from somewhere in the house Jackson heard a sound. He could not be sure: the whisper of a curtain parted in front of an open window. A body coming out of bed. A match being struck or a foot across a floorboard, and Jackson remembered Ramona's father. He had seen him once, big man washing coal dust from a huge neck and shoulders and chest, splashing creek water from a tub on the porch, angry red moustache, muscles alive inside his arms and Jackson dived through the open window, back to the grass and breaking for the fence and the pasture beyond, sure he had heard a sound and it would be Ramona's father filling the doorway of her bedroom and the dog barked and chased him to the fence but Jackson was over, running up the long hill behind the house until his lungs and ribs and legs burned with the effort. A hundred yards out he stopped, panting, turned to look back. The house sat alone and quiet, innocent, small from where he stood. Around him, everywhere, the grass moved like water.

When Jackson heard the music again it was early September and he moved barefoot through the pastures, toward the village where lights flickered across the cover of darkness as if they lived inside his head. He walked and thought *look at me,* tip of his tongue showing between his lips in concentration.

The Snow house rose out of the night: wing-porch, shutters, roof peak. Jackson opened the gate, moved through and closed it behind him and the dog was there, nuzzling at his leg, lying at his feet.

Wading through grass to the back of the house, Jackson saw Ramona's window still open to the cooler nights and he pulled up on the frame, got his feet through and curled his body in and settled on the floor with his hands braced against the sill and the woman in the bed sat up. There was a moment before she whispered *Who's there?*

Jackson held his breath, staring at her, unable to speak.

She pulled the sheet up to cover herself, leaning forward looking at him, at his shape.

"Mr. Stillwell?" She got out of bed. The dread in her whisper was gone. She turned her back and put on a robe, moving to quietly close the bedroom door. He let his breath go, began to breathe again.

Standing in front of him she said, "What are you doing here?" Her voice was soft, and seemed to move over his face like cool air. As if he was hearing her with his skin.

"This is very wrong, Mr. Stillwell. You should know that."

He felt as if his face might slide away. His mouth was moving; he was trying to speak.

"You," he said. "You're not Ramona."

"No," she said. "Ramona's married and gone. A long time gone, nearly eight years."

"You're not Ramona," Jackson said again.

"I'm her younger sister," the woman said. "Becky. You remember me."

Jackson started to speak, and stopped. His mouth was dry. "I came to see Ramona," he said.

"Well," Becky Snow said, gently, speaking to a child. "It's like I told you. She's not here. She doesn't live here anymore."

Jackson studied the room, searching. "I thought this was Ramona's room."

"It was, years ago. Mr. Stillwell? Do you know what time it is?"

Jackson looked at her in wonderment, as if she spoke a foreign language he should understand, but did not.

"Mr. Stillwell? You're going to have to leave now." From deeper in the house a man's voice called her name; she turned to the door and said, "It's alright, Daddy."

Jackson's head made two involuntary beats to the right, a spasm riding down his neck. "I wanted to watch her sleep," he said softly. The muscles in his chest began to drum.

Becky said, "It's proper to visit people during the day. You know that. I don't need to tell you that."

"I wanted to watch her sleep," he said again. "I just wanted to stand here. I would never hurt her."

They looked at each other and Jackson did not speak, hearing the bells. He heard them from under the hills, beyond the horizon. Two heavenly notes ringing over and over, filling the room, coming to eat what little light there was, a spirit he could see at a distance, walking toward him on the air. He could smell a fire, ashes blowing into the house.

Becky said, "I know you only came to see Ramona."

"I only came to see her," he said. His head wobbled against his will.

"It's very sweet of you. I'll tell Ramona you're wanting to visit. But you have to go now."

Jackson saw smoke seeping into the room, pluming from under the bed and he was gone, possessed and flailing, falling backward through the window to rip away the curtain. Beneath the window on his back, convulsing delirious in the bluegrass and chewing away the end of his tongue as the sky rolled and fell open and his mouth filled with blood. Rebecca Snow shouted for her father.

Jackson Stillwell wandered, living on plantain and creek water in parts of the high forest only the Shawnee had seen before him. He had been gone from home for days and imagined himself on horseback, the horse underneath him with the same smoking nostrils and blood-red eyes he had seen in picture books. They climbed together into mist and black water, shapes of wings in silhouette above them. He saw the shadow of his windswept hair gliding on the ground and the shadow of Ramona in the saddle behind him, holding him around the waist. Ramona as he had always wanted her, in a place they could live forever, singing the hymns they learned in church as children. Jackson sang and listened to the music come back to him out of the wind and did not know he was lost, believing his mother's house would rise behind every ridge as he walked on obsessed with what he thought were the voices of angels. On the fifth day out he found a young rabbit cowering in a cave, killed it with a stone and ate the meat raw.

Sleeping in leaves, he woke with spiders on his eyelids. Morning birds called in the reaches of the trees.

There were those prepared to defer to Christ when Jackson turned up missing, arguing for a divine salvation in the wilderness. The search went on for more than a week.

The sheriff organized a posse with six men and hunting dogs. They plotted out the countryside and their campfires could be seen from town on the ridges to the east, north, northwest, finally south along the river. They found no trace of Jackson Stillwell and came home on mud-spattered horses, riding into town in a downpour, the weary dogs stringing behind.

The days moved toward autumn and it was finally Edna alone in the mountains, stopping the few travelers she saw to ask about her lost son, passing the dark hours in half-sleep under the palisades and scree. Night rooted in the wind driving across the canyons' faces, the gone picture of time in an old woman's one good eye. At a summit after a pointless climb she sat down exhausted, knowing he was gone and his disappearance would fade to the quiet turn of mind in the listener hearing the story years away. She thought of the morning in the kitchen he had asked about her first dream. That afternoon he had come home from his traps and sat on the step, pulled out the drawstring on the pouch she had made for him and emptied rabbits' feet onto the porch, eight paws scattered across the planks, blooded stumps. He had looked up at her, his face sweat-rimmed, needing a shave and he said *I gathered these for you. Mama. They will bring you good fortune forever.*

She had nodded and smiled and thanked him.

Jack, she had said, a touch of good fortune is surely what every woman needs.

■ ■ ■ ■ ■ ■ ■ ■ ■ ■ ■

Inside Graciella Gonzales

Charlotte Forbes

I t was the deep center of night when the strange and beautiful emerge and commingle. The subway car was nearly empty, the floor filthy with footprints, the light harsh and disquieting as that of an operating room. In the corner a man slept, chin on chest. Another snored open-mouthed. Graciella Gonzales came upon a book that had been waiting patiently for her.

Graciella was on her way home from a particularly late night of housekeeping for the widower McClanless when she spotted the book across the aisle at the end of the subway car, a paperback book left behind in haste by another rider. The book lay face down and open, a bird with outstretched wings. Graciella lurched over to it before it took flight, and brought it back to her seat. She opened it to a page near the middle and gave a tiny gasp. What she saw so floored her with its beauty that she had to close the book, close her eyes.

The book might have belonged to a child or a student. *Rocks and Minerals* it was called. Timidly, she reopened the book to page one.

Unlike animals, rocks do not run away, it said. Unlike plants, rocks do not die in winter. Simple, obvious facts. But Graciella wasn't prepared to associate rocks with the notions of bravery or honor or eternal life. The gravity of those sentiments caused her to look up anxiously, and sent her quickly to the next page where the picture of a plain brown rock with streaks of electric green and blue so seized her attention that she missed her stop and had to walk ten blocks back to 47th Avenue. At number 3602 she put her key in the door of the sleeping household, tiptoed into the bedroom, put the book under her pillow, and let the pain come.

The pain was her only complaint in life. The pain, or rather pains, had been with her for a very long time; she experienced them as something rough and mass-like rubbing against the underside of her epidermis. They came frequently and in various parts of her short, stout, low-center-of-gravity body.

She told no one about the pains, nor did they register on her peasant face, which always wore the contented half-smile of those who accept their poverty. Graciella had the blessing of youth without its folly, which gave her the stamina to shake off the pain and to see to it every day that the flat she shared with a scar-faced man from the Yucatan and their five children was vacuumed and scrubbed and straightened as neat as a pin, and by weeknight to do the same for the widower Hugh McClanless, attorney at law, and at all other times to indulge the afflicted of the neighborhood. For at the age of thirty-three Graciella had mastered the lost art of comforting the sick of heart and body and, though no one could say what it was she did other than sit there bright-eyed and closed-mouthed, she was known to produce amazing results. After only five consecutive Saturday nights at the bedside of Mrs. Tomasso, a seventy-five-year-old widow whose children plucked her from her ancestral home in the Neapolitan hills and everything she knew and brought her to their home in Queens to live out her days under their overprotective eyes, Graciella hit pay dirt. The poor woman rose, wrapped herself in her black wool shawl, went right to the kitchen and made a tomato sauce in which her children no longer tasted the bitter tears of regret.

In the morning, the family awoke in such a cacophonous din; the book lay in its new resting place, forgotten for the moment. The babies were crying from hunger, the older children argued, the husband complained, grumbled, and demanded to know where he had put his shoes.

With one baby in her arms she retrieved the husband's shoes from beneath the kitchen table and took them to the bathroom where he stood shaving. Fifteen years ago she brought her agrarian body from the peaceful midsection of Mexico to New York where, after a month, she met Pablo at a Day of the Dead celebration. So homesick was she for the beat of the Mexican heart that she latched on to him and never let go. It was only after they married in the small brick church with the wooden statue of the Virgin that she realized the ways of the man from the Yucatan were often as foreign to her as those of New York.

Pablo had the body of a bantamweight, teeth whiter than milk and a long scar on his right cheekbone from a boyhood brush with his father's butcher knife. He had the look of being wound too tight, as if the crush of humanity in this world, in this city, in his own house might suddenly become too much for him. Still, he faithfully made his way into Manhattan each day to work as a counterman at The Sunshine Deli.

In the mirror he saw Graciella approach with the shoes. *Ham, ham,* he growled, flinging the shaving cream from his razor into the sink. *Another day of filling the pigs with ham.*

But it's a good job. It pays and you are able to eat free, Graciella said, putting a hand on his arm.

Pablo jerked his arm away. *I spit on that food,* he cried and stomped his foot. Inside him was strife, the endless strife of the Yucatan, the centuries of warring under the flaming sun. The Yucatan was in him and it was the reason for his torment, Graciella knew that just as she knew there was not a thing to be done about it. She tried to make her words as clear and cool as water to ease the fire in him and went about her tasks.

The older children sat at the kitchen table, not eating their cereal or drinking their milk. *That's mine,* they argued over a napkin, a book, a pencil. *No, it's mine.*

Children, come. The teachers are calling for you. Graciella never shouted, her voice was not a big one, it was soft and small and perhaps incapable of greater decibels, and at the sound of it, especially when it was barely above a whisper, the children perked up their ears and considered what was being said, and usually complied. A great shuffle of chairs against the floor, a clattering of dishes in the sink, hasty kisses, and they were off.

After the door closed and the sound of children and husband disappeared down the walk and into the street, a deep quiet enveloped the house. Graciella did not start to wash the dishes and make the beds and gather the laundry as she usually did. She didn't phone her cousin to come stay with the younger children so she could go arrange the flowers on the altar or cross the street to sit on the front stoop with old Mr. Chu who had not stopped stroking his thin gray beard and mumbling the name of his wife since she passed two months ago from complications of the common cold.

Graciella left Rosa and Ana in their high chairs, playing with their cereal, and went into her bedroom.

The bedroom was dark, the shades were still drawn and the rumpled sheets smelled of sleep. Though no one was there Graciella went on tiptoe to take the book from under the pillow, and returned with it to the kitchen where the babies sat in their highchairs gurgling happily. Absently she rubbed her shoulder where the pains were pushing up from the bone, and opened the book to the middle.

There were rocks that looked like cubes of frozen blood, and sulfur crystals that looked like canary feathers. A diamond sprung from a plain gray rock, a chunky white rock had crevices and craters like the surface of the moon. There were pale pink crystals large and pointed as giants' teeth. Graciella loved them all, so serene and self-contained they were, their benevolence radiating even from their photographs. Hemimorphite, spodumene, realgar, the names were strange and difficult to say, she loved that too, it made them sound intelligent and incomprehensible, which of course they were.

Formed deep inside the earth, some of them, squeezed and heated by the earth's innards. So said the book. Graciella began to think of the dizzying things that went on below ground, private things, the birthing of bizarre concoctions with many faces and resplendent color. Right there under the sidewalk and streets and mountains and meadows.

She sat there until eleven a.m. gazing at her rocks. Her moonstones and rhodonite, her bournonite, her vanadinite. The babies took their morning naps right in their high chairs and were pushing out of sleep to once again be fed and held and fussed over before she realized how much time had passed.

One look at the clock and she raced through the rest of the day of cleaning and fixing and straightening, making the chicken and rice, frying the chicken in the onions and tomatoes as she had learned to do in the way Pablo liked, to do this for him, to make the food he didn't have to spit on, and after school was over, to check the homework of the boys and Maria and ask them how they felt about the world that day and look them straight in their big dark eyes so they could say, yes, I am acknowledged, I exist, and then bathe the babies and kiss the tops of their heads and whisper in their ears the sweet sticky words of love.

Then it was time to go to work.

In the kitchen, the boys argued about who was taller, who was stronger.

At thirteen, Roberto was on the brink of the growth spurt that would propel the rest of him into his huge hands and feet. He was on the lazy side, and possessed of a certain indifferent superiority, the result of having been the kingpin for more than two years before the birth of his brother Juan. Juan was a porky, belligerent boy, whose conception on the heels of a domestic squabble left him continually hankering for a fight, and like many a second son, ready to slay the first.

Maria was dishing out the supper. She was a plain girl of nine, with a thick body born for the toil of the sugar cane fields and a face that was both slightly bewildered to have escaped such a fate and searching for another way to suffer.

Mommy, she said to Graciella, and put her arm in her mother's. *I'll go with you.*

Oh, honey, no, it's woman's work.

I want to go with you. I'll help you.

Graciella put her hand on Maria's cheek, *I'll be home late, and you must get your rest for school. Someday. Someday you will come.*

The TV was spewing forth the news in Spanish.

Pablo was starting on the cerveza.

No, no more, Graciella pleaded with him. *You have the children now. I have to go to work.*

Hey Mami. Pablo grabbed her around the waist and swung her agrarian body in a two-step. *Come on Mami. We are young! You are beautiful! Live a little!*

Graciella blushed like a school girl and let herself be twirled around the kitchen, her legs in the black stretch pants scurrying to keep up, her shoulder purse flying out from her body. She smiled her silent smile of acquiescence, for Pablo's sake, for the sake of the music. The pains were in the back of the legs.

Go Mami! The boys whistled and stamped their feet. Maria lowered her eyes. The babies cried. Gabriella heard their sobs as the subway lurched its way from Queens into Manhattan and she left the heat of the city behind and entered the apartment of Hugh McClanless. Then she forgot.

Although Graciella had worked there for five years now, she was always taken aback by how large and cool and pale as an eggshell the apartment was. After his wife's death, Mr. McClanless kept Graciella on. Graciella preferred to do the work during the day as she always had. But Mr. McClanless was such a gentleman, such a tall, elegant gentleman with such silver hair and magnificent gray suits and he had come to her in such a humble manner with such distress in his eyes and, bowing his fine head in embarrassment, said so earnestly, *I wonder if you'd consider coming in the evening. I'd like to have someone here when I come home,* that Graciella rearranged her life.

She arrived at six-thirty p.m. now, and set straight to vacuuming the spotless carpets, and cleaning the pristine bathrooms and then to prepare the meal.

When Mr. McClanless put his key in the door at eight o'clock the table was set with a glass of claret and, under a silver-domed platter, a chicken quesadilla with yellow rice and red beans.

Good evening, he said to Graciella and sat down to eat. Without so much as a raised eyebrow at the fare before him, he ate everything on his plate, though distractedly, and drank his wine and then adjourned to the study to rattle around, open mail, write checks.

Graciella put the dishes in the dishwasher, tidied the kitchen, and waited.

As always, at nine p.m. Mr. McClanless summoned Graciella to the den.

The television was on. *Nothing unsuitable*, he assured her, *only quality programming*. Graciella nodded and sat in the beige silk armchair beside his while the biography of General Stonewall Jackson and then the history of the Soviet space program rolled before their eyes.

From Sputnik to Aeroflot, he said, halfway through the space program, and a refined chuckle emerged from his throat. Graciella giggled softly and recrossed her ankles as she always did at his jokes, though rarely did she get them.

The thought of the rock book drifted through her mind. Though she longed to hold it in her hands, turn its thin pages and let her eyes wander over the rocks, it didn't occur to Graciella to simply get up and go to the kitchen where her purse hung over the back of the chair and remove the book. Not with McClanless's need filling the room.

Eventually Mr. McClanless dozed off and halfway into the eleven o'clock news, he roused himself, stood up and stretched. *Thank you*, he said to Graciella, *thank you*. He bowed slightly to her and made his way into the marble bathroom for his nightly ablutions. She heard the water, the shutting of drawers, silence. That was her cue to stand just outside the bedroom door and watch the fine gentleman lie alone in his enormous white bed, looking like a small frightened boy.

She waited. Only when she was sure that sleep held him firmly in its blessed grip did she let herself silently out of the apartment. The pains had moved to her hip area, hard and burny against the smooth skin of her hips, and when she reached the lobby and the doorman asked her if she was all right, she allowed herself to stand still for a moment and close her eyes and feel as though she might fall over like a tree in the forest, before answering *Yes, I'm fine*.

L ater that night at home Graciella lay on her back in bed, praying for a breeze to crawl through the window. She tossed and turned and finally sat up and lit the small lamp on the night table. On her lap the book opened to a rock in the shape of a baked potato. Blue-green peaks rose from the middle of it, steep jagged faces. The peaks made her feel cool, as though her body were immersed in a frozen waterfall the color of turquoise.

Pablo woke from a sound sleep and sat straight up in bed and looked at his wife. *Christ,* he cried. *Give me that book. What's so fucking important about this book?* He grabbed it and threw it into the hall. *Go to sleep.*

Once the book was out of the room, Pablo turned on his side and began to snore again. For several minutes Graciella didn't move a muscle. Then she eased herself out of the bed and tiptoed to the hall to retrieve the book, and once again resting against the pillow, set it on her lap. She turned to the pyrite. Her eyes ran up and down the jumbles of small gold cubes spilling this way and that until they grew heavy and she fell asleep with the book in her hands.

During the next few days the pains moved down the left leg from the thigh to the middle of the calf. There was so little chance to take the book and look at it, Graciella resorted to stealing glances in the cracks of time. She began to feel like a thief with a thing in her own possession.

In the morning Rosie and Ana were in the bath, splashing. Two pudgy little ducks, Graciella cooed at them, and sang an old Mexican song about three fishermen going out to sea in small green boats as she knelt on the floor beside the tub, washing them. When they were all soaped and scrubbed and rinsed and began to amuse each other, Graciella did something she never did: she sat back and let them play in the water and splash and sing without her. She sat on the edge of the tub and took the book from her apron pocket and opened it at random to the page on crystals.

If a rock had a lot of time and room to grow, it could grow crystals, the book said. Graciella loved the look of them. The quartz crystals were fuzzy, like white mold. The calcite like chips of ice, the copper crystals dark and long and slim like branches of a tree. How much time, how much room had it taken the crystals to grow? Graciella did not wonder about that, or about where they were found or what use they were put to or what secrets they held. Hers was not an intellectual interest but simply a desire to gaze on their improbable forms, lovely and eternal, and the more she gazed at them, the more she needed to.

So absorbed was she in the world of the crystals that when Rosie cried, *Out Mami, out,* Graciella needed more than a moment to determine where the cry was coming from. No sooner had Graciella turned to get the towels than Rosie reached for the book that lay on the edge of the tub, and pulled it into the water. *Boat, boat,* she sang, and pushed it down to the bottom of the water. Both children squealed with laughter.

Graciella let loose with a barrage in Spanish. So uncharacteristic was the outburst that the children, as young as they were, stopped their laughter and looked down at the water with guilty faces.

Shaking her head and muttering, Graciella wrapped the book in a towel and after the children were dried and dressed brought it outside and attached it with two yellow plastic clothespins to the clothesline that stretched the length of the narrow porch. The book hung at the end of the line, next to the limp underwear and cotton shorts and dresses trying their best to dry in the humid New York summer.

On Saturday night when dinner was nearly finished Graciella quietly rose from the table saying, *Evida, I've got to go to Evida.*

Juan pushed his plate away and jumped up. *No, Mommy, you said we could go get ice cream,* he shouted.

Maria's lower lip began to quiver. *But Mami, we were going to cut out the dress pattern.*

Eh, who's going to do the dishes? sulked Pablo.

Graciella hesitated. Her eyes went out to caress her boys and girls and linger over them in apology. But Graciella knew what she had to do. *I'm sorry,* she said and began to spoon leftover salad and rice into a container and wrap up a piece of pound cake and a bunch of grapes in a red-and-white checkered napkin to bring to the lady in distress down the street. There was comfort to dispense. Evida had suddenly lost the hearing in one ear and had to be soothed and fussed over and then be in the company of someone who would sit next to her good ear and listen without uttering a word so as to not remind her of her recent loss.

Oh, Evida, Graciella said, kissing Evida on one cheek and then the other. *I'm sorry for your trouble.*

Though it was still nearly eighty-five degrees, Evida pulled an afghan up around her. *Ah, Graciella, it's so hard. So many things can happen. You don't know from one day to the next what He has in store for you,* she said and sent a scowl heavenward.

Graciella nodded and smoothed the afghan and sat on the ottoman next to Evida's good ear.

Do you know what they want of me now? Now that I only have the use of one ear? Evida said and put her head in her hands. For the next hour and a half Graciella sat and listened to the crimes and misdemeanors that Evida had suffered that week. The husband's spending their savings on his mechanics shop, the youngest boy's refusal to go to church, the sister-in-law's throat cancer, the mother's telephone call at two in the morning to talk about her swollen legs, the grocer, the landlord, the doctors, the priest hounding them for money, until there was no more to come out and Evida stopped talking and asked to be brought the transistor radio turned to the salsa station.

While Graciella sat at Evida's side, Pablo and the older children sat on their back stoop to escape the heat of the house.

The boys sat idly throwing pebbles into the concrete yard.

Bet I can throw farther than you.

Who cares?

Maria and Pablo sat on the top step. A siren wailed. A dog barked on the next block.

Knock it off you two, Pablo said to the boys.

Juan looked up at the book hanging overhead on the clothesline.

Betcha I can knock it down.

No way.

On Juan's fifth try, the book fell to the ground.

What's that? Roberto asked.

Some stupid kid's book, said Juan.

Shut up. That's your mother's book, Pablo said and gave Juan a swat on the side of his head. *Your mother better not hear you talk like that.*

Ouch. Juan rubbed his head. *She's not here. She won't even know.*

Pablo took a swig of his cerveza. *Mothers know everything.*

They do not, Juan cried. *Mama doesn't even know how to speak English as well as me.*

Pablo thought for a minute. *Your mother doesn't need words. Isn't that right, Maria?*

Maria looked at her father, surprised to be asked for her opinion on anything. *Yes Papa,* she said shyly.

That's dumb, Juan protested. *That's the dumbest thing I ever heard.*

You watch your tongue, Pablo shouted.

The two of them, father and son, went on like that, shouting and arguing about who needed words and why children couldn't ever do what they wanted and who was going to win the soccer match and which was the brightest star in the sky.

Maria got up and went to bed.

Roberto went in to watch TV.

At 9:30 Graciella appeared on the back steps. Her eyes were heavy and her arms folded over her stomach as if in pain.

Eh Mami, how is she? Pablo said.

Better, Graciella managed to get out.

At the sound of his mother's voice Juan began to cry. *Mami, I'm sorry,*

I'm sorry, he blubbered, and rushed to lay his troubled head against her.

What's this, what's this? she asked without expecting an answer, and led him to his bedroom where he lay down on the bed and having cried himself dry, went immediately to sleep.

For a moment Graciella sat over him stroking his forehead which, even in sleep, was clenched in conflict. Many times she sat over him like this, smoothing his face until a kind of peace came over it, until the breathing had passed from rough to fine and regular. But just now her thoughts were not on Juan, they were on herself, and getting into bed and looking over the book of rocks, and she left her son groaning in his sleep and went to the back porch to reclaim the book from the clothesline.

She saw that it was not there, nor was it on the porch, or on the kitchen table or stuck in a living room chair or on her bed or buried in the pile of newspapers at the side of the house.

Eh, Dios, she muttered and went to check on the children. The boys ground their teeth and tossed in their sleep. She gave them each the kiss they would never have allowed when they were awake. The girls' room was quieter. The babies slept soundlessly in their cribs. Maria slept on her side, her face turned toward the wall. Graciella bent over the sleeping girl and saw something that made her smile the smile of gratitude. The plump fingers of Maria's right hand clasped the book of rocks as if it were a stuffed animal or a doll she never slept with.

A t eleven p.m. the doorbell rang.
Pablo got up from watching TV to answer it.

Your wife, said a young man of no more than twenty. He had shaggy dark hair and fear in his eyes. *She must come.*

No way, man. Pablo said. *She's in bed.*

Please. We need her.

Hey, it's late. Go on now.

In a white night dress, and her thick black hair in braids, Graciella appeared behind Pablo. *It's OK,* she said. *It's OK. One minute.*

She dressed quickly and followed the young man three blocks to a small dark apartment where his sister, Faustina, lay on the kitchen table, covered with a cloth. She was shivering. Her face was white and drawn.

In a corner of the kitchen the mother sobbed. With a hand on her shoulder the father, tight-lipped, stared at the opposite wall.

The young man turned to Graciella and began to speak disjointedly. *She's been like this for three days. It just came over her. It's not a fever. Dinner, in the middle of dinner, we were all talking. Arguing possibly,* he said sheepishly. *Yes, arguing. Faustina is a quiet girl. A good girl. But she yelled at us. 'Stop it. You're killing me!' She threw the dishes to the floor and climbed onto the table and screamed, 'Why don't you just eat me alive right now.' Then she just lay there. She won't get up.*

OK, Graciella said.

Do you want us to leave you alone? asked the young man.

If you don't mind, Graciella said softly and accepted the chair the young man pulled up for her right next to Faustina's face.

For three quarters of an hour Graciella never took her eyes off Faustina. Under the force of her gaze, it was inevitable that Faustina react. When their eyes finally met, Faustina gave a small blink. Then she turned her head away and resumed shivering.

Graciella sat still in the wooden chair.

A kind of luxurious tranquility filled the room. A luxurious but stalwart tranquility, not the cursory tranquility of a human, more the deep primitive peace that comes only from an object of nature. It was a tranquility indifferent to its surroundings and not afraid to simply witness the slow passing of the hours and, for those so inclined, the tranquility in the blue kitchen where Faustina Garzan lay on the table was lovely to behold.

The clock ticked.

The refrigerator hummed.

The dog got up to change position and clunked back down on the floor.

Somewhere outside the brakes of a car screeched.

At two a.m., the girl stopped shivering.

Graciella got up to call the brother. *It's OK now*, she mumbled. *It's OK*, and smiled a tired smile.

The young man saw that there had been a change in his sister. *A million thanks, a million thanks*, the young man murmured and made the sign of the cross. *I'll take you home*, he offered.

It's OK, Graciella said, *it's only a short way*. The pains now were in the belly and up into the chest and they were so sharp that she held her breath as she walked out of the house and down the walk. She stopped and held the iron railing in front of the garbage cans. The street was deserted.

Graciella rubbed her belly and walked a block, as far as the El, and sank down on the steps.

Three teenagers ran past her up the steps. The one with the pocked face and the black net T-shirt came back. He knelt down with his face close to Graciella's. *You OK lady?*

No, Graciella managed to mumble.

By the smell, Graciella knew she was in the hospital. She was lying on her back in a very small, bright room. People dressed in light green stood over her. They were feeling her belly, her arms, everywhere. Their faces looked startled, then worried. Instructions were shouted back and forth. Graciella closed her eyes. Seemingly, days passed. Then came the sensation of movement, wheels turning under her, passing through swing doors. Into a white room without a temperature, without air. The clock on the wall said three a.m. Someone with sympathetic eyes pricked the vein in her forearm.

The operating room was crowded. There were seven doctors and eight nurses, all sober-faced. There was none of the usual glib operating room chatter.

They opened the belly first. Two of the doctors gasped. One turned away. Not one person spoke. There were tumors all through the woman's belly, odd, inexplicable tumors. Tumors of translucent lilac. Sulfur spikes. Blue as the bluest sky. Sparkling. Blocks of deep cherry. Gold.

For a brief moment the doctors and nurses stood motionless, as though they felt themselves in the presence of something strange though exceptionally beautiful. Then reason prevailed. The head surgeon broke the silence. *E-god, it's all through her*, he said. *Sew her back up and send her home.* He nodded to the others to carry on, and left the operating room muttering to himself what they had all known the moment they encountered Graciella's pain. *There's nothing we can do for her here.*

■ ■ ■ ■ ■ ■ ■ ■ ■ ■ ■

The Wavemaker Falters

George W. Saunders

Halfway up the mountain it's the Center for Wayward Nuns, full of sisters and other religious personnel who've become doubtful. One time a few of them came down to our facility in stern suits and swam cautiously. The singing from up there never exactly knocks your socks off. It's very conditional singing, probably because of all the doubt. A young nun named Sister Viv came unglued there last fall and we gave her a free season-pass to come down and meditate near our simulated Spanish trout stream whenever she wanted. The head nun said Viv was from Idaho and sure enough the stream seemed to have a calming effect.

One day she's sitting crosslegged a few feet away from a dumpster housed in a granite boulder made of a resilient synthetic material. Ned, Tony, and Gerald as usual are dressed as Basques. In Orientation they learned a limited amount of actual Basque so that they can lapse into it whenever Guests are within earshot. Sister Viv's a regular so they don't even bother.

So I look over to say something supportive and optimistic to her and then I think oh geez, not another patron death on my hands. She's going downstream fast and her habit's ballooning up. The fake Basques are standing there in a row with their mouths open.

So I dive in and drag her out. It's not very deep and the bottom's rubber-matted. None of the Basques are bright enough to switch off the Leaping Trout Subroutine however, so twice I get scraped with little fiberglass fins.

Finally I get her out on the pine needles and she comes to and spits in my face, and says I couldn't possibly know the darkness of her heart. Try me, I say. She crawls away and starts bashing her skull against a tree trunk. The trees are synthetic too. But still.

I pin her arms behind her and drag her to the Main Office, where they chain her weeping to the safe. A week later she runs amok in the nun eating hall and stabs a cafeteria worker to death.

So the upshot of it all is more guilt for me, Mr. Guilt.

Once a night Simone puts on the mermaid tail and lip-synchs on an Astroturf mat on a raft in the wave pool while I play spotlights over her and broadcast "Button Up Your Overcoat." As I'm working the lights I watch Leon, Subquadrant Manager, watch Simone. As he watches her his wet mouth keeps moving. Every time I accidentally light up the Chlorine Shed the Guests start yelling at me. Finally I stop watching Leon watch her and try to concentrate on not getting written up for crappy showmanship.

Afterwards he follows us into the Break Area and chats her up while helping her pack away the tail. On the wall is a picture of him jello-wrestling a traveling celebrity jello-wrestler. That's pure Leon. Plus he had her autograph it. At first he tried to talk her into dipping her breasts in ink and doing an imprint but she said no way. My point is, even traveling celebrity jello-wrestlers have more class than Leon.

He praises Simone's fake singing and the sexy thing she does with her shoulders whenever the animatronic Sea Prince emerges from the pond to wink at her. Do I tell him to get lost? No. Do I knock him into a planter just to remind him just whose wife Simone is? No. I go out and wait for her by Loco Logjam. I sit on a turnstile. The Italian lights in the trees are pretty. The night crew's hard at work applying a wide range of commercial chemicals and cleaning hairballs from the filters.

Finally Simone's ready and we walk over to Employee Underground Parking. Some exiting guests are brawling in the traffic jam on the access road. Through a federal program we offer discount coupons to the needy, so sometimes our clientele is borderline. Once some bikers trashed the row of boutiques and once Leon interrupted a gang guy trying to put hydrochloric acid in the Main Feeder. Bald Murray logs us out while trying to look down Simone's blouse. On the side of El Guapo Boulevard a woman's sitting in a shopping cart, wearing a grubby chemise.

For old time's sake I put my hand in Simone's lap.

Promises, promises, she says.

At the roadcut by the self-storage she makes me stop so she can view all the interesting stratification. She's never liked geology before. Leon takes geology at the community college and is always pointing out what's glacial till and what's not, so I suspect there's a connection. We get into a

little fight about him and she admires his self-confidence to my face. I ask
her is that some kind of put-down. She's only saying, she says, that in
her book, a little boldness goes a long way. She asks if I remember the
time Leon chased off the frat boy who kept trying to detach her mermaid
hairpiece. Where was I? Why didn't I step in? Is she my girl or what?

I remind her that I was busy at the controls.

It gets very awkward and quiet. Me at the controls is a sore subject.
Nothing's gone right for us since the day I crushed the boy with the
wavemaker. I haven't been able to forget his little white trunks floating out
of the inlet port all bloody. Who checks protective screen mounting screws
these days? Not me. Leon does when he wavemakes of course. It's in the
protocol. That's how he got to be Subquadrant Manager, attention to
detail. Leon's been rising steadily since we went through Orientation
together, and all-told he's saved three Guests and I've crushed the shit
out of one.

The little boy I crushed was named Clive. By all accounts he was a
sweet kid. Sometimes at night I sneak over there to do errands in secret
and pray for forgiveness at his window. I've changed his dad's oil and
painted all their window frames and taken the burrs off their Labrador.
If anybody comes out while I'm working I hide in the shrubs. The sister
who wears cat-eye glasses in this day and age thinks it's Clive's soul doing
the mystery errands and lately she's been leaving him notes. Simone says
I'm not doing them any big favor by driving their daughter nuts.

But I can't help it. I feel so bad.

We pull up to our unit and I see that once again the Peretti twins
have drawn squashed boys all over our windows with soap. Their dad's
a bruiser. No way I'm forcing a confrontation.

In the driveway Simone asks did I do my resume at lunch.

No, I tell her, I had a serious pH difficulty.

Fine, she says, make waves the rest of your life.

The day it happened, a great-looking all-girl glee club was laying
around on the concrete in Kawabunga Kove in dayglo suits, looking
like a bunch of blooms. The president and sergeant-at-arms were standing
with brown ankles in the shallows, favorably comparing my Attraction
to real surf. To increase my appeal I had the sea chanteys blaring. I was
operating at the prescribed wave frequency setting but in my lust for the
glee club had the magnitude pegged.

Leon came by and told me to turn the music down. So I turned it up.
Consequently I never heard Clive screaming or Leon shouting at me to kill

the waves. My first clue was looking out the Control Hut porthole and seeing people bolting towards the ladders, choking and with bits of Clive all over them. Guests were weeping while wiping their torsos on the lawn. In the Handicapped Section the chaired guys had their eyes shut tight and their heads turned away as the gore sloshed towards them. The ambulatories were clambering over the ropes, screaming for their physical therapists.

Leon hates to say he told me so but does it all the time anyway. He reminds me of how guilty I am by telling me not to feel guilty, and asking about my counseling. My counselor is Mr. Poppet, a gracious and devout man who's always tightening his butt cheeks when he thinks no one's looking. Mr. Poppet makes me sit with my eyes closed and repeat, "A boy is dead because of me," for half an hour for fifty dollars. Then for another fifty dollars he makes me sit with my eyes closed again and repeat, "Still, I'm a person of considerable value," for half an hour. When the session's over I go out into the bright sun like a rodent that lives in the earth, blinking and rubbing my eyes, and Mr. Poppet stands in the doorway clapping for me and intoning the time-of-day of our next appointment.

The sessions have done me good though. Clive doesn't come into my room at night all hacked up anymore. He comes in pretty much whole. He comes in and sits on my bed and starts talking to me. Since his death he's been hanging around with dead kids from other epochs. One night he showed up swearing in Latin. Another time with a wild story about an ancient African culture that used radio waves to relay tribal myths. He didn't use those exact words of course. Even though he's dead, he's still basically a kid. When he tries to be scary he gets it all wrong. He can't moan for beans. He's scariest when he does real kid things, like picking his nose and wiping it on the side of his sneaker.

He tries to be polite but he's pretty mad about the future I denied him. Tonight's subject is what the Mexico City trip with the perky red-haired tramp would have been like. He dwells on the details of their dinner in the catacombs and describes how her freckles would have looked as daylight streamed in through the cigarette-burned magenta curtains. Wistfully he says he sure would like to have tasted the sauce she would have said was too hot to be believed as they crossed the dirt road lined with begging cripples.

"Forgive me," I say in tears.

"No," he says, also in tears.

Near dawn he sighs, tucks in the parts of his body that have been gradually leaking out over the course of the night, pats my neck with his cold little palm, and tells me to have a nice day. Then he fades, producing farts with a wet hand under his armpit.

Simone sleeps through the whole thing, making little puppy sounds and pushing her rear against my front to remind me even in her sleep of how long it's been. But you try it. You kill a nice little kid through neglect and then enjoy having sex. If you can do it you're demented.

Simone's an innocent victim. Sometimes I think I should give her her space and let her explore various avenues so her personal development won't get stymied. But I could never let her go. I've loved her too long. Once in high school I waited three hours in a locker in the girls' locker room to see her in her panties. Every part of me cramped up, but when she finally came in and showered I resolved to marry her. We once dedicated a whole night to pretending I was a household invader who tied her up. In my shorts I stood outside our sliding glass door shouting, "Meter Man!" At dawn or so I made us eggs but was so high on her I ruined our only pan by leaving it on the burner while I kept running back and forth to look at her nude.

What I'm saying is, we go way back.

I hope she'll wait this thing out. If only Clive would resume living and start dating some nice-smelling cheerleader who has no idea who Benny Goodman is. Then I'd regain my strength and win her back. But no. Instead I wake at night and Simone's either looking over at me with hatred, or whisking her privates with her index finger while thinking of God-knows-who, although probably it's not me.

At noon the next day a muscleman shows up with four beehives on a dollie. This is Leon's stroke of genius for the Kiper wedding. The Kipers are the natural type. They don't want to eat anything that ever lived or buy any product that even vaguely supports notorious third-world regimes. They asked that we run a check on the ultimate source of the tomatoes in our ketchup and the union status of the group that makes our floaties. They've opted to recite their own vows in the Waterfall Grove. They've hired a trumpeter to canoe by and a couple of needy illegal aliens to retrieve the rice so no birds will choke.

At ten Leon arrives, proudly bearing a large shrimp-shaped serving vat full of bagels coated with fresh honey. Over the weekend he studied honey extraction techniques at the local library. He's always calling himself a renaissance man but the way he says it it rhymes with "rent-a-dance fan." He puts down the vat and takes off the lid, and just then the bride's grandmother falls out of her chair and rolls down the bank. She stops face-up at the water's edge and her wig tips back. She is some kind of geriatric mannequin being baptized. One of the rice-retrievers wanders up and addresses her as señora. I look around. I'm the nearest Host. According to the manual I'm supposed to initiate CPR or face a stiff payroll deduction. The week I took the class the dummy was on the fritz. Of course.

I straddle her and timidly start chest-pumping. I can feel her bra clasp under the heel of my hand. Nothing happens. I keep waiting for her to throw up on me or come to life. Then Leon vaults over the shrimp-shaped vat. He shoos me away, checks her pulse, and begins the Heimlich maneuver.

"When your victim is elderly," he says loudly and remonstratively, "it's natural to assume a heart attack. Natural, but, in this case, possibly deadly."

After a few more minutes of Heimlich he takes a pen from his pocket and drives it into her throat. Almost immediately she sits up and readjusts her wig, with the pen still sticking out of her neck. Leon kisses her forehead and makes her lay back down, then gives the thumbs-up.

The crowd bursts into applause.

I sneak off and lay for about an hour on the floor of the Control Hut. I keep hoping it'll blow up or a nuclear war will start so I'll die. But I don't die. So I go over and pick up my wife.

Leon wants to terminate me but Simone has a serious chat with him about our mortgage and he lets me stay on in Towel Distribution and Collection. Actually it's a relief. Nobody can get hurt. The worst that could happen is maybe a yeast infection. It's a relief until I go to his office one day with the Usage Statistics and hear moans from inside and hide behind the soda machine until Simone comes out looking flushed and happy. I want to jump out and confront her but I don't. Then Leon comes out and I want to jump out and confront him but I don't.

What I do is wait behind the soda machine until they leave, then climb out a window and hitchhike home. I get a ride from a guy who sells and services Zambonis. He tells me to confront her forcefully and watch her fall to pieces. If she doesn't fall to pieces I should beat her.

When I get home I confront her forcefully. She doesn't fall to pieces. Not only does she not deny it, she says it's going to continue no matter what. She says I've been absent too long. She says there's more to Leon than meets the eye.

I think of beating her, and my heart breaks, and I give up on everything.

Clive shows up at ten. As he keeps me awake telling me what his senior prom would have been like, Simone calls Leon's name in her sleep and mutters something about his desk calendar leaving a paper cut on her neck. Clive follows me into the kitchen, wanting to know what a nosegay is. Outside, all the corn in the cornfield is bent over and blowing. The moon comes up over Delectable Videos like a fat man withdrawing himself from a lake. I fall asleep at the counter. The phone rings at three. It's Clive's father saying he's finally shaken himself from his stupor and is coming over to kill me.

I tell him I'll leave the door open.

Clive's been in the bathroom imagining himself some zits. Even though technically he's one of the undead I have a lot of affection for him. When he comes out I tell him he'll have to go, and that I'll see him tomorrow. He whines a bit, but finally fades away.

His dad pulls up in a LandCruiser and gets out with a big gun. He comes through the door in an alert posture and sees me sitting on the couch. I can tell he's been drinking.

"I don't hate you," he says, "but I can't have you living on this earth while my son isn't."

"I understand," I say.

Looking sheepish, he steps over and puts the gun to my head. The sound of our home's internal ventilation system is suddenly wondrous. The mole on his eyebrow possesses grace. Children would have been nice.

I close my eyes and wait. Then I urinate myself. Then I wait some more. I wait and wait. Then I open my eyes. He's gone and the front door's wide open.

I think: Jesus, embarrassing, I wet myself and was ready to die.

Then I go for a brisk walk.

I hike into the hills and sit in a cowboy-days graveyard. The stars are blinking like cats' eyes and burned blood is pouring out of the slaughterhouse chimney. My crotch is cold with the pee and the breeze. The moon goes behind a cloud and six pale forms start down from the foothills. At first I think they're ghosts but they're only starving pronghorn come down to lick salt from the headstones. I sit there trying to write Simone off. No more guys ogling her in public and no more dippy theories on world hunger. Then I think of her and Leon watching the test pattern together nude and sweaty and I moan and double over with dread, and a doe bolts away in alarm.

A storm rolls in over the hills and a brochure describing a portrait offer gets plastered across my chest. Lightning strikes the slaughterhouse flagpole and the antelope scatter like minnows as the rain begins to fall, and finally, having lost what was to be lost, my torn and black heart rebels, saying enough already, enough, this is as low as I go.

■ ■ ■ ■ ■ ■ ■ ■ ■ ■ ■ ■

Bodysurfing

Richard Burgin

T here was a rustling, then Lee saw it, fat and gray and big-eyed with an orange crown as it slid across the path. They were going to have the last laugh — the iguanas — that was for sure. There were so many of them Costa Rica was going to be their world some day. The path ended and the boogey board banged against his knee. He swore out loud as he began walking down the road. It was madness, sheer madness to have rented the board. He knew that within two minutes, he knew that when he reached the first wave. There was the wave and his body and nothing ever should come between them, that alone should be pure. Sheer lunacy to think otherwise. He looked at it — baby blue with a dangling wrist strap like an umbilical cord, this boogey board with its silly name — it was idiocy in its purest form to let it ruin his rides, bang about in the wind and hit his knee. Why had he done it, why? It was because he'd remembered his wife saying they were so much fun. Years ago she'd said that, he had a distant memory of it. It was that and the surfboard morons who were taking over the ocean, crowding him out of his space. He'd let them intimidate him, let them infantilize him into thinking he should maybe get some kind of board of his own, so when he left the beach and saw it in the store he'd rented it on an impulse.

It was the same store that was in front of him now. The Palm Store, a combination travel agency and gift shop run by a good-looking man and his wife with a yellow-haired kid who didn't look like either of them, certainly not the man. So he would return it now, eleven minutes after he took it. Of course he wouldn't ask for his money back. He would take responsibility. They would wonder why, perhaps ask him why, but he wouldn't let himself worry about it. He was about to lose his job in two weeks, to be transferred to a lower job in the bank in a different city, to be screwed over like that at his age, and with his mother at death's door too, no, he wasn't going to worry about returning a boogey board to a store that looked like it was made out of cards, with its pathetically corny painting of a sun sinking below the waves, a store that rented surfboards and goggles and boogey boards and tickets for turtle tours!

He went inside The Palm Store. A tall good-looking blond man, a surfboardoron, perhaps two inches taller than he was, perhaps a dozen years younger, perhaps with fourteen better defined muscles than he had, had finished talking to the owner and was fingering a surfboard as Lee placed the boogey board beside it. He is going to ask me how I liked the boogey board, Lee thought, he is going to try to have a conversation with me. The blond man turned toward Lee. He is from California, Lee thought. "How did it ride?" the blond man said.

"How did it ride? *It* didn't ride at all. I didn't have any use for it."

"Surf too strong today?"

"Board too superfluous today, or any day."

"OK. I hear you."

Lee was struck by how straight the surfer's teeth were, which perhaps accounted for the extraordinary hang-time of his smile.

"I don't like anything to come between me and the wave, me and the water. I think that relationship ought to stay pure. Today I violated that relationship, I'm sorry to say. Today I let myself be conquered by a product and I corrupted that relationship."

The blond man's smile vanished and Lee felt vindicated.

"I don't think I get what you mean."

"These boards," Lee said, indicating the blond man's surfboard with his gesture, "they're just another way people've found to make money off the water. They're about buying and selling, that's all."

The blond man showed a second smile, a quizzical but still friendly one. "I guess I don't see it that way," he said.

"Really? How do you see it, then?"

"They're just a piece of equipment for a sport, they're just a means to an end. Like you can't play baseball without a bat or football without a ball, can you?"

Lee felt an adrenaline rush. Apparently the man really wanted to discuss this. "There was a time when you could play sports without buying things," Lee said. "To me, the more a sport costs the less its value. The more it's about buying these accessories, the more of a fetish it becomes instead of a sport. By the way, I hope I didn't desecrate the flag, so to speak, with my remarks about surfboards. I know you guys get sensitive about that."

"No, man, I don't mind. I just never met anyone who thinks like you. It's kind of interesting, really."

Lee felt flattered in spite of himself. Ridiculous to feel that in this situation, though he did for a moment, and thought he should soften himself. Besides he was beginning to get an idea and he needed time to figure it all out. Just before he spoke he made a point of looking at the surfer's eyes.

"And by the way I know whereof I speak," Lee said. "I'm a banker and you can't be much more of a whore than that. My whole life is buying and selling. I'm in middle management at Citibank. Need I say more? Or I soon will be. I was actually at a somewhat higher level of management but that's like bragging about being in a higher circle of hell, isn't it? But at least on my vacation I want to stay pure when I'm in the water. I said to my secretary, 'I don't care what kind of hotel you get me (and she got me Le Jardin del Eden, the most expensive one in Tamarindo), but I insist on big, world-class waves. I want you to research that for me.' Well, the waves here are certainly world class and they deserve the best from me."

Lee looked at the man closely, who in turn appeared to be concentrating intensely on what he said. "So, I'm on my way now. I'm going to have my twilight drink, and again, I hope I haven't offended you at all."

"No way, I enjoyed talking with you. You're the first American I've spoken to in three days. I don't speak Spanish so I've practically been talking to myself since I've been here."

Lee looked at him closely once more, wondering if he were gay or just needy, or perhaps one of those friendly New Age types. He had decided something important, something definitive in the waves yesterday, but this young man might make it even better. Besides he was a surfer and that would make him the cherry on the sundae and his possible gayness would never enter into it.

"I've enjoyed it too," Lee said. "Hey, you know the restaurant, Zullymar?"

"Sure."

"That's where I'm going for my drink. Why don't you join me and have one on the bank?"

The blond man laughed and extending his hand, said, "Sure. My name's Andy."

"I'm Lee Bank or should I say Le Bank, and we all know what shape banks are in."

Lee turned and walked out of the store and Andy followed after him laughing.

"Is Bank really your last name?"

"I'm sometimes known as Lee Bastard or when I'm in Paris as Le Bastard. But we are far from Paris now, aren't we?"

Lee looked straight ahead as they walked down the dirt road and seemed unaware that Andy was walking beside him. It was not much of a road, Lee thought, full of holes and rocks and puddles so they could have, should have left it alone and not put up so many toy-like stores. Laughable really how small they were — the little shack that probably doubled as someone's home — with the giant sign saying Nachos and Ice Cream, a sign that was half as big as the shack. Pathetic really, the hut beside it called Jungle Bus that advertised Killer Burguer and Munchies. If it rose a couple of inches, the puddle on the road in front could swallow it.

Zullymar was on the other side of the road, facing the Jungle Bus on one side and the beach on the other. It was a big (by Tamarindo standards) open-air restaurant and bar filled with surfers, the same crowd that forced him off his path two days in a row in the water and actually made him yearn for a lifeguard to patrol things. A wall mural that clashed with the red floor depicted a pink pelican, circling over some anchored boats and a small island beyond that — the approximate scene outside. Across the street at another bar, a man was playing the marimba with two little boys.

Lee and Andy sat down at a table facing the water and looked briefly at the half-filled room. As soon as they focused on each other Lee said, "You'll want a beer, won't you? Isn't that the drink you guys favor?" He had a tight semi-sarcastic smile and Andy smiled back.

"What do you mean?"

"You surfers, you surf wizards. You don't want to drink anything too hard, anything that might put you at risk when you go out on your boards again."

"I'm done surfing for the day and I drink lots of things. No routine."

"Fine. Dos mai tais," Lee said to the waiter.

The incredulous smile reappeared on Andy's face. Lee was going to say something to try to get rid of it but Andy spoke first.

"You've got some negative feelings toward surfers, don't you?"

Lee shrugged. "What did they do to you, man?" Andy said, half-laughing, his hand absently caressing his board for a moment, Lee noticed, as if he really thought the goddamn thing was alive. "Did they run into you once or something?"

"No, that would never happen, though they have crowded me out more than once here in Tamarindo, kept me from where I wanted to go, but believe me I stick to my own path. I don't mingle. I am not only on a different path from them, I'm in a different world."

"But what's so different about your world?"

"Night and day, Andy. Night and day."

"Why, what do you do? You bodysurf, right? I respect that. So I get up on a board and you bodysurf. Have you ever surfed?"

"I do surf."

"I mean with a board."

"Years ago when I was actually young."

"So what do you have against it?"

The drinks came. Andy took a big swallow while Lee let his sit.

"It's about buying and selling again. Kids see it on TV in ads and think 'that's it.' Then they make movies about it and create a surfing tour and sell all this equipment, all these fetishes and the young guys think 'if I do this I'll be a man, if I do this I'll get some first-class pussy. It will all happen if I can just buy the right board.'"

Andy was laughing now. He was not an easy man to offend, Lee concluded, as he sipped his drink.

"I'm not agreeing with you, by the way," Andy said. "I just think what you're saying is funny and interesting in a way."

"Of course you think that surfboarding is the greater sport, the greater challenge, don't you? After all, you stand up, you are Homo Erectus, whereas I am still on all fours. You go out further to sea whereas I am nearer the shore. You walk on water like Jesus Christ whereas I only ride with it like a fish. And then when gravity must eventually bring you down you take the deeper, more heroic fall. You think all those things, don't you?"

"I just enjoy surfing. I haven't thought it out like that really. And like I say, I respect what you do."

"I wonder if you know what I do. Because there are a number of bodysurfers out there — it isn't just me — and very few of them know when or how to jump, and once they do jump how to go with the wave. They almost always start too late."

"I probably wouldn't know, man," Andy said. "Isn't that the way it is with everything? We don't really understand the other person's thing or point of view."

"Dos mai tais," Lee said, catching the waiter's attention, although he had not yet made significant progress on his first drink.

"So, now tell me your story, Andy. What brings you to glorious Tamarindo?"

Andy looked flustered, ran his fingers twice through his longish blond hair. He could be Kato Kaelin's younger brother, Lee thought.

"I just came here to surf."

"From whence did you come then?"

"Santa Cruz, in California."

Lee smiled tightly again. "This is your vacation then. You came to Tamarindo directly on your vacation?"

"Not exactly. I was in Monteverde first. I went to Costa Rica directly, but I went to Monteverde first, you know, in the mountains."

"Then you are a mountain man, too."

Andy lowered his head a little. Lee couldn't tell if he were burying his smile or giving birth to a new one. In Tamarindo smiles were the iguanas on every surfer's face. Lee distrusted smiles in general because he had discovered that if you believed in them a time would come when that belief would hurt you. He remembered he had once been very moved by his wife's smile.

"So how were the mountains?" he finally said.

"Some bad stuff happened there, so I came here earlier than I expected."

"I'm sorry to learn that. What exactly was the bad stuff?"

The waiter came with the new drinks and Andy took a big swallow as the waiter took his first glass, while Lee carefully placed his second glass next to his first (which was still almost three-quarters full) as if he were positioning two bowling pins.

"The woman I was with went bad on me. She met a dude on the tour we took in the cloud forest. He was older than me, around your age I guess, and he had a lot more money than me, you know, I was never very good at making money. I just help run a little Xerox store. But this rich guy was a businessman, a big businessman, though he was in the same hotel as us, only he was in some luxury suite. Anyway, she told me she was sorry, she said she didn't plan it that way, that it was a one-in-a-million thing, but she thought he was the man for her and she was going to go with him for the rest of her vacation and beyond. So . . . "

"So what could you do?"

"Just got drunk. Woke up alone the next morning and got in my Suzuki and came down here 'cause they said this was where the surf was, and they didn't lie about that. The last couple of days I took it out on the waves, six, seven hours a day and just flushed that bitch right out. It hurt though, I'll tell you. So when you talk about money corrupting things I really hear you."

"And when you talk about women being bitches I hear you. I lost my sense of smell from a woman once."

"How'd that happen?" Andy's incredulous smile had sneaked back, Lee noted, as if it were taking a curtain call.

"I discovered my female friend had cheated on me and I got extremely ill in an odd way. I developed a sinus condition that's never really gone away. I think it was my ex-wife who did me wrong, though it might have been someone else before her. Over the years people tend to blur together, don't they? Anyway I have very little to do with women now. The only woman in my life besides Mother Sea is my secretary and she's far too valuable to bother having sex with. I am completely dependent on her. It was she who arranged this trip for me. Of course I'll lose her when I'm transferred to my next job, but that's the way it is with women, we always lose them. They were put here on earth so we would know what losing is. Even when we have them we lose them — did you ever think about that?"

"What do you mean?"

"We watch them lose their looks, their charm, their ability to have children, their sex. We lose our mothers, too, and then our wives become our mothers and we lose them again. We lose our mothers a second time."

"But men age too," Andy said.

"But we don't notice it as much since we don't desire men, do we? Anyway, you don't have to worry about all this now. It'll be years before you'll have to realize this."

"I realize it, I realize some of it now."

"Then you might consider giving them up as I have. You can get a greater high than the orgasm from bodysurfing, at least you can the way I bodysurf."

Andy looked away morosely. Lee waited a minute. There was a rustling sound in the restaurant as if the waiters were really iguanas. Lee couldn't stand hearing it so he spoke. "Thinking about her?"

"Yah."

"How long were you two an item?"

"Just a couple of months but . . . "

"Impact can be made in a couple of months. Impact can be made in a minute if we allow it to happen. I understand."

"Yah, I thought this one would work out. I had hopes . . . "

"Ah, hopes," Lee said, gesturing vaguely toward the sea. "Listen, I have an idea for you, a proposal to make to you. It does not involve 'hope' but something better. It involves a challenge."

"Go on."

"Something very special happened to me yesterday. Do you know that inlet that separates our beach from the other one, the one that goes straight to the mountains?"

"Yes."

"Have you ever been on that other beach?"

"No. No one surfs over there so I just assumed there wasn't much there."

"That's precisely the point. The beach goes on for miles but because there's no access from the road, because there is a thick jungle of trees to walk through and no other way to reach it unless you swim across the inlet, there is almost no one there. Well, yesterday I swam across that inlet. It was sunset, a little earlier than now and the swim wasn't easy but I found the beach deserted and astonishingly beautiful. There were no footprints on the sand, just the swerving lines of hermit crabs and the twisted branches from trees. I don't think there were even any butterflies, it wasn't civilized enough for them. It was like being on the moon or on a new planet. The waves were enormous and there was no one around to get in my way. My path was totally clear. Why don't you go there with me now and bodysurf with me? Leave your board at your hotel room and just go there with me now. I know you've only known me thirty minutes or whatever it's been. I know it's getting dark and it's a little dangerous."

"It's not that dangerous. I could do that."

"Fine, marvelous. Here, why don't you have my other drink, I haven't touched it, and I'll finish my first one and then we'll go out together and meet the waves with our bodies alone. I promise you it will be extraordinary."

"Yah, OK," Andy said, looking Lee straight in the eye. "I'll go with you. I'm open to it."

They finished their drinks quickly and Lee paid the bill. The moment he put the money in the waiter's hand he saw the sun slip below the water. Some people were watching it in the restaurant and beyond them others watched from the beach. It was an understandable ritual, Lee thought. It had been advertised, like a Citibank card, and people needed to see the promise delivered. In her condominium in Florida, his mother was probably watching it too from her wheelchair, perhaps with one of her nurses. She more than anyone believed in advertised beauty. All her life she believed in Jackie Kennedy and Marilyn Monroe and Marlon Brando and Holiday Inns and sunsets. It would not do any good to tell her the deeper beauty came after the sunset, came with the night when the whole world slid below water. She had never listened to him. They should have switched positions. She should have worked for Citibank and he should have been the cripple. He might have done well in a chair . . .

There were only occasional street lamps outside but he could see the night was thick with moths. They were not talking now, so he could hear another iguana slide past in front of him. Then he decided it wouldn't have mattered if they were talking, he would have heard it anyway. In Tamarindo every sound on earth was an iguana, you could only escape them in the water.

"There's your hotel," Lee said, pointing to the Diria, barely bigger than the travel agency it seemed. "Why don't you drop your board off here. You won't be needing it. It'll only get in the way."

"OK," Andy said softly. He walked off in the dark and Lee waited in the road, thinking he should have told him *go put your dick away there too. That's what your board really is. You won't be needing it where we're going. There aren't any dicks in the ocean, not in the night ocean.*

Andy came back. Lee had never really considered that he wouldn't.

"Let's go," Lee said. There were about fifty yards of road before they reached the path that led to the beach. It will be a bakery of iguanas, Lee thought, but they would be left in their ovens.

The deep orange of the sky had passed. It was now a dark purple and silver, tinged with spots of fading pink. There were not many people on the beach and most of them were leaving. Except for the white of the waves, the ocean was dark.

"It gets dark quickly," Andy said.

"Drops like a plank," Lee said. He is very young, Lee thought, and his fear is showing. Lee thought of himself as a thousand years old. This will be good for him. He needs to put on a hundred years. Then he didn't think about him anymore.

They walked the length of the beach toward the inlet. Andy was talking about the girl who had dumped him, whose name was Dawn.

"Forget the girl," Lee said. "Drown her in the ocean."

When they reached the inlet the sky was nearly black. There were lots of stars out and a quarter of a moon.

"I was hoping it'd be low tide so we could walk across," Andy said.

"We can swim it," Lee said. He threw the towel he'd been carrying into the sky and the black swallowed it.

"What did you just do?"

"I threw my towel away. I won't be needing it. It's a hotel towel."

"Yah, you told me about your hotel. Very impressive. It's supposed to be the best hotel in Tamarindo." There was sarcasm, even a trace of contempt in Andy's voice that stung Lee for a second.

"The hotel can drop dead," Lee said as he walked into the water. He was surprised again by how wide the inlet was but he didn't feel tired this time while he was swimming. He could hear Andy breathing heavily, almost gasping, as he swam beside him and thought for a moment that he shouldn't have let him drink three mai tais.

"Stop racing," he said, nearly yelling. "Stop trying to beat me. It's not a race. You have to pace yourself."

Andy slowed down the rest of the way. When they reached the shore of the deserted beach there were only a few slivers of sky that weren't black.

"I wish it were lighter, man," Andy said.

"Why?"

"I can't see the things you said would be here. I can't see the things you promised."

"Yes you can. Look harder."

"I can barely see in front of myself."

"I can look at anything and see the beauty in it. Especially the dark."

"Tell me what I was supposed to see here again, and walk slower, will you. I can barely keep up with you."

"Twisted tree branches and hermit crab lines," Lee said.

Lee walked briskly, saying nothing for the next few minutes. Andy ran after him, stumbling occasionally, trying to keep up with him or at least keep him in sight, feeling like he did when he was a child trying to keep up with his father's longer, relentless stride.

"Come on, we're going in the water. It's time to face the black water now."

Lee walked toward the ocean in fast imperious strides like a fixated scoutmaster.

"Slow down, will you? Why are you racing?" Andy said and then repeated himself, yelling this time because the ocean was so loud he felt he wasn't being heard.

Lee kept walking into the water without changing speed, the big blustery businessman from the fancy hotel who had to know it all, who had to take what he wanted when he wanted it. Why had he listened to him, why had he come with him to this crazy beach? He was chasing after him in the water now while his legs felt like rubber. The water was up to his knees and he knew something was wrong, had known it for some time.

"Lee," he yelled. "Lee. Lee Bastard."

A few seconds before he'd seen him fifteen yards ahead, propelling himself forward, not even ducking for the waves but somehow willing himself forward like a man walking into a wall, into the earth, until the water covered him. Andy heard himself scream. It might have been "Lee," it might have been "help." His legs wouldn't move at first and when they could he knew he wouldn't move them because he'd already known Lee wanted to be witnessed while he disappeared by a sucker like himself, just as Dawn did, and one of those humiliations was enough. Lee Legend gets back at a surfer. "Lee," he screamed, "Lee Bastard," knowing he would see and hear nothing now except the constant roar in the black and his own sickly voice boomeranging back at him like spit in the wind because the bastard had wanted it this way.

■ ■ ■ ■ ■ ■ ■ ■ ■ ■ ■

The Girl with the Blackened Eye

Joyce Carol Oates

This black eye I had, once! Like a clown's eye painted on. Both my eyes were bruised and ugly but the right eye was swollen almost shut, people must've seen me and I wonder what they were thinking. I mean you have to wonder. Nobody said a word — didn't want to get involved, I guess. You have to wonder what went through their minds though.

Sometimes I see myself in a mirror, like in the middle of the night getting up to use the bathroom, I see a blurred face, a woman's face I don't recognize. And I see that eye.

Twenty-seven years.

In America, that's a lifetime.

This weird thing that happened to me, fifteen years old and a sophomore at Menlo Park High, living with my family in Menlo Park, California where Dad was a dental surgeon (which was lucky; I'd need dental and gum surgery, to repair the damage to my mouth). Weird, and wild. Ugly. I've never told anyone who knows me now. Especially my daughters. My husband doesn't know, he couldn't have handled it. We were in our late twenties when we met, no need to drag up the past. I never do. I'm not one of those. I left California forever when I went to college in Vermont. My family moved, too. They live in Seattle now. There's a stiffness between us, we never talk about that time. Never say that man's name. So it's like it never did happen.

Or, if it did, it happened to someone else. A high school girl in the 1970s. A silly little girl who wore tank tops and jeans so tight she had to lie down on her bed to wriggle into them, and teased her hair into mane. That girl.

When they found me, my hair was wild and tangled like broom sage. It couldn't be combed through, had to be cut from my head in clumps. Something sticky like cobwebs was in it. I'd been wearing it long since ninth grade and after that I kept it cut short for years. Like a guy's hair, the back of my neck shaved and my ears showing.

I'd been forcibly abducted at the age of fifteen. It was something that could happen to you, from the outside, *forcibly abducted*, like being in a plane crash, or struck by lightning. There wouldn't be any human agent, almost. The human agent wouldn't have a name. I'd been walking through the mall parking lot to the bus stop, about 5:30 p.m., a weekday, I'd come to the mall after school with some kids, now I was headed home, and somehow it happened, don't ask me how, a guy was asking me questions, or saying something, mainly I registered he was an adult my dad's age possibly, every adult man looked like my dad's age except obviously white-haired old men. I hadn't any clear impression of this guy except afterward I would recall rings on his fingers which would've caused me to glance up at his face with interest except at that instant something slammed into the back of my head behind my ear, knocking me forward, and down, like he'd thrown a hook at me from in front, I was on my face on the sun-heated vinyl upholstery of a car, or a van, and another blow or blows knocked me out. Like anesthesia, it was. You're out.

This was the *forcible abduction*. How it might be described by a witness who was there, who was also the victim. But who hadn't any memory of what happened because it happened so fast, and she hadn't been personally involved.

It's like they say. You are there, and not-there. He drove to this place in the Sonoma Mountains, I would afterward learn, this cabin it would be called, and he raped me, beat me, and shocked me with electrical cords and he stubbed cigarette butts on my stomach and breasts, and he said things to me like he knew me, he knew all my secrets, what a dirty-minded girl I was, what a nasty girl, and selfish, like everyone of my *privileged class* as he called it. I'm saying these things were done to me but in fact they were done to my body mostly. Like the cabin was in the Sonoma Mountains north of Healdsburg but it was just anywhere for those eight days, and I was anywhere, I was holding onto being alive the way you would hold onto a straw you could breathe through, lying at the bottom of deep water. And that water opaque, you can't see through to the surface.

He was gone, and he came back. He left me tied in the bed, it was a cot with a thin mattress, very dirty. There were only two windows in the cabin and there were blinds over them drawn tight. It was hot during what I guessed was the day. It was cool, and it was very quiet at night. The lower parts of me were raw and throbbing with pain and other parts of me were in a haze of pain so I wasn't able to think, and I wasn't awake most of the time, not what you'd call actual wakefulness, with a personality.

What you call your personality, you know? — it's not the actual bones, or teeth, something solid. It's more like a flame. A flame can be upright, and a flame can flicker in the wind, a flame can be extinguished so there's no sign of it, like it had never been.

My eyes had been hurt, he'd mashed his fists into my eyes. The eyelids were puffy, I couldn't see very well. It was like I didn't try to see, I was saving my eyesight for when I was stronger. I had not seen the man's face actually. I had felt him but I had not seen him, I could not have identified him. Anymore than you could identify yourself if you had never seen yourself in a mirror or in any likeness.

In one of my dreams I was saying to my family I would not be seeing them for a while, I was going away. *I'm going away, I want to say good-bye.* Their faces were blurred. My sister, I was closer to than my parents, she's two years older than me and I adored her, my sister was crying, her face was blurred with tears. She asked where was I going and I said I didn't know, but I wanted to say good-bye, and I wanted to say *I love you.* And this was so vivid it would seem to me to have happened actually, and was more real than other things that happened to me during that time I would learn afterward was eight days.

It might've been the same day repeated, or it might've been eighty days. It was a place, not a day. Like a dimension you could slip into, or be sucked into, by an undertow. And it's there, but no one is aware of it. Until you're in it, you don't know; but when you're in it, it's all that you know. So you have no way of speaking of it except like this. Stammering, and ignorant.

W hy he brought the water and food, why he decided to let me live, would never be clear. The others he'd killed after a few days. They went stale on him, you have to suppose. One of the bodies was buried in the woods a few hundred yards behind the cabin, others were dumped along Route 101 as far north as Crescent City. And possibly there were others never known, never located or identified. These facts, if they are facts, I would learn later, as I would learn that the other girls and women had been older than me, the oldest was thirty, and the youngest he'd been on record as killing was eighteen. So it was speculated he had mercy on me because he hadn't realized, abducting me in the parking lot, that I was so young, and in my battered condition in the cabin, when I'd started losing weight, I must've looked to him like a child. I was crying a lot, and calling *Mommy! Mom-my!*

Like my own kids, grown, would call *Mom-my!* in some nightmare they were trapped in. But I never think of such things.

The man with the rings on his fingers, saying, There's some reason I don't know yet, that you have been spared.

Later I would look back and think, there was a turn, a shifting of fortune, when he first allowed me to wash. To wash! He could see I was ashamed, I was a naturally shy, clean girl. He allowed this. He might have assisted me, a little. He picked ticks out of my skin where they were invisible and gorged with blood. He hated ticks! They disgusted him. He went away, and came back with food and Hires Diet Root Beer. We ate together sitting on the edge of the cot. And once when he allowed me out into the clearing at dusk. Like a picnic. His greasy fingers, and mine. Fried chicken, french fries and runny cole slaw, my hands started shaking and my mouth was on fire. And my stomach convulsing with hunger, cramps that doubled me over like he'd sunk a knife into my guts and twisted. Still, I was able to eat some things, in little bites. I did not starve. Seeing the color come back into my face, he was impressed, stirred. He said, in mild reproach, Hey, a butterfly could eat more'n you.

I would remember those pale yellow butterflies around the cabin. A swarm of them. And jays screaming, waiting to swoop down to snatch up food.

I guess I was pretty sick. Delirious. My gums were infected. Four of my teeth were broken. Blood kept leaking to the back of my mouth, making me sick, gagging. But I could walk to the car leaning against him, I was able to sit up normally in the passenger's seat, buckled in, he always made sure to buckle me in, and a wire wound tight around my ankles. Driving then out of the forest, and the foothills I could not have identified as the Sonoma hills, and the sun high and gauzy in the sky, and I lost track of time, lapsing in and out of time but noticing that highway traffic was changing to suburban, more traffic lights, we were cruising through parking lots so vast you couldn't see the edge of them, sun-blinded spaces and rows of glittering cars like grave markers: I saw them suddenly in a cemetery that went on forever.

He wanted me with him all the time now, he said. Keep an eye on you, girl. Maybe I was his trophy? The only female trophy in his abducting/ raping/killing spree of an estimated seventeen months to be publicly displayed. Not beaten, strangled, raped to death, kicked to death and buried like animal carrion. (This I would learn later.) Or maybe I was meant to signal to the world, if the world glanced through the windshield of his car, his daughter. A sign of—what? *Hey, I'm normal. I'm a nice guy, see.*

Except the daughter's hair was wild and matted, her eyes were bruised and one of them swollen almost shut. Her mouth was a slack puffy wound. Bruises on her face and throat and arms and her ribs were cracked, skinny body was covered in pus-leaking burns and sores. Yet he'd allowed me to wash, and he'd allowed me to wash out my clothes, I was less filthy now. He'd given me a T-shirt too big for me, already soiled but I was grateful for it. Through acres of parking lots we cruised like sharks seeking prey. I was aware of people glancing into the car, just by accident, seeing me, or maybe not seeing me, there were reflections in the windshield (weren't there?) because of the sun, so maybe they didn't see me, or didn't see me clearly. Yet others, seeing me, looked away. It did not occur to me at the time that there must be a search for me, my face in the papers, on TV. My face as it had been. At the time I'd stopped thinking of that other world. Mostly I'd stopped thinking. It was like anesthesia, you give in to it, there's peace in it, almost. As cruising the parking lots with the man whistling to himself, humming, talking in a low affable monotone, I understood that he wasn't thinking either, as a predator fish would not be thinking cruising beneath the surface of the ocean. The silent gliding of sharks, that never cease their motion. I was concerned mostly with sitting right: my head balanced on my neck, which isn't easy to do, and the wire wound tight around my ankles cutting off circulation. I knew of gangrene, I knew of toes and entire feet going black with rot. From my father I knew of tooth-rot, gum-rot. I was trying not to think of those strangers who must've seen me, sure they saw me, and turned away, uncertain what they'd seen but knowing it was trouble, and not wanting to know more.

Just a girl with a blackened eye, you figure maybe she deserved it.

He said: There must be some reason you are spared.

He said, in my daddy's voice from a long time ago, Know what, girl? — you're not like the others. That's why.

They would say he was insane, these were the acts of an insane person. And I would not disagree. Though I knew it was not so.

The red-haired woman in the khaki jacket and matching pants. Eventually she would have a name but it was not a name I would wish to know, none of them were. This was a woman, not a girl. He'd put me in the back seat of his car now, so the passenger's seat was empty. He'd buckled me safely in. OK, girl? You be good, now. We cruised the giant parking lot at dusk. When the lights first come on. (Where was this? Ukiah. Where I'd never been. Except for the red-haired woman I would have no memory of Ukiah.)

He'd removed his rings. He was wearing a white baseball cap.

There came this red-haired woman beside him smiling, talking like they were friends. I stared, I was astonished. They were coming toward the car. Never could I imagine what those two were talking about! I thought *He will trade me for her* and I was frightened. The man in the baseball cap wearing shiny dark glasses asking the red-haired woman — what? Directions? Yet he had the power to make her smile, there was a sexual ease between them. She was a mature woman with a shapely body, breasts I could envy and hips in the tight-fitting khaki pants that were stylish pants, with a drawstring waist. I felt a rush of anger for this woman, contempt, disgust, how stupid she was, unsuspecting, bending to peer at me where possibly she'd been told the man's daughter was sitting, maybe he'd said his daughter had a question for her? needed an adult female's advice? and in an instant she would find herself shoved forward onto the front seat of the car, down on her face, her chest, helpless, as fast as you might snap your fingers, too fast for her to cry out. So fast, you understand it had happened many times before. The girl in the back seat blinking and staring and unable to speak though she wasn't gagged, no more able to scream for help than the woman struggling for her life a few inches away. She shuddered in sympathy, she moaned as the man pounded the woman with his fists. Furious, grunting! His eyes bulged. Were there no witnesses? No one to see? Deftly he wrapped a blanket around the woman, who'd gone limp, wrapping it tight around her head and chest, he shoved her legs inside the car and shut the door and climbed into the driver's seat and drove away humming, happy. In the back seat the girl was crying. If she'd had tears she would have cried.

Weird how your mind works: I was thinking I was that woman, in the front seat wrapped in the blanket, so the rest of it had not yet happened.

It was that time, I think, I saw my mom. In the parking lot. There were shoppers, mostly women. And my mom was one of them. I knew it couldn't be her, so far from home, I knew I was hundreds of miles from home, so it couldn't be, but I saw her. Mom crossing in front of the car, walking briskly to the entrance of Lord & Taylor.

Yet I couldn't wave to her, my arm was heavy as lead.

Yes. In the cabin I was made to witness what he did to the red-haired woman. I saw now that this was my importance to him: I would be a witness to his fury, his indignation, his disgust. Tying the woman's wrists to the iron rails of the bed, spreading her legs and tying her ankles. Naked, the red-haired woman had no power. There was no sexual ease to her now, no confidence. You would not envy her now. You would scorn her now. You would not wish to be her now. She'd become a chicken on a spit.

I had to watch, I could not close my eyes or look away.

For it had happened already, it was completed. There was certitude in this, and peace in certitude. When there is no escape, for what is happening has already happened. Not once but many times.

When you give up struggle, there's a kind of love.

The red-haired woman did not know this, in her terror. But I was the witness, I knew.

They would ask me about him. I saw only parts of him. Like jigsaw puzzle parts. Like quick camera jumps and cuts. His back was pale and flaccid at the waist, more muscular at the shoulders. It was a broad pimply sweating back. It was a part of a man, like my dad, I would not see. Not in this way. Not straining, tensing. And the smell of a man's hair, like congealed oil. His hair was stiff, dark, threaded with silver hairs like wires, at the crown of his head you could see the scalp beneath. On his torso and legs hairs grew in dense waves and rivulets like water or grasses. He was grunting, he was making a high-pitched moaning sound. When he turned, I saw a fierce blurred face, I didn't recognize that face. And the nipples of the man's breasts, wine-colored like berries. Between his thighs the angry thing swung like a length of rubber, slick and darkened with blood.

I would recall, yes, he had tattoos. Smudged-looking like ink blots. Never did I see them clearly. Never did I see him clearly. I would not have dared as you would not look into the sun in terror of being blinded.

He kept us there together for three days. I mean the red-haired woman was there for three days, unconscious most of the time. There was a mercy in this. You learn to take note of small mercies and be grateful for them. Nor would he kill her in the cabin. When he was finished with her, disgusted with her, he half-carried her out to the car. I was alone, and frightened. But then he returned and said, OK, girl, goin' for a ride. I was able to walk, just barely. I was very dizzy. I would ride in the back seat of the car like a big rag doll, boneless and unresisting.

He'd shoved the woman down beside him, hidden by a blanket wrapped around her head and upper body. She was not struggling now, her body was limp and unresisting for she too had weakened in the cabin, she'd lost weight. You learned to be weak to please him for you did not want to displease him in even the smallest things. Yet the woman managed to speak, this small choked begging voice. Don't kill me, please. I won't tell anybody. I won't tell anybody don't kill me. I have a little daughter, please don't kill me. Please, God. Please.

I wasn't sure if this voice was (somehow) a made-up voice. A voice of my imagination. Or like on TV. Or my own voice, if I'd been older and had a daughter. *Please don't kill me. Please, God.*

For always it's this voice when you're alone and silent you hear it.

A fterward they would speculate that he'd panicked. Seeing TV spot announcements, the photographs of his "victims." When last seen and where, Menlo Park, Ukiah. There were witnesses' descriptions of *the abductor* and a police sketch of his face, coarser and uglier and older than his face which was now disguised by dark glasses. In the drawing he was clean-shaven but now his jaws were covered in several days' beard, a stubbly beard, his hair was tied in a ponytail and the baseball cap pulled low on his head. Yet you could recognize him in the drawing, that looked as if it had been executed by a blind man. So he'd panicked.

The first car he'd been driving he left at the cabin, he was driving another, a stolen car with switched license plates. You came to see that his life was such maneuvers. He was tireless in invention as a willful child and would seem to have had no purpose beyond such maneuvers and when afterward I would learn details of his background, his family life in San Jose, his early incarcerations as a juvenile, as a youth, as an adult "offender" now on parole from Bakersfield maximum security prison, I would block off such information as not related to me, not related to the man who'd existed exclusively for me as, for a brief while, I'd existed exclusively for him. I was contemptuous of "facts" for I came to know that no accumulation of facts constitutes knowledge, and no impersonal knowledge constitutes the intimacy of knowing.

Know what, girl? You're not like the others. You're special. That's the reason.

D riving fast, farther into the foothills. The road was ever narrower and bumpier. There were few vehicles on the road, all of them minivans or campers. He never spoke to the red-haired woman moaning and whimpering beside him but to me in the back seat, looking at me in the rearview mirror, the way my dad used to do when I rode in the back seat, and Mom was up front with him. He said, How ya doin', girl?

OK.

Doin' OK, huh?

Yes.

I'm gonna let you go, girl, you know that, huh? Gonna give you your freedom.

To this I could not reply. My swollen lips moved in a kind of smile as you smile out of politeness.

Less you want to trade? With her?

Again I could not reply. I wasn't certain what the question was. My smile ached in my face but it was a sincere smile.

He parked the car on an unpaved lane off the road. He waited, no vehicles approaching. There were no aircraft overhead. It was very quiet except for birds. He said, C'mon, help me, girl. So I moved my legs that were stiff, my legs that felt strange and skinny to me, I climbed out of the car and fought off dizziness helping him with the bound woman, he'd pulled the blanket off her, her discolored swollen face, her face that wasn't attractive now, scabby mouth and panicked eyes, brown eyes they were, I would remember those eyes pleading. For they were my own, but in one who was doomed as I was not. He said then, so strangely: Stay here, girl. Watch the car. Somebody shows up, honk the horn. Two-three times. Got it?

I whispered yes. I was staring at the crumbly earth.

I could not look at the woman now. I would not watch them move away into the woods.

Maybe it was a test, he'd left the key in the ignition. It was to make me think I could drive the car away from there, I could drive to get help, or I could run out onto the road and get help. Maybe I could get help. He had a gun, and he had knives, but I could have driven away. But the sun was beating on my head, I couldn't move. My legs were heavy like lead. My eye was swollen shut and throbbing. I believed it was a test but I wasn't certain. Afterward they would ask if I'd had any chance to escape in those days he kept me captive and always I said no, no I did not have a chance to escape. Because that was so. That was how it was to me, that I could not explain.

Yet I remember the keys in the ignition, and I remember that the road was close by. He would strangle the woman, that was his way of killing and this I seemed to know. It would require some minutes. It was not an easy way of killing. I could run, I could run along the road and hope that someone would come along, or I could hide, and he wouldn't find me in all that wilderness, if he called me I would not answer. But I stood there beside the car because I could not do these things. He trusted me, and I could not betray that trust. Even if he would kill me, I could not betray him.

Yes, I heard her screams in the woods. I think I heard. It might have been jays. It might have been my own screams I heard. But I heard them.

A few days later he would be dead. He would be shot down by police in a motel parking lot in Petaluma. Why he was there, in that place, about fifty miles from the cabin, I don't know. He'd left me in the cabin chained to the bed. It was filthy, flies and ants. The chain was long enough for me to use the toilet. But the toilet was backed up. Blinds were drawn on the windows. I did not dare to take them down or break the window panes but I looked out, I saw just the clearing, a haze of green. Overhead there were small planes sometimes. A helicopter. I wanted to think that somebody would rescue me but I knew better, I knew nobody would find me.

But they did find me.

He told them where the cabin was, when he was dying. He did that for me. He drew a rough map and I have that map! — not the actual piece of paper but a copy. He would never see me again, and I would have trouble recalling his face for I never truly saw it.

Photographs of him were not accurate. Even his name, printed out, is misleading. For it could be anyone's name and not *his*.

In my present life I never speak of these things. I have never told anyone. There would be no point in it. Why I've told you, I don't know: you might write about me but you would respect my privacy.

Because if you wrote about me, these things that happened to me so long ago, no one would know it was me. And you would disguise it so that no one could guess, that's why I trust you.

My life afterward is what's unreal. The life then, those eight days, was very real. The two don't seem connected, do they? I learned you don't discover the evidence of any cause in its result. Philosophers debate over that but if you know, you know. There is no connection though people wish to think so. When I was recovered I went back to Menlo Park High and I graduated with my class and I went to college and married him and had my babies and none of my life would be different in any way,

I believe, if I had not been "abducted" when I was fifteen.

Sure, I see him sometimes. More often lately. On the street, in a passing car. In profile, I see him. In his shiny dark glasses and white baseball cap. A man's forearm, a thick pelt of hair on it, a tattoo, I see him. The shock of it is, he's only thirty-two.

That's so young now. Your life all before you, almost.

Downstream

Janet Kauffman

I've had it with cow towns," Tatia said. "This place is the past tense."

So it was.

We were out at the stream on my farm last summer, in fine ripply shade. Tatia straddled an oak tree fallen over the water, and she looked off through the woods, right through the pawpaw leaves fanned out near her face.

"I'm going that-a-way," she said. She was pointing east.

The water of the stream flowed clear, right down to the mottled rocks, blue and brown, and the fine gravel fingers of the streambed. The stream was spring-fed, with no cows, no cow shit, upstream. I was lucky to have good water. In the swirls and eddies, we'd often found freshwater clams, and under the rocks, mayfly larvae and stoneflies with forked tails.

"If you move downstream, it's won't be like this. It gets ugly," I said. "Foul. Things don't get better."

Tatia didn't care about water quality. She was on her way out. She'd moved here a couple of years ago, into the rented house across the road. She read books and she edited manuals for technology companies. She had it backwards, I told her. She could move downstream six times and never get closer to anything.

But that didn't make a dent. With her shiny black hair, those fine long toes, you'd think she'd have wanted some softer ground, an upstream pasture, or forest.

But Tatia thought the sea was kin to her, and she'd somehow been stranded up here where water was just getting started. She never said ocean. She said sea. Kin. The sea was kin to her.

Some people don't talk enough to their neighbors. Their language suffers, they are so literate. Tatia couldn't think what to call ordinary sounds, like the smack of a hand on a thigh. She wouldn't make up words, she thought it wasn't right. That's the smarts that got her as far as Toledo, the last I heard. She has a thousand more miles to the sea, downstream — though it looks on the map like up — to Niagara Falls, and Montreal, and the mouth of the St. Lawrence opening wide into the Atlantic.

M arvin says that's how it goes, reverse migration, now that we've got to the end of the line. He's stopped along the road where I'm sampling water from the ditch. He wants to talk about Tatia.

"I'm sorry to see her go," he says. "She was sweet." He means unlike me, and he says it. "Unlike you," he says, and pats my arm. "The only clean place to go is outer space, but who can afford it? Not even me," he says.

For a dairyman, Marv has the perfect name, Rindhoof, and he's worked it into the logo on his cap — Rind ribboned around planet Earth, hoof trailing into space. Tatia liked to drive to Ohio with him, to the bar in Archbold, the nights he could get away from the house.

Oh, cow town it is. Marv in his white truck is duke of the fiefdom. He isn't as tall as his brothers the accountants. He looks a lot like the ag engineer Eddie Tea from Michigan State, with a small round face and blond hair in a crease across his forehead, as eyebrow. When they go around checking manure draglines or drainage pipes, they look like twins, walking in step, with the forehead half frown, half goof-ball smile.

Tatia hated the boomtown spurt the big dairies brought, with the miles of steel confinement buildings along the dirt roads. She liked all the men, though, and got them to talk, no matter how pissed they were when they sat down at the bar. They told her about their wives, about problems with plumbing and liquid manure, about trouble with those goddamned water-testers, and Tatia would come back, sit on the fallen-down tree, and tell me.

She had no principles. She liked men with problems, and of course there are plenty of them, upstream and down. I'm sure she's found more, wherever she is.

Tatia and I disagreed about a few things, but not much. I thought certain men should not be allowed to touch taxpayer money, for instance.

"Just men?" Tatia said. "Which ones?"

"Well," I said. "Dairymen. Maybe the Road Commissioner, with that dull skin . . . "

"I know him!" she said. "He told the road crew to chop the flowers in Bobbie's front yard. You know her? The name Bobbie got to him. It's one of those things, he said, who knows if it's a man or a woman. If it's Bobbie, chop the goddamned flowers, pal. Chop the goddamned shrubbery. Say it's for safety. You can't be a Road Commissioner and not worry about safety."

"You've had some conversations," I said.

"You said it," she said.

But we did disagree about travel, and now that she's gone, I don't think she'll write. It's been months since somebody saw her in Toledo, and I haven't heard anything. She had the idea that I was too settled. Stuck, in fact. In mire, she said. She laughed at the black rubber pig boots I wore, and she'd kick out her legs once in a while, to show off the slipperette sorts of shoes she always wore, even walking in the woods, in mud. Tatia said she was a dancer for a few years, and I believe it. She had the posture, and could cross the stream without getting her shoes wet, with one long leap, her legs in a split.

Marvin talks to me because he wants to talk about Tatia. He hasn't heard from her either. We sit on the running board of his truck, while I take off my rubber gloves and fill out the sampling log.

He says, "She has no animosity." His voice is formal, careful. He's from the Netherlands, drawn across the sea to the big dairy cash-flow.

"She didn't care about the water," I said.

"Just because she didn't drive around all the time, causing trouble?"

"She didn't care about this water. She wanted to see the ocean."

"Well, people like her should get what they want," he says. "I'm glad she got the chance. I would go to see the ocean, too, if I could," he says. He stands up and steps out into the sunlight.

"So go. You've traveled." I take the sample bottle to the car and put it in a cooler in the trunk. "Do you miss the sea?"

Marv turns my way and he looks over into the ditch, at the brown water. "You can wait for goddamned forever," he says, "and this water won't turn blue. If you want to see blue water, go to the ocean."

"I'm not going anywhere, you know that. I asked about you."

"I've thought about it," Marv says. "If the government would buy me out, I'd get out for sure. I get nothing but grief from you people."

I take out the dissolved oxygen meter with the twelve-foot cable. "You want to test your water?"

Marv takes the meter, and I drop the cable into the stream.

"Watch the numbers drop," I say, because I know they will. "If it gets below 5, it's no good for fish."

He stands there very quiet holding the meter, and he holds it gently because it's digital and he knows about delicate technologies.

"What is it?" I ask.

"3.3," he says.

He respects the machinery, and he shakes his head. "I do everything right," he says. "I'm doing exactly what I'm supposed to do. Some of this stuff drains through the soils. This could come from septic, you know."

"Then that's yours, too. There's nothing between us and your place."

"Tatia had the idea she was a saint," Marv says, out of the blue.

I just sit down where I am, on the slope of the ditch. Marv hands me the meter and sits down, too. The ditch is a pretty place when you sit in it, with lobelia blooming, and clumps of sedges near the water.

"She told me one time she was pure in heart and had never done anything wrong," Marv says.

"I never heard that," I say. "I heard plenty of other things."

"I know, I know, she slept around a little. But she kept above the fray, you know what I mean?"

"No, I don't have a clue what you mean, Marv."

"Well, she wasn't attached to things, she didn't give anybody a hard time or make them feel guilty, did she?"

"She laughed at my boots," I say.

"But it didn't make you feel bad, that's what I mean. Not like the tack you take."

"I do not take a tack. I sample the water, I tell people about it. Don't you want clean water?"

"I'm talking about Tatia here. She tread lightly, you know what I mean?"

Now there I do know what he means. Tatia would have used those words, too, tread lightly. She who treads lightly is kin to the sea.

"She took me to Harrison Lake one time," Marv says. "At night. We left the bar, and she drove the truck. She told me I ought to get outside more."

Marv leans back. He's halfway down the slope, and his head rests against the weeds. "It's true, I don't get outside much. I manage more than farm."

"You could downsize," I say. "Go back to real farming."

He ignores me. "The park was closed but we drove in anyway. She pulled off the road, and we walked up this grassy berm, like a dam maybe. She pushed me down on the grass, flat on my back, and came at me with her mouth open and gave me this big mouth kiss."

Marv shuts his eyes as he tells this, going back into the dark. "A big wide kiss," he says, "like the sky came down and just laid itself on my face."

"The kiss of a saint?" I say.

"Yes, it was," Marv insists. "I am only telling you because she is gone, and because she was better to me than anybody. She didn't ask for anything. She didn't want anything."

"Then why did she leave?"

"That's just the point. She wasn't attached to anybody. She could go where she pleased. She was here, now she's someplace else. It doesn't matter to her."

We watch the water for a while. Some dead snails float by. He's right, Tatia is probably kissing some guy in Cleveland, or walking along Lake Erie, her feet hardly making prints in the sand.

Marv shakes his head. "These days, it's like waking up," he says, "in a less favorable climate."

Although he is basking today in this climate, his face catching the full brunt of the sun, and a bird even, nearby, singing like crazy.

Tatia had a routine in the mornings. She woke at sunrise and took a cup of coffee outside, even in winter. She sat in a deck chair facing east. I saw her sit there in the rain, in the wind, it didn't matter. On her refrigerator, she'd taped a sheet of paper listing the hour and minute of all the year's sunrises.

"It's what I do," she said, "to get started. Work is easy after that."

Through the day, she didn't open the door. Maybe she worked steadily at the computer, maybe she watched the soaps, I have no idea. But evenings, she'd take off. And weekends. That's mostly when I saw her, on Sundays. She'd walk across the road after lunch, and we'd head back the lane to the woods. She said her next job would be some kind of manual labor. She was sick of working inside. She talked about Marvin, or one of the other guys, not in a gossipy way, just the facts. "Marv says the pit's full. They'll be spraying manure downstream of you this week. Anders wore that white cowboy hat again, he doesn't get it. He thinks it's an American thing to do. He had a spill from the Terragator down on Packard. Did you know about that?"

Tatia heard everything that was going on. By Monday, I had a pretty good idea where to test the water.

She had such a clear mind," Marv says. "No clutter."

"If nothing matters to you, I guess there's no clutter. Is that a clear mind, or empty-headedness?"

"Now that's not fair," Marvin says.

I don't like the sound of it either. I just hate to agree with him. "No, I know, she's smart," I say, as apology to Tatia. "She always says what's on her mind."

Nearby, the bird is still singing, a song sparrow, what a racket. There's a breeze whipping the tall grasses above us. Purple loosestrife is taking over where it shouldn't be. The water smells. A sheen of something floats on the surface, with brilliant paisleyed colors, iridescent. Yellow bur-marigold is blooming, big bouquets, at the water's edge.

I take the DO meter back to the car. Marv doesn't budge. Sprawled on the slope of the ditch with his eyes shut, he looks like somebody knocked him there, knocked him out.

"Rindhoof!" I call down. "I'm headed to the stream on the other side. Want to see what's what?"

He doesn't move.

"Marv, are you OK?" I slide back down the slope to check.

He lifts his head because I guess he has to sometime, and he sits up. His feet are almost in the water.

"We're the grunts," he says. "That's all there is to it."

And now he's done it — stuck me and him together forever in the same ditch. While Tatia in her sainthood rises far beyond us, leaps skyward someplace, into the blue.

"There's nothing we can do," he says, "to bring her back."

The Torturer's Apprentice

John Biguenet

T here once was a boy of good heart but meager prospects whose father apprenticed him to a torturer. It was, unfortunately, a period of decline for the guild. The Inquisition was winding down, and the great witch trials were still a century away. It is true that, here and there, in Toledo, Cologne, Toulouse, Genoa, elderly masters of the trade still practiced their skills on those unlucky enough to run afoul of the authorities. But upon their deaths, the duchies and baronies and city-states and kingdoms declined, one after another, to fill their vacant posts. So traveling on business or pilgrimage through the countryside, one more and more frequently encountered itinerant torturers bringing their expertise to the smaller jurisdictions of mountain villages and rural parishes. It was to such a journeyman that young Alain Macheret was apprenticed.

With twenty years of experience behind him in southern France and northern Spain, Guillem Vouze was well schooled in the art of persuasion. (He remembered with pride a Dominican in Barcelona who had once complimented him on his "eloquence in the rhetoric of the body.") His only weakness was his devotion to his craft. Unslakable in his thirst for knowledge of human physiology and tireless in his enthusiasm for the latest inventions of discomfort, he had indebted himself as his collection of tools grew. His expertise, in fact, was explained in whispers by the malicious and vengeful relatives of his confessed criminals and heretics as the fruit of secret experiments performed upon corpses by the torturer. He worried less, though, about such serious allegations and about the cost of his investments in more and more sophisticated machinery than he did about the simple problem of hauling all his equipment over the rutted springtime roads and the frozen mountain passes of winter.

So when, on his regular circuit through the farming hamlets of Provence, he was approached by Alain's father seeking a craft for the boy, he quickly came to terms with the old man. Such a muscular youth could shoulder a great burden. Perhaps, it also occurred to the torturer, the boy might be trained to operate the basic functions of the machinery, freeing the master to concentrate on more intricate applications of pain.

But though Guillem would not admit it to himself, the idea of a traveling companion to share the rainy distances between villages and to commiserate on the paltry accommodations of the parish houses may have influenced his decision to accept the apprentice. The demands of the road and the fearsome reputation of torturers had intervened on the few occasions when romance might have bloomed in Guillem's life; distracted by his career, he had not recognized the dull ache of loneliness that throbbed in his heart. But offered a kind of son in young Alain, he did not hesitate to embrace the opportunity to escape his solitude.

The apprentice's education was thorough. Many of the techniques Guillem patiently explained on their long journeys have been lost to us; the secrets of the guild were inviolate, and manuals would have been of little use to the illiterate practitioners of the craft. So one can only guess at the body of knowledge bestowed upon the young man by the torturer. Surely there were stories of the fabled masters, anecdotes of odd experiences, tales of inadvertent discoveries of techniques. But the bedrock of his education must have been a comprehensive study of anatomy, a thorough training in the mechanics of a torturer's tools, and a demanding drill of procedures and applicable laws of Church and State. Considering the debt under which his master labored, Alain must have had at his disposal a full panoply of contemporary instruments of torture. He certainly would have had the opportunity to tighten with his own hands the screw of a garrote, to test the pulleys of a strappado, to unbuckle the iron girdle of a twisting stork, to set a tongue lock between jaw and collarbone, perhaps even to clean the bloody spikes of an Inquisitor's chair.

Alain's education continued for some years under the increasingly fond supervision of his master. Though each spring their circuit would return the two torturers to Alain's remote village and the joyful embrace of his large family, the boy came more and more to think of Guillem with the respect he had once accorded his father.

Certainly a bond had been forged between apprentice and teacher in the smoky dungeons that served as the boy's classrooms. Alain had grown up to the pitiful squeals of slaughtered sheep and the rough butchery of hogs in the yard; he had watched the women render goats' heads and pigs' feet to jelly in the village's great pot and had licked from his mother's fingers the thick blood she had boiled for sausage. But the cry he elicited from the first heretic on whom he was allowed to tighten a leg-brace echoed in him for days afterwards. Annoyed at first by the boy's squeamishness, Guillem came to appreciate his apprentice's gentleness. He had often sensed that cruelty was the enemy of the torturer. In fact, cruelty seemed to him a kind of arrogance that a professional would disdain; it was an intoxicant of amateurs. Though he knew the boy would harden soon enough to the pathetic entreaties of the accused, he hoped the young man would never entirely cease to wince at the screams produced through his handiwork.

Guillem also admired the quiet religious faith that sustained his apprentice. Tested again and again through the cynical application of torture by avaricious clerics greedy for the land of the condemned, his own faith had shriveled. He, of course, still observed the Sabbath and the holy days, tithed what the clergy demanded, and honored the Virgin. But these were the empty practices of a faithless man. Though belief eluded him, Guillem was nonetheless moved by Alain's gentle charity. Who knows? Perhaps he secretly hoped that he might follow the boy back to God. None knew better than a torturer that, without the comfort of religion, life was a vale of tears.

In their years together, Alain had grown to early manhood under the harsh rigors of the road, and the simple girls of the countryside mooned over his dark eyes and shy smile. Confined for life to their muddy fields and thatched huts, the girls bribed Alain with sweet milk and bread for stories of the great towns and markets through which he had passed.

But Alain, himself a simple and innocent farm boy, was unprepared when a young woman of Axat, a small town in the Pyrenees where the torturers had been marooned for a week by late snowfalls, offered the apprentice a sweeter temptation than a ladle of milk. Shocked by her whispered invitation, Alain preserved his innocence through prayer and through his infatuated devotion to another girl of the town whom he had seen at Mass. Martine, the young woman who had failed once to seduce him, tried again the next day, this time threatening to make trouble for him if he refused. Foolishly, he told her that he loved another. The jealous young woman cursed him furiously. Alain, frightened, ran back to his master, whose questions he moodily ignored.

Martine, already experienced in the consequences of love, snared a little mouse whose burrow she knew. Crushing it against a stone, she smeared her thighs and stained her smock with its blood. Then, having rolled in the snow, she stumbled back to her home, dazed and weeping. Her sly refusal, at first, to allow her mother to examine her brought all the neighbors to her door before she at last relented and lifted her skirt for the old women. When her father pushed past the women back into the house, Martine again refused, at first, to divulge anything. But when the big man threatened to beat her, she quickly confessed that the torturer's apprentice had raped her.

Only the presence of the parish priest in the rectory where the two visitors were staying saved Alain from the violence of the townsfolk. But within days, the young man had been delivered to the authorities at Quillan for trial.

Guillem had served the bustling town of Quillan for years. In fact, he had developed a polite acquaintance with the jurisdiction's magistrate, Bertran d'Uzes. Though he knew he could expect no consideration from the judge, the torturer comforted his apprentice with his confidence that the learned jurist would uncover the truth. Alain insisted that he was an innocent in God's hands and so feared nothing.

Guillem, troubled by the boy's behavior the afternoon the townsmen had stormed the rectory, was not certain of his innocence. Returning from a walk in the snowy fields where Martine was to testify that he had forced himself upon her, the usually happy and open young man refused to talk, acting as if he were ashamed of something. But Guillem's affection for the boy and his distrust of the strange girl weighed more heavily than his doubts.

Presented with Martine's accusation, Bertran d'Uzes accepted the witnesses' corroboration of her story as a legitimate half-proof, but in the absence of an eyewitness, he insisted upon the Queen of Proofs, a confession. The judge solemnly ordered Alain Macheret to be put to the question. Bertran directed the court's torturer, Guillem, to apply the strappado to his apprentice for the length of a recitation of the Creed. Alain would be put to the question three times.

Guillem, profoundly distressed by the judge's decision to employ the strappado, had hoped for the rope tortures reserved for women and children. (He still saw Alain as the young boy waving farewell for the first time to his tearful mother.) But the seriousness of the charge and the muscular frame of the young man condemned him to the Queen of Torments.

A priest and a guard led Alain to the room where Guillem had hoisted the creaking pulleys of the strappado. The apprentice, so often having assisted in the deployment of the device, slipped his own hands into the noose held behind his back. Pulling the lines taut, Guillem watched the twisted arms lift above the boy's bent back. The moan that slipped from Alain's lips when his feet left the floor and the wretched sigh that escaped with each breath as he dangled above them tormented Guillem. The judge, reverently reciting his Creed, would not be hurried. As soon as the priest responded to Bertran's final words with "Amen," the torturer lowered his flushed and agonized apprentice to the ground. Crumpled on the cold floor, Alain raised his head to whisper his innocence into the ear of the judge, who had begged him to confess.

Intoning for a second time the formula of the question, the magistrate nodded to his torturer to raise the accused. Again Bertran recited the Creed. Over the judge's head, moans yielded to desperate screams as each shift of Alain's weight strained beyond endurance another strap of muscles. Guillem grew pale.

Bringing the boy down too quickly at the priest's "Amen," Guillem heard the body against smack the stone floor like a sack of turnips dropped from a loft. The magistrate was dismayed but stooped to ask the accused again to declare his guilt and save himself from further torment.

Guillem almost hoped that Alain would confess, but the judge raised himself up and for the last time repeated the formula of the question.

The torturer had seen it before. A man would endure the agony of two flights in the strappado. He would tell himself that if he could simply keep silent for a few moments more the judge would declare him innocent. He could return to the arms of his wife. He could sleep in his own bed that very night. He could escape the dreadful executioner, who waited to exact the punishment for the crime of which he had been accused. But swaying gently above his tormentors as muscle after muscle was exhausted into spasm, as cramps contorted his body into more and more painful postures at the end of the rope, he forgot his wife and his bed. He even forgot his fear of death. There was no future, no past—only the hideous present. The cry of confession that would interrupt the judge's prayer was very different from the screams that had preceded it: never once had the torturer heard a judge ask the accused to repeat the low moan of submission. Everyone in the room recognized its meaning immediately. The torturer would lower the whimpering body, the judge would already be entering the verdict in the court's log, and the priest would celebrate the divine intervention that had cast the light of truth upon the shadowy crime of this condemned sinner.

With each tug of the lines, Guillem's experienced hands could feel the effect of the first two flights on Alain's body. Where there had been taut resistance in the beginning, now at the other end of the pulleys and ropes hung dead weight. But not the most horrific apparition from the grave could have produced the chilling moans that issued from the body floating above their heads. Even the judge was unsettled, stumbling in his Creed at the sudden bursts of screams that punctuated the agony of young Alain.

Guillem could not stand another moment of the suffering. He had secretly tutored his apprentice in how to hold the body to lessen the effects of the strappado, but now the boy was adrift in a sea of pain and could not remember how to swim. While the judge continued to enunciate with the most careful deliberation each syllable of the Creed, Guillem surreptitiously let out one line and drew in another to ease the pressure on Alain's back. It was difficult to manipulate the device without attracting the attention of the others, but they were transfixed by the ecstasy of pain above them. All at once, the boy seemed to awaken as if from a dream. He suddenly shifted his weight just as Guillem was jerking a line taut. Beneath the piercing scream, Guillem heard the tendons snap, the muscles rip away from the bone, the joints pop from their sockets. Then he heard the priest say, "Amen."

He lowered the boy as gently as they must have lowered the Savior from the Cross. The judge bent to the broken body and asked whether Alain wished to confess. The young man with a single word refused.

In open court, the innocence of Alain Macheret was declared. Martine's father was ordered to pay the boy blood money for the false accusation of his daughter. Martine herself eventually was consigned by her family to the convent at Foix where, after some brief notoriety as a visionary, she contracted a fever and died.

No one but Guillem was aware of his role in the crippling injury to his apprentice. The boy's left arm hung slack as he dragged his leg after him down the dusty summer roads, and his drooping shoulder gave him the appearance of a hunchback. Though he still had the face of an angel, girls turned away from him as he hobbled past their farms. Parents began to threaten unruly children with a midnight visit from the disfigured torturer. The mere sight of him at trials would sometimes persuade the guilty to confess without being put to the question. And everywhere he traveled, he edified the faithful with the tale of how he had been preserved from condemnation by a just and loving God.

Guillem was confounded by the faith of the young man, but to dispute that faith would have been to put himself in jeopardy with the inquisitors and their agents. He felt guilty about the crippling of Alain, but having discovered in Quillan that pity was as dangerous a distraction to the torturer as cruelty, he learned to ignore the scrape of his apprentice's boot against the floor. So, as the two men wandered with their terrifying machines through the labyrinth of narrow streets in the booming towns and across the empty stretches between, Guillem writhed in the harness of a torture for which he had no name and from which no confession would ever set him free.

■ ■ ■ ■ ■ ■ ■ ■ ■ ■ ■

Hockey Angels

Peter LaSalle

I was eleven years old in 1958, and I had a paper route. Our small mill city was deep in the woods of northern Rhode Island. In the thin sunlight of the December afternoons, everything — the red brick of the mills along the icy river, the buff-and-chocolate combo they inevitably painted the wooden three-deckers — took on the diluted softness of a watercolor. I used to read my way through the evening edition as I delivered, my unbuckled rubber galoshes clanking, the rocky weight of the worn canvas sack on my shoulder lightening. Once on the city page there was a headline and a photograph.

MIRACULOUS MEDAL SAVES TEXTILEVILLE YOUTH

The accompanying story told how Eugene Ouellette, of the Textileville neighborhood, had fallen through the ice while playing choose-up hockey with a group of pals. They were skating at the mill basin pond near the abandoned properties of the Leighton Lace Company. His friends managed to pull him out by making an impromptu chain of themselves linked together by their hockey sticks. The story told how the Textileville "youth" later said to the reporter that he was never scared in the course of the ordeal, where he sank maybe clear to the leafy black muck at the bottom of the frigid water and was actually stuck beneath the ice's surface for a while. He probably pressed his palms against it, his body surely twice its weight in the soaked winter clothes. Yes, his friends eventually tugged him out, and, yes, he had no fear about it all, because he was wearing an item commonly called a miraculous medal. He said that as soon as the cold weather hit every October his mother gave him a new one, to protect him on the ice for the next several months till the earth in the gardens smelled as rich as coffee grounds again and the first crocuses bloomed.

The photograph was grainy. It was of a decidedly goofy-looking kid a little younger than me. He grinned through crooked teeth. He wore a checkered wool jacket and a knit toque pulled almost to his nose. And in one hand he held up the miraculous medal, dangling it like a minnow for the camera.

I knew what the medal was like. A small embossed oval, cheaply plated gold, showed the robed Blessed Virgin, her arms outstretched and stars all about her. It hung from a baby-blue ribbon, in turn attached to a pin, cheaply plated gold too. Maybe at eleven I also already knew that a mother pinning such a medal on her son's jacket was a ritual that could happen only in Textileville, a neighborhood once entirely owned by that lace company. Everybody in our city by this point probably claimed some French ties, even if you were from one of the original blueblood Yankee families who founded all of the mills, or even if you were from the sizeable group of Latvians who came to work the looms not long after the original flow of Quebecois down from Canada. But Textileville was Frencher than French. It was poor as well, and in Textileville you found shrines to St. Joseph in the worn back yards of the tiny white rowhouses, and outdoor stations of the cross, with lurid little oil paintings under glass depicting each stop in Christ's suffering, there on the grounds of the neighborhood church.

I remembered Eugene Ouellette from that picture. His name stuck in my mind. Sometimes dreaming as a kid I seemed to encounter him underwater. In that greenness we were both fully dressed in soaked winter clothes, and as I pushed hard against the underside of the ice in a frantic mime, he just smiled that goofy grin from the newspaper photo. He was wearing the miraculous medal on the checkered wool winter jacket, and he was quite at peace. Call him my first hockey angel.

In my senior year of high school I got into a predictable-enough mess. I was sure my girlfriend Maryanne was pregnant. It was a situation that I could indeed have been dreaming too, it felt so farfetched. I hadn't even taken a girl to a movie before I met her at one of the Mount St. Paul's Academy Friday night "canteen" dances the previous year. And suddenly there I was, thinking about marriage and some kind of a job, and no longer having the heart to look at the catalogues for Williams College in Massachusetts or Dartmouth in New Hampshire. The very scenes of the tweedy, crew-cut undergrads carrying their books along autumnal paths in between classes seemed another assault on any chances of possible happiness for me.

I had studied pretty hard at Mount St. Paul's, honors list all along. I surprised even myself by doing so well on the SATs. I was liked by the other guys at the boys' school enough to be elected either class treasurer or class vice president every year. And my running track in the fall and spring would probably convince any admissions officer that I wasn't simply a grind. My uncle who raised me had only a clerk's job in the city hall, but both colleges were sure that along with my acceptance letter in April — which both were entirely confident about — would be a scholarship offer. What made the situation worse was that I wasn't in love with Maryanne, and I knew she wasn't in love with me, though she went overboard with declarations of that now. Before meeting me she had been dating a guy a half-dozen years older. Maryanne's father was a man who supported a big family with his lifelong job at a tool-and-die shop that had located in one of the former mill buildings. So the ex-boyfriend's having a lot of ready money to spend would understandably impress her. The ex-boyfriend sold insurance for his own father's agency, drove a yellow Chevrolet Impala convertible that could turn heads in a city as small as ours. I knew Maryanne was still in love with him. I knew I could forget college.

Somehow this all eventually involved Brother John Collins, there at Mount St. Paul's. He was maybe my second hockey angel.

In that senior year a group of us from the disbanded Mount St. Paul's varsity hockey team made the long drive from the mill city to Providence to rent ice time. Late on Saturday nights we played hockey amongst ourselves at a rink in a stretch of warehouses that had once been part of a shipyard during World War II. It was 1965.

The hockey was all I had to look forward to then. We got the ice cheap from eleven till one in the morning, and there was always something very special to skating top-speed around the fluorescent whiteness while others slept. Sometimes we convinced the rum-nosed old boozer who ran the place to play Beatles albums over the loudspeakers, and in that smell of refrigeration that could cut like wonderful ammonia as you breathed, the blades ripped, the sticks slammed, and the puck knocked off the scuffed boards with echoes like somebody hammering in the country. Lennon and McCartney came together for that rare Liverpoolian whine that was truly best on "Anna" and "Please, Please Me."

This night, as usual lately, somebody had to stop at the brothers' house at the school to pick up Brother John Collins. A guy about thirty, he was teaching at Mount St. Paul's after a couple of hitches in the order's West

Pakistan missions. He was forced to leave when the fighting there turned dangerous. He somehow received permission from the headmaster, Brother Maurice, to join us for our midnight sessions. He had played a good deal of hockey in upstate New York, I think, and even now he still had his moves. He held his own out there with us teenage guys in his CCM Tacks that looked ready for the museum and a genuine Detroit Red Wings jersey he had picked up somewhere along the line. The three carloads of us usually traveled in a convoy, which was the kind of thing that could be fun then. But seeing I was a little late in my uncle's Dodge Coronet sedan, and seeing I had the duty of giving Brother John a ride that week, those packed in my car couldn't join the caravan of sorts.

Mount St. Paul's sat on a genuine hill. It was a dark silhouette in the blue of that cold January night. I swerved into the parking lot on the lower campus, easing past the shut-down school rink and heading toward the brothers' fieldstone house. Brother John waited outside. He wore full pads and an old army parka opened to reveal the Red Wings jersey. He held his stick like a shepherd's crook, had his equipment bag over his shoulder Santa Claus-style. I approached him—then tromped the accelerator to jet the Dodge past him, jamming on the brakes and jerkingly backing up. He half-jogged toward the car, and when I rolled down the window Brother John was smiling.

"Hey, how ya doing?" I said. "Gordie Howe, right? Look, Gordie, we're looking for this guy, a brother, who's supposed to meet us out here. Brother John Collins."

"Funny," he said in an easy, good-natured way.

"Wow," I said, putting on. "Look, guys, it's him! Sorry, Brother John, I saw the Detroit uniform and I could have sworn you were Gordie Howe."

"Yeah, yeah, yeah. I should put this stuff in the trunk, right?"

I handed him the key. Tommy Cassady sat in the front seat with me. He slid over. He knew all along that I had it in for Brother John, for who knows what reason.

"That Gordie Howe line was funny," Tommy said flatly, then paused. "Funny the first time you pulled it a month ago."

Why did I have it in for Brother John? On one level I could say that it was because the school had taken varsity hockey away from us. Brother Maurice, that new headmaster, had a record for reorganizing some of the order's other financially shaky schools. Despite his name that echoed that of beloved Rocket Richard himself, he looked at the books and was soon convinced that the major drain of money came from keeping a hockey team outfitted, plus the expense of running the decrepit school rink that had a troubled compressor about to huffingly cough its last. He didn't care that Mount St. Paul's had its long hockey tradition. The school attracted day students from that whole pocket of the state. And after World War II Mount St. Paul's in its feared purple-and-gold uniforms tore up the Class A division of the Rhode Island schoolboy league, admittedly with the help of some nasal-accented ringers imported from farms in Quebec. Though the teams hadn't been too strong lately, having slipped into Class C, and a cellar contender in that class too. Still, wasn't it the ultimate irony: the school had taken away hockey, and now one of its brothers showed up on Saturday nights to pitch in his two bucks toward rental, as we had to drive the long forty miles roundtrip to find a rink we could afford.

But, in truth, I had always liked Mount St. Paul's. Around the city even on weekends I wore my shabby blue blazer, the MSP on the pocket in once-white embroidery now as dirty as old string. If I hadn't the problem I currently had I would probably have agreed with that headmaster Brother Maurice that a drain like varsity hockey, as much as all loved it there, would sink the school in the end. And I would probably have been a good pal indeed of a guy like Brother John. He had his easy way. He showed obvious concern for my best, even showed genuine pleasure knowing that it appeared I would be getting an opportunity that most Mount St. Paul's boys never got, the chance to go to one of those top-notch schools on a scholarship. Neither he, nor anybody else, knew that I had gotten a girl pregnant, and that she was a girl who still talked about how "cool" the continental wheel was on her ex-boyfriend's sleek Impala. Brother John didn't know that this time next year I would be working to support a kid and that boring wife who wasn't very interested in me to begin with. So I hated the way Brother John wore his white, rather than black, cassocks around the school. It was a practice supposedly required of brothers who had put in missionary time, and it served as an advertisement for that branch of the order's work. And I hated the friendly way he joked with me in our American history class that he had taken over at midyear. And I hated most the way he could say to me almost dreamily, as if he were wondering if his own life might have taken a different course, that "You've got the whole world waiting for you, Mark. You'll make something of it, I know it, man."

On the ice that night I made sure that when we split into two groups for teams Brother John was on the opposition. I made sure that any chance I had to bang the guy I did. In my tallness I was more skinny than big.

But Brother John with his crooked nose, short-cut hair, and perpetual smile, was thirty, and any shot to somebody thirty from someone eighteen would hurt. The Beatles played, the game raged.

Once I saw him deep in his own corner. He was retrieving the puck, his goalie having routinely flipped it back there. There was nobody else with him, and I was alone too, maybe five yards away. It happened fast, but it was also almost gummy slow motion—as I dug in my skates hard to accelerate, held one elbow up for a spear, and slammed into him with everything I had. The boards were as solid as poured concrete, above them was strung chicken wire, not plexiglas. He could have been a splattered fly on the wall. Play kept going afterwards, but I could see he was shaken when he returned to his bench, and let somebody else take a turn on defense. I returned to ours, huffing.

Tommy Cassady was there. He looked at me, then shook his head.

"That was cute," he said. The sarcasm was overdone.

"What?" I pretended to be interested in the play.

"'What'," he says. "What the hell is the matter with you is *what*. What's this full-time jerk award you're trying for lately is *what*." He left me there, going back to take his turn on the line. Brother John joked about it with me later. We were unlacing our skates. He smiled and admitted that he had surely left himself wide open for that nailing. I didn't joke.

Afterwards we always all went to Mass at the Franciscan chapel in downtown Providence. They offer a service at two on Sunday mornings. With Mass out of the way, we could sleep as late as we wanted the next day at our homes, nicely sore from all that banging. I used to savor that soreness. And it used to be great to doze right till noon—great before my problem, that is.

I had a plan. This was where I was going to really get Brother John, not on the ice. I would expose him. Because wasn't it funny, a little suspicious, that somebody who was a religious brother said he would just as well stay there in the car? He claimed that he would have to go to Mass anyway in a few hours along with the rest of the brothers at the school. The Franciscan chapel in Providence was new and in an alley off Washington Street. In truth this was a drunk's Mass, a lot of tipsy folk attending after the bars closed, and in truth on Saturday night this end of the city's downtown could be seamy. Drug dealers, prostitutes too, in those scarlet go-go boots and ever-so-small mini-skirts they wore even when the temperature on a snow-crusted night like this wasn't much above zero. At Mass we still had on our pads and coats, and I motioned for the other guys to let me slip out of the pew right after the gospel.

The chapel was in the basement and packed. I headed up the stairs and into the cold, determined. In my, well, madness, I was convinced that I would now find what Brother John of the lily-white cassocks and the ongoing understanding was all about, about what he was really up to on these sleazy streets. A Hispanic girl leaned against a Checker cab across the alley, eyeing me. She was younger than me and heavily made-up. She wore the standard go-go boots and a short jack of fuzzy brown stuff that reminded me of a teddy bear. Who was Brother John trying to kid?

So I walked the streets a little crazy for a good fifteen minutes, before I gave up. I finally went to the lot where the car was parked. I suppose I knew all along I should have started there. I suppose that when it looked from a distance that the car was empty I had no doubt either that he was there, that he had been there all along. My desert boots squeaked on the packed white. I stepped up to the car.

Brother John was sleeping. He lay on his side on the back seat. He was in an almost foetal curl, wearing the army-surplus parka and the ridiculous Red Wings jersey. His stubble dark on his face, he nevertheless appeared boyish, the way his hands and knees were tucked close to him. He was sleeping because it didn't, in fact, make any sense for a religious brother or anybody else to go to Mass twice when that exhausted. And what the *hell* had I been thinking? Yet right then I was maybe thinking nothing. The stars above me in the inky sky were huge enough to be matches flickering, and it was somehow so right to be staring through the glass at the man sleeping and sleeping like that. It was somehow so right to be that close to somebody, and also wondering where — all the millions and millions of miles away — he traveled in his peaceful dreams, that hockey angel.

I couldn't remember when I myself had last been as relaxed.

Eugene Ouellette. Brother John Collins. They were just two hockey angels.

I live in Southern California now. All this honeyed sunlight, and streamlined shopping malls, and shrubs like agave and saguaro that might only have been names in a nature text if I hadn't ended up out here. But thinking about Rhode Island, I seem to suspect that there were other hockey angels back so long ago in those winters. Maybe the urchins that I would see hanging around rinks when we played Bantam League games. Bantam League for me would have been in between the Eugene Ouellette story and the Brother John story. You know those scruffy toughs who you still surely see, kids always pug-nosed and pinching cigarettes between their smug lips, who unlatch the gate for the Zamboni resurfacing machine to come onto the ice, who use their big squeegees to smooth the layer of wet around the red goal pipes so it will freeze evenly, who shovel the snowy shavings that the growling robotic contraption sheds in clumps as it bangs back over the threshold bump and through the gate again. Those kids known as "rink rats," who can probably out-skate and out-stick-handle anybody their age, but in their wild delinquency — do they go to school? do they even have parents and homes? — would never submit to anything as square as organized team play. Maybe they live in the rinks like ghosts, haunt the high rafters when nobody else is around, know the peace there that Eugene Ouellette knew as he wore his miraculous medal and smiled so close to death, that Brother John Collins from the dangerous foreign missions knew as he slept like a heavenly whisper in the back seat of my uncle's dark-green Dodge Coronet sedan in the otherworld of 1965.

"Does any of this make sense?" I ask my wife. I have been talking to her in bed in the darkness, long after our three daughters are asleep.

No, my wife isn't Maryanne from the mill city. As it turned out, Maryanne wasn't pregnant after all, and the scholarship to Williams, if not Dartmouth, did come through.

"What?" my wife whispers.

"What I've been telling you now. These stories. This business of hockey angels." She has listened to it all.

"Shhh," she says.

"I'm happy," I say.

"I'm happy too," she says.

"Hockey angels," I say low, to myself.

"Now sleep," she says. "Just sleep."

And I will, dreaming.

■ ■ ■ ■ ■ ■ ■ ■ ■ ■ ■

Wader Man

William Loizeaux

N orm Dickerson was a dispirited man, though it hadn't always been that way. Long ago, when aluminum ladders hit the market and the Dickerson Wooden Ladder Company hit hard times, Norm was determined to never give in.

"Why not sell a few aluminum ladders?" Kay had asked one night.

Norm looked at his wife keenly. Perhaps she just didn't understand. Wood was wood. A family business was a family business. And Norm believed in his ladders as he had believed in himself: though out of fashion, out of use, they must somehow persevere.

So he had refused to deal in aluminum stock. Orders dwindled. He let go of his secretary and salesman, then closed up the New York office. But instead of selling out or getting into another line of work, Norm moved his desk, a chair, his adding machine and Remington typewriter to the basement of their Dutch Colonial in suburban New Jersey. There in the corner near the set tub, furnace, and water heater, beneath a small door that led to the crawlspace; there in his white shirt and clip-on bow tie, with the sump pump humming in the humid air; there with his back to the mildewed wall; there, undaunted, he had made his stand. And tried to sell his wooden ladders again.

N ow, all these years later, Norm was still down in the basement, still banging the keys of his typewriter and cranking his ancient adding machine, but he was only going through the motions. Things hadn't worked out. He had lost his spark. Life, like some extended cold, was just something to put up with. The more he had tried, the more he had sequestered himself in the basement, the fewer ladders he had sold. His hair had turned thin and gray, and except for his trips to the mailbox out front or to his narrowing vegetable garden out back, he seldom left the house anymore.

What did Kay think of this? Apparently not much. She cooked dinners briskly, cleaned the house, and went out on long errands. At night, she slept on the far edge of the bed, cool as an iron rail. She joined a bridge club and the Junior League, and turned more and more to the church. Sometimes on a Saturday as he was working in the basement, Norm would hear their voices in the living room above: Kay and Reverend Spicer whom she'd invited to tea. Norm would climb on his desk, and standing with his head between the beams and his ear to the floorboards, he'd hear them murmuring prayers. "Yea, though I walk through the valley of the shadow..." They were kneeling right above him.

As for his son, Clyde: well, that too was a dispiriting story. He was in his mid-twenties, almost a grown man, though you wouldn't really believe it. He had dropped out of college, and after knocking around at various odd jobs, the kid, who thought he knew everything, still didn't know what he was doing with himself. He was renting a room in a run-down neighborhood in Paterson and painting houses for money. He drove a rusted-out Volkswagen bus crammed with drop cloths, caulk guns, paint cans, and stinking rags. Strapped on the top was a 28-foot extension ladder. An aluminum ladder. Of course.

About once a week, probably when he was running low on cash, Clyde would come roaring up Norm's smoothly raked gravel driveway, unannounced, "just to say hello"—and to stay for dinner, a free meal. He'd smell of cigarettes and mineral spirits. In his scraggly hair there'd be flecks of paint, and often he'd wear a soiled baseball cap, backwards and cockeyed, even when he came into the house.

One evening he arrived carrying a gray cat. He brought it right into the kitchen.

"What's this?" Norm asked. He had come up from the basement for supper which Kay was cooking at the stove.

"This is Phred." Clyde plunked the cat down on the table, letting it arch its back against the palm of his hand. "With a 'Ph'," he added pointedly. "*He* is a *she*."

Norm raised his eyebrows.

"My landlady just gave her the boot," Clyde went on. "Phred ripped down all the curtains. One of us had to go."

Norm nodded just perceptibly, as if to confirm something he had suspected all along.

"She's really a great cat," Clyde said.

Kay peered through the steam above the stove. She was stirring something in a saucepan. "So you think she's staying here — is that it? What about *my* curtains?"

"Don't worry," Clyde said. He lifted the cat and put it in Norm's arms which raised involuntarily to accept it. "She can live in the basement. It'll be all right. You'll like her, I'm telling you."

From his Volkswagen bus, Clyde brought in the cat box, litter, and the two plastic bowls for milk and Meow Mix. Then he carried the cat downstairs, said a quick good-bye, and returned to the kitchen, shutting the door behind him.

So just as he'd suspected, Norm would have to put up with yet another thing, though it wasn't as bad as he'd thought. In the mornings when he opened the basement door, Phred would be waiting on the top step. She'd purr and rub her back against his leg. Then she'd follow him down to his office. It was musty there with the sharp smell of the litter box and the walls stained with seeping groundwater. As the cat lay curled at his elbow, Norm made his phone calls to the warehouse in Pennsylvania, typed his occasional letters and invoices, and cranked his adding machine. At noon he'd go up to the kitchen for a half hour, have a cheese sandwich and Campbell's soup, sometimes right out of the can. Often, he'd walk his letters down his driveway to the mailbox where he'd raise the little red flag. If the weather was hot, he'd get the galvanized can and water his tomatoes out back. Then with some crackers or 'Nilla Wafers, he'd open the basement door, and there would be Phred. Together they'd pad down the stairs.

It was like this for most of a year, until something unfortunate happened.

One afternoon Phred was batting a ping-pong ball on the concrete floor, when she suddenly staggered, swayed like a drunk, and collapsed. In an instant, though, she was up, shook herself, and continued batting the ball. At his desk, Norm watched her for a while. She seemed okay, but she stopped again, crouched, coiled, staring at Norm with her diamond eyes, her gray tail twitching.

And then, incredibly, she lunged. She flew at him, yowling, her teeth and claws whirring, ripping into his calves and thighs. It was appalling, painful, and yet Norm's first impulse was to turn the other cheek, to refrain from striking her, to not even defend himself. She mauled him with wild impunity. "My God!" was the only thing he could say. "What in the world have I done?" As if in answer, the cat suddenly stopped — just as suddenly and mysteriously as it had all begun. The house was quiet. The air in the basement was cool and damp. Phred licked her paws, then curled in Norm's lap and slept.

Twice more it happened that week, without provocation or warning, and so Kay called Dr. Palmer, the vet, who was also a deacon in her church. He said the cat probably had a brain tumor. He had seen it often before: the staggering, and then the aggressive behavior. He hated to tell them, but he had to be honest. There was nothing that he or anyone could do. From here it would only get worse.

Which of course it did. The following week, Norm emerged each evening from the basement, sad and haggard, his khakis scratched and bloodied, as if all day he had suffered some punishment, had waded through great fields of brambles.

"Don't you think this is getting a little ridiculous?" Kay asked during one of their suppers when Clyde had joined them. She was serving mashed potatoes, plopping them down on the plates. "You know, you can have her put to sleep. That's the humane thing. Say your last fond farewell, put her in a box, and take her over to Palmer's."

"Or I can do it," Clyde said bravely, still wearing his cockeyed cap.

But Norm would have none of it. It was out of the question. "I wouldn't do that to anyone, or anything."

"She's a *cat!*" Kay said.

Norm didn't answer. He was moved by a righteousness, as thick and warm as the potatoes before him. On this, as on the matter of wooden ladders, he was a man resolved.

So every morning Norm filled the bowls and cleaned the litter box with a slotted spoon. Each evening he emerged, sad, puzzled, bloodied but unbroken. It occurred to him that this was the feeling that saints might have when they are tested by a stern and fickle God. Forty days in the wilderness. His time in the basement. These scratches, scars: strange stigmata. This blood on his legs and hands.

For two weeks he endured this trial, and then, like a veil, it lifted. He was working at his desk on a Saturday afternoon, as Kay and Reverend Spicer were praying in the living room above. Already that day, Phred had attacked three times, and Norm himself, though a secular man, was in a state that was something like prayer. All open and vulnerable, he waited—for what he didn't know. He was gazing at the door to the crawlspace—at the hinge, at the hasp—when all at once it struck him, like a flash of clearest light. He got up on his desk and opened the door. On hands and knees he crawled in. It was dim and dank with the smell of earth. The ground was cool on his palms. He could make out the long blade of a rusted sled, an old Flexible Flyer. Further in were the damp stacks of *National Geographics* and Kay's poles and wooden skis with bear-trap bindings. Pressing on, he reached the thick pipe that came through the floor of the bathroom above and disappeared into the ground. He moved aside a soup tureen or a goldfish bowl. He pushed through nets of cobwebs. Toward the rear of the crawlspace and in utter darkness, he reached blindly before him with his hands. He felt the canvas creel with its mesh bottom. He felt the squat tackle box and beside it the long, cool, metal tubes that held his bamboo rods. Then his hands fell on what he was after — feet, calves, thighs, chest — his fingers moving on vulcanized rubber: his old fishing waders, just as he remembered them. Yes, they were still there!

Taking the long suspenders in one hand, and still on his knees, Norm dragged the waders back toward the lighted doorway, as though he was pulling some hollowed-out man with his toes pointing up in the air. When he reached the thick pipe, he heard steps just above him, the slow steps of the reverend. Norm stopped, dead quiet, and then with wonder he heard the pious man pee, a ribbon of silvery bells. Next came the rush of water through the pipe, and Norm continued his journey. With Phred watching quizzically from her perch on the water heater, Norm emerged from the crawlspace, rumpled and triumphant, the waders behind him, sliding into the light.

They were Army-green and covered with dust. The leather suspenders were stiff and cracked, but the rubber was smooth and pliant. Norm held them up before him, as high as his shoulders, and as he took them to the set tub, they moved gracefully together, he and the waders, almost as though they were dancing. With soap and a sponge he washed them until they shined like oiled skin. Then he anointed the suspenders with neat's-foot oil, rubbing it in with a rag. Beside his desk again, he took off his shoes, and like a man fitting into an astronaut's suit, one leg at a time he got in. He hiked the top of the waders up to his armpits and buckled the suspenders over his shoulders. He took a step. And then another, the rubber scrunching and squeaking as he moved. He took a slow lap around the furnace, and then he walked at normal speed. He thought he'd feel awkward, encumbered, a man in a heavy tube. Yet as he moved about the basement on his rubber soles, with the fluorescent light shining on his chest, he felt a strange and wonderful upward rush. He felt buoyant, as though he could run, fly, dance on waves, as though he had grown wings. Back at his desk, he pulled out his swivel chair and sat down to work in his waders. Though he didn't know exactly what it could be, he felt like someone possessed of an insight, some truth he might give to the world. Gazing at Phred, he seemed to say, "There. Now, I've solved it."

And he was right. An hour later, the cat crouched on the floor, her tail twitching, and then she lunged, flailing, but only to slide harmlessly down Norm's smooth rubberized calf, like a fireman coming down a pole. She tried again and again with the same result, without even distracting Norm from his work. Some moments later, she hopped on his desk and lay curled and purring at his elbow.

That evening when Kay called him to dinner, Norm went upstairs, and in his old bow tie and new shining skin, stood on the kitchen linoleum.

Kay stared at him, astonished in her red-checked apron. "Good Lord!" was all she could say.

At this moment, Clyde waltzed in from the driveway, and seeing Norm, he also stopped dead in his tracks. "What the hell . . . ?" Then, amazed, he moved slowly forward to touch the waders. "Smooth," he said as though convinced of something doubtful. "Pretty cool. Kinky."

At the dining room table, Norm said grace with his hands folded in his rubbery lap. The words were the same — "Bless these gifts we are about to receive . . . " — and yet his voice tonight was filled with a strange depth and authority. For it seemed that in fact he had received a gift, and now he could feel it warming his loins, a gift that literally girded him. "In the name of the Lord Jesus Christ," he intoned with all the gravity of Reverend Spicer. "Amen."

Each evening, then, he came up and ate dinner, unscathed in his rubber waders. Afterwards, he loaded the dishwasher and, still without changing his attire, sat in his usual living room chair with the newspaper and a ball game on the radio beside the lamp.

Except for her first astonished exclamation, Kay barely mentioned the waders again. She came and went as always, though now with a curious look, without reproach, a faintly quickened interest. Clyde, on the other hand, was openly enthusiastic. There was something in his father's wearing waders around the house that suggested another strain of his personality, perhaps something repressed by bourgeois life, something vaguely bohemian, counter-cultural. For the first time in years, Clyde brought over a few friends. In their baggy jeans and torn T-shirts, they sprawled in the living room, "checking out" Norm's rubber waders. His father was "making a statement," Clyde said, "about the callousness of contemporary life."

For his part, Norm neither confirmed nor denied any of this. He just felt better, more alive in his waders, and so naturally he devised ways of wearing them as comfortably and continuously as possible. He avoided eating beans and onions. With a razor blade, he carefully cut a fly in the crotch of the waders and a rectangular flap in the back, either of which he could open and reseal with duct tape, when the calls of nature sounded. Only at night did he take the waders off and hang them over the bed post where he could step into them right after his morning shower. Then he'd eat his breakfast and go downstairs to work, where periodically Phred would pounce, then subside, and nestle like a child in his lap.

At lunchtime, Norm began going outside in his waders, down the driveway to the mailbox, and out back to his garden. On a Sunday afternoon in May, he cut the lawn while wearing them, pushing the mower before him. It was hot in the sun, his face florid and his breath coming out in gasps. The waders were clammy; they smelled like old tires; his sweat soaked his socks. He felt Kay watching him through the dining room curtains, and finding some last, vital reserve of strength, he straightened his back and pushed even harder, showing her the deep-grooved soles of his waders, kicking clots of grass up behind him.

At noon the next day, he drove his letters to the post office, instead of leaving them in the mailbox at home. He parked, and in his waders and usual white shirt and bow tie, he walked across the town green where some old-timers were sitting on benches. They squinted over their glasses, then quickly hid back behind their newspapers. "Nice day!" Norm said, keeping a brisk pace. "Cheerio!" And he went on to post his letters.

Soon Kay began getting reports from her friends at bridge club. Norm had been seen in his waders at the Peppermill Deli, at the pharmacy, the Dairy Queen, at Freeman's garage getting a rubber patch on his knee, and even as far away as a sporting goods store in Morristown. He was known to stop and talk with the regulars who sat in front of the firehouse. When the police passed him, they'd wave from their squad cars, and at Friendly's restaurant where he stopped in for lunches, he was becoming a small celebrity.

"Wader Man," the waitresses called him. "What'll it be, the usual?" He'd sit at his accustomed spot at the counter. He'd chat with the people on either side of him, while now and then a child would timidly approach.

"Mister, are they real?"

"Why sure!" he'd smile and slap his thighs. "They're really real!"
He'd swivel on his stool so the child could touch, believe, and sometimes
he'd lift the kid and bounce him on his dazzling knees.

The older teenage kids had another idea, something that Norm didn't
immediately understand, though it pleased him nonetheless. They'd come
up to him with earnest looks and with felt-tipped pens in their hands.
He'd say, "Sure. Go ahead," and one by one the kids would sign their
names and leave little messages or designs, all up and down his legs.

"Graffiti," the boys at the firehouse would tease. "You're as pretty
as a New York subway car."

Yet as Norm worked in his basement office with Phred at his elbow,
as he gazed now and then at his rubber waders, he was filled with all
the humility and pride of one who, unwittingly, has been chosen to
embody the hopes and aspirations of others. On his waders, he was
literally carrying their names, their lives, their dreams.

> Go for it! —Bruce
> Peace —From Joyce
> Be Bold! —Duke
> We Luv U Wader Man —Jennifer
> Never say die —Vinny

And just as Norm was carrying *them* on his waders —these names, these
lives of those around him —they in turn seemed to carry *him*. He felt
embraced, uplifted, and carried upon their collective shoulders. He felt
their needs, their yearnings, their strength, and now the weight of his
own responsibility. Sudden tears of gratitude filled his eyes. He, of all
people, had been called upon, entrusted —for what, he didn't know. Yet
he knew that sometime, somewhere there'd be something he must do.
And he knew —he was sure —that he could do it.

This exhilaration, however, was shattered one morning in mid-June,
two months after he had first put on his waders. When Norm went
down to the basement, he found Phred sprawled and stiff, her tongue
locked between her teeth, dead beside the adding machine on his desk.
After he had held her for a while in his arms, he slid her into his canvas
fishing creel and buried her in his garden out back. Returning to the
basement, and with no reason now to wear them, Norm took off his
waders, folded them neatly, and put them back in the crawlspace. At
noon, he didn't drive his letters to the post office. He didn't say hello to
the boys at the firehouse, or slide onto his stool at Friendly's. At the

kitchen table, in his wrinkled khakis, he had a cold Campbell's soup, straight from the can, and a Coke from which he had stirred the carbonation. When Kay saw him like this, she breathed out a little knowing sigh, and shaking her head, turned her eyes to the floor. Things again were as they had been — and as they probably would be forevermore. During the next few weeks, Norm remained in the basement, banging at his typewriter and cranking his old machine, except to come up for meals and to read his paper in the evenings. When it rained, he listened to the hum of the sump pump, and on Saturday afternoons, sitting at his desk, he heard that mumbled praying overhead.

B ut then came the Fourth of July, a warm, blustery day, the day of the Kiwanis Fair, the social event of the summer.

At ten that morning, Kay called down the stairs, "I'm on my way. See you." She grabbed the car keys and turned toward the kitchen door, though to her surprise, she heard steps quietly mounting the stairs, and then Norm appeared in the basement doorway, resplendent once more in his waders.

She was stunned, wordless.

"I'll take the keys," he said with gentle magnanimity, and she dropped them into his palm. He led her out to the car, held her door, then slid in behind the wheel.

At the fairground along the bank of the Passaic River, the big tents rippled in the breeze and, as he pulled into the lot, Norm could see the Ferris wheel and carousel which hadn't yet begun to turn. The air was thick with smells of hot dogs and hamburgers charring on grills. Somewhere a marching band was playing, though the parade, it seemed, had already ended, for the floats, constructed by troops of Boy and Girl Scouts, were parked in the center of the fairground: the big pâpier-maché figures of Ben Franklin, George and Martha Washington, and the squat, cracked Liberty Bell.

Norm bought tickets for himself and Kay. They went in, and as they moved around the fair, he in his bow tie, waders, and she with her wicker purse, a small crowd gathered around them. Norm waved and nodded to folks he knew: Elsie the librarian, Jake from the garage. He gave the thumbs-up sign to Officer Strout and shook hands with the animal warden. People clapped him on the back and said, "How you doing? Good to see you again!" Some kids asked for his autograph, and Trish, from Friendly's, kissed him on the cheek. At the food pavilion, he bought cotton candy for Kay who, through all of this, was strangely

quiet, shy, maybe a little frightened. Norm gave five dollars to the
Ladies' Auxiliary, and on their way to the Volunteer Fireman's display,
they ran into Clyde who was roving with a pack of old friends.

"Hey, that's my dad!" he said, breaking into the entourage. Then
admiring his father, head to toe: "Man, you look great!"

At this moment, the crackling voice on the loudspeaker announced
that before today's big activities began, the pastor of the First Presbyterian
Church would offer a short invocation. The crowd hushed and stilled;
even Clyde took off his cap. With microphone in hand, Reverend Spicer
climbed awkwardly up on the nearest float and stood beside the Liberty
Bell in his collar and flapping surplice. He had barely begun—he was
saying something about freedom, community, and individual responsibility—
when the wind kicked up and a huge gust rocked the reverend and the
floats. Then a mightier gust struck and, as the crowd watched in disbelief,
it dislodged Martha Washington from her moorings and guy wires,
lifted her ponderous shape above the float, and carried her, spinning and
toppling in layers of petticoats, mop hat and puffed sleeves. Out across
the parking lot and an open field, the mother of our nation was borne
rudely away toward the dark, brown, fast-flowing river.

For a petrified moment, no one moved as Martha came sadly to
rest in the current: her skirts aloft, her head submerged, and her arms,
unswimming, still faithfully clutching her husband's three-cornered hat.

It was then that Norm knew just what he must do, as if his whole
life had come to this. Parting the crowd, he ran to the Volunteer Fireman's
display, grabbed a thick coil of rope, and thrust it over his shoulder.
With his breath chuffing and his waders scrunching, he ran across the
fairground, the parking lot, and the open field. Now, as one, the crowd
followed: the Boy and Girl Scouts with their fluttering sashes and merit
badges, the Shriners in their funny hats, the Veterans of Foreign Wars,
the Ladies Auxiliary and Indian Guides, the marching band in disarray,
the Cub Scouts, Brownies, Clyde, the reverend, and Kay with her purse
in the crook of her arm—all ran or hobbled across the field, then
arrived, panting, at the wide river where Martha, so indecorously, was
floating away.

"Hold this!" Norm yelled, and he gave one end of the rope to a
group of men. Then, tying the other around his waist and letting the rest
unfurl from his shoulder, he strode out into the water. The current was
strong and cold, and he could feel its pressure against his waders. It
frothed at his knees. It frothed at his thighs and at his waist, but manfully
he leaned into it, cleaving the river in two. He slid on the rocky bottom.

Twenty yards away, in the middle of the river, Martha drifted as in a dream, rolling and weaving in the quickening flow toward the rapids just beyond the bridge.

If only he had a ladder, a *wooden* ladder! He would float it before him, extending it to her, and she would grab on and, rung by rung, crawl to the safety of his arms.

But ladderless, Norm hurried toward her, aiming to intercept her before her peril, if he could only make it on time. The current moved faster and deeper. He churned his arms like oars. The rope unfurled and unfurled. From behind, he could hear the crowd urging him on. "A little farther! Be careful!" And he could imagine Clyde standing with his cap in his hand, and even Kay in her skirt and ox-blood loafers, like a girl, all wide-eyed, amazed.

The water now was at his chest, and he braced himself with each step. From the shore he appeared like a man without legs, engaged in some balancing act. He held his arms straight out above the water. He teetered and pushed ahead. In the middle of the river, then, they came awkwardly together — he and Martha, like fragile ships, a rendezvous in space. Norm reached out his arms and caught her shoulders, and she pressed her white neck to his lips. He heard a cheer from far away. He felt the rope tighten at his waist — they were trying to pull him toward the bank. Yet it struck him right then as jarring and unpleasant: to be pulled from this moment with his arms around her, with her bloomers clinging to her thighs, and now his face in the plenitude of her bodice . . . to be pulled from this when he could stand on his own, when together they might wring the last from this moment, until, spent but striding in his waders, he would carry her on his own to shore.

There was another, harder jerk on the rope, and even now no one is sure why he did it. Some have said he was off his rocker, while others have said it was the sort of gallantry that you just don't see anymore. In an instant Norm removed the rope from his own waist and hooped it around Martha's. He tightened and knotted it. "Pull in! Hard!" he cried, and he watched her being towed toward safety.

He had done it. He had saved her. And now she seemed to move faster and faster toward the crowd that cheered and beckoned. She planed over the water, a winged hull, her petticoats white as snow. She moved further and faster, and now he too seemed to be moving, buoyed away as on wide shoulders, exalted in his rubber waders. He lay on his back and kicked his feet. He dove under, head first, and raised his legs, a gleaming V in the sun.

From the shore the crowd saw the glimmering waders, and then Norm's head, small as a grape, bobbing on the surface. With Martha rescued, the firemen now ran shouting to Norm along the river. "Hey! Hey! Look out where you're going!" But faster than they ran, he was borne away, his arms uplifted to the sky. Narrowing and descending, the river rushed and boiled, and in a spangle of light near the mouth of the bridge, Norm disappeared from view.

But he didn't perish. No one, not even he, knows exactly what happened in the rapids beyond the bridge. He has no memory of his time in the river after that moment when he rescued Martha Washington. What he does remember is awakening in a sort of marshy nest, surrounded and sheltered by tall reeds that made scissoring sounds in the breeze. He lay on his side, half submerged in muck that held him gently in place. He felt bruised, hungry, wet, dazed, and yet safe, warm, oddly calm and refreshed, as if after a good night's sleep. The light was dim but gaining. Birds sang in the grasses. When he moved, the muck relented with a soft sucking noise, and Norm more or less sat up. He heard a train whistle from far away, and the faint rustle of traffic. With his hands, he felt his bow tie askew and his hair matted with mud. A brownish foam covered his khakis. Then he noticed that his waders were gone.

In his passage through the rapids, he must have slipped out of them, as a snake slides from its skin. Slowly now he crawled out of the muck and stood, peering through the grasses. It was all wide, new, and open out there, the sun edging over a field. He was someplace that he didn't recognize, somewhere, he supposed, downstream from the bridge, perhaps in a whole different town. He straightened his bow tie. He parted the grasses as you'd open a curtain, and then this muddied man, just a man in pants, stepped into the day.

POETRY

■■■■■■■■■■

Building

Gary Snyder

We started our house midway through the Cultural Revolution,
The Vietnam war, Cambodia, in our ears,
    tear gas in Berkeley,
Boys in overalls with frightened eyes, long matted hair, ran
    from the police.
We peeled trees, drilled boulders, dug sumps, took sweat baths
    together.
That house finished we went on
Built a schoolhouse, with a hundred wheelbarrows,
    held seminars on California paleo-indians during lunch.
We brazed the Chou dynasty form of the character "Mu"
    on the blacksmithed brackets of the ceiling of the lodge.
Buried a five-prong vajra between the schoolbuildings
    while praying and offering tobacco.
Those buildings were destroyed by a fire, a pale copy rebuilt
    by insurance.

Ten years later we gathered at the edge of a meadow.
The cultural revolution is over, hair is short,
    the industry calls the shots in the People's Forests.
Single mothers go back to college to become lawyers.

Blowing the conch, shaking the staff-rings
    we opened work on a Hall,
Forty people, women carpenters, child labor, pounding nails,
Screw down the corten roofing and shape the beams
    with a planer,
The building is done in three weeks.
We fill it with flowers and friends and open it up to our hearts.

Now in the year of the Persian Gulf,
Of Falsehoods and Crimes in the Government held up as Virtues,
    this dance with Matter
Goes on: our buildings are solid, to live, to teach, to sit,
To sit, to know for sure the sound of a bell —

This is history. This is outside of history.
Buildings are built in the moment,
    they are constantly wet from the pool
        that renews all things
    naked and gleaming.

The moon moves
Through her twenty-eight nights.
Wet years and dry years pass;
Sharp tools, good design.

■ ■ ■ ■ ■ ■ ■ ■ ■ ■ ■

On Wanting to Grow Horns

Amy Gerstler

Man's envy of animals is ancient,
a damp cave filled to the rafters
with handsome pallid bats, lemurs,
beetles, mallards. *Do I really*
have to walk upright all the time?
Swooping lucidly, melancholy enters
the mind through one's nasal
passages, like the homey smell
of burnt pot roast. Male fruit bats
court females by honking, and flashing
tufts of fur on their shoulders:
not such strange behavior. Less
comprehensibly, child murder's
on the rise. A fly grazes the dog's hide,
which shivers. Primitive brain surgery
involved poking a hole in the sufferer's
skull, a cranial skylight through which
blinding pain or hallucinations
could escape. Sometimes it worked.
Flatworms just grow new heads when needed.
I wear my learned helplessness pinned
to my blouse like a spider's egg sac,
in lieu of your corsage. Brush against me
and it'll rupture, spilling pale
pollen-like spiders. Elephants
ransacked the hunters' tent,
removed a pile of ivory tusks
and buried them. Fascinated to be yanked
out of bed by strange hands.
Vultures can fly 90 miles an hour.
He pulled the quilt tighter
around him, mistaking its stripes
for protective coloring. Male
butterflies and moths can smell

females miles away. *For Christ's sake,*
it was just a love-bite. Sponges
may follow the shapes of rocks
over which they grow. You can't
receive medical attention
at this facility. If a rabbit warren
becomes too crowded, pregnant rabbits
absorb their fetuses till there's
more room. He wakes each morning
feeling like a sore that won't heal.
Pelicans unite to drive fish
into shallow water where they're
more easily caught. For our soundtrack,
we thought of using a tape of inmates
gibbering as they defaced gravestones,
dug up and scattered the bones of those
they hated. Imagine that tenacity:
to despise your enemies' skeletons,
savoring rancor toward brittle rods
of calcium. Ranks and classes
are highly developed among insects.
Each time I pay my rent, my hoarse
landlord growls: "My dentist's Jewish.
My lawyer's Jewish. There are so many
of you." The dog lies quietly
by the stove, gnawing a cow's hoof
I have given her. My mother claims
I was born with a tail, cut off
by some short-sighted obstetrician.

■ ■ ■ ■ ■ ■ ■ ■ ■ ■

Buddha, Christ & the Clock

Gary Soto

I knew Buddha with his belly laughter,
And Christ with his ribs deep
With the shadows of every living grief.
I knew clocks, too, the twist of the knob —
Slashing long hand and small hand hobbling to keep up.
All three sat on my brother's desk.
And made me worry about my own dying.
With watery clouds living behind my eyes,
I crossed myself and prayed in bed,
My hands folded under my head, both feet skyward.
Eyes closed, I prayed
With most of my heart until I saw Buddha and Christ
Sitting together on an ancient rock.
Neither of them was arguing. Buddha was pulling
On an earlobe, fat as a pear on a tree,
And Christ was touching one of his wounds,
Gapes that were like the mouths of pulsating fish.
It was dusk. The stream was hauling
The sunlight west, where Rome lay in incense
And scandal. I wanted to ask
About my sick lungs, vest of yellowish ooze,
And wanted to ask about my three sins —
Rock, flesh, and toad run over by my bike.
I was nine. I had pared skin from my thumb
And was worried about disease.
I got up from bed, wobbling, my heart bled of most
Of its sorrow. I looked closely at these gods
On my brother's desk, and then the clock,
Its hand cutting wedges in its round face.
I weighed Buddha and Christ in my palms,
Surprised that they were light, not like sin itself
Or the furrow one wears when the casket closes
And the sobbing starts. I picked up the clock,
Heavy with machinery, its oily gears and chimes.

I shook it once, hard.
And then lay it face down.
I knew the clock didn't care like Buddha or Christ,
And that my good thoughts mattered little.
It didn't ask for prayers.
When I stood the clock between these gods,
The cogwheel nevertheless nudged ahead
The iron-colored hours.

■ ■ ■ ■ ■ ■ ■ ■ ■ ■ ■

A Walker in the City

Alicia Ostriker

What you see is what you get,
An inventory of garbage lying loose —
The poor are always with us, but the rich
Lurk behind one-way glass in limousines
And an entire class of attractive youth
Increasingly able to make money
Without actually working
Increasingly are into arts and leisure.

There's power and there's glamor and there's grief,
That's what a city is for, it's why we come,
There's violence more or less unchanged
Apart from a brief spike on nine-one-one.

The movies and TV are minting it.
Maybe the city should publish maps
Showing the areas of greatest crime
For the benefit of the interested tourist
With special blue stars for locations
Of especially famous crimes, the way in London
Two shillings lets you follow the career
Of Jack the Ripper with a little booklet.

Midtown East Side, here's where Robert Chambers
Strangled his pretty girlfriend during sex
In Central Park. Up by the reservoir
Someone from lower Harlem jumped and raped
And beat for kicks, get it, a woman jogger
Into not death but coma. We thought it was
Five boys, but that was wrong. Running between
A playground and a lake, Strawberry Fields,
Some blackbirds in the shady sycamores
Mark where across the street on 72nd
The Beatles fan Mark Chapman killed John Lennon.

Imagine there's no heaven, and imagine
The people living in a world of peace.

You have to take the A train to see where
Bernie Goetz pulled out his .44
And stopped the boy he thought another mugger
From sneering with his friends, from making fun.
They come on with their nasty stares, unlaced,
It's so hard to be white, to be a man,
When black kids don't respect you. Here's Howard Beach,
Another white on black question of turf
And good-bye Yusef Hawkins. Here's where the woman guard
In the parking garage got herself shot
Between bright eyes for being eyewitness
To some drug dealer's murder. Here a Bronx housewife
Weary of scrubbing cracked linoleum
Trying to clean her street of crack, lost it,
And the proud Haitian in his candy store the same,
As he wiped his hands on his apron,
And half a dozen children caught in crossfire
One steamy week in summer. "Mama, mama
Ayudame, no puedo" — Here's the house
Where Joel Steinberg hit his little daughter
For pleasure, or for anger, breaking bone
After bone, yanking the soft blond curls
While the mom cowered in her druggie daze.
The case is special because he was a lawyer
And had a lot of money, otherwise it wouldn't count.
It wouldn't count. And in this very courtyard
Of comfortable brick and stone
Kitty Genovese, mother of them all,
Ushering in an era,
Screamed, in 1960, being stabbed
Several times in the chest by her old boyfriend,
"Help me! Somebody help me!"
None of the neighbors who heard that woman scream
For an entire hour called the police,
A sensible restraint, all things considered.
That was the sort of thing that shocked us then.

Alicia Ostriker

It is important to keep the selection of crimes
Racially balanced and symmetrical
For tourist purposes, as the mayor says.
Right now everyone seems worried
About black people killing white people.
That's the disturbing thought if you are white,
Though naturally most of the people killed
Are men of color. There could be a key
At the map's bottom explaining what was what
If you are here on a self-guided tour.
Maybe the sponsors of the map could be
The NRA, and maybe they'd agree
To have an advertisement on the back,
Like flower shops and banks in high school yearbooks.

We'd need another color code to show
Where most non-violent crimes have taken place,
Wall Street, City Hall, Police Headquarters, The Board
Of Education (Bored of Ed) and Columbia University.
Some people rob you with a knife
Some with a fountain pen
Some with an IBM.
And a map to show the areas
Of crimes of omission?
Color the whole map red.
Color the city red.
Color it ghost white
For the death of compassion.

■■■■■■■■■■■

When Threshing Time Ends

Robert Bly

There is a time. Things end.
All the fields are clean.
Belts are put away.
And the horses go home.

What is left endures
In the minds of boys
Who wanted this joy
Never to end.

The splashing of hands,
Jokes and oats:
It was a music
Touching and fervent.

The Bible was right.
Presences come and go.
Wash in cold water.
The fire has moved.

■ ■ ■ ■ ■ ■ ■ ■ ■ ■ ■

Mortal Shower

Bob Hicok

I met my butt in a Pittsburgh
hotel room. My face
still looks like my face
but not my butt, my hair

no longer resembles an ad
for Jell-o pudding, people thought
it was chocolate pudding for years,
so thick

and rich. There was fog
in the bathroom and then not fog,
I faced my face
and then not my face, the mirror

staring at my ass
winked in the mirror
staring at my face

and the future was defined
as an effort
to use the word sag in my resume.
Have sagged, will

sag, am looking for a position
in which to maximize my sagging
potential. I once cared
what went on back there, about

the extent of grip and rise, just
as some birds crave
the reddest plumage, and I propositioned

mirrors, watched women's eyes
follow, turned in shop windows
to see if my pants
fit their purpose. Then love

and car payments, love and the sofa
needs to be moved, love and her grandmother
dies, my grandmother
dies, love
and she comes home and I'm thrilled
by her coat and voice
and the brown habit of her eyes. She

likes my ass and lies
about its travels, how it's lost
focus, and there are wattles
to come, please God
if dentures,
only partials, may Depends

be cheap in bulk and the earth
generous with its telepathy. I'm

in Pittsburgh tonight
                            and with her,
mirrors don't scare me,
room service is a gas
because she's alive, I'm a giant,
a tight-assed
titan because she's alive
and says

            come home, the Honda needs
new brakes, a robin flew
into the window today
but shook it off, just
dizzy, stunned
by reflection.

■■■■■■■■■■

The Waitress Angels Speak to Me in a Vision

Jan Beatty

Another tough Friday night of waitressing,
only fifty bucks to show for it, I throw
my stash of dirty bills on the kitchen table,
leave the change in the apron, the one that
smells like two weeks of road kill & smoke,
the mayonnaise stains gleaming, otherworldly
in the beam of cheap kitchen light. I'm tired
of waiting on drunks, tired of coming home
to myself and these 4:00 a.m. flashbacks
of men trying to put their hands on me, regulars
who think they own me, I'm sitting here staring
at the cobwebs hanging from the ceiling corner,
and that's when they came to me: the waitress angels.
I know you won't believe me — it was dust,
ordinary, paltry dust, the kind that hangs
in long fuzzy strands — don't make me say
cotton candy — but it had that oh-so-precious
softness to it — those threads became a whirling
vortex (white light and all), the change
in my apron began to clatter (throw in
a freight-train roar) and there they were:
angels at my kitchen table. You've heard of
dust to dust, well this was dust to angels,
but these were real women with hard faces,
these were waitress angels, lifers in white,
these were tough broads, broads with cigarettes,
pockets full of guest checks and loose change —
I'm just telling you what I saw — these were
sassy babes with big hair, gravely laughs
and downtown talk, they were smackin'
each other on the back, saying, "Honey,
you're full o' shit," the whole time
my chest bursting open with pride and relief
at the end of sweet obedience, the end

of virginal blue, pressed palms, and bowed heads.
Death to Silent Acceptance! These were my kind
of angels! Death to Perfunctory Humility!
No More Vale of Tears! Their hands on their
hips said: *Hey, we're angels, we're brash,*
we're trashy, we're happenin' — you got
a problem with that? These were no
walking-behind-Jesus kind of babes,
no eyes-to-the-floor floaters, these dolls
were sportin' jewelry and mascara, they were
intact, straight-on, and serious as a heart-attack —
and there I was, ready to flee the corporeal glut
of my life for this hip heaven, when I asked to
join them and they shut me down: "Look, sweetie,
this ain't no picnic here — we're on break right now —
we're flyin' out to shake down some bad tippers —
besides, this celestial trip is overrated. Check it out,
your life ain't so bad."

She Wipes Out Time

Tess Gallagher

She wipes out time
like shaking horseflies from her white mane.
She would like to mail a postcard to
the place she was born. Not just to anyone,
but to the postmaster. "When I stopped to
see him they said he'd gone out into
his fields. He had forty acres," she says. "I didn't
go looking for him." I gaze across America, across death
to the postmaster walking his Missouri fields
in the wide sweep of farmland, woods, rivers and caves
I explored as a child by horseback.

"A thousand acres," she would say, restoring
them to herself and bequeathing them
to us. "Your grandfather had a thousand acres."
That sentence, still a kingdom.
The land gone, but the words of it sustaining,
as if those acres — the slack, timbrel memory
of them — somehow allowed one to carry
an expanse of loss. But who needs
a thousand acres? Better to have the thought
without the bother, to walk the mind under walnut trees
on the slope behind a barn that has long since
fallen away — as the mind
falls away with the roots exposed so
the dry tendrils of small bushes that cling
bird-footed to air remind us that air itself
is a soil apparitional to desire.

I too want to go back. To go
through the long stride of her wish
to make this sign of remembrance: a postcard
to the postmaster. In my mother's memory
of home, on which I lean, he still walks his forty acres
though I know he is long dead. Is it cruel to tell her
and obliterate that switch-back her yearning makes
to resurrect him — he who now represents a place
she can't quite reach in her mind, except
through the hyphenated corridor
of his perpetual looming up as a broken promise?
I said I'd stop and see him . . . calm disappointment
in her voice. But why blot even false hope
to certify a useless truth? Any God would let him
have this saunter in the mind-works of another, so I
say nothing, let him live, beckoning
across time and death.

I am attracted to this new fold in time
by which the postmaster escapes death through having
gone for a walk. But I am also a selfish steward
of the moment and want her
with me. "Mother," I ask, "when did you last see
him?" Her voice has the lilt of truth. Memory's strange
accordion crumples expertly under the tail of
the monkey: "Oh, a couple of years ago."
"Mother, it's twenty years since you were back."
Then, making her arrow sing: "How time flies!"

By custodial violence I yank her to my template,
offer the card she wanted to send. She forgets what it
was for, used it all day as a page marker
in her handbook on African violets. Later she reads
aloud: *Water them from the top*
and you'll rot the crown. Always let them take
what they need from the bottom — her reprimand steely
with innocence, so I suspect language itself
has flown defensively from the page into her
mouth with the audacity of particulate, unquenchable
matter that is, at any moment, fully able to restore
girlish laughter to the high veranda, the postmaster's
hand closing vast distances to my father's courtship letters
ten years of handing them over to her — letters
from her lover, far away in the desperate burrowings of
the coal mines. And now depths darker.
Twenty years toiling under us in the black ore of absence,
as the violets drink on their sills
from little bowls of the mind.

■ ■ ■ ■ ■ ■ ■ ■ ■ ■ ■

A Summer Afternoon

Mary Oliver

From the third-story corner of the house, from a hole in the bricks, the bees swarmed. Then they fell, a glittering heap, to the lawn. We lay on the grass and watched them, hoping to see the Queen.

Then we saw her! But, alas, her wings were torn to shreds. Never again could those wings lift her into the air! Perhaps the scouting bees brought news of distant gardens, for occasionally the bees rose and whirled through the air. But always they returned; the bees would never leave their Queen, and the Queen could not fly.

We brought a box and put the Queen into it. She was frantic in the light, in her uncovered state. Some of the bees followed her into the box and covered her with their own bodies.

So we understood that the bees must be given a city. We found a beekeeper — in an hour he came, with a hive which he lifted from his truck and carried onto the lawn. His movements were slow, almost gracious. He removed the lid from the hive and softly tapped the glittering mass from the box into it. The bees sank from sight.

Quickly the news passed among the other bees — the Queen is in the hive! They did not hesitate. They floated to the hive entrance. By the thousands, trembling, they entered.

■

Now, it is the end of the first day. The hive sits on the lawn, very white in the gathering twilight. The last bees are swirling at the entrance. By dark every one will have entered.

We lean close to hear their humming, which is loud and vigorous. The beekeeper says, this is the sound of satisfaction. The beekeeper tells us how, in the quiet grove where he has arranged a dozen white cities, he often lingers to listen. It is a privilege, he says, to stand among the hives, to hear such happiness.

217

Homo Will Not Inherit

Mark Doty

Downtown anywhere and between the roil
of bathhouse steam — up there the linens of joy
and shame must be laundered again and again,

all night — downtown anywhere
and between the column of feathering steam
unknotting itself thirty feet above the avenue's

shimmered azaleas of gasoline,
between the steam and the ruin
of the Cinema Paree (marquee advertising

its own milky vacancy, broken showcases sealed,
ticketbooth a hostage wrapped in tape
and black plastic, captive in this zone

of blackfronted bars and bookstores
where there's nothing to read
but longing's repetitive texts,

where desire's unpoliced, or nearly so)
someone's posted a xeroxed headshot
of Jesus: permed, blond, blurred at the edges

as though photographed through a greasy lens,
and inked beside him, in marker strokes:
HOMO WILL NOT INHERIT. Repent & be saved.

I'll tell you what I'll inherit: the margins
which have always been mine, downtown after hours
when there's nothing left to buy,

the dreaming shops turned in on themselves,
seamless, intent on the perfection of display,
the bodegas and offices lined up, impenetrable:

edges no one wants, no one's watching. Though
the borders of this shadow-zone (mirror and dream
of the shattered streets around it) are chartered

by the police, and they are required,
some nights, to redefine them. But not now, at twilight,
permission's descending hour, early winter darkness

pillared by smoldering plumes. The public city's
ledgered and locked, but the secret city's boundless;
from which to these tumbling towers arise? I'll tell you

what I'll inherit: steam, and the blinding symmetry
of some towering man, fifteen minutes
of forgetfulness incarnate. I've seen flame

flicker around the edges of the body,
pentecostal, evidence of inhabitation.
And I have been possessed of the god myself,

I have the temporary apparition
salving another, I have been his visitation, I say it
without arrogance, I have been an angel for minutes

at a time, and I have for hours believed
—without judgment, without condemnation—
that in each body, however obscured or recast—

is the divine body—common, habitable—
the way in a field of sunflowers
you can see every bloom's

the multiple expression
of a single shining idea,
which is the face hammered into joy.

I'll tell you what I'll inherit:
erasure, stupidity, hell, exile
inside the chalked lines of the police,

who must resemble what they punish,
the exile you require of me,
you who's posted this invitation

to a heaven nobody wants.
You who must be patrolled,
who adore constraint,

I'll tell you what I'll inherit:
no pallid temple but the real palace
of risk and longing, pleasure and erasure.

Always in the man's body overcoming mine
the uncontrollable legacy:
open, permeable, brightness rising

side by side with the darker enactments
of longing. When I say I "want" a man,
it isn't nearly as simple as you think.

It isn't possession; I am not long
in being done with him, no matter how
beautiful. But the anticipated and actual

memory, the moment flooded by skin
and the knowledge of it, the gesture
and its description — do I need to say it? —

the flesh *and* the word. And I'll tell you,
you who can't wait to abandon your body,
what you want me to, maybe something like

what you've imagined, a dirty story:
Years ago, in the baths,
a man walked into the steam,

the gorgeous deep indigo of him gleaming,
solid tight flanks, the intricately ridged abdomen —
and after he invited me to his room,

nudging his key toward me,
as if perhaps I spoke another tongue
and required the plainest of gestures,

after we'd been, you understand,
worshipping a while in his church,
he said to me, *I'm going to punish your mouth.*

I can't tell you what that did to me.
My shame was redeemed then;
I won't need to be punished in the afterlife.

It wasn't that he hurt me, more
than that: the spirit's transactions
are enacted here, now — no one needs

your eternity. This failing city's
radiant as any we'll ever know,
paved with oily rainbow, charred gates

jeweled with tags, swoops of letters
over letters, indecipherable as anything
written by desire. I'm not ashamed

to love Babylon's scrawl. How could I be?
It's written on my face as much as on
these walls. This city's inescapable,

gorgeous, and on fire. I have my kingdom.

■■■■■■■■■■■

Don't Mention It

Michael Casey

first of all you don't refer
to scars on someone's face
and you don't mention to Gregory Dano
anything about cute Vietnamese kids
just don't do it
don't say a syllable OK?
for one thing he might be
on the down side of being
awake for three days
for another
once this little kid
walks up to us
throws a grenade beats feet
Gregory didn't even see the kid
we had to tell him about it later
why his face looks like someone
scraped it with a grate-o-matic
didn't even see the grenadier
as it happened Greg was unconscious
before hitting the ground
the kid on the other hand was dead
before he hit the ground
so just eat your can of potato chips
watch the movie
and shut the fuck up OK

■ ■ ■ ■ ■ ■ ■ ■ ■ ■ ■

The Road to Son Tay

Kevin Bowen

How many paintings like this one?
A run of low hills stretching above a plain,
a river drifting slowly past a scene of tea fires,
ochre fans set out, red and purple umbrellas
planted for shade. Out here, a man or woman's legs
might spread like continents. For miles nothing
but the paddies' green and yellow stalks,
narrow lines of kilns white smoke rising,
wash hung out from new brick houses,
orchards of eucalyptus, banana, pepper trees,
green lily ponds, white stone markers inching out
like fingers to mark the number of kilometers
back to the capital. Here, a woman runs gracefully
across a field; in her arms she carries a bouquet
of sugar cane. Behind her stick-like figures move
in that familiar stiff-legged walk, bottoms of pants
skirting mud and dust, carts tilted off in every direction,
the impossible angles of bicycles left at crossroads.
Here and there, the tin barns, the scarves of brown
or yellow bent across paddy fields, or moving like
lines of monks. By the duck pond, a lone water buffalo
leans to the afternoon sun as farmers raise their sweaty
white shirts ready to break off from their labors.
The sweet aroma of fresh manured fields fills the air
as pigs nuzzle in the gray mud by the river bank.
Somewhere out there, Tay Phuong Pagoda, the tired
buffalo lying down, its head facing West.

*Son Tay is a village 23 miles west of Hanoi, the site of a North Vietnamese
prisoner-of-war camp during the Vietnam War.

■■■■■■■■■■■

Rabbit Hole

Laura Kasischke

Not a hole you could live in. Not

a hole you could use to climb into or out of
any trouble at all. For

a long time I thought
I was the only one. The only
one this beautiful, the only one who'd ever been

so madly in love I could die. Then I got old.

Truly, I got old. I saw a girl today who was

the girl I was. Head thrown back in laughter. She didn't
see me, and never dreamt . . .

Full of love, made of lies. The lies
were like a lot of shiny pins
sticking the self that wasn't me
to the one I could have been. That

pinned-self, it used to make
a thin whisper as I walked, rustle
its see-through taffeta in the breeze. It smelled

like ether, and didn't bleed. That

rabbit freezes, smelling me — its
blank eye wide. Finally

it hurries into
a narrow hole in the snow, a place
where it's no less cold. But no noise.
A sense that there's a sun, but that it's far away —

light weakened
by the effort of shining, like

light shining through lingerie.

■■■■■■■■■■■

Ararat

Stuart Dybek

No one even noticed that the downpour
had let up. By then, the entire
mangy menagerie was engaged
in the orgy that passes for procreation:
donkeys mounting elephants, lions
laying down with lambs, or llamas,
or lemurs, or whatever was available;
boy, we got some strange new mutts,
and by the time the alleged dove
came back with the olive branch
(it was actually a vulture with a bone)
me and Mrs. Flood had battened down the hatches
and locked ourselves into the cabin.
With no one at the wheel, the drifting Ark
groaned and squealed like a flophouse bed
with swayback springs, then banged aground
flinging passengers forward and aft
as if they were commuters on a rush-hour bus.
Mrs. Flood, she never missed a beat.
"Give it to me again, you crazy old bastard,"
she said. "Stick it here or here
or anywhere, just do me, daddy,"
and that's when through the porthole,
emitting light reflected in the sweat
along her spine, I glimpsed
what might have been a rainbow.

■ ■ ■ ■ ■ ■ ■ ■ ■ ■ ■

Pantoum, with Swan

Maxine Kumin

Bits of his down under my fingernails
a gob of his spit behind one ear
and a nasty welt where the nib of his beak
bit down as he came. It was our first date.

A gob of his spit behind one ear,
his wings still fanning. I should have known better,
I should have bitten him off on our first date,
and yet for some reason I didn't press charges;

I wiped off the wet. I should have known better.
They gave me the morning-after pill
and shook their heads when I wouldn't press charges.
The yolk that was meant to hatch as Helen

failed to congeal, thanks to the morning-after pill
and dropped harmlessly into the toilet
so that nothing became of the lost yolk, Helen,
Troy, wooden horse, forestalled in one swallow

flushed harmlessly away down the toilet.
The swan had by then stuffed Euripides, Sophocles
— leaving out Helen, Troy, Agamemnon —
the whole house of Atreus, the rest of Greek tragedy,

stuffed in my head, every strophe of Sophocles.
His knowledge forced on me, yet Bird kept the power.
What was I to do with ancient Greek history
lodged in my cortex to no avail?

I had his knowledge, I had no power
the year I taught Yeats in a classroom so pale
that a mist enshrouded the ancient religions
and bits of his down flew from under my fingernails.

■ ■ ■ ■ ■ ■ ■ ■ ■ ■ ■

Wrestling with Each Other

Albert Goldbarth

When the President declares the war over,
the other wars aren't over. The dust
is still at war with the subatomic needles
of electrical charge, that stitch the flesh together.
The light is still at war with the sour dark
in the toe of the shoe. The woman besieges the man;
the man, the woman. The white; and the yolk.
When the Holy Benevolent Tyrant of Tyrants says
the bloody crusade is ceased, the opposition of Eternity
and History continues. That's not funny; and can't you
take a joke. Reality; and "reality." It's dawn, you
wake; mind rises into the body like sun
above the horizon. Another morning.
Fire; and water. Hook; and eye.

■

It's raining, a light gray skein of it, and
she sees this as the house's being woven
ever tighter into a viable notion of family. She
wants a child. She hugs herself at the window,
repeating the feel of that tightening weave
and everything it means: a nest,
I guess, comes close as a symbol. Meanwhile,
the weather is ruining his plans
for hunting dove this afternoon. I love
these friends of mine, and with the priceless coin
of their marriage I can't choose sides. He
doesn't want children. All day
it rains. The stream; and the bank.
The rush of flood; and stasis. All day and into the night.

■

228

In this 14th century Sienese *Virgin and Child,* Mary
is stolidly shapeless under her mantle, certainly
her gold leaf chest is breastless, is as flat as the panel
it's painted on — and yet the infant suckles,
from a small flesh-colored ball the painter's set
against the gold and purple cloth around Her armpit,
so it is and isn't corporeal, so it might be something
pliant and taut and mammalian, something as veined
as a ball of blue cheese, something soapy and nubbled,
or might be just the brief, begrudged idea of this
in the overwhelming gold holiness of the scene.
The ageless incompatibility. One night: "You
creep, you only want me for my titties." The next: "*Now*
what's the matter? *Look* — doesn't this turn you on?"

■

When the emir waves his feathered wand, declaring
the border skirmishes at an end, there's still that line
in quantum physics where the particles of "our" "time" meet
the tachyons of "backwards" "time," there's still
conflicting powers in our voids and sines and serums.
When the pasha and the brigadier sign their treaty,
God continues needing feuding with Darwin,
cop with robber, rust with iron, "truth" with "subjectivity."
It rains; it sounds like a tommygun on the roof.
The earthworms swell and slither. And then, of course,
the early birds. When clan and clan lay down their swords
beneath the Tree of Truce, even so, one still is drawn
to that line by Dickens: " ... misery and magnificence
wrestling with each other upon every rood of ground in the prospect."

■

Mary, Mother of God and Secret Agent from Space, is
one scenario. Fantasy novels in which the Earth's
a war zone, and our species is the working out
of another galaxy's battles, or another, eldermost
pantheon of dark deities'. Then every brachiate
dwindle or surge of our evolution, every noted
fascicle of devotion or gumption or dumbfuck luck
in History, is one more moving-forward
of foreign hostilities. Even the most benign of mornings
on the patio. Or we're warriors controlled by our genes.
Their needs. The tides of fortune, and the nucleotides.
The Cross. The cross look. Sun in the puddles
left by the train. A man and a woman sitting down
to breakfast in that relentless machine.

■

I've weighted the game; she *doesn't* want a child,
it's dissatisfaction airier, slipperier, than this, though
no less painful when it stabs or when her own reflection
stares back from the window filled with thick gray weather
inside her skull. He *doesn't* bag dove: I couldn't pass up
that mild bird with the olive branch
heraldically nipped in its beak. But
their distress is true. The rain and whatever
pall of contention it's come to mean is true,
and will return, with all of its fierce life
and erasure. It will be there at the end,
whatever the dialogue, it will have the last word.
It was here at the origin, stirring the mix.
The first sex on Earth was division.

■

Hegemony; and the subaltern. Particle; and wave.
The neocortex; and the hypothalamus. Honey;
bitter herb. Having spoken just now to both of them,
I set the phone back in its plastic cradle
as if it could explode. When every military wallah
lauds the ways of peace, the lamb beside the lion,
there will still be my two friends. My head
is feverish with their bicker, a simmer
of helplessness won't leave my brow,
and I lean my head against the cool,
the impartial, glass of the window — feeling it leach
this fever away, with the press of its clarity.
And, from the other side: the tapping,
the reminding, almost the arguing now, of the rain.

The Psychic Detective: Fantasy

Ai

The victim is lying on her side
as if trying to hide the imprint
of the boot heel that smashed her cheek.
As the river runs through her wounds
(and there are many)
I am coldly examining her body this morning.
"What do you think, Bob?" I ask my partner.
"Do you think she was out shopping?
See that empty shopping bag there
the one from that fancy mall."
"Who cares?" he says.
"She's dead, end of story."
It isn't ordinary as crimes go,
because she's so mutilated.
He hated her naturally,
because he imagined that she was his mother,
or some other female who wronged him
and he's in payback mode,
cracked her skull maybe with a bat,
probably his kid's. "What do you say, Bob?"
He shrugs. Psychology is not his thing.
He likes putting it together
like a math problem he can solve by adding one plus two,
but that doesn't work with psychos.
They hide from the average crime solver.
Somebody like me has to go down into hell with them
and bring them back,
even though they're radioactive with an evil
that clings to your skin.
I'm still hot from the last crime.
Hear the crackle and pop
as I pass through the mind of this killer.
There he is on his knees, his eyes filled with a red glow.
He has to pee and does into the water

that runs over her shattered face,
then he zips up, he leaves
just as the sun rises as big and as orange
as those lollipops
his mom used to buy him
when the first urge to destroy
made him tear apart his toy rabbit.
No, it was her, naked, her big breasts
swinging over him that first set him off,
as she bent down to say good night
as he lay in bed,
the odor of alcohol and a fight with his dad
suffocating him, making him reach up
and pinch the nipple inches from his face.
His mom said, "Suck on it, go ahead,
if you're man enough."
He wasn't then, but he is now
and I'm on his trail.
I'm going to swallow him
like the whale did Jonah.
Who am I kidding? He's gone, Bob.
I won't catch this one,
because he's disappeared into the ether
of ordinary life.
Can't you feel it?
This kill wasn't planned.
It was some kind of post-traumatic thing
where a scent, a sound, maybe a glance
threw him into his murderer's trance
and he entered his mother's spread thighs,
his eyes closed tightly
as he felt those breasts press against his head
like two feather pillows, so soft, so . . .
Then he came out of it
in his driveway.
His rosebushes, his azaleas,
the big cedar tree
and the kid's swing reassured him
that what had happened

was only a fantasy
and he told himself so over and over,
even as he cleaned a few remaining drops of blood
from his hands,
then watered his rosebushes
and greeted his wife with a kiss
when she came home from the store.
He did not acknowledge, or go near that door
behind which his mother
said "just once more, son, once more"
and he tried, he really did,
before he fell asleep,
only to wake in his own bed
and tell himself he'd had a bad dream
and leave it at that
and leave us with another unsolved murder,
another body to send to the morgue
to be claimed by relatives
who'll never have another peaceful day like his
when it's hard to believe he's the one who's alive
and not on the other side
with that girl he met at the mall and his mother
beating on a door
even the psychic detective can't open.

■ ■ ■ ■ ■ ■ ■ ■ ■ ■ ■

Eddie

John Balaban

Hadn't seen Eddie for some time,
wheeling his chair through traffic,
skinny legs in shorts, T-shirted,
down at the corner off Dixie Highway,
lifting his Coke cup to the drivers
backed up, bumper-to-bumper, at the light.
Sometimes he slept on the concrete bench
up from Joe's News. Sometimes police
would take him in and he said he didn't mind
because he got three squares and sometimes
a doctor would look at his legs, paralyzed,
he said, since the cop in New York shot him
when he tried to steal a car. Sad story,
of the kind we've learned to live with.

One rainy day he looked so bad, legs
ballooned, ankles to calves, clothes soaked,
I shoved a $20 in his cup. But, like I said,
I hadn't seen him around so yesterday
I stopped and asked this other panhandler
where's Eddie? "Dead," he said. Slammed
by a truck that ran the light, crushed
into his wheelchair. Dead, months ago.

My wife says he's better off dead,
but I don't know. Behind his smudged glasses
his eyes were clever. He had a goofy smile
but his patter was sharp. His legs were a mess
and he had to be lonely. But spending days
in the bright fanfare of traffic and
those nights on his bench, with the moon
huge in the palm trees, the highway quiet,
some good dreams must have come to him.

■ ■ ■ ■ ■ ■ ■ ■ ■ ■ ■

The Animals of America

Stephen Dunn

The animals have come down from the hills
and through the forests and across the prairies.
They are American animals, and carry with them
a history of their slaughter. There's not one
who doesn't sleep with an eye open.

Out of necessity the small have banded
with the large, the large with the large
of different species. When dark comes
they form an enormous circle.

It's all, after years of night-whispers
and long-range cries, coming together.

To make a new world the American animals
know there must be sacrifices. Every evening
a prayer is said for the spies who've volunteered
to be petted in the houses of the enemy.
"They are savages," one reported,
"let no one be fooled by their capacity for loving."

NONFICTION

■ ■ ■ ■ ■ ■ ■ ■ ■ ■ ■ ■

The Big Game

Peter Najarian

I didn't know I was the supreme reality. I thought I was a young man with a passport and a destination. When my friend, Bob Hass, tells this story he likes to make me into a budding intellectual who had just come from London wearing a foreign correspondent raincoat with a copy of Sartre in my pocket. The truth is I actually did have one of those long coats with the big flaps and all those buttons, though Bob thought he was making it up. It was a very old one that my other friend, Bill Belli, gave me and that he got from his friend, James Jones, who used to wear it all the time in Paris until he finally bought a new one. I loved *From Here To Eternity* in those days and so I would wear that old relic as if it were my big brother's, but then it got stolen and I didn't really have it when I got back to the States. Nevertheless it was true that I was still carrying a lot of baggage from the Old World.

I had been gone three very important years. I remember sitting in Jimmy's, a cheap Greek restaurant in Soho where I often had supper, and waiting for my usual stew and *fasulyah* I would read the *Evening Standard* which was covering a new cultural revolution in California. It seemed to have started with the Free Speech Movement in the autumn of 1964, or just after I had left, and by the time I was reading about it the streets of Berkeley and San Francisco seemed covered with flowers. I wanted to go back, I felt I was missing out on something. Then one day I got a letter from my friend, Robert Pinsky, who was in his last year at Stanford, and he suggested I apply for a grant called a Stegner Fellowship. He had something similar and he'd put in a good word for me.

He was gone when I arrived but he gave me some names to look up in case I felt disoriented. Ed McClanahan was one and I liked him right away. He was also a friend of Ken Kesey and I told him how much I liked Kesey's second novel, *Sometimes a Great Notion*. *Cuckoo's Nest* was okay, I said, but *Notion* was really special. He must have remembered because a few days later he woke me up and said Kesey just got out of the joint and was crashing at his place for a few days. He needed a ride to his probation officer in Redwood City that morning, and Ed had to teach a class. Maybe I could take him? Sure, I said, and since I had to rush I couldn't have had more than a slice of toast, if I remember right, because my empty stomach was going to play a big part in the rest of the day.

Kesey was only in his early thirties at the time, but I was even younger and I looked up to him a bit. He was by then quite famous, which is why he got busted for grass and had to spend six months in a work farm near Soledad. He was a very good young man, wise for his years, and his big handshake was gentle and confident. He had a very strong presence and yet he looked rather odd. He had good posture and was planted solid and straight, and yet wearing those old free-box clothes that were too small and tight for his chunky limbs he looked like an enormous child, especially with his shiny bald head and his curly blond hair around his ears. Later I would learn that innocence was indeed his best quality and he was the kind of person who could trust you immediately because why shouldn't he trust you? Was there something bad about you that he should beware of? Getting ready to go I took a closer look at one of his front teeth and noticed it had a patch of blue and some red stripes. His dentist did that for him, he said. He lost his cap in the joint and his hip dentist made a new one dyed like the U.S. flag.

We got in my bug with the sunroof down and he introduced me to his wife, Fay, a quiet and attractive young woman with a solidness not unlike his own, and she asked where I was from. West Hoboken, New Jersey, I said, and they both chuckled. Why were they chuckling? Oh nothing, they said, it was just that McClanahan hurried the message and not getting it straight they thought they were going with someone who was either a Nigerian from Armenia or an Armenian from Nigeria.

We chatted along the way, Kesey about the joint and I about social work in Harlem before I went abroad. They were invaluable experiences and through them we got a closer look at the underside of our America and the forces of the straight world. We were kinfolk in a way, at least I like to think we were. All sentient beings are kin of course, but we are so limited in our separate shells that, especially when we're young, we look for others who share our way of life. Kesey was one of the family; he was not only an artist but a seeker with a free-box wardrobe and I felt at home with him. Many of us had grown up feeling so alone in an alienating society that it was a tremendous boost to find others like ourselves and to roam our continent sharing pads and simple meals. We all need each other but very often our separate paths become narrow and nuclear, as we used to say, and should something go wrong with them we find ourselves in deep water. Many of us, then as now, had come from deep water and were looking for a shore where we could be at home again.

Back at McClanahan's everyone was at work or school, and after Fay took off to meet someone Kesey and I hung out in the rec room which was a cozy little space with a warm rug and batik spreads. One of the walls was covered with a huge blow-up of the Marx brothers fooling around and Harpo smoking a hookah. He was popping his trademark eyeballs and his curly hair looked a little like Kesey's. Kesey was no Harpo but he would've liked to have been, I think. There was a heaviness about him that he wanted to lighten and his shoulders curved under whatever that burden was that he carried so silently. We each have a burden and I felt his in the quietness and gentleness of his powerful body that could hurt someone if he ever let go. I haven't seen him in twenty years, and I'm mostly imagining now for I never got to know him well, but in person, at least with me, he was very different from the unleashed and abandoned voice I heard in his prose.

We lounged around the rug and he opened a book and started reading from it. He discovered it in the joint, he said, and he wanted to share it with me. It was called the *I Ching*. I had never heard of it before; I was reading *Being and Nothingness* in those days, and when he asked me to throw coins on the rug I began to feel a little uncomfortable. But then the phone rang and when he returned he said the Doctor just called and would be over in a few minutes. Expecting a real doctor I was naturally a bit surprised to see a guy wearing denims and looking like an exquisite hood who had just stolen a tank of gas. He wasn't, of course, he was just a sweet young man like your favorite cousin or the familiar delivery boy who brings your goodies each week. What the tank was for I had no idea but Harpo Marx and the *I Ching* and the beautiful weather were all in progress and I was not about to stop it. I was ignorant in many ways but I had been around, I was familiar with hemp and poppies and even ate a few moldy cactus buds way back when I lived in the Village. And yet I had never tasted what may have been the subject of that familiar line I had heard so many times but never thought of before: "It's a gas, man."

They put it in the middle of the rug, inhaled their fill and then let me have some. It was great stuff, to say the least. You can get a mild taste of it from your local dentist if he's hip. It's not paradise, but even with fingers in your mouth and your gums bleeding it can be a moment of bliss, as William James might say, and it wasn't long before we were rolling around the rug and hugging each other, the *I Ching* open to an auspicious page and Harpo raising his eyebrows. It was then that Kesey turned to me and said softly:

"*Cosmo*, that's your name. The Armenian Cosmo."

It sounded good. I liked it. It had a nice full sound to it. *Cosmo*. Sure, why not?

The tank was not full when we started and we finished it much too soon. Once you start sucking you don't want to stop, and Kesey, to keep the high going I guess, passed around some uppers. I never liked them but I was careless and took one as a gesture of friendliness. Fay happened to return around then and said so and so were waiting in a car for the ride up to San Francisco. I thought it was a private trip and was about to say so-long when Kesey asked me if I wanted to come. Sure, why not, I'd leave my car by McClanahan's and return when I'd return. I was young, I was strong, I could go and do whatever I wanted, right?

We arrived around dusk, which in mid-November must have been just after five o'clock, and we parked by a little church. Why were we going to a little church? Because, Kesey said, his friend and lawyer, an Armenian if I'm not mistaken, had bought this old church and renovated it into a high-class pad. It may have been, Kesey said, an Armenian church.

I was jittery by then. The high from the gas was over and with an empty stomach I couldn't have relaxed even without the dexedrine. There were a bunch of people inside and I was told that some of them were from a new rock group called the Grateful Dead. It felt like an ominous name and seemed to float above the new faces like the tobacco smoke purling in the nacred light of the huge space, everyone hanging around quietly and waiting for the chicken that was frying in the kitchen way back there behind where the altar used to be. Kesey, wanting me to feel at home, touched my shoulder and said he wanted me to meet someone. He said her name was Black Maria and he introduced me as Cosmo. Yes, he took on the role of a paterfamilias, but he sincerely liked people and wished them well. He left with her and mingled with the others.

She must have been in her early twenties then, just a child. But with her long wild hair and her silence she really did seem like a Black Maria and not the young and innocent Jane Doe from an ordinary suburb she had just recently fled. We didn't say much and then the chicken came out, but my stomach was shriveled by now and all I wanted was something to drink. I saw some guys in the corner passing around a big cup and though I figured it was more than tea, what did it matter? I joined the circle and when the cup came to me I finished it, thinking there'd be more. The others looked at me and in my dim memory it seems that one of them may have even said, "Groovy, man."

Meanwhile someone said the Doors were playing in Winterland, neither of which I had ever heard of, and Kesey was calling a Bill Graham to ask if we could all get in. Yes, we could, and so we all piled into the back of a big truck and we were there in a matter of minutes.

As we walked in I asked the Doctor if I could get a ride back to Palo Alto with him later and he said sure, just meet him by this door in the lobby. We walked through the door and Kesey said let's go nearer the stage, but I was starting to feel a little whoozy so I just sat in the last row of seats by the door where I was to meet the Doctor. I'd just sit there, I thought, and observe everything. I was the observer type and this was my first rock concert. The Doors, eh? Why were they called the Doors?

Then I noticed the whoozy feeling was something in particular. What was it? Oh yes, the tea, there was something in the tea. There was something in the tea like those putrid cactus buds way back in the Village. I recognized the same uncoiling flow inside my navel. It reminded me of the slow and mesmeric swirl of tiny bubbles inside those amoebas and cells of grass we once studied in freshman biology. The cactus trip had been mild and thinking it would happen again I decided to just sit back and flow with it. I could handle it, I thought, I could handle anything. I'd just sit there and wait for the Doctor who was going to meet me by the door.

Black Maria came instead. "C'mon," she said. "Let's go join the others." "Oh no," I said very seriously, "I can't." "Why can't you?" she asked, smiling. "Because," I said, and it was then I noticed my hands gripping the seat as if I were on a plane that had suddenly lost a wing, "because . . . because if I leave this seat I'll never get back to Palo Alto." "Oh sure you will," she said. "Why shouldn't you?" "Oh no," I said, and I was gripping with not just my hands but every muscle I could find as if I would unravel into bubbles should I ever let go. "No . . . no, the Doctor said he was going to meet me by this door and take me back to Palo Alto. I have to get back to Palo Alto." My car, my passport, my typewriter, everything that glued me together was in Palo Alto and if I left that seat I would lose them forever. "Oh, you'll get back to Palo

Alto," she said, her voice more and more like a siren's. "Come with me and I'll show you the way." "You will?" I whimpered, and suddenly I was three years old and lost in a sea of alien faces and she might be the great Maria who could lead me home. "Sure I will," she said, and letting go of the seat that was my raft I grabbed her skirt as if it were a lifeline through the maelstrom of the crowd. "Are you sure?" I pleaded. "Are you sure you will show me the way?" "Sure," she said, and looking over her shoulder with a Mona Lisa smile that could have been lethal, her wild hair flowing in the strobes and her eyes like jewels, she said again but now languidly, "Sure, I'll show you the way, and . . . ," her voice suddenly selfish and lascivious, "you'll show *me* the way." Oh no, I moaned, she also drank that tea, and I let go of her and fell to the floor with Jim Morrison bellowing in a voice that seemed to echo through the prehistoric mews of an endless labyrinth, *Show me the way . . .* yes, yes, show me the way, please show me the way *to the next whiskey bar . . .* Oh no, I cried, I would never get back, I would never get back, and it was there on the floor of a former ice rink and now a phantom carnival that this I who is typing these words first encountered what could never be expressed in words and is that part of us where we can't hold on any longer nor have any reason to hold on. Yes, there was something in that tea much stronger than a few cactus buds from Smith's Cactus Ranch, something very pure, which was still around in those days, and which, with an empty stomach and some dexedrine, was more than enough to float me through the door and lead me not to Palo Alto but to you know what and if you don't you should. We should all know that place inside us where there is no outside and we're all together in the flesh and blood, yes, this very flesh and blood. Why we ever left it is the great mystery.

But don't misunderstand me, I don't refer the same travel agent. There are different trips and you should have a guide or at least a friend who can stand by so you don't get trampled. Once you're there you're there, but you don't stay there forever, you get up from the floor and if you're three years old again you want to be in a familiar garden, otherwise you're on a bummer, as we used to say.

After the deep crying and the waves of ecstasy *et cetera*, I got up from the floor and had I not resisted losing "my life" I suppose I might have continued through the gates of illumination a while longer. But I was freaked out, as we say, and the more I resisted the further I went through the other gates where everyone was not only a freak but a possible threat. I knew I drank something but I didn't know if knowing could be trusted. As far as I knew I was not me anymore and I might never be

again, I was gone forever and yet I kept struggling to get back, and I
mean this physically, with every muscle in my vital centers all struggling
to hold myself together lest I dissolve into the overwhelming chaos and
the Doors singing, *Light My Fire*. Were you ever lost when you were
very small? Do you remember how it felt to panic on an alien planet? Or
did you ever go swimming and feel an undertow pull you out where you
thrash as hard as you can and yet get no closer to shore? I stood up and
searched desperately for some way out or in or back or wherever and
suddenly someone like a ghost was saying hello to me. "What are you
doing here?" she asked.

It was Marjorie Katcher. Marjorie Katcher was Bill Belli's old girlfriend.
In fact I introduced them when she was at Douglass and I was at Rutgers
and so forth and so on like buried and hermetic heiroglyphs on a Dead
Sea scroll. Bill and I had lost touch with her and now with a face more
elastic than flesh she was staring at me and saying, "This is really not the
Marjorie you once knew." "It's not?" I asked, taking her more literally
than she could have known. "Oh no," she said, "the Marjorie you knew
is dead." "She is?" I said, not at all with doubt. "Yes," she said, "I'm
reborn now." "Oh," I said, "that's good, that's very good. How did you
do it?" "I'm a mother now," she said. "I have a baby daughter." "Oh,"
I said in despair, "I don't think I can do that." "No," she said, "you
can't." "No, I can't," I said, and unable to talk with any logic I wandered
off and left her with her daughter on the other side of the universe.

How I got back to the door I don't know and though useless by now
it was the only bearing I had. Yet when I walked to the lobby who was
suddenly coming in and wearing a Captain Marvel suit?

"Hey, man!" he said. "Good to see you here." It was Ed McClanahan.
But not really. The Ed McClanahan I once knew, the one person who was
my link back to a face in a mirror, was a jeans-and-flannel young writer
with a wife and kids and a warm solid home, not a flashing Captain
Marvel suit in a lobby full of beads. Oh no, I moaned, I would never get
back, I would never get back.

"What's the matter?" he asked. "Are you all right?" No, I said, I
was not all right, and I wandered outside like a street person who's
mentally disturbed, as they say, and I would have kept going had he not
rescued me. Where would I have gone had he not rescued me? Where
was there to go without the ground always tilting? The police? The
hospital? Or perhaps a diner or a laundromat? Did you ever see what
a city looks like when you have no eyelids? I got a glimpse before he
grabbed my arm and led me back.

He understood what was happening. I told him I drank some tea and he knew what was in it. The police didn't know, the hospital didn't know, most of what we called our society didn't know, but there was a growing number who would learn and he was among them, dear Ed McClanahan, who gave up his good time with the gang so he could sit with a lost soul the rest of the night. Where is he now? I just called the English department at Stanford but they didn't know. I haven't seen him in twenty years but I'm still grateful for his kindness. He's out there somewhere, I hope. Someone told me one of his novels was published a while back. I must try and find it.

"Are you sure you're Ed McClanahan?" I kept asking him. Yes, he said, or at least he was the one I needed him to be. Then who was Captain Marvel? Captain Marvel was a little crippled boy who said the magic word and became a god. The magic word. Ah yes, the magic word.

We had come back to Palo Alto but it was not the same of course. We were back with Harpo and the *I Ching* and now I knew what they were trying to say. Now I knew what *far out* meant and *blow your mind*. Now I knew why the Doors were called the *Doors* and why Kesey called me *Cosmo*.

"Are you sure you're Ed McClanahan?" Yes, he was sure and yes, everything would be okay and tomorrow would be the Big Game just like always.

"The Big Game? What Big Game?" The Big Game, I knew what the Big Game was, didn't I? "Sure, I know what the Big Game is. Do you know what the Big Game is?" Yes, he said, but he meant the other one, the Big Game between Stanford and Cal. "Oh, " I said, "they play the Big Game too?"

And so on until dawn, the protoplasmic swirl of galaxies and atoms becoming less and less visible until tables and lamps, Harpos and McClanahans, slowly became solid again, or at least seemed so, and I was back to these fingers that know the alphabet.

The trip was over and I was wiped out, I would never be the same as before. I walked through the door on the porch in the violet glow of dawn and I felt as if . . . no, not *as if,* but that I had actually just returned from a world that is here and now while I am always somewhere else. I felt perhaps a tiny bit of what Helen Keller must have touched when the letters of her first word were spelled on her fingertips. It was the word *water* and it meant life. "I left the well-house eager to learn," she wrote, "and every object which I touched seemed to quiver with life. That was because I saw everything with a strange new sight that had come to me."

A couple weeks later I drove up to Kesey's farm for Thanksgiving. His family just moved in while he was gone. There were other families and friends as well and they were all trying to live together. It was a simple and beautiful scene and not anything like what is in Tom Wolfe's book, which, if I'm not mistaken, was being written at the time. It was quiet and natural and full of earth colors and the odor of wood. They had just built a communal dining hall and it was like a vision to a city boy who had just come from a world of apartments and burglars. The fresh unpainted fir smelled clean and eternal and the long table had just been covered with a kind of resin that preserved inside its amber their photos from the past when they roamed around the country full of youth and hope. Maria was there and she was now just another girl on a farm who wanted to make yogurt and have kids. I hope she did. Wherever you are, Maria, or whatever your name is now, I wish you well. Everyone wished each other well. We all felt there was so much food and clothing around that all we had to do was share it. Why would anyone want to hoard it? Why would anyone want to live otherwise? I remember asking for the bathroom and I was directed to a room at the side of a barn and walking in I saw a guy on a bowl and a young woman taking a shower. They didn't have such things in London or New York and after I got over the initial surprise I remembered my own childhood where we always left the bathroom door open and when I didn't know I was supposed to close it until I went to someone else's home. It was the tea full of stars that helped us to communal bathrooms, helped to show us that everyone's crap was alike and that no one's was special. I fell in love with that farm up there; it reminded me of a home I had lost and I felt very grateful for sharing all that bread and fresh milk.

Then Neal Cassady came with a few other folk. I didn't know much more about him than that he was Kerouac's pal and I was a little curious. He was in very bad shape and he died not too long afterwards. He was coming down from a lot of speed I was told, and he looked old and decrepit. If he was Kerouac's age he was only about twenty years older than I, or in his forties, my age now. I spent just a few minutes with him but they stuck with me. He was hanging out in the barn and mumbling a bunch of monotony I would have walked away from were he someone else, but I felt a kind of respect and sympathy for where he came from and what he went through. He seemed somehow like one of an Old Guard. He was one of the big guys in that schoolyard that became my hunting ground when I first left my mother's kitchen and wandered into the wilderness of America. He was one of the alumni when I first moved to the Village at the age of nineteen and made friends with other exiles from the wasteland. He was one of those who passed on to us a tradition that went all the way back to young rebels in every age who can't live in America without searching for a way out or in or wherever. And here he was now, mumbling in a boring voice and very close to death. If he ever drank any tea full of stars it didn't seem to lead him to yoga and meditation. It's one thing to see heaven in a flower and another to survive where there are no flowers. Perhaps he died looking for one on a railroad track that kept going.

I drove back to California with a double image of him bobbing nervously by an electric heater and the kids playing outside with a donkey, a sunny landscape all green and sienna and a shivering old soldier who talked to himself. How beautiful the hills were after a rain, how sad and broken he looked.

I stayed in California and took part in that process we call the Sixties, as if it were special and had not been going on forever. And a couple of months later I met Richard Brautigan. I had moved to Bolinas by then.

My new friend, Gatz Hjortsberg, had found me a cheap cabin near his place on the mesa, and his friend, Tom McGuane, lived nearby. But in those days there was hardly anyone else there. You really needed a mate to survive the long rain and grisly fog, and I would drive over the mountain as much as I could. Richard was living in a small apartment in San Francisco and I went to visit him once.

It was a poor writer's apartment, bare and cheap, and though he had girlfriends he lived there alone. "Every once in a while it depresses me," he said, "and then I paint it and it feels like home again." His voice was soft and gentle and his shoulders curved as if he was holding something in his heart that would fall away if he pulled them back. He was about Kesey's age but they were very different. He was very shy and private and yet not at all good at hiding and you could feel his sweetness immediately. Sure, he was sick with selfhood like the rest of us, but he was a very generous and sensitive soul, most good artists are I think, and with Kesey he is one of the figures who stands tall when I remember twenty years ago and try to sketch how much it meant to me. I didn't know him well either, though years later I would hang out with him some more when he moved to the farmhouse next to Gatz in Montana, but he felt like a brother, and his suicide always hovers in the darkness when I wake at four in the morning and feel so far from home and family.

"You want some lambchop?" he asked me that first time I dropped

by. He had just fried some lambchops after writing all day and he was
very hungry. I was a meat-eater in those days and I was very grateful,
though he wasn't much of a cook. He wasn't much of anything, I suppose,
except a writer. He loved to write, just as Kesey did, though in a very
different way. I was very surprised when Gatz told me he never had any
acid or even smoked grass. He just tuned in with his own special antennae
and was able to transmit that wonderful music which was, beneath the
humor, so fresh, delicate, and sincere. He himself was fresh, delicate,
and sincere. There were other sides of him, of course, we all have our
other sides, but when he was in the spirit of what he loved he was able
to gather from the air a certain music that seemed to come through a
door from a very special place. And he wanted to share it, freely. Those
were the days of the free-box and the Diggers dishing free food in the
Panhandle and visions upon visions of everyone living together freely,
from each according to their means, to each according to their needs,
and he stood with his big hat and sloppy mustache and handed out free
packets of flower seeds with his poems printed on them and the label:
PLANT THIS POEM. Not as a gimmick, not in any way like the stunts
performers pull to get attention, but more sincerely and deeply than
even he probably realized. He really wanted to believe it was possible;
he really wanted his work to plant him in the common earth he felt he
had lost.

Then he got famous and that was the beginning of the end. He got
famous just about when the flowers got trampled in People's Park and
the refugees started pouring in from the murderous suburbs. He was not
one who could handle fame and fortune. He never gave interviews, never
had anything to do with the media or Hollywood, but America had caught
up with him and he could buy as much booze as he wanted. He was
drinking hard then. He would get drunk and sit in his kitchen and shoot
the clock on his wall. I dropped by one afternoon and when he didn't
answer I went to the back and the kitchen door was open. I walked in
and the wall and the clock were full of holes like a scene from one of his
later books. He wasn't home. He was in his new studio on top of the barn.
The valley where he lived was the most beautiful I had ever encountered,
and his typewriter was by a wide window that opened to the vast and
incredible landscape with the great mountains in the background. He sat
there and looked out the window and tried to keep writing but the words
didn't come out as they did in that little room on Geary Street that didn't
even have a window. I remember talking with him one morning in Gatz's
kitchen where he would visit and have a cup of coffee. He had the spread

248

in Montana, a house in Bolinas, a studio in North Beach, but he still kept that bare apartment where he shared his lambchops and his flower seeds. "I don't want to lose touch with it," he said. "It's a part of me I don't want to lose touch with."

He died of "the great American loneliness," someone said after his death, quoting Kerouac or was it Fitzgerald? His father, who had abandoned him at birth, learned of his suicide through the news and remembered he had a son way back in the past. His mother may have disappeared also and he grew up an isolated child, especially during a period when he was very small and got very sick and had to stay in a room by himself.

As I reread *Trout Fishing In America* now, its darkness feels much stronger and therefore its light as well. It is not just an amusing book for the young. The winos, the poor kids, the hermits and the freaks, are not only Richard himself but parts of our America that struggle to survive in the nightmare of our history, and that they do is what makes the book so magical. Like the Kool-Aid wino, it creates its own reality and illuminates itself without sugar because there isn't any sugar to put in it. Richard was no simple-minded naif. He was extremely intelligent and perceptive, perhaps too intelligent and his acute perception too close to paranoia. That he was able to overcome, at least for a while, all those demons I encountered one night in Winterland was a real act of courage and faith. He believed in art so deeply that his belief was able to lead him through the manic crowd and take him back to a Palo Alto where he could survive until dawn. For a while at least. Then came the time, I guess, when there was no Ed McClanahan to rescue him, and he just couldn't do it alone anymore.

Read *Trout Fishing* again now. Read it and think of a little boy locked in a room with no parents around. Read it next to his death. It was written at a time when a flower was able to grow out of all the crap we all had accumulated since childhood, both as a country and as individuals. There were many such flowers, and though they lasted such a very short time they bore many seeds and will grow again someday.

I just came back from a walk in the hills. How beautiful they were just before sundown. Like quiet buffalos tufted with evergreen and glowing around the canyon, their flanks mottled with chaparral and the trail ablaze with lovely college girls jogging in shorts. I climbed to the top and gazed across the bay as the sun sank behind the pylons of the Gate. Then I heard music rising from the stadium below. It was the band practicing their marching songs for the Big Game tomorrow. The sun fell and the clouds took over with their beauty, their copper and ruby all burnished above the Farallons and the Tamalpais range reclining into the bay like a great serpent. Percussion and brass echoed up the redwood grove like atavistic rhythms that would never die, another generation getting ready for the Big Game. The freeway moaned in the distance and the cities spread below like a cancer. I entered my navel through my lungs and imagined how it all might look had I drunk some special kind of tea. They were not really clouds above the horizon and that was not really a bridge. They were the sea breathing and the cable was the smile of Eden, the city of St. Francis a castle across the waves and the island of Alcatraz a prisoner who longed to sail through the Gate. Not as metaphor, not in the mind alone, but in the flesh and blood. Pulsing, streaming, like the metamorphic pods of an eternal amoeba and the tiny bubbles in the cell of a leaf. All those kids driving down to Palo Alto tomorrow and listening to the Doors and the Grateful Dead on their cassettes, a singer bellowing like the ghost of an Indian along the polluted shores of the Peninsula, *Show me the way, oh show me the way.*

■ ■ ■ ■ ■ ■ ■ ■ ■ ■

Apologia

Barry Lopez

A few miles east of home in the Cascades I slow down and pull over for two raccoons, sprawled still as stones in the road. I carry them to the side and lay them in sunshot, windblown grass in the barrow pit. In eastern Oregon, along U.S. 20, blacktailed jackrabbits lie like welts of sod—three, four, then a fifth. By the bridge over Jordan Creek, just shy of the Idaho border, in the drainage of the Owyhee River, a crumpled adolescent porcupine leers up almost maniacal over its blood-flecked teeth. I carry each one away from the tarmac into a cover of grass or brush out of decency, I think. And worry. Who are these animals, their lights gone out? What journeys have fallen apart here?

I do not stop to remove each dark blister from the road. I wince before the recently dead, feel my lips tighten, see something else, a fence post, in the spontaneous aversion of my eyes, and pull over. I imagine white silk threads of life still vibrating inside them, even if the body's husk is stretched out for yards, stuck like oiled muslin to the road. The energy that held them erect leaves like a bullet; but the memory of that energy fades slowly from the wrinkled cornea, the bloodless fur.

The raccoons and, later, a red fox carry like sacks of wet gravel and sand. Each animal is like a solitary child's shoe in the road.

Once a man asked: why do you bother? You never know, I said. The ones you give some semblance of burial, to whom you offer an apology, may have been like seers in a parallel culture. It is an act of respect, a technique of awareness.

In Idaho I hit a young sage sparrow—*thwack* against the right fender in the very split second I see it. Its companion rises a foot higher from the same spot, slow as smoke, and sails off clean into the desert. I rest the walloped bird in my left hand, my right thumb pressed to its chest. I feel for the wail of the heart. Its eyes glisten like rain on crystal. Nothing but warmth. I shut the tiny eyelids and lay it beside a clump of bunchgrass. Beyond a barb wire fence the overgrazed range is littered with cow flops. The road curves away to the south. I nod before I go, a ridiculous gesture, out of simple grief.

I pass four spotted skunks. The swirling air is acrid with the rupture of each life.

Darkness rises in the valleys of Idaho. East of Grand View, south of the Snake River, nighthawks swoop the road for gnats, silent on the wing as owls. On a descending curve I see two of them lying soft as clouds in the road. I turn around and come back. The sudden slowing down and my U-turn at the bottom of the hill draw the attention of a man who steps away from a tractor, a dozen yards from where the birds lie. I can tell by his step, the suspicious tilt of his head, that he is wary, vaguely proprietary. Offended, or irritated, he may throw the birds back into the road when I leave. So I wait, subdued like a penitent, a body in each hand.

He speaks first, a low voice, a deep murmur weighted with awe. He has been watching these flocks feeding just above the road for several evenings. He calls them whip-poor-wills. He gestures for a carcass. How odd, yes, the way they concentrate their hunting right on the road, I say. He runs a finger down the smooth arc of the belly and remarks on the small whiskered bill. He pulls one long wing out straight, but not roughly. He marvels. He glances at my car, baffled by this out-of-state courtesy. Two dozen nighthawks career past, back and forth at arm's length, feeding at our height and lower. He asks if I would mind—as though I owned it—if he took the bird up to the house to show his wife. "She's never seen anything like this." He's fascinated. "Not close."

I trust, later, he will put it in the fields, not throw the body in the trash, a whirligig.

North of Pinedale in western Wyoming on U.S. 189, below the Gros Ventre Range, I see a big doe from a great distance, the low rays of first light gleaming in her tawny reddish hair. She rests askew, like a crushed tree. I drag her to the shoulder, then down a long slope by the petals of her ears. A gunny sack of plaster mud, ears cold as rain gutters. All of her doesn't come. I climb back up for the missing leg. The stain of her is darker than the black asphalt. The stains go north and off to the south as far as I can see.

On an afternoon trafficless, quiet as a cloister, headed across South

Pass in the Wind River Range, I swerve violently but hit an animal, and then try to wrestle the gravel-spewing skid in a straight line along the lip of an embankment. I know even as I struggle for control the irony of this: I could pitch off here to my own death, easily. The bird is dead somewhere in the road behind me. Only a few seconds and I am safely back on the road, nauseous, light-headed.

It is hard to distinguish among younger gulls. I turn this one around slowly in my hands. It could be a Western gull, a mew gull, a California gull. I do not remember well enough the bill markings, the color of the legs. I have no doubt about the vertebrae shattered beneath the seamless white of its ropy neck.

East of Lusk, Wyoming, in Nebraska, I stop for a badger. I squat on the macadam to admire the long claws, the perfect set of its teeth in the broken jaw, the ramulose shading of its fur, how it differs slightly, as does every badger's, from the drawings and pictures in the field guides. A car drifts toward us over the prairie, coming on in the other lane, a white 1962 Chevrolet station wagon. The driver slows to pass. In the bright sunlight I can't see his face, only an arm and the gesture of his thick left hand. It opens in a kind of shrug, hangs briefly in limp sadness, then extends itself in supplication. Gone past, it curls into itself against the car door and is still.

Farther on in western Nebraska I pick up the small bodies of mice and birds. While I wait to retrieve these creatures I do not meet the eyes of passing drivers. Whoever they are, I feel anger toward them, in spite of the sparrow and the gull I myself have killed. We treat the attrition of lives on the road like the attrition of lives in war: horrifying, unavoidable, justified. Accepting the slaughter leaves people momentarily fractious, embarrassed. South of Broken Arrow, at dawn, I cannot avoid an immature barn swallow. It hangs by its head motionless in the slats of the grill.

I stop for a rabbit on Nebraska 806 and find, only a few feet away, a garter snake. What else have I missed, too small, too narrow? What has gone under or past me while I stared at mountains, hay meadows, fencerows, the beryl surface of rivers? In Wyoming I could not help but see pronghorn antelope swollen big as barrels by the side of the road, their legs splayed rigidly aloft. For animals that large people will stop. But how many have this habit of clearing the road of smaller creatures, people who would remove the ones I miss? I do not imagine I am alone. As much sorrow as the man's hand conveyed in Nebraska, it meant gratitude too for burying the dead.

Still, I do not wish to meet anyone's eyes.

253

In southwestern Iowa, outside Clarinda, I haul a deer into high grass out of sight of the road and begin to examine it. It is still whole, but the destruction is breathtaking. The skull, I soon discover, is fractured in four places; the jaw, hanging by shreds of mandibular muscle, is broken at the symphysis, beneath the incisors. The pelvis is crushed, the left hind leg unsocketed. All but two ribs are dislocated along the vertebral column, which is complexly fractured. The intestines have been driven forward into the chest. The heart and lungs have ruptured the chest wall at the base of the neck. The signature of a tractor-trailer truck: 78,000 lbs. at 65 m.p.h.

In front of a motel room in Ottumwa I finger-scrape the dry stiff carcasses of bumblebees, wasps, and butterflies from the grill and headlight mountings. A young man strolls up. He really must admire anyone, he says, who tries to keep his car looking sharp on a long trip. I nod, go on with my task. He describes a Jeep he owns, a spotless, cherry-red vehicle he does not drive on muddy roads or during winter. I have begun to scrub with a wet cloth to soften and wipe away the nap of crumbles, the insects, the aerial plankton of spiders and mites. I do not tell him the reason: I am uneasy carrying so many of the dead. The carnage on the bumper and the grill, the lip of the hood, the rearview mirrors is so obvious. I recall a sign on the back of a truck in Mexico: *El azote de las carreteras*, road punisher.

In Illinois, west of Kankakee, two raccoons as young as the ones in Oregon. In Indiana another raccoon, a gray squirrel. When I make the left turn into the driveway at the house of a friend outside South Bend, it is evening, hot and muggy. I can hear cicadas in a lone elm. I'm glad to be here.

From the driveway entrance I look back down Indiana 23, toward Indiana 8, remembering the farm roads of Illinois and Iowa. I remember how beautiful it was in the limpid air to drive Nebraska 2 through the Sand Hills, to see how far at dusk the land was etched east and west of Wyoming 28. I remember the imposition of the Wind River mountains in a hard, blue sky beneath white ranks of buttonhook clouds, windy hay fields in the Snake River Plain, the welcome of Russian olive trees and willows in creek bottoms. The transformation of the heart such beauty engenders is not enough tonight to let me shed the heavier memory, a catalog too morbid to write out, too vivid to ignore.

I stand in the driveway now, listening to the cicadas whirring in the dark tree. My hands grip the sill of the open window at the driver's side, and I lean down as if to speak to someone still sitting there. The weight

I wish to fall I cannot fathom, a sorrow over the world's dark hunger.

A light comes on over the porch. I hear a deadbolt thrown, the shiver of a door pulled free. The words of atonement I pronounce are too inept to offer me release. Or forgiveness. My friend is floating across the tree-shadowed lawn. What is to be done with the desire for exculpation?

"Later than we thought you'd be," he says.

I do not want the lavabo. I wish to make amends.

"I made more stops that I thought I would," I answer.

"Well, bring this in. And whatever I can take," he says.

I anticipate, in the powerful antidote of our conversation, the reassurance of a human enterprise, the forgiving embrace of the rational. It waits within, beyond the slow tail-wagging of two dogs, standing at the screen door.

■ ■ ■ ■ ■ ■ ■ ■ ■ ■ ■

The Clan of One-breasted Women

Terry Tempest Williams

I belong to a Clan of One-breasted Women. My mother, my grandmothers, and six aunts have all had mastectomies. Seven are dead. The two who survive have just completed rounds of chemotherapy and radiation.

I've had my own problems: two biopsies for breast cancer and a small tumor between my ribs diagnosed as "a border-line malignancy."

This is my family history.

Most statistics tell us breast cancer is genetic, hereditary, with rising percentages attached to fatty diets, childlessness, or becoming pregnant after thirty. What they don't say is living in Utah may be the greatest hazard of all.

We are a Mormon family with roots in Utah since 1847. The word-of-wisdom, a religious doctrine of health, kept the women in my family aligned with good foods: no coffee, no tea, tobacco or alcohol. For the most part, these women were finished having their babies by the time they were thirty. And only one faced breast cancer prior to 1960. Traditionally, as a group of people, Mormons have a low rate of cancer.

Is our family a cultural anomaly? The truth is we didn't think about it. Those who did, usually the men, simply said "bad genes." The women's attitude was stoic. Cancer was part of life. On February 16, 1971, the eve before my mother's surgery, I accidentally picked up the telephone and overheard her ask my grandmother what she could expect.

"Diane, it is one of the most spiritual experiences you will ever encounter."

I quietly put down the receiver.

Two days later, my father took my three brothers and me to the hospital to visit her. She met us in the lobby in a wheelchair. No bandages were visible. I'll never forget her radiance, the way she held herself in a purple velour robe and how she gathered us around her.

"Children, I am fine. I want you to know I felt the arms of God around me."

We believed her. My father cried. Our mother, his wife, was thirty-eight years old.

Two years ago, after my mother's death from cancer, my father and I were having dinner together. He had just returned from St. George where his construction company was putting in natural gas lines for towns in southern Utah. He spoke of his love for the country: the sandstone landscape, bare-boned and beautiful. He had just finished hiking the Kolob trail in Zion National Park. We got caught up in reminiscing, recalling with fondness our walk up Angel's Landing on his fiftieth birthday and the years our family had vacationed there. This was a remembered landscape where we had been raised.

Over dessert, I shared a recurring dream of mine. I told my father that for years, as long as I could remember, I saw this flash of light in the night in the desert. That this image had so permeated my being, I could not venture south without seeing it again, on the horizon, illuminating buttes and mesas.

"You did see it," he said.

"Saw what?" I asked, a bit tentative.

"The bomb. The cloud. We were driving home from Riverside, California. You were sitting on your mother's lap. She was pregnant. In fact, I remember the date, September 7, 1957. We had just gotten out of the Service. We were driving north, past Las Vegas. It was an hour or so before dawn, when this explosion went off. We not only heard it, but felt it. I thought the oil tanker in front of us had blown up. We pulled over and suddenly, rising from the desert floor, we saw it, clearly, this golden-stemmed cloud, the mushroom. The sky seemed to vibrate with an eerie pink glow. Within a few minutes, a light ash was raining on the car."

I stared at my father. This was new information to me.

"I thought you knew that," my father said. "It was a common occurrence in the fifties."

It was at this moment I realized the deceit I had been living under. Children growing up in the American Southwest, drinking contaminated milk from contaminated cows, even from the contaminated breasts of their mothers, my mother—members, years later, of the Clan of One-breasted Women.

It is a well-known story in the Desert West, "The Day We Bombed Utah," or perhaps, "The Years We Bombed Utah." Above ground atomic testing in Nevada took place from January 27, 1951, through July 11, 1962. Not only were the winds blowing north, covering "low-use segments of the population" with fallout and leaving sheep dead in their tracks, but the climate was right. The United States of the 1950s was red, white, and blue. The Korean War was raging. McCarthyism was rampant. Ike was it and the Cold War was hot. If you were against nuclear testing, you were for a Communist regime.

Much has been written about this "American nuclear tragedy." Public health was secondary to national security. The Atomic Energy Commissioner, Thomas Murray said, "Gentlemen, we must not let anything interfere with this series of tests, nothing."

Again and again, the American public was told by its government, in spite of burns, blisters, and nausea, "It has been found that the tests may be conducted with adequate assurance of safety under conditions prevailing at the bombing reservations." Assuaging public fears was simply a matter of public relations. "Your best action," an Atomic Energy Commission booklet read, "is not to be worried about fallout." A news release typical of the times stated, "We find no basis for concluding that harm to any individual has resulted from radioactive fallout."

On August 30, 1979, during Jimmy Carter's presidency, a suit was filed entitled *Irene Allen vs. the United States of America*. Mrs. Allen was the first to be alphabetically listed with twenty-four test cases, representative of nearly 1200 plaintiffs seeking compensation from the United States government for cancers caused from nuclear testing in Nevada.

Irene Allen lived in Hurricane, Utah. She was the mother of five children and had been widowed twice. Her first husband with their two oldest boys had watched the tests from the roof of the local high school. He died of leukemia in 1956. Her second husband died of pancreatic cancer in 1978.

In a town meeting conducted by Utah Senator Orrin Hatch, shortly before the suit was filed, Mrs. Allen said, "I am not blaming the government, I want you to know that, Senator Hatch. But I thought if my testimony could help in any way so this wouldn't happen again to any of the generations coming up after us . . . I am really happy to be here this day to bear testimony of this."

God-fearing people. This is just one story in an anthology of thousands.

On May 10, 1984, Judge Bruce S. Jenkins handed down his opinion. Ten of the plaintiffs were awarded damages. It was the first time a federal court had determined that nuclear tests had been the cause of cancers. For the remaining fourteen test cases, the proof of causation was not sufficient. In spite of the split decision, it was considered a landmark ruling. It was not to remain so for long.

In April, 1987, the 10th Circuit Court of Appeals overturned Judge Jenkins' ruling on the basis that the United States was protected from suit by the legal doctrine of sovereign immunity, the centuries-old idea from England in the days of absolute monarchs.

In January, 1988, the Supreme Court refused to review the Appeals Court decision. To our court system, it does not matter whether the United States government was irresponsible, whether it lied to its citizens or even that citizens died from the fallout of nuclear testing. What matters is that our government is immune. "The King can do no wrong."

In Mormon culture, authority is respected, obedience is revered, and independent thinking is not. I was taught as a young girl not to "make waves" or "rock the boat."

"Just let it go — " my mother would say. "You know how you feel, that's what counts."

For many years, I did just that — listened, observed, and quietly formed my own opinions within a culture that rarely asked questions because they had all the answers. But one by one, I watched the women in my family die common, heroic deaths. We sat in waiting rooms hoping for good news, always receiving the bad. I cared for them, bathed their scarred bodies and kept their secrets. I watched beautiful women become bald as cytoxan, cisplatin and adriamycin were injected into their veins. I held their foreheads as they vomited green-black bile and I shot them with morphine when the pain became inhuman. In the end, I witnessed their last peaceful breaths, becoming a midwife to the rebirth of their souls. But the price of obedience became too high.

The fear and inability to question authority that ultimately killed rural communities in Utah during atmospheric testing of atomic weapons was the same fear I saw being held in my mother's body. Sheep. Dead sheep. The evidence is buried.

I cannot prove that my mother, Diane Dixon Tempest, or my grandmothers, Lettie Romney Dixon and Kathryn Blackett Tempest along with my aunts contracted cancer from nuclear fallout in Utah. But I can't prove they didn't.

My father's memory was correct, the September blast we drove through in 1957 was part of Operation Plumbbob, one of the most intensive series

of bomb tests to be initiated. The flash of light in the night in the desert
I had always thought was a dream developed into a family nightmare.
It took fourteen years, from 1957 to 1971, for cancer to show up in my
mother — the same time Howard L. Andrews, an authority on radioactive
fallout at the National Institutes of Health, says radiation cancer
requires to become evident. The more I learn about what it means to be
a "downwinder," the more questions I drown in.

What I do know, however, is that as a Mormon woman of the fifth
generation of "Latter-Day-Saints," I must question everything, even if it
means losing my faith, even if it means becoming a member of a border
tribe among my own people. Tolerating blind obedience in the name of
patriotism or religion ultimately takes our lives.

When the Atomic Energy Commission described the country north
of the Nevada Test Site as "virtually uninhabited desert terrain," my family
members were some of the "virtual uninhabitants."

One night, I dreamed women from all over the world circling a
blazing fire in the desert. They spoke of change, of how they hold
the moon in their bellies and wax and wane with its phases. They mocked
at the presumption of even-tempered beings and made promises that they
would never fear the witch inside themselves. The women danced wildly
as sparks broke away from the flames and entered the night sky as stars.

And they sang a song given to them by Shoshoni grandmothers:

Ah ne nah, nah
nin nah nah —
Ah he nah, nah
nin nah nah —
Nyaga mutzi
oh ne nay —
Nyaga mutzi
Oh ne nay —

The women danced and drummed and sang for weeks, preparing
themselves for what was to come. They would reclaim the desert for the
sake of their children, for the sake of the land.

A few miles downwind from the fire circle, bombs were being tested.
Rabbits felt the tremors. Their soft leather pads on paws and feet
recognized the shaking sands while the roots of mesquite and sage were
smoldering. Rocks were hot from the inside out and dust devils hummed
unnaturally. And each time there was another nuclear test, ravens watched

the desert heave. Stretch marks appeared. The land was losing its muscle.

The women couldn't bear it any longer. They were mothers. They had suffered labor pains but always under the promise of birth. The red hot pains beneath the desert promised death only as each bomb became a stillborn. A contract was being drawn by the women who understood the fate of the earth as their own.

Under the cover of darkness, ten women slipped under the barbed wire fence and entered the contaminated country. They were trespassing. They walked toward the town of Mercury in moonlight, taking their cues from coyote, kit fox, antelope, squirrel, and quail. They moved quietly and deliberately through the maze of Joshua trees. When a hint of daylight appeared they rested, drinking tea and sharing their rations of food. The women closed their eyes. The time had come to protest with the heart, that to deny one's genealogy with the earth was to commit treason against one's soul.

At dawn, the women draped themselves in mylar, wrapping long streamers of silver plastic around their arms to blow in the breeze. They wore clear masks that became the faces of humanity. And when they arrived on the edge of Mercury, they carried all the butterflies of a summer day in their wombs. They paused to allow their courage to settle.

The town, which forbids pregnant women and children to enter because of radiation risks to their health, was asleep. The women moved through the streets as winged messengers, twirling around each other in slow motion, peeking inside homes and watching the easy sleep of men and women. They were astonished by such stillness and periodically would utter a shrill note or low cry just to verify life.

The residents finally awoke to what appeared as strange apparitions. Some simply stared. Others called authorities, and in time, the women were apprehended by wary soldiers dressed in desert fatigues. They were taken to a white, square building on the other edge of Mercury. When asked who they were and why they were there, the women replied, "We are mothers and we have come to reclaim the desert for our children."

The soldiers arrested them. As the ten women were blindfolded and handcuffed, they began singing:

> *You can't forbid us everything*
> *You can't forbid us to think—*
> *You can't forbid our tears to flow*
> *And you can't stop the songs that we sing.*

The women continued to sing louder and louder, until they heard the voices of their sisters moving across the mesa.

Ah ne nah, nah
nin nah nah —
Ah he nah, nah
nin nah nah —
Nyaga mutzi
oh ne nay —
Nyaga mutzi
Oh ne nay —

"Call for reinforcement," one soldier said.

"We have," interrupted one woman. "We have — and you have no idea of our numbers."

On March 18, 1988, I crossed the line at the Nevada Test Site and was arrested with nine other Utahans for trespassing on military lands. They are still conducting nuclear tests in the desert. Ours was an act of civil disobedience. But as I walked toward the town of Mercury, it was more than a gesture of peace. It was a gesture on behalf of the Clan of One-breasted Women.

As one officer cinched the handcuffs around my wrists, another frisked my body. She found a pen and pad of paper tucked inside my left boot.

"And these?" she asked sternly.

"Weapons," I replied.

Our eyes met. I smiled. She pulled the leg of my trousers back over my boot.

"Step forward, please," she said as she took my arm.

We were booked under an afternoon sun and bussed to Tonapah, Nevada. It was a two-hour ride. This was familiar country to me. The Joshua trees standing their ground had been named by my ancestors who believed they looked like prophets pointing west to the promised land. These were the same trees that bloomed each spring, flowers appearing like white flames in the Mojave. And I recalled a full moon in May when my mother and I had walked among them, flushing out mourning doves and owls.

The bus stopped short of town. We were released. The officials thought it was a cruel joke to leave us stranded in the desert with no way to get home. What they didn't realize is that we were home, soul-centered and strong, women who recognized the sweet smell of sage as fuel for our spirits.

■ ■ ■ ■ ■ ■ ■ ■ ■ ■ ■

Jessica, the Hound & the Casket Trade

Thomas Lynch

She went to a long-established, "reputable" undertaker. Seeking to save the widow expense, she chose the cheapest redwood casket in the establishment and was quoted a low price. Later, the salesman called her back to say the brother-in-law was too tall to fit into this casket, she would have to take the one that cost $100 more. When my friend objected, the salesman said, "Oh, all right, we'll use the redwood one, but we'll have to cut off his feet."

— Jessica Mitford, *The American Way of Death*

T he same mortician who once said he'd rather give away caskets than take advantage of someone in grief later hung billboards out by the interstate — a bosomy teenager in a white bikini over which it read *Better Bodies by Bixby* (not the real name) and the phone numbers for his several metro locations.

I offer this in support of the claim that there are good days and there are bad days.

No less could be said for many of the greats.

I'm thinking of Hemingway's take on Pound when he said, "Ezra was right half the time, and when he was wrong, he was so wrong you were never in any doubt of it." But ought we be kept from "The River-Merchant's Wife" by his mistaken politics? Should outrage silence the sublime?

The same may be asked of Mr. Bixby's two memorable utterances.

Or, as a priest I've long admired once said, "Prophesy, like poetry, is a part-time job — the rest of the time they were only trying to keep their feet out of their mouths." I suppose he was trying to tell me something.

Indeed, mine is an occupation that requires two feet firmly on the ground, less for balance, I often think, than to keep one or the other from angling toward its true home in my craw.

I sell caskets and embalm bodies and direct funerals.

Pollsters find among the general public a huge ambivalence about funeral directors. "I hope you'll understand it if I never want to see you again," the most satisfied among my customers will say. I understand.

And most of the citizenry, stopped on the street, would agree that funeral directors are mainly crooks, "except for mine . . . " they just as predictably add. "The one who did my *(insert primary relation)* was really helpful, really cared, treated us like family."

This tendency to abhor the general class while approving of the particular member is among the great human perogatives — as true of clergy and senators as it is of teachers and physicians. Much the same could be said of time: "Life sucks," we say, "but there was this moment . . . " Or of racial types: "Some of my best friends are *(insert minority)* . . . " Or of the other gender: "*(Insert sex)*! You can't live with them and you can't live without them!"

Of course, there are certain members of the subspecies — I'm thinking lawyers, politicians, revenue agents—who are, in general and in particular, beyond redemption and we like it that way. "The devil you know's better than the one you don't" is the best we can say about politicians. And who among us wants a "nice" divorce attorney or has even one fond memory involving a tax man? Really, now.

But back to caskets and bodies and funerals.

When it comes to caskets I'm very careful. I don't tell folks what they should or shouldn't do. It's bad form and worse for business. I tell them I don't have any that will get them into heaven or keep them out. There's none that turns a prince into a frog or, regrettably, vice-versa. There isn't a casket that compensates for neglect nor one that hides true love, honorable conduct or affection.

If worth can be measured by what they do, it might help to figure out what caskets "do" in the inanimate object sense of the verb.

How many here are thinking HANDLES? When someone dies, we try to get a handle on it. This is because dead folks don't move. I'm not making this part up. Next time someone in your house quits breathing, ask him to get up and answer the phone or maybe get you some ice water or let the cat out the back door. He won't budge. It's because he's dead.

There was a time when it was easier to change caves than to drag the dead guy out. Now it's not so easy. There's the post office, the utilities, the closing costs. Now we have to remove the dead. The sooner the better is the rule of thumb, though it's not the thumb that will make this known.

This was a dour and awful chore, moving the dead from place to place. And like most chores, it was left to women to do. Later, it was discovered to be a high honor — to bear the pall as a liturgical role required a special place in the procession, special conduct and often a really special outfit. When hauling the dead hither and yon became less the chore and more an honor, men took it over with enthusiasm.

In this it resembles the history of the universe. Much the same happened with protecting against the marauding hordes, the provision of meaty protein sources, and more recently, in certain highly specialized and intricate evolutions of food preparation and child care.

If you think women were at least participants and perhaps instrumental in the discovery of these honors, you might better keep such suspicions to yourself. These are not good days to think such thoughts.

But I stray again. Back to business.

Another thing you'll see most every casket doing is being horizontal. This is because folks that make them have taken seriously the demonstrated preference of our species to do it on the level. Oh, sure—it can be done standing up or in a car or even upside down. But most everyone goes looking for something flat. Probably this can be attributed to gravity or physics or fatigue.

So horizontal things that can be carried—to these basic properties, we could add a third: it should be sturdy enough for a few hundred pounds. I'm glad that it's not from personal experience that I say that nothing takes the steam out of a good funeral so much as the bottom falling out.

And how many of you haven't heard of this happening?

A word on the words we're most familiar with. *Coffins* are the narrow, octagonal fellows—mostly wooden, nicely corresponding to the shape of the human form before the advent of the junk food era. There are top and bottom, and the screws that fasten the one to the other are often ornamental. Some have handles, some do not, but all can be carried. The lids can be opened and closed at will.

Caskets are more rectangular and the lids are hinged and the body can be both carried and laid out in them. Other than shape, coffins and caskets are pretty much the same. They've been made of wood and metal and glass and ceramics and plastics and cement and the dear knows what else. Both are made in a range of prices.

But *casket* suggests something beyond basic utility, something about the contents of the box. The implication is that it contains something precious: heirlooms, jewels, old love letters, remnants and icons of something dear.

So casket is to coffin as tomb is to cave, grave is to hole in the ground, pyre is to bonfire. You get the drift? Or as, for example, eulogy is to speech, elegy to poem, or home is to house or husband to man. I love this part, I get carried away.

But the point is a *casket* presumes something about what goes in it. It presumes the dead body is important to someone. For some this will seem like stating the obvious. For others, I'm guessing, maybe not.

But when buildings are bombed or planes fall from the sky, or wars are won or lost, the bodies of the dead are really important. We want them back to let them go again — on our terms, at our pace, to say you may not leave without permission, forgiveness, our respects — to say we want our chance to say good-bye.

Both coffins and caskets are boxes for the dead. Both are utterly suitable to the task. Both cost more than most other boxes.

It's because of the bodies we put inside them. The bodies of mothers and fathers and sons, daughters and sisters and brothers and friends, the ones we knew and loved or knew and hated, or hardly knew at all, but know someone who knew them and who is left to grieve.

In 1906, John Hillenbrand, the son of a German immigrant, bought the failing Batesville Coffin Company in the southeastern Indiana town of the same name. Following the form of the transportation industry, he moved from a primarily wooden product to products of metal that would seal against the elements. *Permanence* and *protection* were concepts that Batesville marketed successfully during and after a pair of World Wars in which men were being sent home in government boxes. The same wars taught different lessons to the British for whom the sight of their burial grounds desecrated by bombs at intervals throughout the first half-century suggested permanence and protection were courtesies they could no longer guarantee to the dead. Hence the near total preference for cremation there.

Earth burial is practiced by "safe" societies and by settled ones. It presumes the dead will be left their little acre and that the living will be around to tend the graves. In such climates the fantasies of permanence and protection thrive. And the cremation rate in North America has risen in direct relation to the demographics and geographies of mobility and fear and the ever more efficient technologies of destruction.

The idea that a casket should be sealed against air and moisture is important to many families. To others it means nothing. They are both right. No one need explain why it doesn't matter. No one need explain why it does. But Batesville, thinking that it might, engineered the first "sealed" casket with a gasket in the 1940s and made it available in metal caskets in every price range from the .20 gauge steels to the coppers and bronzes. One of the things they learned is that ninety-six percent of the human race would fit in a casket with interior dimensions of twenty-five inches and exterior dimensions of six-foot, six-inches.

Once they had the size figured out and what it was that people wanted in a casket — protection and permanence — then the rest was more or less the history of how the Hillenbrand brothers managed to make more and sell more than any of their competition. And they have. You see them in the movies, on the evening news being carried in and out of churches, at gravesides, being taken from hearses. If someone's in a casket in North America chances are better than even it's a Batesville.

We show twenty-some caskets to pick from. They're samples only. There are plenty more we can get within a matter of hours. What I carry in blue, my brother Tim, in the next town, carries in pink. What I have tailored, Tim carries shirred. He carries one with *The Last Supper* on it. I've got one with the *Pietá*. One of his has roses on the handles. One of mine has sheaves of wheat.

You name it. We've got it. We aim to please.

We have a cardboard box (of a kind used for larger appliances) for seventy-nine dollars. We also have a mahogany box (of a kind used for Kennedy and Nixon and Onassis) for nearly eight grand. Both can be carried and buried and burned. Both will accommodate all but the tallest or widest citizens, for whom, alas, as in life, the selection narrows. And both are available to any customer who can pay the price.

Because a lot of us tend to avoid the extremes, regardless of how we elect to define them, we show a wide range of caskets in between and it would look on a chart like one of those bell curves: with the most in the middle and the least at either end. Thus, we show three oak caskets and only one mahogany, a bronze, a copper, a stainless steel, and six or seven regular steels of various gauges or thicknesses. We show a cherry, a maple, two poplars, an ash, a pine and a particle board and the cardboard box. The linings are velvet or crepe or linen or satin, in all different colors, tufted or ruffled or tailored plain. You get pretty much what you pay for here.

I should probably fess up that we buy these caskets for less than we sell them for — a fact uncovered by one of our local TV news personalities, who called himself the News Hound, and who was, apparently, untutored in the economic intrigues of wholesale and retail. It was this same News Hound who did an exposé on Girl Scout cookie sales — how some of the money doesn't go to the girls at all, but to the national office where it was used to pay the salaries of "staff."

It was a well-worn trail the News Hound was sniffing—a trail blazed most profitably by Jessica Mitford, who came to the bestselling if not exactly original conclusion that the bereaved customer is in a bad bargaining position. When you've got a dead body on your hands it's hard to shop around. It's hard to shop for lawyers when you're on the lam, or doctors when your appendix is inflamed. It's not the kind of thing you let out to bids.

Lately there has been a great push toward "prearrangement." Everyone who's anyone seems to approve. The funeral directors figure it's money in the bank. The insurance people love it since most of the funding is done through insurance. The late Jessica, the former News Hound, the anti-extravagance crowd—they all reckon it is all for the best, to make such decisions when heads are cool and hearts are unencumbered by grief and guilt. There's this hopeful fantasy that by prearranging the funeral, one might be able to pre-feel the feelings, you know, get a jump on the anger and the fear and the helplessness. It's as modern as planned parenthood and prenuptial agreements and as useless, however tidy it may be about the finances, when it comes to the feelings involved.

And we are uniformly advised "not to be a burden to our children." This is the other oft-cited *bonne raison* for making your final arrangements in advance—to spare them the horror and pain of having to do business with someone like me.

But if we are not to be a burden to our children, then to whom? The government? The church? The taxpayers? Whom? Were they not a burden to us—our children? And didn't the management of that burden make us feel alive and loved and capable?

And if the planning of a funeral is so horribly burdensome, so fraught with possible abuses and gloom, why should an arthritic septuagenarian with blurred vision and some hearing loss be sent to the front to do battle with the undertaker instead of the forty-something heirs-apparent with their power suits and web browsers and cellular phones? Are they not far better outfitted to the task? Is it not their inheritance we're spending here? Are these not decisions they will be living with?

Maybe their parents do not trust them to do the job properly.

Maybe they shouldn't.

Maybe they should.

The day I came to Milford, Russ Reader started prearranging his funeral. I was getting my hair cut when I first met him. He was a massive man still, in his fifties, six-foot-something and four hundred pounds. He'd had, in his youth, a spectacular career playing college and professional football. His reputation had preceded him. He was a "character" — known in these parts for outrageous and libertine behavior. Like the Sunday he sold a Ford coupe off the used-car lot uptown, taking a cash deposit of a thousand dollars and telling the poor customer to "come by in the morning when the office is open" for the keys and paperwork. That Russ was not employed by the car dealer — a devout Methodist who kept holy his Sabbaths — did not come to light before the money had been spent on sirloins and cigars and round after round of drinks for the patrons of Ye Olde Hotel — visiting matrons from the Eastern Star, in town with their husbands for a regional confab. Or the time a neighbor's yelping poodle — a dog disliked by everyone in earshot — was found shot one afternoon during Russ' nap time. The neighbor started screaming at one of Russ' boys over the back fence, " . . . when I get my hands on your father!" Awakened by the fracas, Russ appeared at the upstairs window and calmly promised, "I'll be right down, Ben." He came down in his paisley dressing gown, decked the neighbor with a swift left hook, instructed his son to bury "that dead mutt" and went back upstairs to finish his nap. Halloween was Russ' favorite holiday which he celebrated in more or less pre-Christian fashion, dressing himself up like a Celtic warrior, with an antlered helmet and mighty sword which, along with his ponderous bulk and black beard and booming voice, would scare the bejaysus out of the wee trick-or-treaters who nonetheless were drawn to his porch by stories of full-sized candy bars sometimes wrapped in five-dollar bills. Russ Reader was, in all ways, bigger than life so that the hyperbole that attended the gossip about him was like the talk of heroes in the ancient Hibernian epics — Cuchulainn and Deirdre and Queen Maeve, who were given to warp-spasms, wild couplings, and wondrous appetites.

When he first confronted me in the barber's chair, he all but blotted out the sun behind him.

"You're the new Digger O'Dell I take it."

It was the black suit, the wing tips, the gray striped tie.

"Well, you're never getting your mitts on my body!" he challenged.

The barber stepped back to busy himself among the talcums and clippers, uncertain of the direction the conversation might take.

I considered the size of the man before me — the ponderous bulk of him, the breathtaking mass of him — and tried to imagine him horizontal and uncooperative. A sympathetic pain ran down my back. I winced.

269

"What makes you think I'd want anything to do with your body?" I countered in a tone that emphasized my indignation.

Russ and I were always friends after that.

He told me he intended to have his body donated to "medical science." He wanted to be given to the anatomy department of his alma mater, so that fledgling doctors could practice on him.

"Won't cost my people a penny."

When I told him they probably wouldn't take him, on account of his size, he seemed utterly crestfallen. The supply of cadavers for medical and dental schools in this land of plenty was shamefully but abundantly provided for by the homeless and helpless who were, for the most part, more "fit" than Russ was.

"But I was an All-American there!" Russ pleaded.

"Don't take my word for it," I advised. "Go ask for yourself."

Months later I was watering impatiens around the funeral home when Russ screeched to a halt on Liberty Street.

"OK, listen. Just cremate me and have the ashes scattered over town from one of those hot-air balloons." I could see he had given this careful thought. "How much will it cost me, bottom line?"

I told him the fees for our minimum services — livery and paperwork and a box.

"I don't want a casket," he hollered from the front seat of his Cadillac idling at curbside now.

I explained we wouldn't be using a casket as such, still he would have to be *in* something. The crematory people wouldn't accept his body unless it was *in* something. They didn't *handle* dead bodies without some kind of handles. This made tolerable sense to Russ. In my mind I was thinking of a shipping case, a kind of covered pallet compatible with forklifts and freight handlers, that would be sufficient to the task.

"I can only guess at what the balloon ride will cost, Russ. It's likely to be the priciest part. And, of course, you'd have to figure on inflation. Are you planning to do this very soon?"

"Don't get cute with me, Digger," he shouted. "Whadasay? Can I count on you?"

I told him it wasn't me he'd have to count on. He'd have to convince his wife and kids — the nine of them. They were the ones I'd be working for.

"But it's *my* funeral! *My* money."

Here is where I explained to Russ the subtle but important difference between the "adjectival" and "possessive" applications of the first-person singular pronoun for ownership — a difference measured by one's last breath. I explained that it was really *theirs* to do—his survivors, his family.

It was really, listen closely, "the heirs"—the money, the funeral, what was or wasn't done with his body.

"I'll pay you now," he protested. "In cash—I'll prearrange it. Put it in my Will. They'll have to do it the way I want it."

I encouraged Russ to ponder the worst-case scenario: his wife and his family take me to court. I come armed with his Last Will and Pre-need documents insisting that his body get burned and tossed from a balloon hovering over the heart of town during Sidewalk Sale Days. His wife Mary, glistening with real tears, his seven beautiful daughters with hankies in hand, his two fine sons, bearing up manfully, petition the court for permission to lay him out, have the preacher in, bury him up on the hill where they can visit his grave whenever the spirit moves them to.

"Who do you think wins that one, Russ? Go home and make your case with them."

I don't know if he ever had that conversation with them all. Maybe he just gave up. Maybe it had all been for my consumption. I don't know. That was years ago.

When Russ died last year in his easy chair, a cigar smoldering in the ash tray, one of those evening game-shows flickering on the TV, his son came to my house to summon me. His wife and his daughters were weeping around him. His children's children watched and listened. We brought the hearse and waited while each of the women kissed him and left. We brought the stretcher in and, with his son's help, moved him from the chair, then out the door and to the funeral home where we embalmed him, gave him a clean shave, and laid him out, all of us amazed at how age and infirmity had reduced him so. He actually fit easily into a Batesville Casket—I think it was Cherry, I don't remember.

But I remember how his vast heroics continued to grow over two days of wake. The stories were told and told again. Folks wept and laughed out loud at his wild antics. And after the minister, a woman who'd known Russ all her life and had braved his stoop on Halloween, had had her say about God's mercy and the size of Heaven, she invited some of us to share our stories about Russ and after that we followed a brass band to the grave, holding forth with "When the Saints Go Marching In." And after everything had been said that could be said, and done that could be done, Mary and her daughters went home to the embraces of neighbors and the casseroles and condolences and Russ' sons remained to bury him. They took off their jackets, undid their ties, broke out a bottle and dark cigars and buried their father's body in the ground that none of us thought it would ever fit into. I gave the permit to the sexton and left them to it.

And though I know his body is buried there, something of Russ remains among us now. Whenever I see hot-air balloons — fat flaming birds adrift in evening air — I sense his legendary excesses raining down on us, old friends and family — his blessed and elect — who duck our heads or raise our faces to the sky and laugh or catch our breath or cry.

In even the best of caskets, it never all fits — all that we'd like to bury in them: the hurt and forgiveness, the anger and pain, the praise and thanksgiving, the emptiness and exaltations, the untidy feelings when someone dies. So I conduct this business very carefully because in the years since I've been here, when someone dies, they never call Jessica or the News Hound.

They call me.

■■■■■■■■■■■

Son of a Gun

Josip Novakovich

Before getting to know Sam, an Australian blue-heeler, outside of Winnetoon, Nebraska, I used to take pride in belonging to the cat-loving rather than the dog-loving breed. In Croatia as a kid I had once thrown iced snowballs at a German shepherd, struck him on the muzzle, and he chased me, gaining on me; I jumped into a ten-foot hole. The dog growled at the edge of the pit for hours before he gave up. Frozen, I had barely managed to crawl out. That had confirmed my dislike of large dogs, and Sam did nothing to convert me, at first. I met him outside of my wife's uncle's farmhouse. Sam leaped at me, dug his thick and sharp claws into my belly, tearing my T-shirt and skin, and despite my anxiety and pain, I could see by his sloppy tongue that he groveled for affection. Next time when he did the same type of greeting, when nobody could see what I was doing—I believed that everybody around me loved him—I kneed his ribcage.

Jeanette's uncle Al offered us Sam to take care of. Al had moved into town and married a woman who hated dogs—not having animals around somehow proved to her that she was a city person. My tomcat and I were alarmed by the generous loan, but Jeanette thought it was an excellent idea, since we would live in a dilapidated farmhouse with lots of wildlife around us. And true enough, soon I appreciated his chasing away badgers and skunks.

I even played with Sam. I teased him with the Toyota siren; the pitch irritated his ears so that he'd lift his head straight up and howl, adjusting his pitch to merge with the car's. I tossed him antlers in the field, and he'd bring them back to me; I held them high, above my shoulder, and he'd leap and snatch them.

Despite Sam's treeing our cats, slurping calves' dung, climbing the roof of our car and scratching it, pissing on our tires, tearing our clothes, and howling at three in the morning, I reluctantly became fond of his shifty eyes, and of his waiting for us on the porch, even when we were gone for days.

His previous caretaker, John, who lived alone in a cabin in the woods and occasionally helped out in the fields, claimed that Sam used to fetch newspapers from the mailbox every morning. I failed to get Sam to fetch my mail; my presence must have demolished his discipline. Or, John, who'd in the meanwhile become a law student, lied — though, since he recently dropped out, he may not have been a liar. (A poor joke about law — poor logic, but, don't jokes mostly depend on poor logic?)

Sam was certainly a smart dog; an article in a recent *Atlantic* laid a claim to the blue-heeler's credit: as the only distinct variety of dog whose genes the American Kennel has not messed with, narrowing the genetic pool, etc., the blue-heeler has retained wolfish vitality and cunning.

Though we had such a brave dog, I wanted a gun. All our neighbors had guns hanging in the backs of their pickups — if not because of coyotes, I wanted a gun because of the neighbors. My father-in-law, a full-time cowboy and ecology professor emeritus, carried a pistol — with a criss-crossed, engraved, wooden handle and a long barrel — in a little plastic case resembling a briefcase. On the morning of the first snow of the year, as the environmentalist, enshrouded in blue smoke, chain-sawed trees to extend his pastures, I drove past him to borrow the gun at his house in the town of Center, population 120, six miles away. In the first curve, I ran into the Holzer brothers. I waved and they waved, although our cars kept sliding. It was our point of honor—no matter what bind you were in, no matter how difficult it was to steer, you lifted one hand and waved. We may not have liked each other, we may have never talked to each other except about the precip and subsoil moisture, but here on the road we were a tight-knit community, good Cornhuskers. (Actually, we had talked several months before in a Creighton bar, below coyotes, horned owls and barn owls prepared and jutting forth from the wall. When I mentioned I had seen a horned owl, one brother said he'd shot two and just the other day, he'd killed a barn owl, of all places, in his barn. To him that perhaps counted as the love of owls.) My topsy-turvy Corona slid left and right, but steadied itself back like a pair of skis.

In another downhill curve, the mailman's car showed up. Greedy for job offers and good news from Croatia, I braked. He'd be happy he didn't have to take the long detour to our mailbox, he should be smiling at the thought, was he smiling? My car swerved, and it didn't slow down. Would I smash into him, die, and kill him? My car spun, straightened out, but dragged along a ditch and dipped into sumac brush. The mailman, a VFW, stopped gracefully — clearly he suffered no PTSD, grinned out the window, and said, "Braking downhill in snow, a useless proposition. You want a ride to the old Becker place? He's got a four-wheeler."

"No, thanks, I'll walk."

"Are you sure?"

But soon Becker showed up in his old beat-up pickup and gave me a ride to the car. "Did the mailman tell you I got stranded?" I asked.

"No, I saw how fast you were going and I heard the noises, so I said, what the heck, I might help." With his engine idling next to my ditched car he talked. "You young people ought to be ashamed of yourselves. My generation, we built all the roads and most of the rails, and you can't even repair them!"

He could have said we could not even drive on them decently, but he did not, though he did say a provocative thing: "Do you pay taxes?" I hesitated with the answer, wishing I made enough money to pay taxes, and nodded slightly, ambiguously, taking the question to be merely a rhetorical introduction to one of his points, which I guess it was.

He continued: "If we all honestly paid taxes, we'd have more than enough, no three-trillion dollar deficits, for sure. We'd be able to rebuild the roads, send men to Mars, keep everybody health-insured, but because everybody's a cheat, we can't do that. When I was a young man, I paid all my taxes, and I went to Lincoln to see whether our honorable community members did their share. I found out that many rich farmers cheated, and I, a poor dumb farmer, didn't. So I said, I'll show you who's dumb. I visited the state treasurer, but he wouldn't let me examine his records, so I went to the governor, and by golly, pretty soon I had them all back-to-back! Even the governor was embarrassed, by golly!"

The old man roped my bumper — while his little mutt barked at me with genuine animosity, perhaps smelling Sam's urine — and pulled out the car, and now I drove back. The mailman had left something in my box — he had not bothered to deliver it to me while I was in the ditch.

Junk mail, bills, and a package. Musical Heritage Society sent us more tapes because I had not canceled the membership on time. I thought I would mail the tapes back, but I tore the package to peep in. Beethoven's five piano concertos. (I know, it would be perhaps less hickish to say that five tapes of Philip Glass monotones came, and that I assassinated the cassette player just as a long heralded change in pitch was about to occur.) As soon as I shook the snow off my work shoes, I stuck a tape in the stereo and listened to the prolonged wistful variations of a quiet piano, which filled me with grandiose gloom as though it was I who had experienced all the inspiration. But amidst the great sadness, imported from Beethoven, I experienced the small sadness, that I had not managed to get the gun, that somehow I was doomed to be gunless.

I walked out on the tilting porch and shouted for Sam to come back — in the white fields with yellow stubble, the blue-heeler was chasing Anguses; Al certainly wouldn't allow him to do that. Sam came back, leaped at me, which in the winter I did not mind — the claws did not reach me through my thick sweater. I scratched his neck, pulled his blue-gray hair — in softness resembling small porcupine needles — and thought about how Sam would not be so ornery if he weren't lonely.

To assuage his loneliness, we got two puppies, one male, one female. In the reprieve from the cold, Sam played with the young dobermen (or doberdogs). The boy had huge paws and promised to become larger than Sam. As the two tumbled over the yard, Sam must have appreciated that prospect, for soon he led the pup farther and farther into the hills, and after one such escapade, the pup did not return. The coyotes probably ate him. Sam feigned some sadness, blinking cleverly; his body hunched as though he were depressed or as if he expected a blow, but he did not keep up the act for long. Now the true game started, with the female pup. He rolled and tumbled with her, got carrot-like erections, rubbed against her back, but did not enter her, at least not with me around.

The pup grew so fast that she too would soon be larger than Sam, and rather than "fix" her and have two dogs to feed, I gave her to Dave, a community college student — I taught full time for a part-time salary — along with forty dollars for dog food. Forty dollars of booze later, that same evening, Dave got nabbed for drunk driving, was sent to the regional jail, got into a fight, and plucked a man's eye out of the socket with his fingers. When I heard that, I despaired: you give away a sweet pup, and pretty soon, somebody's eye is torn out.

Sam pined away for his vivacious jail-bait. But, as soon as Holzer's young beagle showed up — the Holzers came over to cut some wood, Al's present to them — Sam cheered up and rolled with her in the grass; they bit each other's ears and licked foreheads, howled, rushed through crumbling barns, hunted possum, and when she faltered from exhaustion, with her tongue on a shoe, Sam mounted her tenderly, his tongue on her nape. Even three weeks later, Sam and the beagle kept tumbling, rolling across the yard among tumble weeds, which, driven by dusty winds, hopped over dried tire marks, and accumulated on the fence before the cow watering drum. Who knows how long their intimacy would have lasted — but a Holzer, who did not like a dog who would not stay close to his home, shot her, and killed her.

Now Sam ran around, looking for her and perhaps for the doberwoman, and after two days of disconsolate rushing over the country, he collapsed on our porch and moaned for days, barely opening his blood-shot eyes.

After that he grew even more viciously lonely. When Jeanette's young niece and her friends visited, he gazed into their eyes with his tongue sentimentally loose, licked their cheeks, and they hugged him. Because he yearned for company so much, he was no guard dog. If a total stranger with a gun showed up — sometimes Al allowed pheasant and deer hunters on the land — he'd leap and grovel for joy. Whenever Jeanette and I took walks, he followed us in the fields. For Jeanette and me it was a little awkward to cross wire fences, press the top-most one, step on tiptoe and lift one leg over the wires, or crawl beneath or between them. Sam simply jumped the fence.

In the field we once found a stillborn calf, with gaping bloody red holes in the black fur. Sam took quite a few big bites out of the carcass, and when he was done he pissed around it, reserving it for later, though this was not his territory, but coyote land. Only when we walked him could he go this far away from the house and eat carcasses. He could take the road to villages six miles away, in either direction; there, the coyotes could not stop him, but here in the field, he had to yield.

Rather than managing to expand his territory by marking far afield, Sam lost it. Every night coyotes seemed to come closer and closer to the house, so that Sam was circumscribed into an area of three to four acres, and during the day double that, but still mostly outside of the range of dead calves (each spring there were at least three stillbirths).

Coyotes came so close that they dug a nest beneath our defunct Chevy pickup left alone in the pastures. One sunny noon a mother with half a dozen pups as yellow as the dry prairie grass peeped out from beneath the shelter. Rusty, tilting, the pickup merged with the landscape, for what is iron but a sort of stone, and what is landscape but stone with a bit of green and yellow life cracking through it — or green and yellow life with a bit of stone cracking through? Almost every round hill had an old stripped pickup growing yellower among bones of abandoned cows now blazingly, stonily, white. To my mind, pickup bodies weren't junk at all, unlike in junkyards, and to coyotes' minds, far from junk, they became homes.

Once, before having a cup of coffee, I looked out the window and saw half a dozen cats in trees. "Look," I said to Jeanette, "even our small kittens love to climb trees." She interrupted proofreading her essay on *Paradise Regained*—she studied for an English degree across the Missouri River, in Vermillion—and pointed out a detail which I had missed: Sam. I went out and shouted at him, trying to sound as forbidding as possible. Sam rolled on the ground, contritely, and looked at me sideways. Often, if he had done something wrong—like chewed my wool sweater or ate my shoe—even before I knew it because he must have assumed I did know it, he'd coil on his back with his paws in the air, as though to defend himself. The difference now was that as I kept shouting at him, he got an erection, and he looked slyly at me, one of his eyes closing and opening, winking—as though to say. You look pretty when you're angry!—or fearful that I would kick him. I told him to go away, pointing to a barn, and he went there, looking from a distance as I collected the precariously perched kitties and let them into the house, where Sam was allowed only if temperatures dipped below zero. Before us, he'd had to weather minus twenties. The first time we invited him inside, he would not enter the house, as though crossing the doorstep was a grave violation of laws human and canine. And in rural Nebraska it was. Once, after Sam had jumped on a kitchen table, Jeanette's uncle—not Al but his older brother Jim—had beaten Sam with a tractor chain. Clearly remembering the punishment, Sam would not enter our house, and even as I pulled him in, he squealed. Soon however he got used to being inside; in the morning, rather than squeal to be let out, he stood in the kitty-litter box, his back feet in the sand, front outside, aiming precisely at the middle of the box. And then he covered his crap, while cats, in utter alarm, watched from cupboards and bookshelves.

In sub-zero temperatures it seemed that Sam was simply too old— seven or eight, nobody knew precisely—to take the weather, although local ranchers would have deliberately made him stay outdoors, as they did with their dogs and cows. Old barns which used to protect cows now fell apart, some dismembered for lumber or new pasture, and the cows huddled together in windchills as low as minus seventy.

Sometimes Sam left us for several days because he participated in "cattle drives." These were organized nearly by a movie script: local cattle farmers, in boots and cowboy hats, rode horses and bullied cattle, moving them to winter pastures with corn-stubble in a festival of manhood. Women were not welcome—neither were city-slickers, like myself—to the chagrin of Jeanette, who although an excellent and experienced rider, was allowed to join only once, to take pictures of the cowboys. Sam thrived then, living up to his reputation as a heeler—he ran after straying cows in an outside loop so that they would return to the herd. He could not do that with bulls, but on the other hand, bulls always stayed in the same pastures, with their impressive bulk tightening into well-defined muscles under shiny black fur.

While Sam was away, I missed him particularly when I went into the basement to throw logs into the furnace, because now, without the canine, possums and badgers began to return. I walked down the wooden steps with a long poker in my hands, so that if one of these creatures startled me, I could chase it away, which I did by banging a big metal sheet rolled upright in a spiral (I thought I would use it to repair a furnace duct, but never came around to doing it). At the metallic bang, possums ambled away slowly and awkwardly like aging ducks in the dark. Basement light bulbs quickly burnt out because the high mineral content of our water from leaky pipes corroded the wiring which sent waves of stray voltage, so that our cats, when we wanted to pet them, jumped away before fire from our fingertips would leap crookedly, as though cats were a prairie hill and our fingers clouds. I felt ashamed of being uncomfortable in the dark basement, listening to the sounds of meek wildlife, with faces of badgers, bullsnakes and foxes merging surreally in my imagination into an infernal painting by Bosch. But rabies was a good excuse for the discomfort. So, although we grew used to a baby skunk who ate cat food on the porch without stinking up the place, we beheld Sam joyously.

For a couple of days Sam ran, threatened, and even killed the sampling of prairie wildlife, until my going downstairs to light a fire became a delightfully hearthy rite: I'd toss in some ash and red hardwood, after chopping stray branches and edges of thick logs to fit into the large mouth past its thick iron lip, a door with the name of Marshaltown, Iowa, bulging in cast iron. Orange fire in my eyes, smoke in my nostrils, and tar on my fingers gave me many sensations, and among them this: that I was loading the steam engine of a train and crossing the continent, and what a luxurious train it appeared when I climbed out to face a briskly black firmament, a frosty Milky Way, coyotes howling, and among them, a child of love—Sam's?—barking. Some dogs did seem to be a cross between coyote and dog. The Holzers' mutt, with his thick orange fur and narrow muzzle, looked like a coyote.

Several nights after Sam came back from the cattle drives, we certainly appreciated him. Sam growled, with his back to our window. The light

279

from the window usually reassured him, but not enough that night — he moaned and squealed when he did not pant or bark.

"I wish we had a gun," I said. "If there's a pack of rabid coyotes there, I could scare them. Poor Sam has to do all the work himself."

"Do rabid coyotes get scared?" Jeanette asked.

Sam, perhaps tired of fear, ran into a grove in our yard. Late at night we heard bulls hollering and somewhere a cow screamed as though a beast were slaughtering her.

"Something big is out there," Jeanette said.

In the morning we forgot about the incident, but in the afternoon, as I hadn't seen Sam, I wondered about him. I was taking a crap in the grove, aiming at the hole of the previous outhouse site, because our outhouse was now occupied by a crew of wasps, who had already stung me four times so that I was somewhat reluctant to go back. And my way, although not dignified, seemed environmentally sound — the stuff was biodegradable. (That was the downside of living in the country, in what would otherwise be a deserted country house, as an alternative to living in crap-congested cities.) Standing up from my innocuous way of dealing with nature, I noticed Sam, not far, watching me, a plea in his eyes. A red stripe went straight from his neck down his chest on one side, and a dark red stripe on another.

I scrutinized the stripes and asked Jeanette, "Have you seen Sam lately?"

"It is blood, isn't it?"

Sam limped to the porch and lay down.

"Boy, that's strange," I commented. "Sam is so fast, I can't see how another dog would get him."

"Coyotes may have ganged up on him."

"Or could it be a bobcat?"

"Oh, I forgot to tell you, there's been a cougar around. The Holzers have seen it, and so have the Kruppels, near Winnetoon. I bet it's the cougar."

"Come on, he wouldn't survive that, would he?"

"The cougar must have had him by the neck, see the big marks?"

"What a brave dog! He probably attacked the cougar!"

"I am going to town to ask my brother about the cougar reports."

"Ask him to finally give you a gun."

She was gone.

Faithful Sam: he was always there, guarding us, and we didn't even feed him much except for his dry food. True, lately he'd been piling rabbits and squirrels in the yard, letting them rot — his version of cooking. I went to the fridge and gave him a piece of a dead cow, which he devoured in two gulps and growled. "Sure thing," I said. "You understand the importance of iron in your blood. Here, have some more." I was heartened. Sam would recover.

So now while Jeanette was away, I tried to examine Sam's wounds, but he ducked. I didn't insist because I could hurt him. He stood and walked with a surprising amount of strength. I admired what a broad genetic pool could do for your stamina.

Soon Tim and Jeanette were back. Tim called Sam, Sam jumped at him, gave him a lick on his chin below his cigarette. Tim pulled Sam by the neck, right by the wound. (I resented that bit of cowboy machismo — Tim played rough and independent, and yet though he was twenty-eight, he stayed at his parents' place and constantly begged for loans.) Sam didn't squirm; his tail — a little bitty stump, cut by his first owner because of a peculiar tail-hating esthetic — continued to wag.

"Oh, my God," shouted Tim. "That's no blood. It's shit! It's shit!" His voice grew shrill.

"It can't be," I said. "Look at how red it is."

Jeanette smelled it and said, "No, it's blood. Old blood smells like this."

"Like shit? You are crazy," Tim said.

"I worked in a hospital, you haven't. This is old stinky blood."

"You two are crazy, man!"

"You are crazy," I said. "Have you brought us a gun? You know, here without a neighbor in a mile radius, we need it."

"I'll bring you a pistol. It's louder, if you want to scare coyotes, cougars and shit." Now he went through Sam's wounds again, "It's shit. At least I can tell shit. Yuck."

"Come on, it's a wound."

"There's no wound crust, no scratch, nothing deep in the hairs!" His fingers groped through the hairs.

"It was a tooth that pierced just in one spot," I said.

"What's wrong with the two of you?"

"We are sorry to see the romance go: Our dog fighting a cougar," Jeanette said.

"Sick," he commented.

I grew impatient with Sam's being insulted like that so I examined the wounds. I smelled my fingers. "Shit, it is shit!" I felt mixed emotions but no mixed sensations.

Tim was about to leave.

"You know, Tim," I said, "the worst thing about this is that I think the shit is mine." I put warmth into my voice, confiding. (In my Italophilia, I had lasagna before reading the offal sections from the *Inferno*, about a third of that wonderful excretory poem. Pope portrayed the *Odyssey* as that *wonderful eating poem*, so why not dub the *Inferno* the wonderful scatological—more than eschatological—poem?)

"How disgusting!" Tim squealed.

"I was joking. I don't think he would have gone into the outhouse, but then, again . . . "

Tim was in the car and down the lane, mad as Inferno.

"That was the last time he'll come here," Jeanette said.

"He'll be back before long to bum for two bucks for cigarettes. But he hasn't even brought us a gun."

"You know, I don't really think we need one," Jeanette said.

Our brave dog cowered away, inexpressible sadness in his eyes, perhaps for the loss of glory. At least he got a steak, and now I understood why he was reluctant to have his wounds examined. But he kept the stripes—they probably worked as a kind of diplomatic passport that allowed him to cross into the coyote land with the aura of human prestige and immunity.

The following morning, pretty early, I stole my wife's slippers and went into the yard. "Where are you going?"

"I am going out to free the cougars. They've been caged for too long."

I freed the cougars in the outhouse and when I stood up, I stood like a monkey, pretty low, so the wasps from the nest on the roof wouldn't swoop down to sting me.

Sam squealed and jubilantly ran out of the yard and into the woods near a thin creek among cottonwoods, where ordinarily he would not dare run during the day.

It was July 4, and one event excited Knox County. A Desert Storm war hero delivered speeches amidst fireworks and flags. Later his wife—who had had several lovers while he had been in the desert and left him for good—had supposedly slept with another man, her daughter's boyfriend. She was found in her bed with her skull smashed. Before police could question the hero, he drove into a field, put a gun barrel below his chin, and pulled the trigger. The trouble was he did not seem to know where the vital part of the brain was. He blew off his chin, his tongue, his nose, his eyes, and the frontal lobes of his brain, but he stayed alive, despite blood clogging his throat and filling his lungs. After that, I did not desire to get a rifle that bad.

Just when we began to treat Sam as a great pal—we now combed his hair with a rough brush and bought medicine for his lingering eye infection (one eye seemed constantly blood-shot)—we had to leave. Our time of poverty seemed to be up. I got a job offer at a university in Minnesota. In two years we had made hardly any friends in the area; it seemed it would take fifty years to begin to fit in. So why not leave? We dropped a tomcat off behind a cheeseburger joint. This may sound cruel, but a month before, we had picked him up as a stray in Center because his ears were torn, and we bought cream for him and nursed him back to good health, and then, as we packed our car, he snuck into the house, and in a couple of seconds killed two kittens, biting through their necks, and wounded the third, before we noticed and kicked him out. When we dropped him off, he was better off than he had been before. We gave away some cats to Jeanette's relatives; others, we had advertised in the local papers, and then we left sacks of food atop the furnace for the toms who had not showed up. We asked Jeanette's brother and her father and uncles to take care of Sam. Guiltily, with heavy hearts and a couple of dearest cats, we drove away from our muddy driveway.

Three months later, when we came for a visit, there were no cats and no Sam. Skunks had moved under our porch, droves of bickering badgers and raccoons into the barns, and old possums, who looked like ancient balding professors, into the basement. I started a reluctant, heavy, smoky and stinky fire, which smoked us out of the house. We found out that nobody would have Sam; people feared that he would bark and urinate too much, scratch up car roofs, bite through ropes, eat shoes, and he would not stay on a chain. Al, his owner, had died of a stroke. In his will he did not mention Sam. So, Sam kept visiting the Holzers, who could not stand a dog that left too much, and now apparently, the dog that stayed too much. The old Holzer paterfamilias killed Sam with a hunting rifle, and dumped his body in the ravine nearby, his garbage dump.

■■■■■■■■■■■

Notes from the Country Club

Kimberly Wozencraft

T hey had the Haitians up the hill, in the "camp" section where they used to keep the minimum security cases. The authorities were concerned that some of the Haitians might be diseased, so they kept them isolated from the main co-ed prison population by lodging them in the big square brick building surrounded by eight-foot chain-link with concertina wire on top. We were not yet familiar with the acronym AIDS.

One or two of the Haitians had drums, and in the evenings when the rest of us were in the Big Yard, the drum rhythms carried over the bluegrass to where we were playing gin or tennis or softball or just hanging out waiting for dark. When they really got going some of them would dance and sing. Their music was rhythmic and beautiful, and it made me think of freedom.

There were Cubans loose in the population, spattering their guttural Spanish in streams around the rectangular courtyard, called Central Park, at the center of the prison compound. These were Castro's Boat People, guilty of no crime in this country, but requiring sponsors before they could walk the streets as free people.

Walking around the perimeter of Central Park was like taking a trip in microcosm across the United States. Moving leftward from the main entrance, strolling along under the archway that covers the wide sidewalk, you passed the doorway to the Women's Unit, where I lived, and it was how I imagined Harlem to be. There was a white face here and there, but by far most of them were black. Ghetto blasters thunked out rhythms in the sticky evening air, and folks leaned against the window sills, smoking, drinking Cokes, slinking and nodding. Every once in a while a joint was passed around, and always there was somebody pinning, checking for hacks on patrol.

Past Women's Unit was the metal door to the Big Yard, the main recreation area of three or four acres, two sides blocked by the building, two sides fenced in the usual way — chain-link and concertina wire. It was generally in the Big Yard entrance that you would find people "jumping." Prison sex was fast and furious; even the threat of shipment to a maximum security joint did not entirely subjugate the criminal libido. I walked out to breakfast one morning and saw a set of brown buttocks pumping between a pair of upraised knees; they were halfway hidden in the shrubbery, but the tableau leaped out at me like a sudden close-up in a movie. The important thing was not to stare or look startled. I could see a hack at the far side of Central Park, strolling along in the six o'clock morning, oblivious to the goings-on directly across the courtyard from him. As I walked past the entryway, I nodded to a young man standing at the edge of the courtyard and smoking a cigarette. He had the hack under surveillance. If the blue-suited guard came too close the fellow would warn his friends in the bushes to get out fast.

Sex in prison always involved at least three people, two to copulate, one to pull jiggers. It was sex in the bathrooms, sex in the bushes, sex in the closets, sex in the little out-of-the-way coves at the end of the unused hallways. I just wanted to do my time and get out, but by the morning of the sixth month, I was waking up aching, so when the chance presented itself, I took it. It was the right time of the month not to get pregnant (that's always a little risky but desperation pushed me to play the odds), and the boss was out sick. The hack in charge of the Sewage Plant was forced to keep an eye on Landscape as well as his own crew. Rick, a fellow inmate who kept the Landscape tractors running, was a genuinely decent fellow, a real friend who was hurting as much as I was, and when he raised his eyebrows at me in the shop that morning I nodded yes. The whole crew paired off that day, one woman even doing double duty. Rick and I did it in the safest place on the entire compound — in the Warden's back yard. After, he held me gently for a long time, and it was so good just to touch another human being that I felt like crying.

Past the Big Yard you entered the Blue Ridge Mountains, a sloping grassy area on the edge of Central Park, where the locals, people from Kentucky, Tennessee and the surrounding environs, sat around playing guitars and singing, and every once in a while passing around a quart of hooch. They made it from grapefruit juice and a bit of yeast smuggled out of the kitchen. Some of the inmates who worked in Cable would bring out pieces of a black foam rubber substance and wrap it around empty Cremora jars to make thermos jugs of sorts. They would mix the grapefruit juice and yeast in the containers and stash them in some out-of-the-way spot for a few weeks until Presto! you had hooch, bitter and tart and sweet all at once, only mildly alcoholic, but entirely suitable for evening cocktails in Central Park.

Next, at the corner, was the Commissary, a tiny store tucked inside the entrance to Veritas, the second women's unit. It wasn't much more than a few shelves behind a wall of plexiglas, with a constant line of inmates spilling out of the doorway. They sold packaged chips, cookies, pens and writing paper, toiletries, some fresh fruit, and the ever-popular ice cream, sold only in pints. You had to eat the entire pint as soon as you bought it, or else watch it melt, because there weren't any refrigerators. Inmates were assigned one shopping night per week, allowed to buy no more than seventy-five dollars worth of goods per month, and were permitted to pick up a ten-dollar roll of quarters if they had enough money in their prison account. Quarters were the basic spending unit in the prison; possession of paper money was a shippable offense. There were vending machines stocked with junk food and soda, and they were supposedly what the quarters were to be used for. But we gambled, we bought salami or fried chicken sneaked out by the food service workers, and of course people sold booze and drugs. The beggars stood just outside the Commissary door. Mostly they were Cubans, saying "Oye! Mira! Hey, Poppy, one quarter for me? One cigarette for me, Poppy?"

There was one Cuban whom I was specially fond of. His name was Shorty. The name said it, he was only about five-two, and he looked just like Mick Jagger. I met him in Segregation, an isolated section of tiny cells where prisoners were locked up for having violated some institutional rule or another. They tossed me in there the day I arrived; again the authorities were concerned, supposedly for my safety. I was a police woman before I became a convict, and they weren't too sure that the other inmates would like that. Shorty saved me a lot of grief when I went into Seg. It didn't matter if you were male or female there, you got stripped and handed a T-shirt, a pair of boxer shorts and a set of Peter Pans—green canvas shoes with thin rubber soles designed to prevent you from running away. As if you could get past three steel doors and a couple of hacks just to start with. When I was marched down the hall between the cells the guys started whistling and hooting and they didn't shut up even after I was locked down. They kept right on screaming until finally I yelled out, "Yo no comprendo!" and then they all moaned and said, "Another fucking Cuban," and finally got quiet. Shorty was directly across from me, I could see his eyes through the rectangular slot in my cell door. He rattled off a paragraph or two of Spanish, all of which was lost on me, and I said quietly, "Yo no comprendo bien Espanol. Yo soy de Texas, yo hablo ingles." I could tell he was smiling by the squint of his eyes, and he just said, "Bueno." When the hacks came around to take us out for our mandatory hour of recreation, which consisted of standing around in the Rec area while two guys shot a game of pool on the balcony above the gym, Shorty slipped his hand into mine and smiled up at me until the hack told him to cut it out. He knew enough English to tell the others in Seg that I was not really Spanish, but he kept quiet about it, and they left me alone.

Beyond the Commissary, near the door to the dining hall, was East St. Louis. The prison had a big portable stereo system which they rolled out a few times a week so that an inmate could play at being a disk jockey. They had a good-sized collection of albums and there was usually some decent jazz blasting out of there. Sometimes people danced, unless there were uptight hacks on duty to tell them not to.

California was next. It was a laid back kind of corner near the doors to two of the men's units. People stood around and smoked hash or grass or did whatever drugs happened to be available and there was sometimes a sort of slow-motion game of handball going on. If you wanted drugs, this was the place to come.

If you kept walking, you would arrive at the Power Station, the other southern corner where the politicos-gone-wrong congregated. It might seem odd at first to see these middle-aged government mavens standing around in their Lacoste sport shirts and Sans-a-belt slacks, smoking pipes or cigars and waving their arms to emphasize some point or other. They kept pretty much to themselves and ate together at the big round tables in the cafeteria, sipping cherry Kool Aid and pretending it was Cabernet Sauvignon.

That's something else you had to deal with—the food. It was worse than elementary school steam table fare. By the time they finished cooking it, it was tasteless, colorless, and nutritionless. The first meal I took in the dining room was lunch. As I walked toward the entry, a tubby fellow was walking out, staggering really, rolling his eyes as though he were dizzy. He stopped and leaned over, and I heard someone yell, "Watch out, he's gonna puke!" I ducked inside so as to miss the spectacle. They were serving some rubbery, faint pink slabs that were supposed to be ham, but I didn't even bother to taste mine. I just slapped at it a few times to watch the fork bounce off and then ate my potatoes and went back to the unit.

Shortly after that I claimed that I was Jewish, having gotten the word from a friendly New York lawyer who was in for faking some of his clients' immigration papers. The Kosher line was the only way to get a decent meal in there. In fact, for a long time they had a Jewish baker from Philadelphia locked up, and he made some truly delicious cream puffs for dessert. They sold for seventy-five cents on the black market, but once I had established myself in the Jewish community I got them as part of my regular fare. They fed us a great deal of peanut butter on the Kosher Line; every time the "goyim" got meat, we got peanut butter, but that was all right with me. Eventually I was asked to light the candles at the Friday night services, since none of the real Jewish women bothered to attend. I have to admit that most of the members of our little prison congregation were genuine *alter kokers*, but some of them were amusing. And I enjoyed learning firsthand about Judaism. The services were usually very quiet, and the music, the ancient intoning songs, fortified me against the screeching pop-rock vocal assaults that were a constant in the Women's Unit. I learned to think of myself as the *shabot shiksa*, and before my time was up, even the Rabbi seemed to accept me.

I suppose it was quite natural that the Italians assembled just "down the street" from the offending ex-senators, judges, and power-brokers. Just to the left of the main entrance. The first night I made the tour, a guy came out of the shadows and whispered to me, "What do you need, sweetheart? What do you want, I can get it. My friend Ahmad over there, he's very rich, and he wants to buy you things. What'll it be, you want some smoke, a few Ludes, vodka, cigarettes, maybe some Kosher salami fresh from the kitchen? What would you like?" I just stared at him. The only thing I wanted at that moment was Out, and even Ahmad's millions, if they existed at all, couldn't do that. The truth is, every guy I met in there claimed to be wealthy, to have been locked up for some major financial crime. Had I taken all of them up on their offers of limousines to pick me up at the front gate when I was released and take me to the airport for a ride home in a private Learjet, I would have needed my own personal cop out front just to direct traffic.

Ahmad's Italian promoter eventually got popped for zinging the cooking teacher one afternoon on the counter in the Home Economics classroom, right next to the Cuisinart. The Assistant Warden walked in on the young lovebirds, and before the week was up, even the Cubans were walking around singing about it. They had a whole song down, to the tune of "Borracho Me Accoste a Noche."

At the end of the tour, you would find the jaded New Yorkers, sitting at a picnic table or two in the middle of the park, playing gin or poker and bragging about their days on Madison Avenue and Wall Street, lamenting the scarcity of good Deli, even on the Kosher line, and planning where they would take their first real meal, upon release.

If you think Federal correctional institutions are about the business of rehabilitation, drop by for an Orientation session one day. There at the front of the classroom, confronting rows of mostly black faces, will be the Warden, or the Assistant Warden, or the Prison Shrink, pacing back and forth in front of the blackboard and asking the class, "Why do you think you are here?" This gets a general grumble, a few short, choked laughs. Some well-meaning soul always says it — Rehabilitation.

"Nonsense!" the lecturer will say. "There are several reasons for locking people up. Number one is incapacitation. If you're in here, you can't be out there doing crime. Secondly, there is deterrence. Other people who are thinking about doing crime see that we lock people up for it and maybe they think twice. But the real reason you are here is to be punished. Plain and simple. You done wrong, now you got to pay for it. Rehabilitation ain't even part of the picture. So don't be looking to us to rehabilitate you. Only person can rehabilitate you is you. If you feel like it, go for it, but leave us out. We don't want to play that game."

So that's it. You're there to do time. I have no misgivings about why I went to prison. I deserved it. I was a cop, I got strung out on cocaine, I violated the rights of a pornographer. My own drug use as an undercover narcotics agent was a significant factor in my crime. But I did it and I deserved to be punished. Most of the people I met in Lexington, though, were in for drugs, and the majority of them hadn't done anything more than sell an ounce of cocaine or a pound of pot to some apostle of the law.

It seems lately that almost every time I look at the *New York Times* Op-Ed page, there is something about the drug problem. I have arrested people for drugs, and I have had a drug problem myself. I have seen how at least one Federal Correctional Institution functions. It does not appear that the practice of locking people up for possession or distribution of an insignificant quantity of a controlled substance makes any difference at all in the amount of drug use that occurs in the U.S. The drug laws are merely another convenient source of political rhetoric for aspiring office-holders. Politicians know that an anti-drug stance is an easy way to get votes from parents who are terrified that their children might end up as addicts. I do not advocate drug use. Yet, having seen the criminal justice system from several angles, as a police officer, a court bailiff, a defendant, and a prisoner, I am convinced that prison is not the answer to the drug problem, or for that matter to many other white-collar crimes. If the taxpayers knew how their dollars were being spent inside some prisons, they might actually scream out loud.

There were roughly 1,800 men and women locked up in Lex, at a ratio of approximately three men to every woman, and it did get warm in the summertime. To keep us tranquil they devised some rather peculiar little amusements. One evening I heard a commotion on the steps at the edge of Central Park, and looked over to see a Rec Specialist with three big cardboard boxes set up on the plaza, marked 1, 2 and 3. There were a couple hundred inmates sitting at the bottom of the steps. Dennis, the Rec Specialist, was conducting his own version of the television game show, "Let's Make a Deal!" Under one of the boxes was a case of soda, under another was a racquetball glove, and under a third was a fly swatter. The captive contestant picked door number 2, which turned out to contain the fly swatter, to my way of thinking the best prize here. Fly swatters were virtually impossible to get through approved channels, and therefore cost as much as two packs of cigarettes on the black market.

Then there was the Annual Fashion Show, where ten or twenty inmates had special packages of clothing sent in, only for the one evening, and modeled them on stage while the baddest drag queen in the compound moderated and everyone else oohed and aahhed. They looked good, up there on stage in Christian Dior and Ralph Lauren instead of the usual fatigue pants and white T-shirts. And if such activities did little to prepare inmates for a productive return to society, well, at least they contributed to the fantasyland aura that made Lexington such an unusual place.

I worked in Landscape, exiting the rear gate of the compound each weekday morning at about nine, after getting a halfhearted frisk from one of the hacks on duty. I would climb on my tractor to drive to the staff apartment complex and pull weeds or mow the lawn. Landscape had its prerogatives. We raided the gardens regularly and at least got to taste fresh vegetables from time to time. I had never eaten raw corn before, but it could not have tasted better. We also brought in a goodly supply of real vodka, and a bit of hash now and then, for parties in our rooms after lights out. One guy strapped a six-pack of Budweiser to his arms with masking tape and then put on his prison issue Army field jacket.

When he got to the rear gate, he raised his arms straight out at shoulder level, per instructions and the hack patted down his torso and legs, never bothering to check the arms. The inmate had been counting on that. He smiled at the hack and walked back to his room, a six-pack richer.

I was fortunate to be working Landscape at the same time as Horace, a fellow who had actually lived in the city of Lexington before he was locked up. His friends made regular deliveries of assorted contraband, which they would stash near a huge elm tree near the outer stone fence of the reservation. Horace would drive his tractor over, make the pickup, and the rest of us would carry it, concealed, through the back gate when we went inside for lunch or at the end of the day. "Contraband" included everything from drugs to blue eye shadow. The Assistant Warden believed that female inmates should wear no cosmetics other than what she herself used — a bit of mascara and a light shade of lipstick. I have never been a plaything of Fashion, but I did what I could to help the other women prisoners in their never-ending quest for that Cover Girl look.

You could depend on the fact that most of the hacks would rather have been somewhere else, and most of them didn't really care what the inmates did, as long as it didn't cause any commotion. Of course, there were a few you had to look out for. The Captain in charge of Security was one of them. We tried a little experiment once, after having observed that any time he saw someone laughing, he took immediate steps to make the inmate and everyone around him acutely miserable. Whenever we saw him in the area, we immediately assumed expressions of intense unhappiness, even of despair. Seeing no chance to make anyone more miserable than they already appeared to be, the Captain left us alone.

Almost all of the female hacks, and a good number of the males, had outrageously large derrières, a condition we inmates referred to as "the Federal Ass." This condition may have resulted from the fact that most of them appeared, as one inmate succinctly described it, to simply be "putting in their forty a week to stay on the government teat." Employment was not an easy thing to find in Kentucky.

Despite the fact that Lexington is known as a "country club" prison, I must admit that I counted days. From the first moment that I was in, I kept track of how many more times I would have to watch the sun sink behind eight feet of chain-link, of how many more days I would have to spend eating, working, playing and sleeping according to the dictates of a "higher authority." I don't think I can claim that I was rehabilitated. If anything I underwent a process of dehabilitation. What I learned was what Jessica Mitford tried to tell people many years ago in her book, *Kind and Usual Punishment*. Prison is a business, no different from manufacturing tires or selling real estate. It keeps people employed and it provides cheap labor for NASA, the U.S. Postal Service, and other governmental or quasi-governmental agencies. For a short time, before I was employed in Landscape, I worked as a finisher of canvas mailbags, lacing white rope through metal eyelets around the top of the bags and attaching clamps to the ropes. I made one dollar and fourteen cents for every one hundred that I did. If I worked very hard, I could do almost two hundred in a day.

It's not about justice. If you think it's about justice, look at the newspapers and notice who walks. Not the little guys, the guys doing a tiny bit of dealing, or sniggling a little on their income tax, or the woman who pulls a stunt with welfare checks because her husband has skipped out and she has no other way to feed her kids. I do not say that these things are right. But the process of selective prosecution, the "making" of cases by D.A.s and police departments, and the presence of some largely unenforceable statues currently on the books (it is the reality of "compliance": no law can be forced on a public which chooses to ignore it, hence, selective prosecution), make for a criminal justice system which cannot realistically function in a fair and equitable manner. Criminal justice—I cannot decide if it is the ultimate oxymoron or a truly accurate description of the law enforcement process in America.

I think about Lexington almost daily. I will be walking up Broadway to shop for groceries, or maybe riding my bike in the original Central Park and suddenly I'm wondering who's in there now, at this very moment, and for what inane violations, and what they are doing. Is it chow time, is the Big Yard open, is some inmate on stage in the auditorium singing "As Time Goes By" in a talent show? It is not a fond reminiscence, or a desire to be back in the Land of No Decisions. It is an awareness of the waste. The waste of tax dollars, yes, but taxpayers are used to that. It is the unnecessary trashing of lives that leaves me uneasy. The splitting of families, the enforced monotony, the programs which purport to prepare an inmate for reentry into society but which actually succeed only in occupying a few more hours of the inmate's time behind the walls. The nonviolent offenders, such as smalltime drug dealers and the economically deprived who were driven to crime out of desperation, could remain in society under less costly supervision, still undergoing "punishment" for their crime, but at least contributing rather than draining the resources of society.

Horace, who was not a subtle sort of fellow, had some T-shirts made up. They were delivered by our usual supplier out in Landscape, and we wore them back in over our regular clothes. The hacks tilted their heads when they noticed, but said nothing. On the front of each shirt was an outline of the state of Kentucky, and above the northwest corner of the state were the words, " Visit Beautiful Kentucky!" Inside the state boundary were:

- Free Accommodations
- Complimentary Meals
- Management Holds Calls
- Recreational Exercise

In small letters just outside the southwest corner of the state was "Length of Stay Requirement." And in big letters across the bottom:

Take Time to Do Time
F.C.1. Lexington

I gave mine away on the last day I finished my sentence. It is a time-honored tradition to leave some of your belongings to friends who have to stay behind when you are released. But you must never leave shoes. Legend has it that if you do, you will come back to wear them again.

■ ■ ■ ■ ■ ■ ■ ■ ■ ■ ■

The Abstract Wild

Jack Turner

> *The tigers of wrath are wiser than the horses*
> *of instruction.*
> —William Blake, *The Prophetic Books*

The mountains have many moods. Even under clear summer skies I require my clients to pack warm clothing, to be prepared for the worst. I am a mountain climbing guide, and like all mountain climbing guides I am a skeptic about mountain weather. We abide by a local adage: only fools and newcomers predict the weather in the Tetons. If someone does not have the right equipment—a hat or a pair of warm pants—I send them to Orville's, a nearby Army surplus store that sells cheap wool clothing. Once, however, I sent a client to Orville's for pants and he came back without them, although he did not reveal this until later, after the climb was well underway. Since he was ill-prepared for our venture I was annoyed, and said so. He replied that the only pants available at Orville's were old German army pants; he would not wear them.

My client was a Jew. He offered no further explanation, no list of principles; he expressed no hate. The decision was visceral, as private as the touch of fabric and skin.

His action suggests a code: if justice is impossible, honor the loss with acts of remembrance, acts that count for little in the world, but which, if sustained, might count for oneself, might shore up a portion of integrity. Refuse to forgive, cherish your anger, remind others. His code was old-fashioned, almost Biblical. A less impassioned attitude, indeed, an almost indifferent one, was expressed by then Vice-President Bush when he visited Auschwitz in September, 1987: "Boy, they were big on crematoriums, weren't they?"

I understood my client. His conviction opposes our tendency to tolerate everything, to accept, to forget, to forgive, to get on with life, to be realistic, to get over our losses. We accept living with nuclear weapons, toxic wastes, oil spills, rape, murder, starvation, smog, racism, teenage suicide, torture, mountains of garbage, genocide, dams, dead lakes, and the daily loss of species. Most of the time we don't even think about it.

I, too, abhor this tolerance for anything and everything. My client's refusal stems from the Holocaust; mine started with the damming of the Glen Canyon of the Colorado River and its tributaries, especially the Escalante River, and specifically Davis Gulch, which I visited twice in 1963 just before it was drowned by the waters of Lake Powell. Visitors now houseboat and water-ski hundreds of feet above places where I first experienced wilderness. It broke my heart then; I am still angry about it now. I am angry that Wallace Stegner and the late Edward Abbey would boat around Lake Powell as guests of universities and the U.S. government, I am angry with those who vacation on houseboats there, I am angry with friends who kayak and skin-dive its waters. I make a point of being nasty about it.

Some find it obscene to mention the loss of six million people and the loss of one ecosystem in the same breath. I am not ignorant of the difference in magnitude, but I refuse to recognize a difference in causation. In the September 11, 1989 *High Country News*, there is a picture of eleven severed mountain lion heads stacked in a pyramid at the base of a cottonwood tree. You can see the details of their faces; they are individuals. The association with death camps is involuntary. These are only eleven of the 250,000 wild predators killed by the U.S. government in 1987. No one raised a voice to the Animal Damage Control division of the U.S. Department of Agriculture. No one got angry. These deaths, the destruction of the rain forest, and the death of 2 million Cambodians have a common source, a source that deserves our rage, but a source that we do not yet comprehend.

It is now often said (ever since Wendell Berry stated it so clearly and forcefully) that our ecological crisis is a crisis of character, not a political or social crisis. This said, we falter, for it remains unclear what, exactly, is the crisis of modern character; and since character is partly determined by culture, what, exactly, is the crisis of modern culture. Answers to these questions are not to be found in the writings of Thoreau, or Muir, or ecologists ("deep" or otherwise). Answers, always controversial, are found in the study of the Holocaust, the study of "primitive" peoples untouched by our madness, and in the study of the self.

Although the ecological crisis appears new (because it is now "news") it is not new; only the scale and form are new. We lost the wild bit by bit for 10,000 years and forgave each loss and then forgot. Now we face the final loss. Although no other crisis in human history can match it, our commentary is strangely muted and sad, as though catastrophe was happening to us, not caused by us. Even the most knowledgeable and enlightened continue to eat food soaked in chemicals (herbicides, pesticides, and hormones), wear plastic clothes (our beloved polypropylene), buy Japanese (despite their annual slaughter of dolphins), and vote Republican — all the while blathering on in abstract language about our ecological crisis. This is denial, and behind denial is a rage, the most common emotion of my generation; but it is suppressed, and we remain silent in the face of evil.

Why is this rage a silent rage, a quiet impotent protest that doesn't extend beyond the confines of our private world? Why don't people speak out, why don't they *do* something? The courage and resistance shown by the Navajos at Big Mountain, by Polish workers, by Blacks in South Africa, and, most extraordinarily, by Chinese students in Tiananmen Square render much of the environmental protest in America shallow and ineffective. With the exception of a few members of Earth First!, Sea Shepherd, and Greenpeace, we are a nation of environmental cowards. Why?

Effective protest is grounded in anger, and we are not (consciously) angry. Anger nourishes hope and fuels rebellion; it presumes a judgment, presumes how things ought to be and aren't, presumes caring. Emotion is still the best evidence of belief and value.

Our most recent conceit is that certain places and animals and forests are "sacred." We have forgotten that sacred is a social word and that "sacred for me" is as irrelevant as "legal for me." We ignore that our culture is as sacred as any other because we do not distinguish between formal and popular religion. If it is true that our national parks are sacred, it is also true that Disneyland is sacred, and that the location of President Kennedy's assassination is sacred. But these pilgrimage sites are sacred because of the function of entertainment and tourism in our culture. In a commercial culture the sacred will have a commercial base.

We have forgotten the relation between violence and the sacred, forgotten that the wars in Ireland, Palestine, and Kashmir are, in part, about sacred land (and, in part, as Joseph Campbell points out, about mistaking a piece of real estate for the "Kingdom of God"). If you go to Mecca and blaspheme the Black Stone the believers will feed you to the midges, piece by piece. Go to Yellowstone and destroy grizzlies and grizzly habitat and the believers will dress up in bear costumes, sing songs, and sign petitions. This is charming, but it is not rage, and it suggests no sense of blasphemy. The sacred must be more than personal preference.

It would be helpful to acknowledge that we fear our rage for two reasons: it might lead us to do something illegal, thus threatening our freedoms; and it might lead to violence. This fear is justified. Any form of resistance to public or private authority that is *effective* (e.g., spiking trees) must of necessity become a felony. Historically, continued effective disobedience has been met with violence. At Amritsar, India, in 1919, the British slaughtered 379 non-violent demonstrators in cold blood and wounded more than 1,000. In 1930 they murdered 70 more at Peshawar. The non-violent demonstrators in Norway who successfully resisted German attempts to teach Nazi ideology in Norwegian schools were sent to concentration camps. Remember Kent State?

Violence breeds violence. In the October 1967 demonstrations at the Pentagon, protesters were non-violent until U.S. Marshals began dragging women by their hair and beating them in the groin with clubs. Only then did the demonstrators riot. The cant of messianic humanism conceals our culture's highest command: thou shalt not defy authority. To effectively protest the destruction of the earth we will have to face these facts, surmount these fears.

A *sacred* rage does often surmount these fears. The belief, emotion, and action of the little old Christian lady arrested for protesting abortion can reasonably be connected to the sacred. So can the non-violent protest of a Buddhist peace activist. So can the terrorist activities of a Moslem fanatic. Whether we like or dislike these acts, think them good or bad, or right or wrong, is irrelevant to their being sacred. They are sacred because of their origin. For the believer, the sacred is the *source* of belief, emotion, and action, what is good and what is right; it *determines* life and is immune to merely secular legal and ethical judgments. This is vital religion, lived belief. Old forests will be sacred, and their destruction blasphemous, when we demonstrate that *our* rage is immune to secular judgment. The hard question is this: do we want an environmental *religion?* Do we want nature to be *sacred?* I am inclined to agree with Dogen Zenji: "Clearly nothing is sacred—hard as iron."

Effective protests are grounded in a refusal to accept what is normal. We accept a diminished world as normal; we accept a diminished way of life as normal; we accept diminished human beings as normal. What was once considered pathological becomes statistically common and eventually "normal"—a move that veils a move toward abstraction. Decayed teeth are statistically common, just like smog and environmentally caused cancers. That a statistically common decayed tooth is also an abnormal tooth, a pathological tooth, a diminished tooth, a painful, horrible, mind-bending tooth, is a fact we ignore. Until it is our tooth. At present most of us do not experience the loss of the wild like we experience a toothache. That is the problem. The "normal" wilderness most people know is a charade of areas, zones, and management plans which is driving the real wild into oblivion, but we deny this, accepting the semblance instead of demanding the real. This too is normal. The real loss is not experienced.

Effective protests are grounded in a coherent vision of an alternative; we have no coherent vision of an alternative to our present maladies. Deep Ecology does not, as yet, offer a coherent vision. Our main resources for Deep Ecology, the books by Sessions, Devall, and LaChapelle, are hodgepodges of lists, principles, declarations, quotations, clippings from every conceivable tradition, and tidbits of New Age kitsch. The authors do not clearly say what they mean; they do not forcefully argue for what they believe; they do not create anything new. That some are professional philosophers is all the more confounding. Presented as revolutionary tracts aimed at subverting Western Civilization, these works embarrass us with their intellectual timidity and flaccid prose. Compare them with other revolutionary works — *Leviathan*, the *Social Contract*, the *Communist Manifesto* — or even the work of contemporary European thinkers such as Foucault or Habermas and we glimpse the depth of our muddle.

Deep Ecology is suspicious. It lacks passion, an absence that is acutely disturbing given the current state of affairs. A reading of Marx's theses on Feuerbach is in order, especially the 11th: "Philosophers have only interpreted the world in various ways; the point, however, is to change it." If we do not change the world soon, Deep Ecology will become an obtuse form of necrophilia.

Apathy, complacency, docility and cowardice are not new; they were, for instance, major subjects of both *Walden* and "Resistance to Civil Government." (It is always helpful to recall that for most of their lives Thoreau and Muir were considered maladjusted failures, even by those that knew and loved them.) But for the present let it be, at best, controversial, and at worse improper, to have strong moral feelings about the treatment of animals, plants, and places — an emotional mistake — like being in love with the number 2. Let the case for the destruction of the earth rest — we are smothered with facts; they are both depressing and endless. What is shocking is that we are all "good Germans." That is *our* problem, and a problem we can attempt, at least, to solve.

The social reasons for our apathy are numerous: religious traditions (Christian and Buddhist) that glorify acceptance and condemn emotion (particularly anger) and judgment; a political ideology that extols relativism, pluralism, tolerance, and pragmatism in internal affairs (although not in external affairs—until recently it was all right to hate the "Commies" and be enraged at *their* "evil"); the inertia of any social structure; a claustrophobic conformity behind a mask of individualism; and a love of expediency that is short-sighted and self-serving. The most readily accepted social criticism in our society is cloaked in humor—the political cartoons of Gary Trudeau and Gary Larson, for example. Ordinary people don't talk of normal and abnormal. We no longer talk of good and evil; we talk about what we like and dislike, as if discussing ice cream. To defend our likes and dislikes we quote opinion polls and surveys that track the gentle undulations of the true, the good, and the beautiful.

There are also private reasons for apathy and indifference. As Marcuse noted twenty-five years ago: "The intellectual and emotional refusal 'to go along' appears neurotic and impotent." Even as citizens of the alleged high-point of Western Civilization, we are ridiculed for equating public pathology and personal tragedy. Criticize the greed of the rich and you are *envious*; become enraged at the killing of 100,000 dolphins every year and you are *infantile*; protest the FBI's harassment of dissident organizations and you *have a problem with authority*; condemn the state for exposing citizens to radiation from nuclear-arms testing and you are *unpatriotic*. The reduction of social criticism to private defect is incessant in our culture and has the crippling effect of diminishing our outrage and numbing our moral imagination. Convinced that it is really *our* problem, we fail to be astonished by evil; living nightmares no longer awaken us. We are put down, so we shut up, abandoning the prospect of autonomy, self-respect, and integrity.

Signing more petitions, giving money, or joining another environmental organization helps some, but is too abstract to help *us* and *our* problem. These means are too far from the end, the intention unachieved. Indeed, our apathy and cowardice stem, in part, from this: these abstractions *never* work; they *never* achieve for us a sense of power and fulfillment; they correct neither the cause nor the effect. We end up feeling helpless, and since it is human nature to want to avoid feeling helpless, we become dissociated, cynical, and depressed. Better to live in the presence of the wild—feel it, smell it, see it—and do some small thing that is real and succeeds—like Gary Nabhan's preservation of wild seeds, or Doug

Peacock's study of grizzlies. Thoreau's "In Wildness is the preservation of the World" is exact truth. We know that in the end moral efficacy will manifest knowledge and love — our intimacies. We only value what we know and love. We no longer know or love the wild. So we no longer value it. Instead, we accept substitutes, imitations, semblances, and fakes — the diminished wild. We accept abstract information in place of personal experience and communication. This removes us from the true wild and severs our recognition of its value. Most people don't even miss it. Most people *literally* do not know what we are talking about.

In 1928, Walter Benjamin sadly remarked, "The earliest customs of peoples seem to send us a warning that in accepting what we receive so abundantly from nature we should guard against a gesture of avarice. For we are able to make Mother Earth no gift of our own." Now a gift is possible: knowledge, passion, courage, and a long list of heresies (often called felonies). We must become so intimate with wild animals, with plants and places, that we answer to their destruction from the gut. Like when we discover the landlady strangling our cat.

If anything is endangered in America it is our experience of wild nature — gross *contact*. There is knowledge only the wild can give us, knowledge specific to it, knowledge specific to the experience of it. These are its gifts to us. In this, wilderness is no different from music, painting, poetry, or love: concede the abundance, respond with grace. The problem is that we no longer know what these gifts are. In our noble effort to go beyond anthropocentric defenses of nature, to emphasize its intrinsic value and right to exist independently of us, we forget the reciprocity between the wild in nature and the wild in us, between knowledge of the wild and knowledge of the self that was central to all primitive cultures.

Once the meaning of the wild is forgotten, because the relevant experience is lost, we abuse the word, literally, misuse it. The savagery and brutality of gang rape is now called "wilding," and in New Age retreats men search for a "wild man within." It is doubtful these people have been in a wilderness. They don't know what wild means. They don't "know," that is, in the sense of having experienced it, though they may "know" it abstractly. (Bertrand Russell put the difference nicely: knowledge by acquaintance and knowledge by description.)

Why do we associate the savage, the brutal, and the wild? The savagery of nature fades to nothing compared to the savagery of human agency. The most civilized nations on the planet killed 60 to 70 million of each other's citizens in the 30-year span from the beginning of World War I to the end of World War II. Dante, Shakespeare, Goethe, Kant, Rousseau, Dogen, Mill, Beethoven, Bach, Mozart, Manet, Basho, Van Gogh, and Hokusai didn't make any difference. The rule of law, human rights, democracy, the sovereignty of nations, liberal education, tradition, scientific method, and the presence of an Emperor God didn't make any difference. Protestantism, Catholicism, Greek and Russian Orthodoxy, Buddhism, Shintoism, and Islam didn't make any difference. How can we, at this time in history, think of a bear or a wolf as savage? Why laugh at the idea of the noble savage when we have discovered no "savage" as savage as civilized man?

Why equate the wild only with the masculine, as though the feminine were not also wild? The wild is neither and both. The easiest way to experience a bit of what the wild was like is to go into a great forest at night alone. Sit quietly for a while. Something very old will return. It is well described by Ortega y Gasset in *Meditations on Hunting*: "The hunter . . . needs to prepare an attention which does not consist in riveting itself on the presumed but consists precisely in not assuming anything and in avoiding inattentiveness. It is a 'universal' attention, which does not inscribe itself on any point and tries to be on all points." This is very close to a description of certain meditation techniques, especially "shikantaza," a practice of the Soto sect of Zen. (It is not an accident that Lama Govinda believed meditation arose among the hunting cultures of the Himalayan foothills; it is not an accident that the Baiti and the Golok handle utensils like masters of the Tea Ceremony.) Alone in the forest, time is less "dense," less filled with information; space is very "close"; smell and hearing and touch reassert themselves. It is keenly sensual. In a true wilderness we are like that much of the time, even in broad daylight. Alert, careful, literally "full of care." Not because of principles or practice, but because of something very old.

The majority of Americans have no experience of the wild. We are surrounded by national parks, wilderness areas, wildlife preserves, sanctuaries and refuges. We love to visit them. We also visit foreign parks and wilderness; we visit wild, exotic cultures. We are deluged with commercial images of wildness: coffee table books, calendars, postcards, posters, T-shirts, and placemats. There are nature movies. A comprehensive bibliography of nature books would strain a small computer. There are hundreds of nature magazines with every conceivable emphasis: Yuppie outdoor magazines, geographical magazines, philosophy magazines, scientific magazines, ecology magazines, and political magazines. Zoos and animal parks and marine lands abound, displaying a selection of beasts exceeded only by Noah's.

From this we conclude that modern man's knowledge and experience of wild nature is extensive. But it is not extensive. Rather, what we have is extensive experience of a severely diminished wilderness — animal or place — a *caricature* of its former self; or, we have extensive indirect experience of wild nature via photographic images and the written word. This is not experience of the wild, not gross contact.

The national parks were created for and by tourism and they emphasize what interests a tourist — the picturesque and the odd. They are managed with two ends in mind: entertainment and preservation. Most visitors rarely leave their cars except to eat, sleep, or go to the john. (In Grand Teton National Park, 93% of the visitors never visit the backcountry.) If visitors do make other stops, it is at designated picturesque "scenes" or educational exhibits presenting interesting facts — the names of the peaks, a bit of history — or, very occasionally, for passive recreation, a ride in a boat or an organized nature walk. None of this is accidental. It results from carefully designed "management plans" that channel the flow of tourists according to maximum utility — utility defined by the ends of entertainment, efficiency, and preservation.

The problem is not what people do in the parks; it is what they are discouraged or prevented from doing. No one, for instance, is encouraged to climb mountains, backpack, or canoe alone. Hikers are discouraged from traveling off-trail, especially in unpatrolled areas with difficult rescue. They are often prohibited from remote areas where they might encounter bears, or else travel is restricted to groups. Their movements are always tracked. It is *illegal* to wander around the national parks without a permit defining where you go and where you stay and how long you stay. In every manner conceivable national parks separate us from wildness.

If we go into a designated wilderness area, say the Bridger-Teton, we are slightly less restricted, but we find as much degradation of the wild environment. We see signs and hike horse trails and cross sturdy bridges and find maps on large boards at trail junctions. We meet patrolling rangers. Boy Scout and Girl Scout troops working on character, and the National Outdoor Leadership School teaching "wilderness" skills in a corporate management seminar. We meet trail crews, pack trains, and hikers galore.

At night we see the distant lights of cities and highways and sodium vapor lamps in the yards of farms and ranches. Satellites pass overhead.

By day, contrails from commercial jets mar the sky; military planes, private jets, small aircraft, and helicopters are a common presence. We camp by a lake, the outlet of which is filled with spawning golden trout. We notice they are thin as smelt. They are not indigenous to these mountains. Around camp, many small trees have been cut down by Basque sheepherders. The trails of their herds are ubiquitous; domestic sheep still graze this wilderness. In autumn we find hunting camps the size of military installations, the hunters better armed than Green Berets. Many of the camps use salt licks to lure the elk, deer, and moose. If we wander out of this narrow "wilderness zone," we walk straight into clear-cut forest, logging roads, and oils wells.

This is no longer the wild, no longer a wilderness; and yet we continue to accept it as wilderness and call our time there "wilderness experience." We *believe* we make contact with the wild, but this is an illusion. In both the national parks and wilderness areas we accept a reduced category of experience, a semblance of the wild nature, a fake.

And no one complains.

We visit the zoo or Sea World to see wild animals, but they are not wild; they have been tamed, rendered dependent and obedient. We learn nothing of their essential life in nature. We do not see them hunt or gather their food. We do not see them mate. We do not see them interact with other species. We do not see them interact with their habitat. Their numbers and their movements are artificial. We see them controlled. We see them trained. In most cases they are as docile, apathetic, and bored as the people watching them. If we visit wild animals in sanctuaries we are protected by buses and Land Rovers and observation towers. We are separated from any direct experience of the wild animals we came to visit. No *contact?* Why call it a visit?

The majority of people who feel anguish about whales have never seen a whale at sea; the majority who desire to reintroduce wolves to Yellowstone have never seen a wolf in the wild, and some, no doubt, have never been to Yellowstone. We feel agony about bludgeoned seal pups and shredded dolphins without ever having touched one or smelled one or watched it swim. However much these emotions promote environmental causes, they remain suspect, for the object of the emotion is experienced through a *medium*, via movies, TV, the printed word, or snapshots. They pass as quickly as our feelings about the evening news or our favorite film. They are the emotions of an *audience*, the emotions of *sad entertainment*. We cry our hearts out about "Old Yeller"; the

Humane Society has to destroy thousands of dogs and cats because homes cannot be found for them.

Dissatisfied with the semblances and imitations at home we travel abroad in a search for the real thing. But there isn't anything different out there, no *exotic* context by which to judge the absence of context in our lives. The context remains, in the apt phrase of George Trow, "the context of no context." We do not find the Other. We can spend a lifetime in parks and wilderness areas and on adventure travel trips and remain starved for wild country and wild people.

Thirty years ago no foreigner had set foot in Khumbu, the beautiful valley that approaches Everest from the south. When I started going there thirteen years ago it was advertised as a remote wilderness, despite the presence of thousands of Sherpas in dozens of villages. Sometimes it is still advertised that way — an exotic Shangri-la. That this is false is not the point; it is the form and magnitude of the con that is important, the "size" of the illusion.

Now, tens of thousands of foreigners visit the region every year. Most arrive by plane at the village of Lukla. The trail from there to the old Everest Base Camp — Interstate "E" — is always crowded with tourists, many of them in shorts and sandals with Pan Am flight bags over their shoulders containing all they need for several weeks in this wilderness.

In Namche Bazaar I recently stayed at a hotel owned by a Sherpa I worked with years ago. I slept in one of the "special" rooms separated from the dorm used by most tourists. On the wall are two scribbles. One is the signature of former President Jimmy Carter. The other is the signature of Richard Blum, husband of former San Francisco mayor, Dianne Feinstein. Both needed to let us know they slept in this special room in this remote wilderness. In the morning I was served the first omelette prepared in the hotel's new microwave oven, the first microwave in Khumbu. It was so hard I barely got it down. The cook, who happens to be the owner's wife, said "Sherpa way better" and headed back to the kitchen in disgust. Right! That next winter electricity came to Thyangboche monastery and promptly burned it down.

At the old British Base Camp in Tibet, on the north side of Everest, is a bare concrete platform awaiting a communications satellite dish that will improve weather predictions for climbing expeditions. Soon there will be a hotel.

The north side of K2 is more difficult to reach. Fly to Beijing. Fly from Beijing to Urumchi. Fly from Urumchi to Kashgar. Drive two days by Toyota Land Cruiser or Mitsubishi bus to Mazar on the long road between Kashgar and Lhasa. Ride camels for a week (they are required for the many fordings of the Shaksgam River). Walk for several days up a glacier. What do you find? Skeletons of tents, with pieces of nylon flapping in the breeze. Inside are boxes of unused stainless steel pressure cookers, cases of antipasto, and Italian magazines. On a ridge above the glacier is a concrete platform with a radar dish.

Tibet is still described as wild, exotic, and forbidden. When in Lhasa, I stay in a large, modern hotel operated by Holiday Inn. The manager meets me at the door. He is an Englishman dressed in an impeccable three-piece Saville Row suit and speaks with an Oxford accent. My room is like any other Holiday Inn room. It has closed-circuit television. In the lobby, during cocktail hour, there is a string quartet that plays Mozart and Beethoven. I drink Guinness Stout and Corvousier Cognac. I dine on pasta and yakburgers.

In the streets I see a Red Army soldier driving a lime-green Mercedes Benz; another soldier drives a cobalt blue Jeep Cherokee. Golok nomads wander the bazaar wearing yak-skin boots, woolen breeches, and cloaks (Tibetan "chuba") fringed with snow leopard fur. Their hair, entwined with scarlet cloth, is gathered on top of their heads. One carries a ghetto-blaster the size of a small suitcase. The volume makes me wince. He is playing Bruce Springsteen.

The preferred style of dress for young male Tibetans in Lhasa is called "Kathmandu Cowboy": black Hong Kong cowboy boots, stone-washed Levis, a black silk shirt, gold necklace, and Elvis Presley hair cut. Young Tibetan women date Chinese soldiers.

I am thankful for the small things. Once at a monastery outside of Lhasa, I witnessed a senior monk debating with a large gathering of students. He shouted his questions, clapping and stomping to an eight-count beat. His students shouted their answers trying to keep up with his furious pace, and he continued at the same furious pace. When they failed to answer correctly he would brush the back of one hand with the back of the other, dismissively smiling and laughing. The students, animated and responsive, would try again.

Once I saw a pilgrim circumambulating the Jokhang monastery through the Barkhor bazaar. He was wearing only yak-skin boots and woolen breaches; in the middle of his back, a gilded prayer box the size of a gallon of milk hung from a thick leather strap slung over one shoulder. He chanted continuously in a strong voice, first holding his hands in prayer high over his head, then bowing hard to the ground in the middle of the bazaar—first knees, then chest, then elbows, his hands still held in prayer over his head. Then he would rise, take one step to the left, and repeat his prayer. Though the bazaar was packed with people there was a forty-foot circle around him. No one interfered; very few tourists had the temerity to photograph him, and then only from a great distance. He is the only wild human being I have seen during fifteen years of travel in Asia. A modern Milarepa.

At the Dalai Lama's old summer palace—the Norbulingka—there is a zoo, his private zoo. There are long trenches cut in the ground for yaks and buffalo; all they can see is the sky. There are small cages for wolves and fox and cats and bears. In one of the cages there is a bear the Chinese call "ma-shang." We would call it a grizzly. I think of Buddhism's first vow—"Beings are numberless: I vow to enlighten them"—trying to discover the proper relation between the Dalai Lama, enlightenment, and a caged ma-shang. I feel that I have arrived at the end of a long labyrinth and found a mirror.

These places *are* beautiful; these people *are* wonderful. I continue to go there and always will. There are small pockets of wilderness left, and a few wild people, but, in general, the wilderness and the people of the wilderness are gone; wild things cannot necessarily be reached by travel. We perpetuate the idea that it is out there, we console ourselves with feeble imitations, we seek reassurance in nature entertainment and outdoor sports. But it is nearly gone. Unless we change the world soon the wild will be but a memory in the minds of a few people. When they die it will die with them, and the wild will become completely abstract.

What is wrong with all this fun and entertainment, with this imitation of what was once a real and potent Other? Nothing, if it is recognized for what it is—a poor substitute. But we do not note that the wild is missing, and it is not clear how we might re-establish contact with wild things. It is probably best to begin now with what we are emotionally closest to—animals. Plants can come later, places last. Despite all the eco-babble to the contrary, at present we do not understand what it might mean to communicate with a plant or a place as Native Americans did. Unfortunately, the conditions under which we might form a relationship with wild animals are also diminishing.

The story is repeated daily in the media. A natural habitat is eroded or lost, a species suffers, becomes endangered, or is lost. Efforts are made to save it, study it, and arouse public sympathy for its plight. This always sounds so inevitable, as though the loss of habitat is as incorrigible, as implacable as fate. There is no mention of human agency, no suggestion that we are responsible for the loss of wilderness habitat, no possibility that we could have done otherwise, that we could reverse this horrible situation, no suggestion that we have this power, no realization that the abstract language of wildlife management aids and abets the continued loss of wild habitat, no acknowledgment that a zoo, a circus, a Sea World, a national park, is *a business*. Reading these articles, hundreds of them, we never discover why an orca like Shamu has to jump through 10,000 hoops next year to help make 338 million dollars for the parks division of Harcourt Brace Jovanovich Inc.

Zoos are getting bigger and more "natural"; wildlife sanctuaries and national parks are "islands," too small and increasingly artificial. Yellowstone National Park is really a megazoo. *Everything is exploited and managed, now; it's just a matter of degree. Accept this. It's normal. Nothing to be done.*

When we deal in such abstractions boundaries are blurred, between the real and the fake, between the wild and the tame, between independent and dependent, between the original and the copy, between the healthy and the diminished. Blurring takes the edge off loss and removes us from our responsibilities. *Wild nature is not lost; we have collected it; you can go see it whenever you want.* With the aid of our infinite artifice this fake has replaced the natural. It's not really *very* different from the original! Why worry? As Umberto Ecco observes in *Travels in Hyperreality*, "The ideology of this America wants to establish reassurance through imitation." And that ideology has succeeded; we are reassured, we are not angry, we are not even upset.

A bstraction masks horror. A zoo is a very different kind of place from the wild; a caricature requires an original. A zoo, a Sea World is (at best) a fake habitat presenting pseudo-wild animals to the public for entertainment and financial reward. The wild is the original, the wild is home. The bigger and more naturalistic the megazoo, the "better" the fake. But it is still a fake. And why we should or should not accept this fake is a subject that cannot be addressed by the abstractions of wildlife management.

Abstraction displaces emotion, constraining us to relate to the "problems" of wild animals rationally — the excuses of scientific knowledge, commerce, and philanthropy. It leaves us without an explanation of our emotional relations to animals. It cannot explain why I went berserk, amok, at the zoo in Mysore, India, at the sight of a crowd pelting an

American mountain lion trapped in a cage on a small wooden platform. This animal was suffering due to a very un-abstract cause. She had been sold to a foreign business for purposes of amusement and profit, and human beings there were mistreating her. Nothing unusual here. *Normal.*

Her suffering was obscene, the solution simple: she needed to get home. To run along rims through pinyon and cedar and crouch and leap and dance on her toes sideways, her tail curled high in the air to seduce a mate and then hunt with him in the moonlight and eat deer and cows and sheep and make little pumas and die of old age on warm sandstone by a clear spring at the end of a gulch dense with cottonwood and box elder.

The condors need to get home, too. So do the orcas. That they no longer have a home is not their problem. (That homeless humans no longer have a home is not their problem.) It is our problem; *we* have done it. The solution is to give them their home. (The solution for the homeless is equally simple: to give them their home.) Why is this so difficult to conceive or act upon? Part of the answer is this: *we* no longer have a home except in a brute commercial sense; home is where the bills come. To seriously help homeless humans and animals would require a sense of home that was not commercial. The Eskimo, the Aranda, the Sioux, belonged to one place. Where is our *habitat*? Where do *we* belong?

"All sites of enforced marginalization — ghettos, shanty towns, prisons, madhouses, concentration camps — have something in common with zoos." (John Berger, *Why Look at Animals?*) If we add Indian reservations, aquariums, and botanical gardens to this list, then a pattern emerges: removed from their home, living things become marginal, and what becomes marginal is diminished or destroyed. Of bedrock importance is community, for humans, animals, and plants.

We know that the historical move from community to society proceeded by destroying local structures — religion, economy, food patterns, custom, possessions, families, traditions — and replacing these with national, or international, structures that created the modern "individual" and integrated him into society. Modern man lost his home; in the process everything else did, too. That is why Aldo Leopold's Land Ethic is so frighteningly radical; it renders this process *morally wrong.* "A thing is right when it tends to preserve the integrity, stability, and beauty of the biotic community. It is wrong when it tends otherwise." Apply this principle to people, animals, and plants and the last 10,000 years of history is *evil.*

We are repeatedly told that the nature entertainment and recreation industries help the environment. After an orca killed another orca at Sea World the veterinarian responsible for the whales claimed that children often "come away with knowledge they didn't have before and a fascination that doesn't go away... they become advocates for the marine environment." We hear the same general argument about national parks and wilderness areas; they must be entertaining and recreational or the public will not support environmental issues. And contact with exotic cultures is defended by saying it is required to save them.

This argument is no different from the one given by the Marine officer in Vietnam who explained the destruction of a village by saying, "We had to destroy it in order to save it." The first "it" here is real — people, plants, animals, houses: what was destroyed. The second "it" is abstract — a political category: the now non-existent village we "saved" from the Viet Cong.

What, *exactly*, is the "it" we are trying to save in all the national parks, wilderness areas, sanctuaries, and zoos? What are we traveling abroad to find? I suggest that part of the answer is this: something connected with *our home*.

That, of course, is not the usual answer. The usual answer is mass recreation sites and mass entertainment programs. We have succeeded admirably. Nature recreation and entertainment is a multi-billion dollar business — the Nature Business. Hundreds of thousands of people in the government and in the private sector depend on the nature business for their livelihood, *depend* on a caricature defended by obscure abstractions.

If the answer is wild nature and the experience of wild nature, then we have failed miserably. For intimacy with the fake will not save the real. Many people believe that continued experience with caricatures creates a desire to experience the real wild. In my experience it is more likely to produce a desire for more caricatures.

The illusion of contact with the wild provided by national parks, wilderness areas, and Sea Worlds actually *diverts* us from the wild. Knowledge gained from these experiences creates an *illusion* of intimacy that masks our true ignorance and leads to complacency and apathy in the face of our true loss. We are inundated by "nature" but we do not care about nature. We do not care that Shamu is in exile from a home in the sea.

We might call this failure "Muir's Mistake." He did not see clearly enough, if at all, that his experience of the wild — intimate, poetic, and visionary — *could never* be duplicated by Sierra Club trips. In 1895 he told the Sierra Club, " . . . if people in general could be got into the woods, even for once, to hear the trees speak for themselves, all difficulties in the way of forest preservation would vanish." They got into the woods, but they did not hear the trees speak. Muir could not understand then that setting aside a wild area would not, in itself, foster intimacy with the wild. Yosemite Valley is now more like Coney Island than a wilderness. He could not know that the organization and commercialization of anything, including wilderness, would destroy the sensuous, mysterious, empathic, absorbed identification he was trying to save and express. He could not know that even the wild would eventually succumb to commodicide — death by commodification.

The world of Thoreau and Muir — the mid-nineteenth century — was bright with hope and optimism. In spite of that, they were angry and expressed their anger with power and determination. Thoreau went to jail for his beliefs. Our times are darker; such optimism seems impossible at the end of this century. Our world looks backward, obsessed with memory and forgetting. Something vast and crucial has vanished. Our rage should be as vast. Refuse to forgive, cherish your anger, remind others. We have no excuses.

> It was a place for heathenism and superstitious rites —
> to be inhabited by men nearer of kin to the rocks and to
> wild animals than we. We walked over it with a certain
> awe . . . it was a specimen of what God saw fit to make
> this world. What is it to be admitted to a museum, to
> see a myriad of particular things, compared with being
> shown some star's surface, some hard matter in its home!
> I stand in awe of my body, this matter to which I am
> bound has become so strange to me. I fear not spirits,
> ghosts, of which I am one — that my body might — but
> I fear bodies, I tremble to meet them. What is this Titan
> that has possession of me? Talk of mysteries! — Think
> of our life in nature — daily to be shown matter, to come
> in contact with it—rocks, trees, wind on our cheeks!
> the solid earth! the actual world! the common sense!
> Contact! Contact!
> —Thoreau, "Ktaadn"

■ ■ ■ ■ ■ ■ ■ ■ ■ ■ ■

Saturday Night, and Sunday Morning

James Alan McPherson

"One of these days I'm go'n show you how nice a man can be
One of these days I'm go'n show you how nice a man can be
I'ma buy you a brand new Caddilac.
After, always speak some good words about me."
— Muddy Waters

People say it is always cold in Chicago.
Once in the dining room of the Hyde Park Hilton, I saw a father and son arguing over Sunday dinner. The father wore a dark blue gabardine suit with shoulder pads, a colored shirt, and a striped tie. The son's three-piece suit linked him with the commercial life of the city. The father's tentative manner, in that upscale hotel, defined him as self-consciously lower class. The son's manner was smooth, manicured, consciously geared to the decor of the dining room. The father did not "belong" in the dining room of the Hyde Park Hilton. The son did. The son kept saying, "But Dad, can't you see?" The father could not see. The father kept insisting on what the Bible says. The son kept making exceptions. They were discussing the son's responsibility toward a woman who was bearing his child. Each seemed determined to pull the other into an alien world.

The winter of 1985 is bitterly cold. It is the coldest day on record, and people have been warned to stay indoors. It is Saturday. At the entrance to the El station, at State and Randolph, two frostbitten boys try to sell at half-price the Sunday edition of the *Tribune*. Down on the platform, the man selling newspapers behind the concession stand is Asian. Along the platform a young black man, in a formal black suit and white shirt and black bow-tie and black gloves and black sunshades, is tap-dancing. People waiting for the El, mostly white, applaud and toss coins into his top hat, upturned on the cement platform. Still another black man, handcuffed, is being led away by two Chicago policemen. One policeman also leads a lean German shepherd on a leash. The second officer, escorting an enraged white female, follows behind. The polished handcuffs on the young man's wrists catch the cold yellow light. He seems to be crying without sound.

People pretend they do not see.

During the 1980s, as traditionally, *money* best defined what Chicago runs on. People come to this city because they want to do well. Its traditions are rooted in fur trading, riverboats, railroads, stockyards, banks, commodity futures, and in buildings so tall they almost swagger in the wind off Lake Michigan. This city is unabashed in its commitment to material values, ruggedly honest about its areas of corruption. But it is also a city of great contradictions. Its downtown skyline competes with New York, Atlanta, Houston, San Francisco; its neighborhoods are rigidly ethnic and provincial. It is a city always in the process of reforming; it never seems able to get away from the same old gang. Its overt allegiances are to material values; its covert allegiances, the texture of its soul, are extremely complicated. There are probably more active churches in Chicago—Protestant, Catholic and Jewish—than in any other city in the country. Chicago has contributed more to the arts than any other city; it is still self-conscious in comparing itself to New York. It is one of the most racially polarized of American cities; it is a city still capable of profound human gestures.

Perhaps Chicago is all that can be expected of America.

During the 1930s, the young Richard Wright, in search of values to replace those he thought he had left behind in Mississippi, expressed personal contempt for the public values of Chicago. "Perhaps it would be possible for the Negro to become reconciled to his plight," he wrote in *American Hunger*, "if he could be made to believe that his sufferings were for some remote, high, sacrificial end; but sharing the culture that condemns him, and seeing that a lust for trash is what blinds the nation to his claims, is what sets storms to rolling in his soul."

> "*Precious Lord, take my hand, lead me on, let me stand,*
> *I am tired, I am weak, I am worn ...*"
> —Thomas Dorsey

During the same time Wright lived there, Mahalia Jackson, Thomas Dorsey and Muddy Waters came to Chicago. Like many thousands of other Mississippians, they brought with them an idiom, a technique for transcending personal storms, that Wright had somehow bypassed. They used aspects of this idiom to confront, and then to transcend, the hard facts of life. From within their roles as entertainers, from behind the various masks that provided safety, they provided Chicago's material culture with a spiritual optimism. It was Studs Terkel who, back in the 1940s, recognized the value of Mahalia Jackson's music and helped it reach a wider audience. And it was a white Chicago promoter who brought Muddy Waters from the small clubs of the South Side of Chicago to the folk festival at Newport, Rhode Island in 1960.

Several decades later, these two giants still define the blues idiom.

Saturday Night

During his last set that evening at the Checkerboard, Buddy Guy said to his audience, "I would like your support in helping to make it possible for part of 42nd Street to be named for Muddy Waters. He did the most to make this street famous, and I think the city should honor him." Buddy Guy was a young blues artist with a rising reputation. Small clubs like the Checkerboard, and Theresa's further down 42nd Street, supported him. Only those who value authenticity of feeling, the "real" blues, come to these clubs. They are mostly black people, middle-aged or older, whose roots are close to the rural South. For them, the music is not entertainment. It is an organic part of a settled way of life. Groups of white students from the University of Chicago come here, especially on the weekends, but they are not really in the idiom, the felt experience. Still, they brave the cold, and the warnings of black cab drivers ("Don't flash any money. They'll knock you in the head!") to get a feel for the authentic blues. The armed black policemen, or guards, at the doors of the clubs are there to ensure the safety of the white patrons. But still the mostly black audience sets the musical standard. Next to the front door, beside the armed black guard, a sad-faced, middle-aged black woman sits alone, playing her nightly game of solitaire. Next to the bandstand, an old black man, probably a laborer, does a slow grind to the music. Two women, one toothless and wrinkled and the other young, wearing a red headrag, embrace closely as they dance together. They seem to be supporting each other's souls. Behind my table a man is singing to himself. Suddenly he gets up, walks around the room, and says, "I got the blues! I got the blues!" He stops at my table and makes a statement: "My daughter died last week from heroin. Went out to Michael Reece Hospital, she was layin' up in bed, needle holes swole up in her neck big as a basketball. She was the baddest one of my kids. Monday, I'm takin' her ass down to Clarksdale, Mississippi and put her six feet under. I'm go'n bury her right. I ain't go'n bury her wrong."

He asks for a contribution for the funeral and I give it to him. Then he goes up onto the small stage and sings.

I try to hear his feelings for his daughter *beneath* the words of his song. But the electrified guitars, in their mocking commentary, seem much too loud and playful. The singer seems to be crying from within his song. I find myself remembering another blues artist, a much older man named John Jackson — a gravedigger by profession and a musician by necessity — of Rappahannock, Virginia. I remember the night he was told, during a gig, that his second son was dying, this one of cancer. To outpourings of sympathy from friends, John Jackson said, "Yes, m'am. Yes suh. I thank y'all." Then he continued with his music, making very joyful sounds on his blues banjo. John Jackson confirmed for me my suspicion that inside the best musicians is a very delicate mechanism, one guarded at all costs, trained by hard experience to transform deep pain into a kind of beauty. This mechanism, or perhaps it might be called a style, is completely integrated into the fabric of the musician's personal life. The best of them would be incapable of crying. The best of audiences would not allow it.

The blues singer steps down from the platform while the audience applauds politely. He is introduced, to all newcomers, as Muddy Waters, Jr. He passes my table as he moves back to his own. "My *main* man," he whispers to me. "My daughter has some children and I'm tryin' to do the best I can for them."

I give him more money.

While leaving the Checkerboard I observe to the guard how well Muddy is holding up under his tragic loss.

"What loss?" the guard asks.

I detail the circumstances of his daughter's death.

The guard laughs. "Man," he says, "Muddy ain't got no daughter. You give him money? He told that same shit about his Mama last week, right in this club, and she was alive and well up in her own home."

It came to me then that I was only a tourist from Iowa, someone who lives apart from the current uses of the blues idiom. It also came to me that the idiom had gone desperately commercial. The narrative statement had become detached from its ritual base, and survives now as a form of folklore. There was now *crying* in it.

Sunday Morning

Chicago is an urban center that is receptive to black folk art in all its forms. The many blues and jazz clubs, and the hundreds of churches, are expressions of a rural cultural tradition. How peasant traditions have been able to survive within a highly technological and commercial culture is a profound mystery. Perhaps it has to do with the Midwestern lack of pretension, or with a predisposition toward democratic values, or even with Chicago's unofficial policy of ethnic segregation. Whatever has sustained its vitality, it was the cohesive power of this core culture that was the basis of Harold Washington's election as mayor. His sagging campaign finally came together on the coattails of one song, "Move On Up a Little Higher," sung at a rally by Curtis Mayfield.

The core culture is part of the city and at the same time is apart from it. To see the complex simplicity of the connection, one only has to sit on the rear seat in the last car on the El, the one going South, and watch the downtown skyscrapers become toylike and small. One can actually feel the hold of hierarchy diminishing. And, briefly, it becomes clear that Chicago is still a prairie town, one whose various outlying sections have a loose relationship with the controlling powers in the skyscrapers. This arrangement encourages a closeness with one's own ethnic roots.

The purest expression of the blues idiom was once found in the black Baptist churches. Hundreds of them thrive on the South and West sides of the city: First Baptist, Christian Tabernacle, Greater Salem Baptist. It was at Greater Salem that Mahalia Jackson reached a national and international audience. She was the greatest of gospel singers, and her aristocratic presence still dominates this expression of the idiom. Each January 28th, the anniversary of her death in 1972, Studs Terkel plays a retrospective in her honor. He had great love for her. Now, several decades later, in the hums and phrasings of individual singers, one can hear the style she imposed on a folk form. Inside the churches, on Sunday mornings, one can *feel* that her definition of gospel music ("Having faith with a little *bounce* added") still holds true.

Inside Shiloh Baptist, on 49th Street, one feels a sense of redemption and renewal. For almost half an hour, a slender young girl leads a 200-voice choir in urging a full congregation to "Don't Give Up." Although the organ is electrified, and although the choir is being "conducted" as if it were a symphony, the spirit is there, among the people. The call and response between the girl and the choir is hypnotic. Time stops, and she is a priestess performing an ancient ritual function. People shout, dance, wave hands, shake tambourines, are "possessed," transcend private selves and are redeemed into a common spiritual body. They become a collective soul, all essentially equal, before God. The minister comes, now that the preparatory work is over, and begins what soon becomes a jazz-like riff on one line in the Book of Matthew. The message is unimportant. His sole function is to keep the spirit active among his

people. Trained nurses in white uniforms rush back and forth, reviving
those whose souls have been released from tremendous burdens. For a
while, it seems absolutely evident that "Jesus Is On The Main Line,"
and that one only has to tell Him what one wants. Feeling the collective
faith and spirit of the people, it becomes clearer why Christianity
is the most radical of religions, why the bedrock and basic values of
American society cannot erode. The resilience, the optimistic dream of
a foundation in the future, are rooted in churches such as these. It is no
accident that gospel music is an essential idiom in evangelical Christianity.
It speaks directly to the soul.

"When you get a song in your heart," Mahalia Jackson said, "and
you just sing it, it makes you forget about everything. It's good when we
can be on one accord. It's good to be on one accord . . . " The serenity
and eloquent economy, the personal dignity that characterized Mahalia's
rendition of gospel, can still be heard in the voices of some singers. But,
like the blues, the basic form has become somewhat standardized. In
many of the churches, the idiom has shifted back towards its roots in
dance music, threatening to deprive the individual singer of her ritual
significance. It is difficult to appreciate the vocabulary of a moan when
it is heard against a background of electrified music. The orchestration
of the choir, the incorporation of electrified organs and guitars, the
almost predictable up-tempo—these are concessions to trends that have
become a part of *most* American music. One consequence is that the
same arrangements of sounds flow out of a variety of different churches
in Chicago each Sunday morning. It is almost as if the technological
bias in the outside culture has begun to impose its own highest value,
the interchangeability of all parts, on the spiritual values basic to the
transcendent ambitions of the idiom. One has the sense, after listening
to the music for a while, of human souls encased in metal cages
struggling to rise above them. One misses the feel of a *single* human soul
speaking out of its own inner calm to the collective soul. One misses the
silence of the spirit as it descends, or is made manifest, among the
congregants. As one misses the simply lyrical compassion that a single
human voice and a piano once had for each other. Perhaps I miss only
certain people—Mahalia Jackson, Thomas Dorsey—whose personal
sounds said that they had gone through the fires and had come out
redeemed. The purifying work of the fire was in their voices.

In Chicago, the sacred and the secular are inextricably linked. It
is a sophisticated commercial city, but it respects artistic integrity. It is
ethnically segregated, but it allows each group to preserve its own

culture. It is a cold city, but it preserves many islands of human warmth. It has provided a home for the blues idiom, and it has nurtured a few giants. Their influence and the standards they set still dominate the popular culture of the city. The names of developing musicians in the idiom suggest a continuing stance of apprenticeship: Muddy Waters, Jr., Buddy Guy, Sons of Blues. They perform at the Checkerboard and at Theresa's, against the old standard. But they also perform on the North Side, before ethnically mixed, middle-class audiences, at The Kingston Mines, The Blues, The Wise Fool. They seem to know that their roots go back to the South Side, and from there to the rural towns of Mississippi and Alabama, to the tough experiences of *life* that went into the making of the idiom. Many of the current singers seem to have not yet settled the philosophical distinction between the requirements of folk art and the requirements of entertainment. Some of them guide their audiences from one set to another with a certain promise. "We go'n play some Muddy Waters for you. We go'n be right back and play some Muddy Waters for you . . . "

One expects that in time, and through the hard lessons of the *life* behind the expressions of the idiom, some of them eventually will.

O n that trip nine years ago, I went into Chicago looking for something much better than what I saw. Perhaps I expected to see areas of "purity" in my own ethnic community, some kind of muscular resolve, derived from the traditions of the blues idiom, to forego participation in the general cannibalizing of basic values which characterized that bleak time. Instead I saw what was there: human beings trying to make it as best they could.

It has become an easy cliché by now to say that corruption, public as well as personal, became normative during those years. The stance I took, while trying to explore the cultural life of the city, was bemused disbelief. I did not want to believe that those people who were hit the hardest by Reagan's policies would actually participate in the corruption of the very aesthetic forms created by their ancestors to fortify their souls against oppression. I suppose I nursed a romantic expectation that the mere fact of physical segregation would insulate black people, and our values, from the basic corruption of that time. But the cities, as everyone knew except me, had been written off. Poverty and homelessness had been placed on the back burners of national consciousness.

The word "decadence" is now gaining currency as a way of defining, in 1994, the state of the American soul. I would sharpen it to mean a debilitated, spiritless level of existence, such as what I saw in Chicago, and was defined by Ortega Y Gassett in *The Dehumanization of Art*:

> The acute dissociation between past and present is the sign of our times, a generic factor of the epoch, and with it arises a suspicion, more or less vague, which engenders the restlessness peculiar to life in our times. Present day man feels alone on the face of the earth, and suspects that the dead did not die "in jest but in earnest," not ritually, but factually, and can no longer help us. The remnants of the traditional spirit have evaporated. Norms, models, standards are of no further use. We must resolve our problems without the active collaboration of the past, totally confined to the present — whether our problems be in art, science, or politics. Modern man finds himself alone, without any living shadow at his side . . . That is what always happens at high noon . . .

I saw in Chicago nine years ago a period just before "high noon." It is now some time past that hour and little has changed to help renew the vitality of the blues idiom or the Chicago landscape against which it once thrived. The cities have been abandoned as a total loss. Yet there are some hopeful signs. The jazz musician, Wynton Marsalis, in his ongoing attempt to renew the blues idiom, has taken it back to its ritual beginnings in the African American Church. His recent "In This House On This Morning" is the most "pure" and ritually based sound that I have heard in the idiom since Phariah Sander's "Journey To The One" just at the beginning of the madness that was the 1980s. Perhaps the black American community will reclaim through its musicians, after all, its old enclaves of artistic purity.

■■■■■■■■■■■

Chicken 81

Sarah L. Courteau

My mother is a killer.

She knows how to pull a chicken's head off under her size-ten shoe, but she prefers to lay it gently on a chopping block and lop off its head with a clean stroke of the ax. Then she swings the flapping body away from her so its red life spatters the yard.

She's grabbed up a shovel, an ax, a hoe, to hack the heads off copperheads and occasional rattlesnakes that have confused their territory with ours. Once she dispatched an unfortunate blacksnake with a knot in his middle. He'd swallowed the white stone we kept in the chicken coop to fool the hens into thinking we weren't taking all their eggs.

She has stood in the barn and dropped five of a litter of nine puppies with the blunt side of an ax head. We had nothing to feed them but a gruel my mother cooked each day on the stove. Her winsome sketches on handbills and the tearful calls my younger sister Darcy made to numbers in the phone book had failed to turn up any takers for the puppies. The guy at the animal pound said no one would adopt redbone-hound mix pups, and the pound would charge $5 a head to dispose of them.

My father kills with a gun, which my mother knew would terrify the puppies in their last moments. She did the killing because her weapon of choice is an ax wielded with a skill honed by many mornings of chopping kindling for the stove. In the end, he finished the job anyway. My mother had set down her ax after the pup with one blue eye sat down and looked frankly up at her instead of nosing the decoy food bowl like the other pups had done. When my father went out with the gun to deal with the three remaining puppies, he knew — though my mother didn't ask — to save that pup with the blue eye. We named her Annie.

Other killings I can't remember or she's lied to us about. Years after our mutt Brodie had run away and been replaced in short order with an Australian shepherd puppy, my mother let the truth slip at the dinner table. They went for a walk, and my mother shot Brodie in the head with a .22 pistol. I used to kiss little Brodie on the nose, but strangers made her nervous. When a friend's child bent to pet and coo, Brodie bit the girl in the face. On our farm, a dangerous bull might be tolerated, but not a dangerous pet.

Death is supposed to be matter-of-fact on a farm. A flick of the wrist, an arc of the ax, a squeeze of the trigger, and the wriggling animal becomes just another lump of flesh to be plucked, skinned, or buried.

Not for my mother.

This is a woman who has nursed along innumerable baby birds fallen from their nests, foundling rabbits quivering with the anxiety of existence, a hairless baby mouse she tucked away in an old sock, a wild fawn found by the roadside, goats heaving with the effort of holding in their own guts after a dog attack, a calf that lived in a corner of the front room after my father cut it from the womb of its dying mother, a small king snake with a broken back that lacked the prudence to stay out from underfoot. For weeks, as I remember, she carried bits of food out to him in a protected brush pile behind the house as he wasted slowly toward death.

I've asked her how she forced past that moment of hesitation when, ax in hand, she eyed the chicken and it eyed her back with the uneasy sideways look a chicken gets when it knows something bad is going to happen. The answer was always the same: It had to be done. We had to eat, she had to protect us, an animal's pain had to be extinguished.

When our neighbors gave us several white geese to butcher one fall, Darcy stood in the haymow while my mother and father killed them, wailing over and over, "Can't we keep just one?" The answer was as inevitable as the coming winter. Survival was not negotiable.

My mother doesn't kill much any more. Maybe it's because my grandmother died a few years ago and left my father a little nest egg. Maybe it's because the last of my six siblings is in school and my mother's job as a part-time sculptor has vaulted her into the ranks of money-makers who buy their hamburger in plastic instead of on the hoof. The chief reason, I think, is her summer job three years ago at a chicken farm a mile up the road.

"I went into it with the same attitude of a Quaker going into the medical corps in Vietnam," she says. She wasn't there to send these chickens to the swift, steely deaths she had witnessed working at a Campbell Soup factory before she met my father. She was just there to care for them and make a little money at a job close to home.

The neighbors paid her $25 a day to shepherd the chickens through six weeks of life, until their muscles were just the right consistency for Tyson chicken patties and nuggets. Then the chicken catchers would descend in big trucks, stuff the three-and-a-half-pound birds into crates, and haul them away to processing plants, from which they would emerge breaded and boxed.

My mother had charge of three chicken houses, 48,000 chickens to a house, and several thousand Cornish hens besides. She had three main duties: feed them, water them, and kill any of the chicks that weren't uniform and spry.

She didn't discover that she would have to kill until her first day on the job, but she learned quickly enough. The man I'll call Alvin Smith, who owned the operation along with his wife, would scoop up a runty chicken. "He'd be talking but I'd be watching that chicken in his hand, small and soft as an egg yolk," she said. "Without looking down, he'd squeeze its head and it would loll limp in his hand, and all the while he'd be talking. Alvin was completely opaque."

It was easy to spot the deviants, the ones that weren't quite big enough or vigorous enough to reach the water line that was raised every two days in accordance with the growth plan plotted by Tyson, a company that has engineered the six-week lifespan of a chicken to the point where it considers its chicken-feed formula a trade secret.

When Alvin or the woman who trained her was around, my mother killed, snapping the necks of as many as 45 chickens a day. When I could picture the scene at all, I imagined her sweeping through the chicken houses like a cross between the Angel of Death and Little Bunny Foo Foo.

My mother has always been a sucker for the underdog, the slow starter, the runt. Now she was to cull any birds that didn't conform to the Tyson life plan. They wrecked the feed conversion ratio, wasting resources better consumed by chickens that would fit Tyson specs come collection day. If she put off killing them when they were young, she wasn't doing them any favors. The further they fell behind the other birds' growth, the harder their life of scavenging became. And, in the end, this was not a system that rewarded game survival. To put off the day of reckoning meant only that the mature chicken would be less easily and painlessly snuffed out.

I was living in St. Louis then. When I called home, I started hearing little cheeps in the background. They were just a few at first, but they swelled to a chorus over the course of the summer. Within a few days of starting work, my mother had become an Oskar Schindler of the chicken farm. Once left alone to do the job, she started smuggling chickens home, a few at a time.

She couldn't save them all, but she chose the birds she called little champions, like the one that would leap up and peck a drop of moisture from the water line when it wasn't tall enough to reach otherwise. One chick she brought home had a leg that stuck out sideways. She had lifted him up to the water line once, and he had the pluck to call to her the next time she made her rounds so she could help him again.

I started hearing scrappy tales of chicken survival during my calls home. She admired the way the misfits scratched for food on the chicken house floors or sought out condensed moisture on the door of the chicken house when they couldn't compete with the bigger birds at the feeders. In her enthusiasm, she held the chick with the sideways leg to the phone receiver so I could hear his reedy chirps, a triumph of life over science.

Even without what happened that summer, I think my mother's association with big agribusiness would have been short-lived. Where before the force of necessity had borne her through each time she took an animal's life, now she was merely a hired killer.

It was a hot summer. Old folks who were too thrifty or poor to turn on their air conditioners were dying in their rocking chairs. Then one of the Tyson plants shut down to fix a wastewater problem, and the chicken catchers stopped coming to pick up birds for slaughter. The temperature controls where my mother worked were crude, and the chickens began to pant in the heat.

The birds passed the three-and-a-half-pound mark and the Tyson pickup date. As they closed in on four pounds, they began to run out of room. They started going lame, and my mother tracked down a Tyson field representative who diagnosed the problem as femur-head necrosis, a disease caused when bacteria fester in a chicken's equivalent of our hip joint. The birds lost even what little range of movement they'd had in the cramped houses. Everything from space allotment to bird weight was controlled by strict adherence to the Tyson schedule. Now that the schedule was disrupted, the precise equations began to jumble. The chickens started to die.

My mother made her rounds day after day, picking up the dead. The freezers in each chicken house that preserved the dead chickens before transport began to overflow, and then they gave out and the dead birds inside started to putrefy. The chickens that lived couldn't keep cool as they put on weight, and they panted miserably.

Chicken 81 clinched my mother's decision to leave. She was fastening chicken wire across a doorway so the chickens could get a little more air from outside while she did her chores. One chicken followed my mother as she moved from one side of the doorway to the other, and finally settled between her feet. She reached down and rubbed its head with her finger. All the other thousands of chickens that summer had run from her or avoided her. When she rubbed the head of this one, she could see the chicken enjoyed it.

My pathologically honest mother decided to commit seventeen cents' worth of larceny—the profit the Smiths made on each bird. She resolved to come back to collect this chicken and take it home after she'd finished her rounds in the house. Even among those tens of thousands of white birds, she knew she'd find it again. Most chickens confined themselves to a fairly small area, and this one had distinctive charcoal feathers on its neck and wing.

When she returned to the spot, she had collected eighty dead chickens. She counted and recorded the dead each time she passed through a house to track the attrition for Alvin. She searched all over for the affectionate chicken, convinced it couldn't have shuffled far. Finally, she gave up. She started to lift the makeshift screen she'd lashed across the door and discovered Chicken 81. In the half hour she was gone, her chicken had crawled partway beneath the screen and died.

My mother wept.

She gave her notice that afternoon but agreed to stay on until the Smiths could find someone else. Ten days past schedule, the Tyson trucks rolled in and the catchers hauled away the chickens in a flurry of feathers. Most of the chickens, anyway. In each house several hundred were left, those too small or too crippled to meet the Tyson specs. In the past, Alvin had orchestrated a chicken roundup, closing in on the rejects with a circle of chicken wire. Then he immobilized them any way he could—snapping their necks, stomping on them—to clean out the house for the next shipment of dandelion-puff chicks. This time, he was working at his job in town and the press was on to prepare the houses, so my mother was left to clean house alone.

She went at night, when she knew the chickens would be sleeping.

She left on her car's parking lights to shine into the house and silhouette the birds where they slept clustered in puddles of white. The water lines, the feeders, all the chicken house equipment, had been hoisted to the ceiling to clear the way for the chicken catchers earlier that day.

She started down the first cavernous house. The chickens had become accustomed to the occasional bump or nudge as part of life in close quarters. My mother would sidle up to one and try to grab it by the neck and give a quick twist before it could utter a sound to alert the others. A clean grab the first time was essential. Even if the chicken flapped afterwards, if it didn't squawk, its companions didn't suspect a death spasm. By the time my mother reached the end of the chicken house, though, the few birds that were left knew a predator was among them. She had to stalk them and chase them down as she pounced and twisted, pounced and twisted.

She stood in the dark to catch her breath, her hands and shoulders sore from her kills. And she started to feel that she wasn't alone anymore.

"It began to grow in me, this feeling that someone else was in this long, dark building. I shouted out loud, 'Who's there?' I felt for a moment as though a shark spirit was there, drawn by the blood itself."

My mother fought down her panic. She finished the job that night by promising herself she would never do it again. The few chickens she missed and discovered the next day she took home.

By mid-August she had trained a young man who lived near the Smiths to tend the chickens, and she was up to her elbows in clay at a local pottery and art studio where she'd been offered a sculpting job fashioning potpourri pigs and whimsical hound dogs. She'd stopped buying chicken in the stores. The chickens she had rescued grew and grew. With a little feed and the run of the place, their bantam-size bodies grew far beyond the three and a half pounds at which their brethren had perished, and they lumbered around the farm producing noises closer to a bellow than a cluck.

A brother of mine dubbed one of the roosters Boots, after its large, muscled legs. Boots had arrived nearly grown, one of the refugees from the final night of extermination. He strutted around the farm and, when he hit puberty, started a reign of terror. He lay in wait in the yard and jumped out at my little brothers. And he raped the hens so often and so viciously that one finally died, sealing Boots' own fate as surely as Brodie's snap at a child had sealed hers.

Whatever brutality Boots himself had suffered, he had transgressed outside the bounds of the life my mother was able to negotiate for him on the farm, requiring the raw life of his fellow chickens in order to sustain his own. As my mother had always done, she gathered herself up and did what she had to do. She put a kettle of water on to boil and brought out her ax.

"Boots, he had seen me killing the other chickens, and he never trusted me after that. In the end, he was fully justified."

Franz Kafka, Metamorphosis, and the Holocaust

Peter Stine

I am separated from all things by a hollow space," Franz Kafka wrote in his diary in 1911, "and I do not even reach to its boundaries." And in another entry of 1913: "Everything appears to me to be an artificial construction of the mind . . . I am chasing after constructions. I enter a room, and I find them in a corner, a white tangle." Such uncanny seizures of alienation are faithfully recorded in the diaries which Kafka clung to as a mode of self-rescue; for he experienced the new century as a "phantom state" in which the self was forever fluctuating under the exigencies of living. Because this state cursed his own relationships with bad faith or the danger of merging into the other, Kafka was to renounce them out of love. As a writer, he would embrace this state of maximum instability. "What one is," he wrote, "one cannot express, for one is just that; one can only communicate what one is not, that is to say falsehood." From this level of submersion in reality, where the self was permanently hidden and to cast it in language was to lie, there was no rescue into meaning, least of all from psychology, which Kafka dismissed as "mirror-writing . . . the description of a reflection such as we, who have sucked ourselves full of earth, imagine; for no reflection actually appears — it is simply that we see earth wherever we turn."

What deepened his exile was that the earth Kafka saw at every turn was Prague, "the little mother with claws," torn apart by virulent strains of German and Czech nationalism in the waning decades of the Hapsburg empire. "The racial doctrines which an Austrian corporal was to translate into genocide half a century later," observes Ernst Pawel in *The Nightmare of Reason*, "were already sprouting in the subsoil of Austro-Hungarian politics." In retrospect, Pawel notes that the Edict of

Toleration in 1782 was calculated not to free the Jews, but to obliterate their ethnic identity through assimilation. This was one of the primary tasks of the German educational institutions Kafka attended in Prague, which he accurately denounced as "a conspiracy of the grown-ups" — and of the Hapsburg bureaucracy in which he later worked. In 1883, the year of Kafka's birth, the first political manipulation of Jew-hatred surfaced as German, Czech, and Hungarian extremists joined ranks to form an abortive movement based solely on anti-Semitism. The ancient Jewish ghetto in the heart of Prague was torn down or "sanitized" at the turn of the century. In 1897, a pogrom struck the city that required the intervention of Austrian troops and martial law. Two years later erupted the infamous "blood libel" Hilsner case, in which a Jewish shoemaker from Polna was baselessly accused of murdering a Christian virgin — thereby freeing psychotic propagandists to spread their ancient mythological "constructions" of the Jew as Christ-killer, rapist, and usurer across Bohemia.

This toxic turn-of-the-century anti-Semitism was fueled not only by widespread poverty and rapid industrialization, but by a new component of irrationality liberated by the weakening of age-old forces of repression. The Jewish middle class of Prague, comprising 85% of the 35,000 German speakers in a total population of 420,000, was caught in a no-man's land. Politically powerless, culturally and linguistically dispossessed, they were viewed as subhuman even by the ruling German minority whose culture and language they loyally supported as a practical matter. Ultimately, what inspired Kafka's literary generation was the failure of assimilation, and perhaps even more insufferable, the familiar denial by the Jewish bourgeoisie of the very existence of anti-Semitism. "The ghetto walls had been razed," Pawel writes, "the age-old traditions were rapidly eroding, but the newly emancipated citizens of the nation-state still found themselves accused of being Jewish — and increasingly unable to understand the nature of the accusation. The harder they tried to defend themselves by being more Czech than the Czechs, more German than the Germans, the harsher the ultimate sentence."

This was Kafka's earth, and it invaded his consciousness with an inexorable linking of accusation, guilt and punishment. "I have never been under the pressure of any responsibility," he wrote, "but that imposed upon me by the existence, the gaze, the judgment of other people." Except for the last nine months, he lived out his entire life with his parents in Prague. Kafka hardly ventured out of the inner city — except to leave town to calm his nerves in sanatoria whose sun-bathing "nature worship" was ironically in harmony with the racist German mythology that would deliver the "ultimate sentence" twenty years later. Already the way was being prepared by the elders of the tribe, whose feats of self-deception amounted on a spiritual level to collaboration in their own extinction. In "The Judgment," the father rises up from his sickbed to quell the son's rebellion by sentencing him to death-by-suicide. "It is not necessary to accept everything as true," the Cathedral priest explains to Joseph K. in *The Trial*, "one must only accept it as necessary." The accused responds that this "turns lying into a universal principle." This injunction to adapt through mendacity leads him to forget himself, leaving only the authority of the other, and inaugurates the metamorphosis of innocence into guilt and punishment. By the end Joseph K. fails to assist in his own execution only out of weariness, and dies "like a dog . . . It was as if the shame of it must outlive him."

Kafka's own father, the owner of a successful wholesale dry-goods store, treated his employees with a vulgar tyranny. His cash-register mentality fulfilled the very anti-Semitic stereotypes he was so eager to dismiss as a marginal phenomenon. The world of the fathers and the world of officialdom converged. Kafka would urge his sister Ottla to send her son to a boarding school so as to shield him from "the special mentality which is particularly virulent among wealthy Prague Jews and which cannot be kept away from children . . . this petty, dirty, sly mentality."

Yet here too he experienced another oscillation of consciousness. For whatever his private grievances, Kafka acknowledged in *Letter to His Father* that Hermann Kafka's desperate bid for assimilation was merely a reflection and escape from the racial prejudice and poverty of his own youth. Given the earth as it was, his betrayal of Judaism was inevitable.

> You really had brought some traces of Judaism from the ghetto-like village community. It was not much, and it dwindled a little more in the city and during your military service; but still, the impressions and memories of your youth did just about suffice for some sort of Jewish life, especially since you did not need much help of that kind but came of robust stock . . . At bottom the faith that ruled your life consisted in your believing in the unconditional rightness of the opinions of a certain class of Jewish society, and hence actually, since these opinions were part and parcel of your own nature, in believing in yourself. Even in this there was still Judaism enough but it was too little to be handed on to the child; it all dribbled away while you were passing it on . . . The whole thing is, of course, no isolated phenomenon. It was much the same with

a large section of this transitional generation of Jews, which had migrated from the still comparatively devout countryside to the cities.

Granted the complexities of Kafka's own case, such an objective grasp of reality became a bondage. "Perhaps the strangest of all my relationships with him," the son wrote in *Letter to His Father*, "is that I am capable of feeling and suffering to the utmost not with him, but *within him*." Given this amazing power of sympathetic merging, even with his own opposite, no wonder Kafka clung to his "hovering nothingness" as a writer. At least it was a privileged position of espionage, offering momentary freedom from the weight of a new and threatening world in which social organization is fate.

Yet this exile into writing was no real escape. Instead what Kafka called "this tremendous world I have inside my head" only martyred him in his own miraculous feats of attention to everything, both good and evil. Consider his stunned response in 1920 when Milena Jesenska asked him if he were Jewish.

> You ask me if I'm a Jew. Perhaps this is only a joke, perhaps you're only asking me if I belong to those anxious Jews. In any case as a native of Prague, you can't be as innocent in this respect as Mathilde, Heine's wife . . . You may reproach the Jews for their specific anxiousness, although such a general reproach shows more theoretical than practical knowledge of human nature . . . The strangest thing is that, in general, the reproach does not fit. The insecure position of the Jews, insecure within themselves, insecure among people, would make it above all comprehensible that they consider themselves to be allowed to own only what they can hold with their hands or between their teeth, that furthermore only tangible possessions give them the right to live, and that they will never again acquire what they once have lost . . . From the most improbable sides Jews are threatened with danger, or let us, to be more exact, leave the dangers aside, they are threatened with threats.

Shortly afterwards, Kafka wrote again to say he intended no reproach.

> . . . I could reproach you for having much too high an opinion of the Jews whom you know (myself included); there are, of course, others. *Sometimes I'd like to cram them all as Jews (including myself) into the drawer of the laundry chest, wait a while, then open the drawer a little to see whether all have already suffocated, and if not, close the drawer again, and so on like this to the end.*

Fueled by all his parricidal and cosmic rages, Kafka's concluding metamorphosis of mind is not Jewish self-hatred, but rather a private "holocaust" directed at those who were not Jewish enough. Yet the vision of ultimate revenge is there, and directed against himself as well. If such a moral being could entertain such a vision, anything was possible. And in view of the earth he saw at every turn, clearly all was permissible.

K afka investigated this condition by writings whose mark of integrity is their resistance to interpretation. "Our art," he wrote, "consists of being dazzled by the Truth. The light which rests on its distorted mask as it shrinks from it is true, nothing else is." Such an aesthetic was continuous with a fluctuating self in all its enigmatic purity. "We burrow through ourselves like a mole," he wrote Max Brod, "and emerge blackened and velvet-haired from our sandy underground vaults, our poor little red feet stretched out for tender pity." His art, far from neurotic, reflects a higher lucidity, the wisdom of a clairvoyant stutterer, due, as he says, to "introspection, which will suffer no idea to sink tranquilly to rest but must pursue each one into consciousness, only itself to become an idea, in turn to be pursued by renewed introspection." There was no escape from this dialogue with the unknown. "Man's own frontal bone bars his way," as the present is perpetually invaded by a dizzy recapitulation of all those discarded "selves" receding into oblivion. Kafka's challenge as an artist, then, was to discover a means for "the exchange of truthful words from person to person." And what his inner dreamlife discovered was *metamorphosis* — an image that was commensurate with the opposite, yet integral modes of being that exist within a single mind.

Under this dispensation Kafka saw the act of forgetting as vital to survival in the new century, a way of editing a metamorphosing self for the sake of a parodic wholeness of being. Memory was not a fixed record, but rather subject to laws of Darwinian selection within an unpredictable environment. Such a saving amnesia allowed one (momentarily) the sensation of being on firm ground, the "efficiency" that Kafka admired, for instance, in Felice Bauer, or the "endurance, will for living, for business, and for conquest" that he respected in his father. Once sealed through repression, such lapses of memory performed on a personal level the task of ordering the psyche once reserved for a viable and interdictive tradition.

But this was no option for Kafka. "Lying is terrible," he told Milena, "a worse spiritual torture does not exist." Any learning for this soul-voyager was an act of recovery, a reversal of time into the past, and here again Kafka turned to his animals, which Walter Benjamin has aptly labeled "receptacles of the forgotten." For Kafka, the private man, what had been forgotten was that alien territory that underlies his superb asceticism—his body or "animality." But the animal world is more that a droll metaphor for his own hidden depths, or the plight of the urban Western Jew. "The unity of mankind," he wrote in a diary entry in 1913, "now and then doubted, even if only emotionally, by everyone . . . on the other hand reveals itself to everyone, or seems to reveal itself, in *the complete harmony, discernible time and again, between the development of mankind as a whole and of the individual man. Even in the most secret emotions of the individual.*" Speaking for the ordinary man in the new century, then, what Kafka had forgotten was an ancestral inheritance of Judeo-Christian values that once offered us wholeness of being and has now degenerated into a tradition in decay.

From this perspective, "A Hunger Artist" becomes not simply a spiritual autobiography, but a glimpse of what religious asceticism looks like to a world that has evolved beyond it. One might say the same relation holds between the Mosaic Law and the first Commandant's torture machine in "In the Penal Colony." Pawel sees in the amorality of the Commandant a "prescient portrait of Adolf Eichmann"—although the latter fainted when he visited the camps—and one might be licensed by hindsight to see in the hunger artist a prescient *muselmann* neglected unto death as the crowd moves on to the panther.

But one thing seems certain. Retreating from humankind for fresh air, Kafka found his own fallen secular state reflected in his animals, who have "forgotten" their sagacious ancestors of the Hasidic fables. By meditating upon their "earth," now a "distorted mask" of his own, Kafka evokes the feeling of endless introspection minus any clarifying doctrine that was to harrow the new century. Shorn of human wisdom, his animals emerge as some far pole of dispossession from ourselves and each other, and we stand in the same relation to them as God does to us. "We are nihilistic thoughts, suicidal thoughts that come from God's head," Kafka told Brod. "There is hope, plenty of hope—but not for us."

What is suicidal about this inward nihilism is that Kafka experienced it as a departure from prevailing norms and hence a "failing to prove one's worth." Whether these tribunals took the form of his own family or secular institutions, Kafka found them stifling; yet out of some deep integrity he had to breathe their polluted air. In *Letter to His Father* he admits: "My writing was all about you; all I did there, after all, was to bemoan what I could not bemoan upon your breast." Of the injured working-class clients who entered the official maze of the Workers' Accident Insurance Institute, he remarked: "How modest these men are . . . They come to us and beg. Instead of storming the institute and smashing it to little pieces, they come and beg."

In both cases the supplicants have suffered an injustice, but they are under the bondage of a nostalgia, or mode of survivor guilt before an ancestral past, forgotten yet extending into the present in the form of what Kafka called "an artificial, miserable substitute . . . for forebears, marriage, and heirs." Clearly the diffidence of his injured clients before the factory owners of Bohemia was an obsolete gesture. More ontological than psychological, Kafka's own guilt bore the weight of vast eras of time. "You think my sense of guilt is a crutch, a way out," he told Felix Weltsch. "No, I have a sense of guilt simply because for me it is the most perfect form of repentance, but you do not have to look very closely to discover that this sense of guilt is really only a longing for the past."

Living among the invisible realities of a lost tradition did not enable Kafka to "foresee" the Holocaust. But looking back gave him a visionary grasp of the wide margin of terror that surrounded a present in ruins. The streets of "the hygienic new town" of Prague were a "launching ramp for suicides." It is revealing that Kafka chose to suppress mention of his encounters with Jew-hatred in his diaries and his voluminous correspondence. Yet one exception suggests that this reality was a primary source of inspiration, indeed the amniotic fluid of his nightmare art.

"I've spent all afternoon in the streets, wallowing in the Jew baiting," Kafka wrote to Milena in 1920. "*Prasive plemento* — filthy rabble — I heard someone call the Jews the other day. Isn't it the natural thing to leave a place where one is hated so much? (For this, Zionism or national feeling is not needed.) The heroism which consists of staying on in spite of it all is that of cockroaches, which also can't be exterminated from the bathroom. Just now I looked out of the window: mounted police, *gendarmerie* ready for a bayonet charge, a screaming crowd dispersing, and up here in the window the loathsome disgrace of living all the time under protection."

K afka had already envisioned the heroism of the cockroach in "The Metamorphosis," written during his first genuine burst of automatic writing in 1912. In turning to his family, he most likely needed the animal world for fear of violating his own sense of wholesomeness while exploring under the rock of repression. Kafka told Brod that, for him, to write out of bad or perverted passions ("I have hundreds of wrong feelings — dreadful ones — the right ones won't come — or if they do, only in rags; absolutely weak") was to let them get the upper hand. Prior to composition, he confessed to Felice that "when I didn't write, I was at once flat on the floor, fit for the dustbin." This becomes the fate of his hero, a vehicle for Kafka to exorcise his own "general load of fear, weakness, and self-contempt" before his father. Upon completing the story, he is reported to have buoyantly asked of a friend on the streets of Prague: "What do you think of the terrible things that go on in our family?"

What went on in Kafka's family was the projected fate of his entire "post-transitional generation" being groomed for a role that invariably led from obedient son to vermin. Gregor Samsa's metamorphosis into his own "troubled dreams" is less a tragedy than a naked clarification of all his relations to the world, a telescoped restoration of Truth — in particular, the hidden rage of the Father who has been battening on him like an insect. Yet Gregor is as far removed from this recognition as the gap between his consciousness and his numerous waving legs. This son and servant of officialdom now feels "guilt and shame" that his Father must work, for he has no existence apart from his filial loyalty. For Gregor and for his creator, metamorphosis is a kind of secret rescue from the loss of self into others, the attending alienation a form of liberation even if it does no good.

Gregor's only real pleasures and resentments — what we might call his real or hidden self — arise out of that despicable, forgotten, yet indestructible side of being, his animality. His relish for garbage, his discovery of the autoerotic freedom of hanging from the ceiling, his possessive gaze at an innocently lewd picture of a lady with a muff on his wall . . . such are the freakish and regressive antics of a sexuality too long deferred. What we witness is a kind of trans-Freudian comedy as Gregor breaks free on three different occasions into the domain of his Mother's living room, only to be repelled with increasing violence by the "giant soles" of his advancing Father. Such humor (as the pun implies) is not psychological, but rather ontological: "The noise in his rear sounded no longer like the force of one single father." Indeed, these primal scenes take us back to the dawn of creation. At one point Gregor is trapped between his Mother, who has fainted in his room in a swamp of petticoats, and the stalking wrath of his Father, and suffers bombardment with apples for bumbling into this tableau that parodies the Biblical Fall. Under this cosmic burden, Gregor might very well choose to forget his "animality" and embrace his "human" consciousness.

But it isn't easy. Gregor touches on reality only when he acknowledges his pain and its causes through his body, a result of the social reorganization of the household. The ministrations of Grete and the bony charwoman, which start to lapse into neglect and indifference, soon oppress him. He grows more rebellious as he moves toward starvation. Hunger is real. And yet his Father's obsequiousness before the three lodgers, followed by his violent purging of them, only anticipates his son's urgencies and extinguishes them. At last Gregor accepts the family verdict upon him, cooperates with their desire he be gotten rid of, and expires "thinking of his family with tenderness and love." There is no resistance to fate here, for what else could have happened given this family and this metamorphosis?*

In the ensuing four years, none of Kafka's animal stories would entertain a metamorphosis from human to animal worlds within a single soul: instead the two worlds converse across an abyss. "Far, far away world history takes its course," he muses in his diary, "the world history of your soul." We might guess two matters intervened now to rarefy Kafka's self into an empty mirror, to lead him beyond his own family to its equivalent in the world at large: tradition in decay. First, there was the failure of his long and tortured relationship with Felice, his yearning for marriage that

---

* It is little wonder that Kafka simultaneously pursued another option with great relish in "The Stoker," the first chapter of a fragmentary novel, *Amerika*, first entitled by Brod as "the man who ran away." But the adventures of young Karl Rossman in a mythological America, armed only with Kafka's sense of justice and love for the underdog, become a series of immigrant nightmares. The capricious authority of a European father who banished Karl reappears in the form of ship officials, a corrupt Uncle Jacob, the head waiter at the Occidental Hotel, rascals like Robinson and Delmarche—indeed all who have a momentary power to ensure his survival in a world of social anarchy. Karl is accused unjustly at every turn, and always "the verdict was determined by the first words that happened to fall from the judge's lips with an impulse of fury." He finds that "it's impossible to defend oneself where there is no good will . . . that all he could say would appear quite different to the others, and that whether a good or bad construction was to be put on his actions depended alone on the spirit in which he was judged." Karl's fall from apprentice secretary to lift-boy to servant of the macabre Brunhilde is accompanied by an engulfing loneliness, and his final flight is checked by the ultimate uniformed judge, a policeman barking: "Show your identification papers." His eventual employment in the Nature Theatre of Oklahoma, where "everyone is welcome" provided he play himself, promises some paradisical hope, yet the sign concludes: "Down with all those who do not believe in us!" Kafka leaves his hero on a train heading toward an unknown destination.

would only have put him in paralyzing competition with his father, eroding his destiny as a writer. The second matter that likely tilted his attention to larger vistas was the scarcely acknowledged presence of World War I in his mind, the atavistic slaughter conducted in 25,000 miles of trenches that crisscrossed the earth of a once-proud Europe. Equipped with new technology, the machine gun and high explosives, World War I was the first "death factory," producing ten million corpses over four years, the flower of Europe's younger generation. (*The Trial* was launched with the outbreak of hostilities in August 1914.) Kafka maintained a pregnant silence about the war in his diaries, except to muse that "it would be a great good fortune to become a soldier"; yet no event more clearly suggested that a whole tradition was committing suicide, and he would be ceaselessly involved in measuring the consequences.

It is tempting, if audacious, to see this very trench warfare with a defunct past at the heart of Kafka's unpublished story of 1914, "The Village Schoolmaster" (or "The Giant Mole"), an investigation of the obstacles in communicating the "forgotten" element in the new century. Once again that element, unspecified, "related to fundamental axioms of whose existence we don't even know," takes an animal form, a giant mole that was seen in a village by an obscure old schoolmaster in the district, whose firsthand account has been dismissed as a rumor by the public and a joke by the scholarly community. The narrator, a man of business with mild curiosity, comes to the aid of the schoolmaster by duplicating his original research — but this provokes hostility in the old man, a pamphlet which competes with his own labors and, as it were, eclipses them. Once alarmed that the narrator "wanted to rob him of the fame of being the first man publicly to vindicate the mole," the schoolmaster is devoured by an ambitious narcissism, as his discovery starts to fade into oblivion, not "completely forgotten," yet outside the radius of "trivial interest that had originally existed." Not much can be salvaged from this realm: the narrator's pamphlet is fated to be wryly disregarded by a prestigious journal as a recirculation of the schoolmaster's — "An unpardonable confusion of identity."

Now the old man takes refuge in a childish daydream of his metamorphosis from rustic obscurity to tawdry public acclaim in the city. About the urban world, however, only the narrator can speak with authority, and he warns the schoolmaster of what he will lose under the weight of modern institutions: "Every new discovery is assumed at once into the sum total of knowledge, and with that ceases in a sense to be a discovery; it dissolves into the whole and disappears, and one must have a trained scientific eye to recognize it." It is ultimately the way work and life are organized in society that confers destiny. "After all," Kafka wrote to Felix Weltsch, "our nervous system does take in the entire city." In this droll way he anticipates the entropic effects of information flow in our era, in which, devoid of any mediating authority, a public response of inert uniformity can be expected even in the face of the miraculous.

One earthly reflection of this vision was the war itself, sending off a generation to be sacrificed to patriotic lies, returning "elements of the forgotten" in the steady stream of destitute refugees and trainloads of wounded soldiers into Prague. At first Kafka wished evil on all the participants, but he admitted in 1915, "I mostly suffer from the war because I am not taking part in it." Deemed indispensable at the Institute, he assumed responsibility for medical benefits for disabled war veterans, working with amazing dedication to establish neurological clinics for shell-shocked survivors of the trenches. Kafka had displayed a similar identification through his "sneak attacks" on conditions in Bohemian factories before the war, producing meticulous reports on the death and mutilation of workers by machinery. "In my four districts," he wrote Brod, "people tumble off scaffolds and into machines as if they all were drunk, all planks tip over, all embankments collapse, all ladders slip, whatever gets put up comes down, whatever gets put down trips somebody up."

Imagined in 1915, the Commandant in "In the Penal Colony" suggests what the idolatry of the machine held for the future. Kurt Tucholsky was one of the few contemporaries to recognize the full implications of Kafka's masterpiece.

> This officer is no torturer, let alone a sadist. His delight in the manifestations of the victim's six-hour agony merely demonstrates his boundless, slavish worship of the machine, which he calls justice and which in fact is power. Power without limits. To be able for once to exercise power without any constraints—do you still remember the sexual fantasies of early adolescence? What stimulated them was not just sex but the absence of restraints. To be able to impose one's will, without any limits ... the torture is eventually cut short not because society, the state, or the law indignantly rise up in protest and put a stop to it but because the spare parts for the machine turn out to be defective; the apparatus, though still tolerated by the higher echelons of bureaucracy, no long enjoys full support at the top ... Don't ask what it means. It means nothing. The book may not even be of our time. It is completely harmless. As harmless as Kleist.

Another "forgotten element" that Kafka encountered now was Eastern European Jewry, pouring into refugee camps in Prague. Their roots and sense of communal strength were exactly what he lacked in his "inner emigration" — while their strident contempt for the city's middle-class German-Jews mirrored his own. Kafka's reunion with Felice at this time seems linked to her work as a volunteer at the Jewish People's Home in Berlin, set up to aid the refugee children of *Ostjuden.* "I am desperately eager for you to participate," he wrote her, " ... to let the dark complexity of Judaism as a whole, so pregnant with impenetrable mystery do its work ... " Yet for him memory was fate. "The synagogue is not something you sneak up on. I could not do this today any more than I could as a child; I still remember how I literally drowned in the terrifying boredom and pointlessness of the temple services. They were hell's way of staging a preview of my later office career. "

S piritually, then, Kafka was still banished to the animal kingdom. He did not idealize the primitive, for there were the war and the blood-and-sex ideologies swirling in the streets of Prague. But he did investigate the impulse with devilish innocence. Brod tells us that Kafka was fond of quoting Kierkegaard's perception that "as soon as a man appears who brings something of the primitive along with him ... a metamorphosis takes place in the whole of nature." What the primitive does is to stir traces of theological crisis, now replayed in terms of secular magic and fairytale — but by itself is no theology at all. Kafka's strict vegetarianism, for instance, a rite he always associated with the early Christians and their persecutions, was merely double-edged spiritual mimicry — a respect for the primitive and a refusal to be polluted by it. Once, at a Berlin aquarium, Brod tells us Kafka began speaking to the fish in their illuminated tanks: "Now at last I can look at you in peace, I don't eat you anymore."

This remark offers a clue to what lies behind the "distorted mask" of Kafka's magical tale, "Jackals and Arabs," written in a sudden release from war depression in 1916. Here a man "from the North" is visited by a swarm of jackals as he falls asleep on an oasis. They have awaited him for "endless years" so that he might be recruited as a messiah to deliver them from Arabs. These vile nomads "kill animals for food," and their meat-eating ways have cleared the desert of carrion. Speaking with aggrieved dignity, the jackals seem to have natural justice on their side — until suddenly the man from the North finds "two young beasts behind me had locked their teeth through my coat and shirt." He protests only to be told this cannot be helped: "We are poor creatures, and we have nothing but our teeth; whatever we want to do, good or bad, we can tackle it only with our teeth." So much for primitive adaptability. The head jackal tries to allay our uneasiness by delivering a speech which is ecologically superb — "We want to be troubled no more by Arabs; room to breathe; a skyline cleaned of them; no more bleating of sheep knifed by an Arab: every beast to die a natural death" — but humanly repulsive — "no interference till we have drained the carcass empty and picked its bones clean."

This sardonic complement to the dream of Jewish deliverance from oppression recurs moments later as visual pun when the man from the North is offered a pair of sewing scissors that the jackals have adopted for the purpose of assassinating Arabs. Such a confusion of realms, however, only exposes their impotence (jackals are dumb as fighters), and suddenly an Arab appears to crush the conspiracy with a crack of his whip (the oppressor regains as sadist what he has lost as carrion). This is happening all the time ("that pair of scissors goes wandering through the desert and will wander with us to the end of our days"), just as it is going on in the barren places of every human psyche. We are left gazing awestruck at what was forgotten as the jackals, once thrown a piece of "stinking carrion," lash themselves into ecstasy in pursuit of primitive cleanliness.

But apes are another matter, as Kafka starts to reduce the evolutionary gap between his animals and the human world, and sharpen the antagonism between them. In "A Report to an Academy," a performing ape reports to a learned body of mankind on his former life, now reduced to a fleeting nostalgia. In imagining how he learned to forget his origins, Kafka gives us a replay of the assimilation process, compressed into five years, that has enabled the ape to "reach the cultural level of an average European." Once a native of the Gold Coast, the ape was bushwacked by technology (hunters with guns) at a watering hole, and the nature of his wounds, one in the cheek and the other "below the hip," suggests that access to the human world is a sexual wound — as the ape's penchant for pulling down his trousers to expose "well-groomed fur and the scar made . . . by a wanton shot" makes clear. His trauma sealed by amnesia and the wall of language, the ape is now locked up where he can only squat, miming the act of human defecation. He experiences only one feeling — "no way out . . . I had to find a way out or die" — and reaches one conclusion: "Well, then, I had to stop being an ape." To do this, he must renounce the heaven of his former freedom for its laughable equivalent in the human world: "self-controlled movement" or acting. Over eras of time mankind has learned this as part of the Darwinian drama; but now that a fluctuating self-consciousness had turned act into acting and all human gestures were losing their traditional supports, Kafka saw his present by a wide curve of irony beginning once more to approximate the ape's. That the first human gesture he learns is a handshake is likely to fill us with the same wonder that led Kafka to describe his encounter with daily life in Prague as "a seasickness on dry land."

The breaking of the ape begins at sea by a sailor who acts out the process of drinking schnapps. "After theory came practice," although the ape is disgusted by schnapps. But torture, a burning pipe held against his fur, simply a necessary cauterization "against the nature of apes," at last enables him to break into the human world "as an artistic performer" by getting drunk and blurting out a brief but unmistakable "Hallo!" This dismal triumph for mankind is merely a matter of survival to the ape: "I repeat: there was no attraction for me in imitating human beings; I imitated them because I need a way out, and for no other reason." Unlike all those invited to join the Nature Theater of Oklahoma, provided they play themselves, the ape must play man and graduates to variety shows as his teachers file into mental hospitals. Yet imitation is only the pragmatics of the void: the ape is a success "provided that freedom was not to be my choice." A wistful sadness remains for what has been lost, captured in the anguish the ape feels for a female chimpanzee that awaits him in his room — and indeed Kafka would not sacrifice freedom in his art ever again.

M y maltreated blood finally burst out," Kafka said of his massive hemorrhage in 1917, diagnosed as tuberculosis of the lungs, which he welcomed as a salvation from marriage. "As you know," he wrote in one of his last letters to Felice, "there are two of me at war with each other . . . one is good, the other evil. At times they switch masks, which further confuses the already confused struggle . . . The blood shed by the good one on your behalf has served the enemy . . . I don't believe this illness to be primarily tuberculosis, but my all-around bankruptcy . . . I shall never get well again." Living in a city filled with war survivors, Kafka's health actually improved during 1918, until on October 14, a month before the armistice, he caught the Spanish flu. This viral infection devastated his body — and soon became a plague that killed an estimated 40 million people. Kafka's early desire for battlefield oblivion may have eluded him, yet he was ultimately the casualty of a disease whose outbreak was made possible by the devastated earth of World War I.

K afka returned to the animal world in 1922. By now Milena had passed through his life as a lost possibility for personal happiness. "I am too far away, am banished," he wrote to Brod, thus echoing what he had said upon the breakup of his second engagement to Felice in 1917: "What I have to do, I can do only alone. Become dear about the ultimate things." This impulse was only more urgent now, for Kafka was clearly dying of tuberculosis (whose cough he called the "animal" in him) and was ready to write from entirely inside the animal world, abjuring personal relations for the isolation of writing, "a sleep deeper than that of death."

A year earlier he had written to Brod that most Jewish writers "who started to write in German wanted to get away from their Jewishness, usually with their fathers' vague consent (the vagueness of it was what made it outrageous). They wanted to get away, but their hind legs still stuck to the fathers' Jewishness, while the forelegs found no firm ground. And the resulting despair served as their inspiration." But personally Kafka allied himself with the wild visionaries and legendary Talmudic scholars on his mother's side.

> All of this literature is an effort to breach the frontier . . . But for the intervention of Zionism, it could easily have developed into a new mysticism, a Cabala. Incipient trends in that direction exist. What is needed, however, is something like an inconceivable genius who either sends out roots into the ancient centuries or else re-creates them all over, yet does not spend himself in the task but only now begins his work.

Kafka assumed this impossible burden in "Investigations of a Dog," among other things a "distorted mask" of his own contribution to the state of Jewish letters. His mute and gazing dog has his own fate, the expansion of a "little maladjustment" into a full-fledged metaphysical riddle, soon divorcing him from the legendary community of dogdom ("All of us in one heap!") and setting him on his investigations. A traumatic episode out of childhood started it, naturally, an encounter with seven dogs conjuring music from the air and walking on hind legs, "blatantly making a show of their nakedness." The dog retreats into an asceticism, the conversion of sexual fear into an investigation of "what the canine race nourished itself upon," what has crumbled away "like a neglected ancestral inheritance." This inquiry pursues the unknowable, generating pedantry and headaches — yet the dog is pledged to "lap up the marrow" of life even if it might be poison. Others along the way only parody real spiritual pursuit, for instance the "roaring dogs," whom he finds "self-complacently floating high up in the air," and whose "dumb senselessness" violates the silence with "an almost unendurable volubility." So much for contemporary gurus (whether fractious Zionists or Jewish revivalists). His real colleagues remain "everywhere and nowhere" — that is, in the collective domain of lapsed memory, and this leads the dog to his pivotal insight: "Our generation is lost, it may be, but it is more blameless than those earlier ones. I can understand the hesitation of my generation . . . it is the thousandth forgetting of a dream dreamt a thousand times and forgotten a thousand times: and who can damn us merely for forgetting for the thousandth time."

Amid this uncertainty, the dog can only improvise his own religious practices. "God can only be comprehended personally," Kafka warned Gustav Janouch. "Each man has his own life and his own God. His protector and judge. Priests and rituals are only crutches for the crippled life of the soul." Science can only offer food in abundance: it begs the question. Traditional rituals seem tempting, but the dog finds them to be mere escapism, an effort to "take flight from it (the earth) forever." At last the dog resorts to fasting, but he can conquer neither physical hunger nor the ensuing guilt that aligns him with a past beyond his reach. Even his asceticism is an empty gesture, for sages have now cast prohibitions on fasting that leave him "only a dog laying here helplessly snapping at the empty air." Polluted by false hope, he starts to vomit blood. At last his investigations return to music, the "ultimate science" that prizes "freedom higher than anything else." The dog ends by coming full circle, with a pledge that seals his isolation as it confirms his campaign of self-transcendence. Kafka often called himself "Chinese," and never was his genius for illuminating the central axiom of these spiritual ancestors more clear: the mind is a monkey.

In an extraordinary letter to Brod in 1922 that recasts these issues, Kafka accused himself as a writer of "devil worship," of creating "a whole planetary system of vanity" as a surrogate for living, of having "not fanned the spark of life to a flame but simply used it to illuminate my corpse." Never was a genius more sensitive to the modern urge toward idolatry of self: it is the basis for Kafka's elevation of life over art, what enabled him to declare, "I despise Literature, but I am it." He concludes that letter by imagining a "nonexistent" writer who might yield up his corpse to the grave: "Although it will never happen now, I am writer enough to . . . tell this story... completely forgetting my self, for in the final analysis writing depends not on vigilance but on the ability to forget one's self."

This literary credo finds a pure manifestation in Kafka's last animal story, "Josephine the Singer, or the Mouse Folk." For here he vanishes into his own creation, evoking an entire world devoid of human wisdom, a "distorted mask" of the human world losing its old supports. "I shall never grow up to be a man," Kafka lamented to Brod. "From being a child I shall immediately become a white-haired ancient." This, as we are told, is exactly the path of spiritual growth among the Mouse Folk, and one need not gaze too long and selflessly (mouselike) upon the present to recognize this metamorphosis as our own.

A sympathetic "opponent" of Mouse culture, yet able to "sink in the feeling of the mass," the narrator proceeds with a patient and wondrous analysis of the power that Josephine holds over the nation. This power resides in her "piping," what remains of a decayed tradition of singing, the voice of music, always in Kafka an intimation of undivided being. But what might have been the dividend of a viable tradition is reduced now among the Mouse Folk to mere daily speech. Josephine makes "a ceremonial performance out of doing the usual thing"; indeed, "we admire in her what we do not admire in ourselves." In the absence of God the miraculous takes up residence in the commonplace — and this is mirrored in Josephine's personality. She is vulgar ("She actually bites"), vain ("She believes . . . she is singing to deaf ears"), clearly an idiot; but that is the point. Under the modem dispensation, in which all of us are holding counsel in empty space, only an idiot might offer help. But this does not deter Josephine. Insulated by her own conceit, she makes large claims for her art and herself as a savior; in national emergencies she rises up "like a shepherd before a thunderstorm" to rally the Mouse Folk. The narrator dismisses these messianic claims by noting that the Mouse Folk "save themselves, although at the cost of sacrifices which make historians — generally speaking we ignore historical research entirely — quite horror-struck." What, then, is the ground for Josephine's appeal? Her piping is "a message from the whole people to each individual," allowing the Mouse Folk merely respite from an existence that threatens extinction, an occasion to "dream . . . at ease in the great warm bed of the community."

"For all this, doubtless," the narrator says, "our way of life is mainly responsible." A tragically brief childhood, incessant work, over-population, the bloody depredations of enemies, a sudden and premature agedness of spirit — under these conditions, we are told, "a little piping here and there, that is enough for us." Too great a gap exists between the "unexpended, ineradicable childishness" of the Mouse Folk (that indulges Josephine) and their "infallible practical common sense" (that ultimately dismisses her) to permit any real musical talent to unfold. What eludes Josephine, any "unconditional devotion" or "permanent recognition of her art," reflects only an absence of tradition among the Mouse Folk and a resulting fall into the quotidian that makes her appeal possible.* She is merely the present, mere rumor and folly, and she can vanish at the end and "be forgotten like all her brothers." Josephine, then, enters the only heaven available to the Mouse Folk (and perhaps to all of us): the redemptive depths of oblivion.

We must take seriously, then, Kafka's choice of just such a heaven for himself when he willed that all his works be destroyed at his death. Impelled as an artist with a messianic urge to "raise the world into the pure, the true, the immutable," he fell wondrously short of his goal. "If I were to define the writer," he wrote in 1922, "I would say: he is a scapegoat for humanity, he enables people to enjoy sin without — or almost without — a sense of guilt." Kafka's experience of sin was a radical empiricism, with the earth his only sacred text; animals offered him a means for endless reflection on that present without presuming to grasp it. Language will never be more than a lurching probe of life, and Kafka's led into the far recesses of negativity of his era — both private alienation and coercion by emerging social norms that are the beneficiaries of our guilt under the evacuated heavens. For this saintly

---

*Only in the degree to which conditions of the human world start to approximate those of the Mouse Folk might we draw a parallel between the two. Yet consider our state of constant warfare, our eschewal of history, our early loss of innocence, our collapse of tradition into mass culture, our hunger for massive doses of nostalgia to retain a sense of continuity. Kafka's generation possessed at least a vestigial piety, but much avant-garde art today — that which sardonically brackets and inflates the dreck of mundane existence, as in the work of Andy Warhol or Donald Barthelme — might be viewed as human "piping." A part of its appeal can be discerned in what we are told of Josephine's art: "Something of our poor brief childhood is in it, something of lost happiness that can never be found again, but also something of active daily life, of its small gaieties, unaccountable and yet springing up and not to be obliterated."

genius, all was a temptation to despair that made his own works suspect. If writing was an "act of prayer," all of Kafka's work reduces to a serene and secular act of attention: he regarded himself as a failure, and everything else followed, including his sense that he was like a banished animal dreaming of home.

"The experience which corresponds to that of Kafka, the private individual," Benjamin wrote, "will probably not become accessible to the masses until such time as they are being done away with." That was observed in 1936, four years before Benjamin himself committed suicide while fleeing the Nazis. All of Kafka's sisters were killed in German extermination camps. Ottia, his favorite, renounced her protection as a wife of a German non-Jew in 1942, and after her divorce was deported to the Terezin Ghetto and then to Auschwitz. Yitzhak Levi, the Yiddish actor and friend of Kafka, gave his final performance in the Warsaw Ghetto and was killed at Treblinka. Milena joined the underground, was arrested by the Gestapo in 1939, and died at Ravensbruck. All of them in their own unimaginable circumstances might have echoed Kafka's last outcry of pain: "Kill me, or else you are a murderer!"

■■■■■■■■■■■

Zip

Floyd Skloot

T he flower song ends and there is distracting movement on stage. Men arrange tables and chairs, a singer slips off his jacket, half-naked women sashay across the nightclub set. It is the first scene in Act II of *Pal Joey*. I can hardly sit still as Melba Snyder and seedy nightclub singer Joey Evans meet stage right to conduct their haphazard interview. The waiter brings them fake Scotch and water. After telling a few casual lies, Joey leaves and the lights start to change: we are finally ready for Melba's song, the racy show-stopper.

But the woman now spotlit on stage looks more like a fullback than a stripper. Short and squat, arms encased in white gloves that reach nearly to her neck, she begins a bump & grind that suggests shedding tacklers rather than inhibitions. The music blares for an instant and she breathes deeply. In her snug gown, lime-green and black with great poufs at the shoulders, she seems to be wearing a football uniform, not evening wear.

The audience, which has filled the auditorium of the synagogue, is not reacting properly. Some chuckle, some laugh, others shift around in their seats. A few people mumble the way I have heard old men mumbling in this place before, lost in their prayers. The couple sitting beside me looks worried. We had expected cheers, maybe even a few whistles or hoots of encouragement as the song progressed, and had rehearsed how she would pause between lines to let the laughter die down. But we never expected confusion.

In the glare of the light, I see now there is a look of rapture on my mother's round face. She reaches toward the heavens. She rotates her palms. Her long-lashed eyes are closed and a smile has just begun to stretch her mouth as the muted trumpet growls to signal her next lines. *Zip! I was reading Schopenhauer last night.* Each *Zip!* is accompanied by a rim shot as she slides another zipper down somewhere on her costume, or slips the glove off another finger. *Zip! And I think that Schopenhauer was right.*

I am eight years old and I know this routine cold, having helped my mother rehearse it every night for the last two months. Schopenhauer, she said to me, was a Swiss poet. Zorina or Corbina, whose names would occur in the next two lines, were Hungarian dancers, married but not talking to each other. She had explained that the line *I have read the great Cabala* referred to an Arabian novelist whose book had been made into a movie starring Humphrey Bogart before I was born. For a few days, she had practiced running her hands down her sides and over her belly, asking me if I thought that worked. I shrugged, which she took to mean No. How about this: she bent forward and tried to make her tightly corseted breasts swing in unison, but lost her balance and decided not to risk it in the performance. She turned around and wriggled the way I had seen her wriggle to get into her girdle, but with her rear end stuck further out. She tried curtseying. She crossed her hands over her lower abdomen like Eve after eating the apple.

"You're no help," she said.

Sitting in the synagogue in my aisle seat, leaning way over to the left so I can see past the people in front of me, I am singing the lyrics along with her but trying to keep my voice down so as not to disturb anyone. *Zip! I'm a heterosexual.*

She is coming to the most difficult part, the final two lines of the refrain, which require that her voice surge into the limits of its upper range. She also has to be finished removing her gloves so she can fling them into the audience, first the left when she sang *Zip! It took intellect to master my art,* then the right when she sang *Zip! Who the hell is Margie Hart?* Even from where I sit, even if I look somewhere else on stage, I can see the strange, inward-turning expression of joy in my mother's eyes.

Though there was no Hungarian blood anywhere in her lineage, my mother saw herself as the lost Gabor sister. There was Magda, Eva, Zsa Zsa and, it turns out, Lil. After all, there were two lost Marx Brothers (Gummo and Zeppo) and a fourth, vanished Stooge (Shemp), and who ever remembered Diana Barrymore? Such things happened all the time. Perhaps this explains her fascination for stories of switched identity: the only book other than *Babar* that I can recall my mother reading to me was *The Prince and the Pauper,* over and over again.

Her father Max was from Cracow, which he left at age fourteen to become what he called "a man from the world." He had traversed

Europe during the first years of the new century, living in Paris for a while, learning a trade before coming to New York. A furrier, he met Rose Landorf when he offered himself as an apprentice in her father's upper West Side shop and demonstrated an especially good hand at sewing chinchilla. The Landorfs, late of Tarnow only forty-five miles east of Cracow, had several daughters working in the family business. The ones Max was most interested in — Eda and Eva — were younger than Rose; if he wanted to marry a Landorf, it had to be Rose, one year his senior. He took what he could get. They were together for the next seventy-two years.

My mother was born in 1910 and grew up in the small fur shops her parents operated. As business improved, they moved gradually downtown from the Bronx, finally landing in the same Manhattan neighborhood as the Landorfs. My mother, alert to the implications of neighborhood boundaries, considered the upper West Side her native land. Max worked in the back of the shop on pelts, Rose waited on customers, and my mother watched everything. It was a busy world her parents moved in, too busy to spare much time for a little girl. But she loved to see the wealthy women parading around in front of the shop's mirrors, admiring themselves as they caressed a sable coat, a fox stole or mink jacket, spinning in an air suffused with exotic perfumes. Men hovered in the background saying flattering things and taking out their money. This was the way to live! Elegance, hauteur, privilege. She enjoyed hearing them speak, especially the extravagantly wealthy immigrant women who seemed to return annually for a new garment, always trailed by a new man, always polite but distant to the shopkeepers and ignoring the child. Lil hardly cared about that; she studied these women. She would be treated this way, treat men this way, treat shopkeepers and workers and herself this way.

From the start, she was a good mimic. Recasting herself, reinventing herself, she assembled a vision of true grandeur.

So despite solidly Polish ancestry, my mother would often lapse into a vaguely Hungarian accent, laced with Yiddish when she was tired. She called people "Dahlink." Sometimes she stopped speaking in mid-sentence, pretending to struggle for a word in English that she knew perfectly well in Hungarian, mumbling and narrowing her eyes as she translated to herself. All her jewelry, regardless of where it was purchased, was reported as being fabricated by Cartier or Faberge. Her closet had sable, fox and mink, which she seldom had occasion to wear. She held her head regally uplifted and her unfiltered Chesterfield aloft, elbow resting on the vast bosom, a woman who would clearly be at home in the Imperial court. Though my father was a poultry butcher and we lived in a cramped Brooklyn apartment, she insisted on having a maid and being rigorous about the class implications of diet. "Only peasants eat stew, dahlink."

On the one bookshelf against our living-room wall, she had an unopened set of red leather-bound books by Balzac, de Maupassant, Zola, names she loved to pronounce, sounding as though she were speaking of beloved cousins. She had a painting, purchased from a street vendor, that she believed to have been painted by Toulouse-Lautrec's bastard son. All piano music was either written or directly influenced by Chopin.

My mother experimented with various dyes to keep her hair, whose natural color I have never seen in my fifty years, properly blonde. She favored lavishly layered dresses, droopy hats wider than her shoulders, shawls or capes in all weather, everything in attention-grabbing colors. She seemed taller when she sat than when she stood, posing with her back arched, neck stiff, ring-laden fingers splayed across her hip, perched rather than settled on a chair or sofa. Her brown eyes, protuberant by nature, were kept wider by a look of perpetual surprise, a look whose meaning I came to understand not as wonder at the world's miracles but as astonishment at one's audacity in addressing her without permission.

Glamour was inherent in certain people, she felt. Regardless of their circumstances, there were people who were just naturally aristocratic. Even if they happened to be married to a butcher. A butcher who lacked culture and breeding. Even if they lived in a six-story Flatbush building across the street from the county hospital where no one in her right mind would allow themselves to give birth and where they locked up the criminally insane. Mistakes, fueled by class jealousy, were made all the time; why, even the Tsar and Tsarina had been locked up like common criminals and executed by thugs.

While some things could not be taught, other things could never be forgotten. Taste, for example, or panache, nobility of heart. The elect, the geniuses of the soul, always knew one another. Her favorite adjective was "exclusive."

The haut monde myth must have been very difficult for her to sustain. For my mother, it was not enough to be looked at and admired, even envied; she had to rule. My father, spending more and more time at his failing chicken market, was not a willing subject. So the next best thing to ruling, I imagine, was being adored, worshipped, which perhaps explains her theatrical aspirations, where she could rule the stage, the world of illusion.

Starring as a performer had been her lifelong ambition. She dropped out of public school after the seventh grade, in the mid-1920s, took art classes and got a job painting mannequins for a theatrical costume designer. She sang pop songs, accompanying herself on the piano, and briefly had a five-minute radio show on WBNX in the Bronx, produced by a family friend named Barney Barnett. She was scheduled opposite Rudy Valee, which explained her small audience. This turned out to be the climax rather than the start of her career, however, and the decade between her radio work and her marriage to my father have always been blurred by an absence of detail.

"I had so many suitors, dahlink," she would say, as though being courted were her full-time occupation. If the facts and sequence may not have supported it, still she always claimed to have given up her burgeoning life as a star in order to marry and raise her two children, spaced eight years apart.

I n 1950, a song from the ten-year-old Rodgers & Hart musical *Pal Joey* was suddenly rediscovered and became one of the most popular songs in America. For sixteen weeks, "Bewitched, Bothered and Bewildered" was featured on Your Hit Parade and occupied the top spot on five different occasions. All in all, seven competing versions made the Top 40, including renditions by Doris Day, Mel Torme, the Harmonicats, and, biggest of all, by pianist Bill Snyder and His Orchestra.

Interest in the old show, which had opened on Christmas night of 1940 and run for eleven months before fading from view, was revived. Back in 1940, audiences were not ready for a story about a two-bit crooner scheming and hustling his way into women's beds and ownership of a nightclub of his own. But the songs were grand. After the success of "Bewitched, Bothered and Bewildered" in late 1950, Columbia Records decided to produce a cast album in the studio, assembling a mix of new and original stars. By 1952, *Pal Joey* was again running on Broadway and this time was a genuine hit, running for nearly two years before going on a 12-city tour. There was talk of a movie version to star the original Joey, Gene Kelly, then talk of a version with Marlon Brando, but the film would have to wait for five more years and Frank Sinatra before being made. Meanwhile, *Pal Joey* began to work its way into local community theater productions, which is where it caught up with my mother in 1955.

By late fall of 1955, season of Sputnik I and polio vaccines and the Brooklyn Dodgers finally winning a World Series, life in Brooklyn was undergoing dazzling changes. The Dodgers' victory suggested a great shift in the loser, wait-till-next-year identity that had long haunted the borough. But that was misleading. The team announced a plan to play eight games the next year in Jersey City, which my father said was the beginning of the end of Brooklyn baseball. Not only were the Dodgers disappearing, but the ubiquitous trolley cars which Brooklyn pedestrians always had to dodge (hence the name Dodgers) were disappearing as well. By 1956, they would all be gone. So was the delightful newspaper, *The Brooklyn Eagle.* Houses were being knocked down everywhere; supermarkets were appearing to threaten my father's livelihood. The vacant lot where I played across the street from our apartment building was being developed and would soon house the Downstate Medical Center. There was a rumor that our apartment building would be purchased for conversion to dormitory space and the two hundred families occupying it would have to relocate. The city was changing, the world was changing, and my parents could not count on anything anymore.

As I look back on this time in our lives, I think of it as the breaking point for my mother. For the last two decades, she had been struggling in the quicksand of mundanity—not only did she fail to marry a Count, a composer, a French surgeon fluent in Hebrew literature or a land-owning son of money, she had married a one-eyed Brooklyn slaughterer of poultry who never heard of Gustave Flaubert or what's-his-name Rimsky-Korsakov. After attending her cousin's wedding in Belgium and stopping in at the 1928 Olympics, she had never again traveled outside the state of New York. It was difficult to keep her tales of European experience sounding fresh. Her husband left home at 3:30 a.m. and returned at 6:30 p.m., ready for dinner and sleep. She herself maintained a shadow schedule, going to sleep at 3:00 a.m. and rising shortly after noon so that, with the exception of Sundays when they visited relatives in Brooklyn or Manhattan, they seldom encountered one another. The older child was always in trouble at school, a big *trombenik*, and the little one was just a *pisher*, always playing with his baseball cards on the floor. Nobody played music but her, nobody thought about culture but her, nobody YEARNED for anything except maybe a good meal, a few laughs, some peace and quiet. My mother had few friends; her only hobby was making table centerpieces out of the cardboard cores of toilet-paper rolls and stacks of handmade greeting cards, out of buttons and scraps of fabric, that she loved too much to sell or send.

It was, I believe, no coincidence that my mother was notoriously difficult to wake from sleep. She did not want to leave her dreams or face the day.

Nightly during 1955 it seemed that my parents always talked about what to do in the face of all those changes on the horizon. He would sell his chicken market. He would open a business of his own, maybe producing a line of clothes especially for short men. We would move, perhaps to Long Island. The children would get rooms of their own. There would have to be new jobs, new friends, new everything.

This kind of talk went right through me. Living with them, I had already learned that in our family change erupted without warning. Fights — verbal and physical — altered the very texture of every evening. Talk and plans were just the background music to dinner. Nevertheless, they often spoke about changing their lives, sending out signals of dissatisfaction with the way things were going. *I gotta have chicken fricassee every goddamn Wednesday?* my father would say. *We never go anywhere,* my mother would say. Then talk flared into actions that distracted them from what they were talking about.

My mother constantly redecorated the apartment's four small rooms, moving furniture around, switching paintings from room to room, getting new towels or drapes or appliances. She had the place repainted and repapered whenever the lease would allow it. She talked on the phone with her friends about whether to get a nose job, discussed it with my father, swore to us that she would, then changed her mind, asking me whether or not I thought her nose was beautiful the way it was. No one sat still; there was a restlessness everywhere we were.

After months of discussion, my mother decided to try out for a play at the temple over on Eastern Parkway. The theater, a word she pronounced with three syllables, was after all her natural calling. Even strangers who met her for the first time told her so. It had been a mistake ever to give it up. Also, I think theatrical performance seemed to her a legitimate, sanctioned way to enact her secret desires. She could be someone else, someone she was supposed to be, and she could be in the spotlight. They were going to do *Pal Joey,* she said, and began to sing "Bewitched, Bothered and Bewildered" while my father ate his flanken.

The role of Melba Snyder is a fascinating cameo in the musical version of *Pal Joey.* She appears in only one scene, has two dozen short speeches to deliver, sings one song and disappears. But she is memorable.

The actress playing Melba routinely gets co-star billing. Shrewd and sassy, the character transforms from buttoned-down professional woman to sizzling sexpot in a matter of moments. She is an authentic female shapeshifter, impossible to predict or know. Everything about her is illusion. It was, I believe, a part my mother felt born to play.

Melba works for a Chicago newspaper, *The Herald*, where she writes a column about the city's nightlife that she signs "M.S." She arrives at Chez Joey, the club financed by Joey's wealthy lover Vera, to interview the hot singer and figurehead, who does not know the famous M.S. is a woman. Once he is set straight, Joey, ever on the make, weaves a shoddy fabric of lies about a past in high society, lost fortunes, and Ivy League education, trying to snow Melba with his false savoir-faire. She sees right through him; she makes Joey look ridiculous in his obvious fabrications and dismisses him, complaining that she must "get some pictures of this tripe. God knows why."

At this point, the nightclub manager steps in and tries to smooth things over, telling Melba "you mustn't mind him." Worldly-wise, she segues into her song by saying "Him? After the people I've interviewed? It's pretty late in the day for me to start getting bothered by the funny ones I talk to."

Her song, "Zip," is a parody of the best interview Melba ever had. Though she has interviewed Pablo Picasso and Igor Stravinsky, her "greatest achievement" was an interview with Gypsy Rose Lee, the burlesque queen, mystery novelist, playwright and actress. Lee had explained to Melba (and showed her) that whenever she stripped, her mind was actually focused on matters of cultural and artistic depth. *Zip! I consider Dali's painting passe. Zip! Can they make the Metropolitan pay?* The ecdysiast as closet critic.

So despite what she looks like and what she does, Miss Lee inside was the exact opposite. *Zip! It took intellect to master my art.* This pleases Melba Snyder, who is also unlike what she seems, and I think it pleased my mother, who believed herself entirely separate from her surface image. Indeed, my mother may have lost touch entirely with her surface image, seeing in the mirror and insisting that others see a precise reflection of her fantasies. The most dangerous question my mother ever asked was: "Do you like the way I look?"

In John O'Hara's novel *Pal Joey,* from which some of the musical's characters emerged, Melba is even more unpredictable than she is on stage. When she first appears in print, wearing a man's suit that Joey considers too masculine even for himself and sporting a crew-cut and eyeglasses, he dismisses her as a "Lesbo." Then, after interviewing him, Melba changes clothes and reappears in panties and bra to pose for photographs with Joey. Suddenly, she is so gorgeous that he "forgot about Lana Turner." Joey says he would do "anything to get my hands on her." Indeed, Melba is a figure of immediate transformative power, able to change herself utterly and to turn Joey's perceptions of her inside-out. She is irresistible.

The layering in this situation is complex, but also evocative of my mother's way in the world. On stage, an actress plays a reporter of uncertain identity — known only by her initials — who exposes a man posing as more accomplished and sophisticated than he really is. She then sings a song in which she imitates a strip-tease artist proclaiming that despite impressions to the contrary she is an intellectual. And here was my mother, of all people, portraying savvy, sexy, no-nonsense Melba strutting her stuff. Surprising everyone out of their complacent and mistaken attitudes toward her. Being irresistible. In the synagogue.

Physically, my mother, who was 4' 10" and continually struggling with her weight, did not look the part. Actresses like tall, slender Eileen Heckart (1959), or the lithe former dancer Bebe Neuwirth (1995), or the one-time cabaret singer and cocktail waitress Kay Medford (1961) typically played the role of Melba on stage. In the 1957 movie starring Sinatra, the role of Melba was cut entirely, but the song "Zip" was delivered by Rita Hayworth (and dubbed by a sultry Jo Ann Greer) in the role of the wealthy heiress who finances Joey's club. Rita Hayworth! I think that even in her fantasies, my mother never went that far. Still, the theater has a long history of successful performances by actors cast against type and there was a peculiar resonance for her in portraying, in essence, two women at once pretending to be something they are not, insisting on their higher-class inner lives, proclaiming their intellectual natures, hiding a torrid but disdainful sexuality, making a life out of being listened to or looked at and admired.

It was all very difficult for a boy to figure out. My mother's particular blend of disconnectedness and flamboyance was at its peak in this situation. So were her confused notions of being a woman in a man's world, pampered and feared. The way her self-loathing and self-adoration blended made a volatile compound; though I was too young to appreciate that, I do know that I was afraid she might come apart on-stage before my eyes. I remember worrying about whether she would make it through her number without tumbling over her spiked heels. Also, despite the director having shortened her song by one chorus, she had had trouble remembering the lyrics near the finale and I worried throughout the song about her fumbling at the end.

I could not tell if people were laughing at her or with her, if she was perceived as ridiculous or brilliant, if there was shame or admiration directed at her. What I felt was relief when "Zip" ended, since that meant I would not have to help rehearse it anymore.

Over nearly sixty years, the material comprising *Pal Joey* has gone through steady transformation until it became the opposite of what it was at the start. Its honest sense of human behavior was abandoned for a fantasy projection of decency, a victory of charm and illusion over fact. It glimpsed the sordidness of actual life and asserted an alternative reality.

Beginning in 1938, John O'Hara began publishing a series of twelve short stories about Joey Evans in *The New Yorker*. These stories were in the form of letters from the second-rate lounge singer and master of ceremonies to his more successful friend, a bandleader named Ned. The letters, signed with regards from your Pal Joey, recounted manipulative antics in which Joey took advantage of one or more young women, sought to con money from people (including Ned), and was forced to move from town to town as his victims got too familiar with Joey's ways. He is last seen saying good-bye to the one woman, Linda, who might truly be able to love and save him, in order to pick up another woman strolling past the site of their farewell. Taken together, these stories paint the dark portrait of an immoral charmer, a louse on the loose among the innocent women and audiences of the Midwest.

O'Hara, who had already written his classic novel *Appointment in Samarra* and the grim roman a clef *Butterfield 8*, as well as two widely praised collections of short stories, quickly tired of Joey Evans. In 1940, he added two more stories and published the group of fourteen as a short novel. Ironically, it went on to make him the sort of fortune that eluded his scheming protagonist.

O'Hara's biographer Matthew J. Bruccoli has said that "although the Joey stories and their spin-offs brought John O'Hara his first great popularity, they are not important in themselves." Derivative of Ring Lardner's epistolary novel *Alibi Ike*, and borrowing mood and language from the stories of Damon Runyon, O'Hara's pieces lack firepower or originality. They are slick and readable, an unhappy man's portrait of his world, but it is difficult to have sympathy for Joey or his troubles and we are never brought inside his disguises to glimpse his inner life. Clearly, O'Hara's heart is not in the writing, which is only a cut above the sort of hack-work that Joey himself did. According to Bruccoli, the stories "delayed O'Hara's development as a novelist, for their earnings relieved him of the pressure to write."

That happened because, in October 1939, O'Hara sent a letter to composer Richard Rodgers. O'Hara said, "I got the idea that the pieces, or at least the character and the life in general, could be made into a book show, and I wonder if you and Larry (Lorenz Hart) would be interested in working on it with me." Rodgers was then in Boston and had been worried about what to do next.

In his autobiography *Musical Stages,* Rodgers recalls that "the letter was a total surprise, and a welcome one." What attracted Rodgers and Hart to the idea of working with O'Hara on a musical about Joey Evans was the uniqueness of a character like Joey as the focus of an American musical. "The 'hero' was a conniver and braggart who would do anything and sleep anywhere to get ahead," Rodgers wrote. "The idea of doing a musical without a conventional clean-cut juvenile in the romantic lead opened enormous possibilities for a more realistic view of life than theatregoers were accustomed to."

Hart was attracted to the material for different, almost complementary reasons. It spoke to his soul. In Frederick Nolan's biography *Lorenz Hart,* the point is made that "writing the kind of cynical, callous, suggestive lyrics needed for characters like Joey and his older benefactress was a paid vacation for Larry Hart." According to Nolan, the singer Mabel Mercer described Hart as "the saddest man I ever knew."

Their reply to O'Hara was swift and positive; correspondence about adapting the material followed. But O'Hara wanted to write something new altogether, using only bits of his existing Joey material and developing a fresh story with characters invented for the stage. It took him longer than any of the participants had anticipated. In fact, Rodgers finally nudged O'Hara with a telegram saying "SPEAK TO ME JOHN SPEAK TO ME." One wonders whether O'Hara took so long in part because he felt the material, slight as it was, slipping away from him, if he was having second thoughts about what was happening. *Pal Joey* was getting spruced up.

The finished book for their musical had mutated into a story of blackmail and intrigue, but its edges were rounded. Rodgers and Hart wrote at least two love songs for it that have entered the canon of popular music, "I Could Write a Book" and "Bewitched." Moderately successful, the show opened to generally favorable reviews. There were only a few dissenters such as Brooks Atkinson, who admired its expertise but wondered "can you draw sweet water from a foul well?" After all, *Pal Joey* was a story in which, as Rodgers noted, "there wasn't one decent character in the entire play except the girl who briefly fell for Joey—her problem was simply that she was stupid." Yet despite its lack of sunny conventionality, the musical tried to reveal a softer heart, which was the key to its success as entertainment.

It was still a story about people trying to disguise their true natures and motives via deception and self-delusion as they conned each other out of money. It was still a relatively unsentimental look at the seedy truth of male-female relations, at casual manipulation and betrayal, but the musical was easier on Joey than O'Hara's stories had been. It was also simpler and less subtle. Joey manages greater success and intimacy before his fall, which comes because Joey is a victim, betrayed by others rather than doing the betraying. He shows more talent and moxie than in the novel. He does not have his old bandleader friend Ned to manipulate, which focuses the action more fully upon his relations with women, which are culturally more normal for the times. Rodgers and Hart viewed the story of Joey as being about someone with "too much imagination to behave himself," someone who "was a little weak." A far cry from the predator O'Hara first imagined, who was neither imaginative nor weak but calculating and hard. As a result, the musical forgave Joey in ways that neither the author's original tales nor Joey himself ever could. It became possible to say, as critic Denny Martin Flinn does in his history of American musical theater (*Musical: A Grand Tour*) that "the gigolo character was irresistibly charming." Much of the cynicism behind O'Hara's stories had lightened. Why, the musical starred the sweet Gene Kelly.

An even greater transformation occurred during adaptation for the screen version, which Pauline Kael has called a "blighted Hollywoodization of the musical." The score, as Kael puts it, has been "purified along with Joey's character." Some changes were superficial—the story takes place in San Francisco, for example. But major changes entirely alter the meaning of the material as Joey falls in love with Linda and does the right thing at the end, abandoning his scheming and potential riches to marry. He has a moral center; he is a decent fellow.

The material was turned virtually inside-out so its sheen could impress. It pandered even more than the stage version by taking the heel beyond lovable to loving. The film is a stunning act of wish-fulfillment and audience manipulation, taking the words of two famously miserable men and shaking them free of despair. Less believable in each incarnation, *Pal Joey* on screen has been distilled into a curmudgeonly story that inadvertently praises the triumph of inauthenticity.

In a technical sense, inauthenticity certainly rules: except for Frank Sinatra as Joey, none of the lead actors actually sings her songs, with Kim Novak's voice being dubbed by Trudy Erwin and Rita Hayworth's by Jo

Ann Greer. Songs that have nothing to do with the story are imported in order for Sinatra to perform an anthology of Rodgers and Hart hits guaranteed to please audiences and sell recordings. These are, of course, customary Hollywood maneuvers. What is more compelling is how deception and flim-flammery have gone from being the problem to being the solution.

No character in the film is authentic, no one is what he or she seems. They seek happiness by making the world accept their act, or by modifying their act until it sells, rather than by being true to themselves. Even Linda, a model of integrity through previous incarnations of the story, succeeds only by pretending to be what she is not—first an exotic dancer willing to strip, then a woman not in love with Joey. We see that Joey is really a man of honor, though he seems a cad; his original lies about himself (that he is honest, that he cares) turn out to be the truth, though he does not know it; the wealthy widow who falls for him and buys him his nightclub is in fact an exotic dancer herself; and when people say No they mean Yes and when they lose everything they win.

I believe that this vision of the world is precisely the one my mother used to write her operating manual. Sham, artifice, fantasy became for her the reality they were enlisted to replace. Looking back to her involvement with *Pal Joey*, I can recognize how slippery the truth always was in her mind. What is authentic and what is counterfeit for her were entwined in ways that made them inseparable. Perhaps no longer vital.

My mother elevated wishful transformation to an art form. Life disappointed her, so she replaced it. The trick was that she always insisted her audience—particularly my father, my brother and me—see it her way. That the performance seldom worked never stopped her from taking the stage again.

Surely the flip-side of my mother's pretensions and fantasies was a deep feeling of inauthenticity about her life. Her return to the theater not only let her temporarily escape the mundane lower-middle class trap she was in, it let her be who she felt she should have been. Portraying Melba, despite what would seem to be her limitations in the role, was a start. After we moved to Long Island, she performed in *Mame, The King and I, Fiddler on the Roof* and many other musicals, always playing a person who was not at all what she seemed.

■ ■ ■ ■ ■ ■ ■ ■ ■ ■ ■

Raging Waters

Brenda Miller

Above me, the loudspeakers croon *All I need is the air that I breathe and to love you.* In this particular hour, at Raging Waters in Salt Lake City, everyone seems to believe it: the many children, and the adults who trot behind them, all of them wet and smiling, their bare legs and arms and belly buttons flashing through the heat. Some of them hoist pink rafts onto their shoulders; some drag blue tubes behind them; some have no rafts at all, just their damp feet slapping on the asphalt, their arms flung high as they slide down the chutes, through the fountains, tumbling into the frothy water. The crowd neither walks nor runs, but moves like one organism with many limbs; it undulates in all directions around the water slides, toward the snack bar, into the wave pool. A flock of boys scatters at the edge of the pool; teenage girls skitter by, the skin of their thighs and bellies radiant. Bathing suits punctuate this expanse of flesh like mere afterthought.

From where I've chosen to sit in the shade, in my black Land's End, Kindest-Cut tank, I have a clear view of the splashdowns from Shotgun Falls, The Terminator, and several loop-de-loop affairs that wind down from on high, their sources impossible to decipher. One slide drops vertically into a pool; the riders tuck themselves onto yellow sleds and plummet down, then bounce across the surface of the water like skipped rocks. For an hour, I watch people zoom out of tunnels and plunge over waterfalls, their legs and arms akimbo, one person after another, skimming around curves, flying, arcing, descending, their screams merging into a pleasant, discordant harmony, like jazz.

Though hundreds of children roam the crowd, carrying with them the opportunity for any number of altercations, I hear no cries, no parents shouting, no slaps, no whines. In the line to the snack bar (hamburgers

$2.50; pretzels $1.00), the children can have whatever they want; they clutch damp dollars in their fists and hop from foot to foot, towels draped over their shoulders, or tucked around their waists.

My charges have already melded into the crowd. Hannah and Sarah are not my children, though I've come to use the word "my" when I speak of them; they are my boyfriend's girls, and I agreed, reluctantly at first, to take them on this outing to give their father a break. I've known them for two years, but I have only a few weeks more to spend with them; I'll be moving to another state, leaving them behind with promises not to forget. Though I know we will, all of us. Already, I can hardly remember their faces, here in this crowd where all the children begin to look alike — their skin slick, their hair one damp color, their bathing suits askew on bodies that take no notice.

With Sarah, who is six, I've already been to Dinosaur Pond, and swum among its sighing palms, slid through the primordial waters. We put our raft into the wave pool ("Utah's Beach") and rode the crest of the waves into shore. With the strength of someone twice her size, she tugged the raft back into deep water. Though she can't yet swim, she showed no fear as the waves broke over her head; she emerged from each one, her eyes wide, her mouth sputtering, her hands splayed at her sides. She staggered and fell back, like someone intoxicated; I lunged for her, but already she was up, laughing, her bathing-suit straps down around her elbows. Her eyes, laser-bright, no longer looked out on this earthly world. I shouted her name, but she had eyes only for the water, searching the waves, baiting them to engulf her once again. Looking at her, I could imagine her face the day she was born: her mouth a puckered exclamation of wonder, her eyes gazing back to a place I'd never be able to fathom. I reached for her again, and she was slippery as a fish, or a newborn, sliding out of my grasp.

I think I could stay cheerfully on the lawn for the rest of the day, but Hannah, the nine-year-old, issues a challenge. *White Lightning.* She knows I'm afraid to go down the slides, we've discussed this. Before we came, I told her I'd had a bad experience on a crude water slide as a child; I've said there's no way I'm going down. But now she stands over me on the grass, her bikini dripping, her hands gripping her shoulders. She knows she has me; her face is alight. She reminds me that I've told her to face her fears head on, to try whatever you think is impossible.

The first, and only, time I'd been on a water slide was almost thirty years ago, when I was twelve years old. I remember the tall slide in an abandoned field outside L.A. No ponds, no dinosaurs, no carefully engineered drops: only a trickle of water splashing down a Plexiglas slope, with three plateaus spaced at irregular intervals. It reminded me of a vertical slip-'n-slide; the riders careened off onto a wet, plastic drop cloth spread over the grass.

I wore a bikini with a halter top whose straps cut into the skin at the base of my neck. It was a hot summer night, the air stagnant and thick, the vapor lights of a distant air field shimmering through the smog. I climbed the ladder with my brother and his friends, those boys from the basketball team who made me breathless with a vague desire. I was aware of my body in the bikini as I climbed, the boys close behind me; I knew my legs were the finest part of me then, slender and long and tanned. I laughed carelessly as we reached the top, and turned to say something witty, but the boys pushed past me to grab their mats and hurtle down the slide, whooping. I watched them go, some of them head first, and in moments they became small distant bodies strewn across the grass. I paused a moment. My brother handed me a mat. "Go," he said, jerking his head. I crouched. He pushed me off, and I was sliding down, fast. Too fast.

No one had said anything about technique. No one had said this task required any finesse at all. I made the mistake of leaning forward at first, off balance, and as I gripped my mat, I *flew* down the side of that mountain, lifting off at each plateau and slamming down on my tailbone, bouncing up, skidding down. My body no longer belonged to me; it uncoiled into space, leaving me behind. At the bottom, when I finally veered off onto land, I was sobbing. Not whimpering in a sad, ladylike way, but crying big, snotty tears I wiped off with the flat of my hand. My brother and his friends already scrambled to go back up, but they hesitated, looking at me with their heads cocked to the side, as if I were a strange animal they'd never before encountered. They looked to my brother. I saw his lips twist with embarrassment as he held out his hand to help me. "It's supposed to be fun," he hissed, then let me go. The boys turned away en masse, their boxer shorts barely hugging their bony hips, their hairy calf muscles bulging as they climbed the ladder again.

It's supposed to be fun. All my life, it seems now, I've murmured that phrase to myself in the most unlikely places: on the playground as a child, at the mall as a teenager, even — as I've grown into middle age — during lovemaking with men both sweet and kind. I've said it with both wonder and despair, as if "fun" were a foreign term I've yet to fully comprehend. Now, nearly thirty years later, I stand with Hannah on the steps to White Lightning. I don't think I've ever seen her so happy, and thus so beautiful; her entire body seems incandescent, lit up with her triumph at getting me here at all, on the wooden stairs high above Raging Waters. Her hair is plastered to her head, outlining the bones so perfectly joined; her belly, midway between a child's and an adolescent's, distends just slightly between the top and bottom halves of her bathing suit. She clutches the front end of our raft, leaning toward the next step up, and the next. We have a view of the entire Salt Lake Valley from here. A haze obscures the Wasatch Front and below us golfers tee off on the 18th hole.

Hannah and I watch slider after slider go down Blue Thunder, the slower of the two rides on this platform, the one most people choose. I look to the left, at White Lightning, at the tight curves and the three sharp descents, the waterfall roaring off the end. "Why isn't anyone going down this one?" I ask, trying to be casual, but my voice squeaks up a little, and Hannah grins. "It's *fast*," she says. "That's why."

Finally we're at the top. A Raging Waters "Guest Assistant," in her white polo shirt and royal-blue shorts, watches us with lazy boredom through her sunglasses. No expression mars her placid face as I situate the raft in the starting gate, no expression of warning or respect. I sit in the back of the raft, with Hannah between my legs, and I look up at the girl a moment, wanting *something* from her — a benediction, perhaps — but she gives us only a little push with her sneakered foot, and we're off.

We enter the first curve fast, sliding up on one wall then the other, straightening out for the first drop where we lift off, *oh god*, into the air, and we bump down hard, but no pain and no time to think of pain, the water rushing us through a tunnel and into the next drop, *please*, and the next; I'm holding on to Hannah and leaning back, *yes!*, as we're spit out into the waterfall. We're sailing over it. My body no longer seems linked to me; it's lifted free of gravity and become only motion and speed and liquid as Hannah and I splash down into the pool.

I'm laughing now, not crying, but laughing so hard I can barely speak. The waters roil and dump us off the raft. Hannah hops out of the pool. She stands taut on the edge, looking down at me, eagerness trembling in all her limbs. There is so much I want to say, so much I *could* say, but all I manage to sputter is: "*That* was so much *fun*."

Hannah nods, smug in her knowledge of what fun is, satisfied to be the one teaching *me* a lesson. She pulls the raft from the water, raises her lovely eyebrows. "Again?" she asks. I look up at her. The chlorine burns my eyes, but I can see Hannah more clearly than I ever have before.

Unlike my vision of Sarah in the wave pool, which rocketed her back to an infant, I imagine Hannah far into the future, as a young woman, gazing with this same intensity at a horse, at a man, at her own child sleeping in her arms. The water magnifies everything about her — her brave lips, her high cheekbones, her capable hands — and makes me believe beyond all reason that I really will know her forever.

Other sliders release into the pool, all hallelujahs and hosannas, splashing me off my feet. So I hoist my heavy body onto the cement. I sit there a moment, catching my breath, and the crowd throbs around me. It's grown larger but no less unified, feet slapping in every direction, voices raised in one keen avowal of fun. But Hannah is the only one to notice me here, a baptized convert in the midst of the masses. She's waiting for my answer. The tape on the loudspeaker has looped around full circle to *All I need is the air that I breathe and to love you.* I can only nod my head yes, when what I mean is: yes, my love, we'll do it again, and again, until the hours have spilled from this day and our time here is finally done.

Notes on Contributors

John Addiego's stories and poems have appeared in *Wisconsin Review, Writers' Forum, Italian Americana, Prairie Schooner,* and elsewhere.

Ai is the author of six books of poems, most recently *Dread* (Norton, 2003) and *Vice: New and Selected Poems* (Norton, 1999), which won the National Book Award for Poetry.

John Balaban is the author most recently of *Locusts at the Edge of Summer* (1997), nominated for the National Book Award, and *Spring Essence: the Poetry of Ho Xuan Huong* (2000), both from Copper Canyon Press.

Jan Beatty's most recent book of poems, *Boneshaker,* appeared from the University of Pittsburgh Press in 2002. She won the Agnes Lynch Starrett Prize for *Mad River* (University of Pittsburgh Press, 1994).

John Biguenet is the author of a novel, *Oyster* (2003), and a collection of stories, *The Torturer's Apprentice* (2001), both from Ecco Press.

Robert Bly's most recent book of poems is *The Night Abraham Called to the Stars* (HarperCollins, 2001). His nonfiction books include *Iron John: A Book about Men* (Addison-Wesley, 1990).

Kevin Bowen is the author of three books of poems, including *Playing Basketball with the Vietcong* (Consortium Books, 1994). He directs the William Joiner Center for the Study of War and Social Consequences at the University of Massachusetts, Boston.

Richard Burgin is the author of nine books, most recently a story collection, *The Spirit Returns* (Johns Hopkins University Press, 2001), and a novel, *Ghost Quartet* (TriQuarterly Books, 1998). He is the editor of *Boulevard.*

Bonnie Jo Campbell is the author of *Women and Other Animals* (Baker & Taylor, 1999), which won the AWP Short Fiction Award.

Ron Carlson is the author of six books of fiction, most recently a collection of stories, *At the Jim Bridge* (Picador, 2002), and a novel, *The Speed of Light* (Harper/Tempest, 2003).

Michael Casey is the author of three books of poems, *Obscenities* (Yale University Press, 1972), *Millrat* (Adastra Press, 1999), and *The Million Dollar Hole* (Carnegie Mellon University Press, 2001).

Sarah L. Courteau's nonfiction has appeared in *Bitch, The Dead Mule, Harper's,* and the environmental anthology *Naked: Writers Uncover the Way We Live on Earth.* She is an assistant editor at *The Wilson Quarterly.*

Richard Currey is the author of two novels, *Fatal Light* (Dutton, 1988) and *Lost Highway* (Houghton Mifflin, 1998), and two collections of stories. He is working with Operation Homecoming, a NEA initiative to assist veterans of Afghanistan and Iraq shape their stories for publication.

Mark Doty is the author of six books of poems, including *Sweet Machine* (HarperCollins, 2002), winner of the Ambassador Book Award, and *Alexandria* (University of Illinois Press, 1993).

Stephen Dunn is the author of eleven books of poems, most recently *Local Visitations* (Norton, 2003) and *Different Hours* (Norton, 2001), which was awarded the Pulitzer Prize.

Stuart Dybek's most recent collection of stories is *The Coast of Chicago* (Knopf/Vintage, 1990). His book of poems, *Brass Knuckles*, appeared from the University of Pittsburgh Press in 1979.

Charlotte Forbes has published stories in *New Orleans Review, Other Voices, Sycamore Review,* and *Prize Stories: The O. Henry Awards 1999.*

Tess Gallagher's most recent books are a collection of stories, *At the Owl Woman Saloon* (Scribner, 1999), and a volume of poems, *My Black Horse* (Blood Axe, 2000).

Amy Gerstler is the author of six books of poems, most recently *Ghost Girl* (2004) and *Medicine* (2000), both from Penguin.

Albert Goldbarth's most recent books are *Saving Lives* (Ohio State University Press, 2001), winner of the National Book Critics Circle Award, and a collection of essays, *Many Circles* (Graywolf Press, 2001).

Bob Hicok's most recent books of poems are *Animal Soul* (Invisible Cities, 2002), a finalist for the National Book Critics Circle Award, and *Insomnia Diary* (University of Pittsburgh Press, 2004).

Lucy Honig is the author of *The Truly Needy and Other Stories* (University of Pittsburgh Press, 1999), winner of the Drue Heinz Literature Prize, and a novel, *Picking Up* (Dog Ear Press, 1986).

Laura Kasischke is the author of four books of poems, most recently *Dance and Disappear* (University of Massachusetts Press, 2002). Her third novel, *The Life Before Her Eyes,* appeared from Harcourt in 2002.

Janet Kauffman's latest books are a novel, *Rot* (Green Rose Books, 2001), and a collection of prose poems, *Five on Fiction* (Burning Deck, 2004).

Maxine Kumin is the author of eleven books of poetry, including *Looking for Luck* (Norton, 1993). Her memoir, *Inside the Halo and Beyond: The Anatomy of a Recovery*, appeared from Norton in 2001.

Peter LaSalle's most recent book is a story collection, *Hockey Sur Grace* (Breakaway Books/Lyons and Burford, 1996). His work has appeared in *The Best American Short Stories* and *Prize Stories: The O. Henry Awards.*

William Loizeaux's nonfiction books include *The Shooting of Rabbit Wells* (Arcade Press, 1998) and *Anna: A Daughter's Life* (Arcade Press), the latter a *New York Times* Notable Book of 1993.

Barry Lopez's nonfiction books include *Of Wolves and Men* (Scribner, 1979) and *Arctic Dreams* (Vintage, 2001), which won the National Book Award. His latest collection of stories is *Resistance* (Knopf, 2004).

Thomas Lynch's most recent book of poems is *Still Life in Milford* (Norton, 1998). His collection of essays, *The Undertaking—Life Studies from the Dismal Trade* (Norton, 1997), won the American Book Award.

Jane McCafferty is the author of two collections of stories, *Director of the World* (University of Pittsburgh Press, 1992), which won the Drue Heinz Literature Prize, and *Thank You for the Music* (HarperCollins, 2004). Her novel, *One Heart,* appeared from HarperCollins in 1999.

James Alan McPherson's two collections of stories are *Hue and Cry* (Macmillan, 1969) and *Elbow Room* (Little Brown, 1977), which won the Pulitzer Prize. A memoir, *Crabcakes*, appeared from Free Press in 1997.

Brenda Miller is the author of *Season of the Body: Essays* (Sarabande Books, 2002). She has won three Pushcart Prizes, and her essays have appeared in *Fourth Genre, The Georgia Review*, and *Utne Reader.*

Peter Najarian is the author of three novels, *Voyages* (Pantheon, 1971), *Wash Me on Home Again, Mama* (Berkeley Poets' Workshop & Press, 1978), and *Daughters of Memory* (City Minor, 1986).

Josip Novakovich's latest collection of stories, *Salvation and Other Disasters* (Graywolf Press, 1998), won an American Book Award from the Before Columbus Foundation.

Joyce Carol Oates' most recent novel is *I'll Take You There* (Ecco/HarperCollins, 2002). Her most recent story collection is *Small Avalanches* (Harper/Tempest, 2003).

Mary Oliver's most recent book of poems is *Why I Wake Early* (Beacon Press, 2004). She has received the National Book Award and the Pulitzer Prize.

Alicia Ostriker's most recent book of poems is *the volcano sequence* (University of Pittsburgh Press, 2002). Her most recent book of nonfiction is *Dancing at the Devil's Party* (University of Michigan Press, 2000).

George W. Saunders is the author of two collections of stories, *Pastoralia* (2001) and *CivilWarLand in Bad Decline* (1997), both from Riverhead Books. *The Very Persistent Gappers of Frip* (2000) appeared from Villard.

Robert Schirmer's collection of stories, *Living with Strangers* (New York University Press, 1992), won the Bobst Award for Emerging Writers. He has won a Pushcart Prize and an O. Henry Award.

Floyd Skloot's collection of essays, *In the Shadow of Memory*, appeared from the University of Nebraska Press in 2003. His book, *The Evening Light* (Consortium), won the 2001 Oregon Book Award in Poetry.

Gary Snyder's recent books are *No Nature: New and Selected Poems* (Pantheon, 1992) and *A Place in Space: Ethics, Aesthetics, and Watersheds: New and Selected Prose* (Washington DC/Counterpoint, 1995).

Gary Soto is the author of ten books of poems, most notably *New and Selected Poems* (Chronicle Books, 1995), a finalist for both the *Los Angeles Times* Book Award and the National Book Award.

Peter Stine's work has appeared in *The Iowa Review, Boulevard, The Threepenny Review, The New York Times,* Harold Bloom's *Modern Critical Views,* and elsewhere.

Jack Turner is the author of *Teewinot: A Year in the Teton Range* (Thomas Dunne Books, 2000) and *The Abstract Wild* (University of Arizona Press, 1996).

John Edgar Wideman is the author of eight novels, most recently *Two Cities* (Houghton Mifflin, 1998). Winner of two PEN/Faulkner awards, he has also written a memoir, *Brothers and Keepers* (Vintage, 1995).

Terry Tempest Williams' books of nonfiction include *Refuge: An Unnatural History of Family and Place* (1991) and *Red: Patience and Passion in the Desert* (2001), both from Pantheon.

Lex Williford's collection of stories, *Macauley's Thumb*, was co-winner of the 1993 Iowa Short Fiction Award. His work has appeared in W.W. Norton's *Flash Fiction, Glimmer Train Stories,* and *Shenandoah.*

Kimberly Wozencraft's most recent novels are *Wanted* (St. Martin's Press, 2004), *Catch* (Doubleday, 1998), and *Notes from the Country Club* (William Morrow, 1994).